Sant   n

P9-CKP-528

Santa Barbara, CA 93101
www.SBPLibrary.org

"The hives refuse to admit to an extermination mandate, and BUR has not yet determined how to prove definitively the vampires are"—he coughed gently—**"trying to kill your child. And by default, you."**

"Monsieur Trouvé's homicidal mechanical ladybugs?"

"Never did trace the vampires' agent in Europe."

"The exploding gravy boat?"

"No appreciable evidence left behind."

"The flaming Mongolian poodle?"

"No connection to any known dealer."

"The poisoned dirigible meal that Mr. Tunstell consumed in my stead?"

"Well, given the general foulness of food while floating, that could simply have been a coincidence." Professor Lyall removed his spectacles and began to clean the clear lenses with a spotless white handkerchief.

"Oh, Professor Lyall, are you making a funny? It doesn't suit you."

The sandy-haired Beta gave Lady Maccon a dour look. "I am exploring new personality avenues."

"Well, stop it."

"Yes, my lady."

Praise for
The Parasol Protectorate Series

"Carriger delivers surprises with every book, and this one is no exception. With action, intrigue, and, above all, proper manners, this excellent series will have broad appeal to readers of steampunk, urban fantasy, and paranormal and historical romance."

—*Library Journal*

"Light-hearted and fast-paced, *Soulless* will please fans of fantasy, historical fantasy and paranormal romance alike."

—*The Miami Herald*

"*Soulless* has all the delicate charm of a Victorian parasol, and all the wicked force of a Victorian parasol secretly weighted with brass shot and expertly wielded. Ravishing."

—Lev Grossman, *New York Times* bestselling author of *The Magicians*

"A series for female fantasy fans that are looking for a stroke of ingenuity amongst the torrents of fanged fiction."

—*SciFi Now*

"Carriger's writing remains crisp and witty, and the affectionate banter between Lord and Lady Maccon will please series fans."

—*Publishers Weekly*

"Laugh out loud funny and refreshingly different, *Soulless* kept me turning pages well into the night. I enjoyed every minute of this wonderfully unexpected twist on paranormals."

—Angie Fox, *New York Times* bestselling author of *The Accidental Demon Slayer*

"I was enchanted from start to finish." —sfrevu.com

"The dialogue is as smart and snappy as ever, full of intelligent humor and artful verbal sparring."

—*All Things Urban Fantasy*

"*Changeless* is the equal of *Soulless*: witty, sexy, graceful, and unpredictable. With a few more novels this delightful, Ms. Carriger will be challenging Laurell K. Hamilton and Charlaine Harris for the top of the *New York Times* bestseller lists." —*Fantasy Magazine*

"Delivers what readers have come to expect: witty style paired with globe-spanning Victorian derring-do."

—*RT Book Reviews*

"Carriger's Parasol Protectorate series beautifully blends together alternate history, steampunk and paranormal romance into stories that are witty, engaging and fun."

—*Kirkus*

By Gail Carriger

The Parasol Protectorate
Soulless
Changeless
Blameless
Heartless
Timeless

The Custard Protocol
Prudence (coming March 2015)

The Parasol Protectorate Manga
Soulless: The Manga, Vol. 1
Soulless: The Manga, Vol. 2

Finishing School
Etiquette & Espionage
Curtsies & Conspiracies
Waistcoats & Weaponry
Manners & Mutiny

HEARTLESS

The Parasol Protectorate: Book the Fourth

GAIL CARRIGER

www.orbitbooks.net

Copyright © 2011 by Tofa Borregaard
Excerpt from *Timeless* copyright © 2012 by Tofa Borregaard
Excerpt from *Charming* copyright 2013 by Elliott James

All rights reserved. In accordance with the U.S. Copyright Act of 1976, the
scanning, uploading, and electronic sharing of any part of this book without
the permission of the publisher constitutes unlawful piracy and theft of the
author's intellectual property. If you would like to use material from the book
(other than for review purposes), prior written permission must be obtained
by contacting the publisher at permissions@hbgusa.com. Thank you for your
support of the author's rights.

Orbit
Hachette Book Group
237 Park Avenue, New York, NY 10017
www.OrbitBooks.net

Printed in the United States of America

RRD-C

Published in Great Britain in 2013 by Little, Brown.

First U.S. trade edition: July 2014

10 9 8 7 6 5 4 3 2 1

Orbit is an imprint of Hachette Book Group, Inc.
The Orbit name and logo are trademarks of Little, Brown Book Group Limited.

The Hachette Speakers Bureau provides a wide range of authors for speaking events. To find out more, go to www.hachettespeakersbureau.com or call
(866) 376-6591.

The publisher is not responsible for websites (or their content) that are not
owned by the publisher.

Library of Congress Control Number: 2014932820

ISBN 978-0-316-40204-0 (pbk.)

HEARTLESS

PROLOGUE

P Is for Preternatural

Notation to the Records, Subject P-464-AT, Alexia Tarabotti

Archivist: Mr. Phinkerlington, junior clerk, aethographic transmission specialist, second class

Subject P-464-AT is with child, sire unknown. Subject removed from London. Subject detached from Shadow Council. Position of muhjah vacant.

Notation to the Notation to the Records, Subject P-464-AT, Alexia Tarabotti

Archivist: Mr. Haverbink, field agent, recognizance and munitions expert, first class

Subject P-464-AT's pregnancy confirmed as direct result of union with Subject W-57790-CM, werewolf. Impregnation duly verified by scientists in good standing and by Italian Templars (preternatural breeding program discontinued circa 1805). (Please note: Templars classified as Threat to the Commonwealth of the Highest Order, yet their research in this is rated Unimpeachable.) Subject P-464-AT reinstated as muhjah.

Addendum to the Notation to the Notation to the Records, Subject P-464-AT, Alexia Tarabotti

Archivist: Professor Lyall, field agent, secretary prime (aka Subject W-56889-RL)

Werewolf howlers consulted on progeny. Child most likely a soul-stealer (aka *skin-stalker* or *flayer*). Templar records reported to indicate this implies ability to be both mortal and immortal. Potentate, Lord Akeldama (aka Subject V-322-XA), concurs. Subject P-464-AT says she believes "the horrible man said something along the lines of . . . a creature that can both walk and crawl and that rides the soul as a knight will ride his steed." (Please note: suspect "horrible man" is reference to Florentine preceptor of the Knights Templar.)

Only previous recorded example of a soul-stealer was Al-Zabba (aka Zenobia, Queen of the Palmyrene, no subject number). Understood to be related to Subject V–322–XA, Akeldama. (He won't reveal the details—you know vampires.) Zenobia most likely result of union between Vampire Queen and Male Preternatural (subjects unknown). It is thus impossible to say if her abilities will be comparable to those of the forthcoming Subject P–464–AT progeny, as this child is the result of Female Preternatural and Alpha Werewolf union. In either case, type of manifestation unknown.

Suggest new classification for progeny: M for metanatural.

Additional Addendum for Consideration: Vampires clearly desire progeny eliminated, at expense of Subject P–464–AT. It is this archivist's belief that it is in the best interest of the Commonwealth to see this child born, for scientific purposes if nothing else. Have consulted with Subject V–322–XA, Akeldama, and believe we have a solution to vampire negativity.

CHAPTER ONE

In Which Lady Alexia Maccon Waddles

Five months! Five months you—dare I say it—*gentlemen* have been sitting on this little scheme of yours and only now you decide to inform me of it!" Lady Alexia Maccon did not enjoy being surprised by declarations of intent. She glared at the men before her. Fully grown, and a goodly number of centuries older than she, yet they still managed to look like shamefaced little boys.

The three gentlemen, despite identical expressions of sheepishness, were as dissimilar as men of fashion and social standing could possibly be. The first was large and slightly unkempt. His perfectly tailored evening jacket draped about massive shoulders with a degree of reluctance, as if it were well aware that it was worn under sufferance. The other two existed in far more congenial partnerships with their apparel, although, with the first, dress was a matter of subtlety and, with the second, a form of artistic, nigh declamatory, expression.

Lady Maccon was not looking fearsome enough to inspire feelings of embarrassment in any gentleman, fashionable or no. Perilously close to her confinement at almost eight months, she had the distinct appearance of a stuffed goose with bunions.

"We didna want to worry you overly," ventured her husband. His voice was gruff in an attempt at calm solicitude. The Earl of Woolsey's tawny eyes were lowered, and his hair might actually have been dampened.

"Oh, and the constant vampire death threats are so very restful for a woman in my condition?" Alexia was having none of it. Her voice was shrill enough to disturb Lord Akeldama's cat, normally a most unflappable creature. The chubby calico opened one yellow eye and yawned.

"But isn't it the most *perfect* solution, my little lilac bush?" exalted Lord Akeldama, petting the cat back into purring, boneless relaxation. The vampire's discomfiture was the most manufactured of the three. There was a twinkle in his beautiful eyes, however downcast. It was the twinkle of a man about to get his own way.

"What, to lose possession of my own child? For goodness' sake, I may be soulless and I am, admittedly, not precisely maternal, but I am by no means heartless. Really, Conall, how could you agree to this? Without consulting me!"

"Wife, did you miss the fact that the entire pack has been

on constant bodyguard duty for the past five months? It's exhausting, my dear."

Lady Maccon adored her husband. She was particularly fond of the way he strode about shirtless in a fit of pique, but she was finding she didn't actually like him at the moment—the fathead. She was also suddenly hungry, a terrible bother, as it distracted her from her irritation.

"Oh, indeed, and how do you think I feel being on the receiving end of such constant supervision? But, Conall, *adoption!*" Alexia stood and began to pace about. Or, to be more precise, waddle fiercely. For once, she was blind to the gilded beauty of Lord Akeldama's drawing room. *I should have known better than to agree to a meeting here,* she thought. *Something untoward always occurs in Lord Akeldama's drawing room.*

"The queen thinks it's a good plan." That was Professor Lyall joining the fray. His was probably the most genuine regret, as he disliked confrontation. He was also the one truly responsible for this plot, unless Alexia was very wrong in her estimation of his character.

"Bully for the ruddy queen. Absolutely not—I refuse."

"Now, Alexia, my dearest, be reasonable." Her husband was trying to wheedle. He wasn't very good at it—wheedling looked odd on a man of his proportions and monthly inclinations.

"Reasonable? Go boil your head in reasonable!"

Lord Akeldama tried a new tactic. "I have already converted the room next to mine into a positively charming nursery, my little *pomegranate* seed."

Lady Maccon was really quite shocked to hear that. She paused in her wrath and her waddling to blink at the vampire in surprise. "Not your second closet? Never that."

"Indeed. You see how *seriously* I am taking this, my dearest petal? I have relocated *clothing* for you."

"For my child, you mean." But Alexia was impressed despite herself.

She looked to Lyall for assistance and tried desperately to calm herself and behave as practically as possible. "And this will stop the attacks?"

Professor Lyall nodded, pushing his spectacles up with one finger. They were an affectation—he had no need of them—but they gave him something to hide behind. And something to fiddle with. "I believe so. I have not, of course, been able to consult with any queens outright. The hives refuse to admit to an extermination mandate, and BUR has not yet determined how to prove definitively the vampires are"—he coughed gently—"trying to kill your child. And by default, you."

Alexia knew that the Bureau of Unnatural Registry was handicapped by a combination of paperwork and proper appearances. That is to say, because it was the enforcing body for England's supernatural and preternatural subjects, it had to seem at all times to be obeying its own laws, including those that guaranteed the packs and the hives some level of autonomy and self-governance.

"Monsieur Trouvé's homicidal mechanical ladybugs?"

"Never did trace the vampires' agent in Europe."

"The exploding gravy boat?"

"No appreciable evidence left behind."

"The flaming Mongolian poodle?"

"No connection to any known dealer."

"The poisoned dirigible meal that Mr. Tunstell consumed in my stead?"

"Well, given the general foulness of food while floating, that could simply have been a coincidence." Professor Lyall removed his spectacles and began to clean the clear lenses with a spotless white handkerchief.

"Oh, Professor Lyall, are you making a funny? It doesn't suit you."

The sandy-haired Beta gave Lady Maccon a dour look. "I am exploring new personality avenues."

"Well, stop it."

"Yes, my lady."

Alexia straightened her spine as much as her protruding belly would allow and looked down her nose at Professor Lyall where he sat, legs crossed elegantly. "Explain to me how you have arrived at this solution. Also, given that you have not proposed this scheme to the hives, how do you know with such confidence that it will stop this annoying little tic they seem to have developed wherein they continually try to murder me?"

Professor Lyall looked helplessly at his coconspirators. Lord Maccon, with a wide grin, slouched back into the golden velvet settee, making it creak in protest. Neither Lord Akeldama nor any of his drones were built to Lord Maccon's scale. The couch was overwhelmed by the experience. It had this in common with a good deal of furniture.

Lord Akeldama merely continued to twinkle unhelpfully.

Clearly surmising that he had been left out to dry, Professor Lyall took a long breath. "How did you know it was my idea?"

Alexia crossed her arms over her very ample chest. "My dear sir, give me *some* credit."

Professor Lyall put his glasses back on. "Well, we know that the vampires are afraid of what your child could be, but I think they are wise enough to know that if raised with the proper precautions, even the most natural-born predator will behave in an entirely civilized fashion. You, for example."

Alexia raised an eyebrow.

Her husband snorted derisively.

Professor Lyall refused to be intimidated. "You may be a tad outrageous, Lady Maccon, but you *are* always civilized."

"Hear, hear," added Lord Akeldama, raising a long-stemmed glass and then taking a sip of the pink fizzy drink within.

Lady Maccon inclined her head. "I shall take that as a compliment."

Professor Lyall soldiered bravely on. "It is vampire nature to believe that any vampire, even—you'll pardon the insult, my lord—Lord Akeldama, will instill the correct ethical code in a child. A vampire father would ensure the baby is kept away from the corruption of Americans, Templars, and other like-minded antisupernatural elements. And, of course, you, Lord and Lady Maccon. Simply put, the hives will feel like they are in control, and all death threats should stop as a result."

Alexia looked at Lord Akeldama. "Do you agree with that prediction?"

Lord Akeldama nodded. "Yes, my *dearest* marigold."

The earl was beginning to look less annoyed and more thoughtful.

Professor Lyall continued. "Lord Akeldama seemed the best solution."

Lord Maccon wrinkled his nose at that and huffed derisively.

Professor Lyall, Lord Akeldama, and Alexia all pretended not to hear.

"He is more powerful than any other rove in the area. He has a goodly number of drones. He is centrally located, and as potentate, he carries the authority of Queen Victoria. Few would dare interfere with his household."

Lord Akeldama tapped Lyall playfully with the back of one hand. "Dolly, you flatterer, you."

Professor Lyall ignored this. "He is also your friend."

Lord Akeldama looked up to his ceiling, as though contemplating possible new canoodling for the painted cherubs depicted there. "I have also implied that because of a certain unmentionable incident this winter, the hives owe me a debt of honor. My potentate predecessor may have taken matters into his own lily-white hands, but *the fact remains* that the hives should have exerted some control over his activities on their behalf. His kidnapping of *my droney poo* was *utterly* inexcusable, and they are very well aware of that *little* fact. I hold a blood debt and intend to bite them back with this arrangement."

Alexia looked at her friend. His posture and demeanor were as relaxed and frivolous as ever, but there was a hardness about his mouth that suggested he actually meant what he was saying. "That is a rather serious statement coming from you, my lord."

The vampire smiled, showing fang. "Better revel in the experience, my little *cream puff.* It will probably never occur again."

Lady Maccon nibbled at her lower lip and went to sit in one of Lord Akeldama's more upright chairs. She found it tricky these days to extract herself from couches and love seats and preferred simply not to get involved with plushy furniture.

"Oh, I can't think." She rubbed at her belly, annoyed at the fuzziness in her own brain, the persistent product of lack of sleep, physical discomfort, and hunger. She seemed to spend all her time either eating or dozing—sometimes dozing while eating and, once or twice, eating while dozing. Pregnancy had given her a new window into the human capacity for consumption.

"Oh, blast it, I'm positively starving."

Instantly, all three men proffered up comestibles extracted from inner waistcoat pockets. Professor Lyall's offering was a ham sandwich wrapped in brown paper, Lord Maccon's a weather-beaten apple, and Lord Akeldama's a small box of Turkish delight. Months of training had seen the entire werewolf household running attendance on an increasingly grumpy Alexia and learning, to a man, that if food was not provided promptly, fur might fly, or worse, Lady Maccon would start to weep. As a result, several of the pack now crinkled as they moved, having desperately stashed snacks all about their personage.

Alexia opted for all three offerings and began to eat, starting with the Turkish delight. "So you are genuinely disposed toward adopting my child?" she asked Lord Akeldama between bites, and then looked at her husband. "And *you* are willing to allow it?"

The earl lost his amused attitude and knelt before his wife, looking up at her. He put his hands on her knees. Even through all her layers of skirts, Alexia could feel the wide roughness of his palms. "I'm taxing BUR and the pack to keep you safe, wife. I've even contemplated calling in the Coldsteam Guards." Curse him for looking so handsome when he came over all bashful and sincere. It quite undid her resolve. "Not that I would do it any differently. I protect my own. But Queen Victoria would be livid if I pulled military strings in a personal matter. Well, more livid than she already is over my killing the potentate. We must be clever. They're older and craftier and they'll keep trying. We canna continue on like this for the rest of our child's life."

Perhaps he has learned something about pragmatism being married to me, Alexia thought. *Oh, but why'd he have to turn all sensible now?* She tried desperately not to fly into a tizzy over his unilateral handling of the situation. She knew that it cost Conall a terrible price to admit to any kind of inability. He liked to think he was all-powerful.

She cupped his cheek with her gloved hand. "But this is *our* baby."

"Do you have a better solution?" It was an honest question. He was genuinely hoping she could think up an alternative.

Alexia shook her head, trying not to come over mawkish. Then she firmed up her mouth. "Very well." She turned to Lord Akeldama. "If you intend to take possession of my child, then I'm moving in, too."

Lord Akeldama didn't miss a beat. He opened his arms wide as though to embrace her. "Darlingest of Alexias, *welcome* to the family."

"You do realize I may have to take up residence in your other closet?"

"Sacrifices, sacrifices."

"What? Absolutely not." Lord Maccon stood and glared down at his wife.

Lady Maccon got *that* look on her face. "I'm already in London two nights a week for the Shadow Council. I'll come in on Wednesday and stay through to Monday, spend the rest of the week at Woolsey."

The earl could do math. "Two nights? You'll give me two nights?! Unacceptable."

Alexia wouldn't budge. "You're in town on BUR business most evenings yourself. You can see me then."

"Alexia," said Lord Maccon on a definite growl, "I refuse to petition for visiting rights with my own wife!"

"Tough cheese. I am also this child's mother. You are forcing me to choose."

"Perhaps, if I may?" Professor Lyall interjected.

Lord and Lady Maccon glowered at him. They enjoyed

arguing with each other almost as much as they enjoyed any other intimate activity.

Professor Lyall called upon the sublime confidence of the truly urbane. "The house adjacent is to let. If Woolsey were to take it on as a town residence, my lord...? You and Lady Maccon could maintain a room here at Lord Akeldama's but pretend to live next door. This would keep up the appearance of separation for when the child arrives. You, Lord Maccon, could spend meals and so forth with members of the pack while they are in town. Of course, parts of the month everyone would have to return to Woolsey for security purposes, and there's hunting and runs to consider. But it might work, as a temporary compromise. For a decade or two."

"Will the vampires object?" Alexia rather liked the idea. Woolsey Castle was a little too far outside of London for her taste, and those buttresses—positively excessive.

"I don't believe so. Not if it is made absolutely clear that Lord Akeldama has complete parental control, proper documentation and all. And we manage to keep up pretenses."

Lord Akeldama was amused. "Dolly, *darling,* so deliciously unprecedented—a wolf pack living directly next to a vampire such as *moi.*"

The earl frowned. "My marriage was also unprecedented."

"True, true." Lord Akeldama was on a roll. He swept to his feet, dumping the cat unceremoniously off his lap, and began sashaying about the room. This evening he wore highly polished oxblood boots and white velvet jodhpurs with a red riding jacket. It was all purely decorative.

Vampires rarely rode—most horses would have none of it—and Lord Akeldama disdained the sport as disastrous to one's hair. "Dolly, I *adore* this plan! Alexia, *sugar drop,* you must make over your town house to complement mine. Robin's-egg blue with silver detailing, don't you think? We could plant lilac bushes. I do so *love* lilac bushes."

Professor Lyall was not to be sidetracked. "Do you believe it will work?"

"Robin's-egg blue and silver? Of course. It will look *divine.*"

Alexia hid a smile.

"No." Professor Lyall possessed infinite patience, whether dealing with Lord Maccon's temper, Lord Akeldama's purposeful obtuseness, or Lady Maccon's antics. *Being a Beta,* Alexia figured, *must be rather like being the world's most tolerant butler.* "Will having your vampire residence adjacent to a werewolf pack work?"

Lord Akeldama raised his monocle. Like Lyall's spectacles, it was entirely artificial. But he did love the accessory so. He had several, set with different gemstones and in different metals to match any outfit.

The vampire regarded the two werewolves in his drawing room through the small circle of glass. "You are rather more civilized under my dear Alexia's tutelage. I suppose it could be tolerated, so long as I do not have to dine with you. And, Lord Maccon, might we have words on the proper tying of a cravat? For my sanity's sake?"

Lord Maccon was nonplussed.

Professor Lyall, on the other hand, was pained. "I do what I can."

Lord Akeldama looked at him, pity in his eyes. "You are a brave man."

Lady Maccon interjected at this juncture. "And you wouldn't mind Conall and myself occasionally in residence?"

"If you see to the cravat situation, I suppose I could surrender yet another closet to the cause."

Alexia swallowed down a broad grin and tried to be as serious as humanly possible. "You are a noble man."

Lord Akeldama tilted his head in gracious acceptance of the accolade. "Whoever thought I would have a werewolf living in my closet?"

"Hobgoblins under the bed?" suggested Lady Maccon, allowing her grin to emerge.

"La, *butterball,* I should *be* so lucky." A gleam entered the vampire's eyes, and he brushed his blond hair flirtatiously off his neck. "I suppose your pack must spend a good deal of time underdressed?"

The earl rolled his eyes, but Professor Lyall was not above a little bribery. "Or not dressed at all."

Lord Akeldama nodded in pleasure. "Oh, my darling boys are going to *love* this new arrangement. They often take a keen interest in remarking upon the activities of our neighbors."

"Oh, dear," muttered Lord Maccon under his breath.

Biffy remained unmentioned, although everyone was thinking about him. Alexia, being Alexia, decided she would bring the taboo subject out into the open. "Biffy is going to be pleased."

Silence met that statement.

Lord Akeldama assumed a forced lightness of tone. "How *is* the newest member of the Woolsey Pack?"

In truth, Biffy was not adjusting as well as anyone would like. He still fought the change each month and refused to try shifting of his own volition. He obeyed Lord Maccon implicitly, but there was no joy in it. The result was that he was having trouble learning any modicum of control and had to be locked away more nights than not because of this weakness.

However, not being inclined to confide in a vampire, Lord Maccon only said gruffly, "The pup is well enough."

Lady Maccon frowned. Had she and Lord Akeldama been alone, she might have said something to him of Biffy's tribulations, but as it was, she let her husband handle it. If they, indeed, moved in to Lord Akeldama's neighborhood and home, he would find out the truth of the matter soon enough.

She made a dictatorial gesture at Conall.

Rather like a trained dog—although no one would dare suggest the comparison to any werewolf—Lord Maccon stood, offering both his hands. He hoisted his wife to her feet. During the last few months, Alexia had taken to using him thus on multiple occasions.

Professor Lyall stood as well.

"So it's decided?" Alexia looked at the three supernatural gentlemen.

They all nodded at her.

"Excellent. I shall have Floote make the arrangements.

Professor, can you leak our relocation to the papers so that the vampires find out? Lord Akeldama, if you would use your very own special distribution methods as well?"

"Of course, my little *dewdrop.*"

"At once, my lady."

"You and I"—Lady Maccon grinned up at her husband, immersing herself, albeit briefly, in his tawny eyes—"have packing to do."

He sighed, no doubt contemplating the pack's reaction to the fact that their Alpha was about to reside, at least part of the time, in town. The Woolsey Pack was not exactly renowned for its interest in high society. No pack was. "How do you manage to drag me into such situations, wife?"

"Oh"—Alexia stood on tiptoe and leaned in to kiss the tip of his nose, balancing her belly against his strong frame—"you love it. Just think how terribly dull your life was before I came into it."

The earl gave her a dour look but ceded the point.

Alexia nestled against him, enjoying the tingles his massive body still engendered in her own.

Lord Akeldama sighed. "You lovebirds, how will I endure such flirtations constantly in my company? How déclassé, Lord Maccon, to love your *own* wife." He led the way out of his drawing room and into the long arched front hallway.

Inside the carriage, Lord Maccon scooped his wife against him and planted a buzzing kiss on the side of her neck.

Lady Maccon had initially thought Conall's amorous attentions would diminish as her pregnancy progressed, but

she was happily mistaken. He was intrigued by the altera-
tions of her body—a spirit of scientific inquiry that took the
form of her being unclothed as often as he could arrange it.
It was a good thing this was the season for such activities;
London was experiencing quite the nicest summer in an age.

Alexia settled against her husband and, grabbing his face
in both hands, directed his kissing toward her mouth for a
long moment. He gave a little growl that was almost a purr
and hauled her closer. Her stomach got in the way, but the
earl didn't seem bothered.

They spent a half hour or so thus pleasantly occupied
until Alexia said, "You really don't mind?"

"Mind?"

"Living in Lord Akeldama's closet?"

"I've done more foolish things for love in the past," he
answered, rather unguardedly, before nibbling on her ear.

Alexia shifted against him. "You have? What?"

"Well, there was this—"

The carriage bucked and the window above the door shat-
tered.

The earl immediately shielded his wife from the flying
glass with his own body. Even fully mortal, his reactions
were fast and military sharp.

"Oh, doesn't that just take the sticky pudding?" said
Alexia. "Why is it *always* when I'm in a carriage?"

The horses screamed and the coach lurched, coming to
a rattling halt. Something had definitely spooked the beasts
into rearing against their traces.

In classic werewolf fashion, Lord Maccon didn't wait to

see what it was but burst out the door, changing form at the same time to land in the road a raging wolf.

He's brash, thought his wife, *but terribly handsome about it.*

They were outside of London proper, following one of the many country lanes toward Barking that would eventually branch off to Woolsey Castle. Whatever had startled the horses seemed to be giving Lord Maccon a bit of stick. Alexia poked her head out to see.

Hedgehogs. Hundreds of them.

Lady Maccon frowned and then looked closer. The moon was only half full, and though it was a clear summer night, it was challenging to make out the particulars. She reassessed her first impression of the roly-poly attackers. These were far bigger than hedgehogs, with long gray spines. They reminded her of a series of etchings she'd once seen in a book on Darkest Africa. *What had that creature been named? Something to do with pig products? Ah, yes, a porcupine.* These looked like porcupines. To her utter amazement, they also seemed to be able to eject their spines at her husband, embedding them into his fur-covered flesh.

As each wickedly barbed spine hit, Conall howled in distress and bent to yank the projectile out with his teeth.

Then he seemed to partly lose control of his back legs.

Numbing agent? wondered Alexia. *Are they mechanical?* She grabbed her parasol and stuck the tip of it out the broken window. Firming her grip with one hand, she activated the magnetic disruption emitter with the other by pulling down on the appropriate lotus leaf in the handle.

The animals continued to attack Conall with no slowing or reaction to the invisible blast. Either the parasol was broken, which Alexia doubted, or the creatures had no magnetic parts. Perhaps they were as biological as they initially appeared.

*Well, if they are biological…*Lady Maccon took out her gun.

The earl had objected to his wife carrying firearms, until the vampires orchestrated the gravy-boat attack. After that, he took Alexia out behind Woolsey Castle, ordered two members of his pack to run about holding trenchers over their heads, and showed her how to shoot. Then he'd gifted her with a small but elegant gun, American made and delectably deadly. It was a .28 caliber Colt Paterson revolver, customized with a shorter barrel and a pearl handle—the former for ease of concealment and the latter to match Lady Maccon's hair accessories.

Alexia named the gun Ethel.

She could hit the Woolsey pot shed at six paces if she concentrated, but anything smaller or farther away was rather beyond her skill level. This didn't stop her from carrying Ethel, usually inside a reticule made to match her gown. However, it did stop her from pointing Ethel at any of the creatures near her husband. She could just as easily damage him as them.

Conall had managed to pull out most of the spines embedded in his body, but new and freshly equipped porcupines only fired at him again. Alexia tried to stop herself from panicking, as those projectiles might, just possibly, be silver tipped. However, while he seemed a tad overwhelmed and groggy, none had managed to hit him in any vital organs. Not yet. He was snapping and snarling, trying to get his deadly jaws about the creatures, but they seemed to move remarkably quickly for such pudgy animals.

In the interest of scientific experimentation, Alexia fired Ethel out the carriage window at a porcupine nearer to the edge of the undulating herd. Proximity and density combined to result in her actually hitting one. Not the one she'd aimed at, but... The animal in question fell heavily to one side and began to slowly bleed, thick black blood, the kind of blood emitted by vampires. Alexia wrinkled her nose in disgust. Once in her past, a certain wax-faced automaton had also oozed such blood.

Another shot rang out. The coachman, a newer claviger, was also firing on their attackers.

Lady Maccon frowned. Were these porcupines already dead? *Zombie porcupines?* She snorted at her own flight of fancy. *Surely not.* Necromancy had long since been disproved as mere superstitious folderol. She squinted. They did seem to have oddly shiny quills. *Wax perhaps? Or glass?*

Alexia's gun was outfitted with sundowner bullets, although no one had authorized her to carry them. Conall had positively insisted, and Alexia was not one to stand against him on matters of munitions. Undead or not, the porcupine she had shot stayed down. That was something to note. Although, truth be told, sundowner bullets would work just as well on any normal porcupine. Still, there were positively masses, and Conall had fallen once more to his side, writhing and howling under the swarm of quills.

Alexia put away Ethel and armed herself with her parasol once more. She poked it fully out the carriage window, opened it up, and then in one practiced movement flipped it about so that she held the tip, her fingers poised on the deadly dial there. Her husband would take some time to recover from the resulting injuries, and she loathed causing him pain, but sometimes circumstances warranted extreme measures. Making very certain she was dialing to the second and not the first or third position, she sprayed out a mixture of lapis solaris diluted in sulfuric acid. The liquid, designed to combat vampires, was still strong enough to burn any living creature—causing severe pain at the very least.

The mist floated out, coating the porcupines. The unmistakable smell of burning fur permeated the air. Her husband, now almost entirely covered in the creatures, avoided most of the spray as the porcupines took the brunt of the falling acid.

Eerily, they made no noise. The acid burned through the fur covering their faces but had little effect on the quills that continued to jab into Lord Maccon. The parasol sputtered and the spray turned to a dribble. Alexia shook it, flipped it up, and caught it in reverse before closing it.

With a roar so loud it was guaranteed to shake the porcupines in their boots, had they been wearing any, her husband shook off the creatures and reared back, as though luring them to follow him. Perhaps he was not so disabled as he pretended. Perhaps he was trying to draw them away from Alexia.

Struck with a sudden inspiration, Lady Maccon yelled to her lupine spouse, "My love, lead them off. Go for the lime pit." She remembered Conall complaining to her about running into the pit by accident only a few nights previous, singeing all the hair off of his forefeet.

Lord Maccon barked his agreement, understanding her completely—as Alpha, he was one of the few who held on to his wits when he lost his skin. He began backing off the road and down the gully toward the nearby pit. If the creatures had any wax components at all, the lime should at least seize them into immobility.

The porcupines followed.

Alexia had only a moment of reprieve to appreciate the macabre sight of a wolf luring away a flock of porcupines like some Aesop's version of the Pied Piper. A thud resounded on the driver's box on the outside of the carriage. Something far larger than a porcupine had hit the claviger coachman and knocked him out. Seconds later, for speed was always their strong point, the parasol was bashed out of Alexia's grasp and the carriage door yanked open.

"Good evening, Lady Maccon." The vampire tipped his top hat with one hand, holding the door with the other. He occupied the entrance in an ominous, looming manner.

"Ah, how do you do, Lord Ambrose?"

"Tolerably well, tolerably well. It is a lovely night, don't you find? And how is your"—he glanced at her engorged belly—"health?"

"Exceedingly abundant," Alexia replied with a self-effacing shrug, "although, I suspect, unlikely to remain so."

"Have you been eating figs?"

Alexia was startled by this odd question. "Figs?"

"Terribly beneficial in preventing biliousness in new-borns, I understand."

Alexia had been in receipt of a good deal of unwanted pregnancy advice over the last several months, so she ignored this and got on to the business at hand.

"If you don't feel that it is forward of me to ask, are you here to kill me, Lord Ambrose?" She inched away from the carriage door, reaching for Ethel. The gun lay behind her on the coach seat. She had not had time to put it back into its reticule with the pineapple cut siding. The reticule was a perfect match to her gray plaid carriage dress with green lace trim. Lady Alexia Maccon was a woman who liked to see a thing done properly or not at all.

The vampire tilted his head to one side in acknowledgment. "Sadly, yes. I do apologize for the inconvenience."

"Oh, really, must you? I'd much rather you didn't."

"That's what they all say."

*   *   *

The ghost drifted. Floating between this world and death. It felt like being trapped in a coop, a cage for chickens, and she a poor fat hen kept to lay and lay and lay. What could she provide but the eggs of her mind? Nothing left. No more eggs.

"Bawk, bawk!" she clucked.

No one answered her.

It was better—this was better, she had to believe—than nothingness. Even the madness was better.

But sometimes she was aware of it, the reality of her coop, and the substantial world around it. There was something very wrong with that world. There were parts of it missing. There were people acting indifferent or incorrect. There were new feelings intruding that had no right to intrude. No right at all.

The ghost was certain, absolutely certain, that something must be done to stop it. But she was nothing more than a specter, and a mad one at that, drifting between undead and dead. What could she do? Who could she tell?

CHAPTER TWO

———

Wherein Alexia Will Not Be Flung

Lord Ambrose was an exceptionally well-formed gentleman. His perpetual expression was one of pensive hauteur exacerbated by aquiline features and brooding dark eyes. Alexia felt that he had much in common with a mahogany wardrobe that belonged to Mrs. Loontwill's great-grandfather and now resided in embarrassed austerity among the frippery of her mother's boudoir. That is to say, Lord Ambrose was immovable, impossible to live with, and mostly filled with frivolities incompatible with outward appearance.

Lady Maccon moved toward her gun, finding the spacious carriage difficult to navigate with her attention focused on the vampire in the doorway and her mobility hampered by the infant in her belly. "Terribly forward of the countess to send you, Lord Ambrose, to do the deed."

Lord Ambrose made his way inside. "Ah, well, our more subtle attempts seem to be wasted on you, Lady Maccon."

"Subtlety usually is."

Lord Ambrose ignored her and continued with his explanation. "I am her *praetoriani*. When you want something done properly, sometimes you must send the best." He lunged toward her, supernaturally fast. In his hands he held a garrote. Alexia would never have thought the most dignified of the Westminster Hive capable of wielding such a primitive assassin's weapon.

Lady Maccon might be prone to waddling of late, but there was nothing wrong with the mobility of her upper extremities. She ducked to avoid the deadly wire, grabbed for Ethel, swung about, pulling the hammer back in the same movement, and fired.

At such close range, even she could hit a vampire full force in the shoulder, surprising him considerably.

He paused in his attack. "Well, my word! You can't threaten me, you're pregnant!"

Alexia pulled the hammer back again. "Take a seat, won't you, Lord Ambrose? I believe I have something to discuss with you that might change your current approach. And I shall aim for a less-resilient part of your anatomy next."

The vampire was looking down at his shoulder, which wasn't healing as it ought. The bullet hadn't passed through but had gone into the bone and lodged there.

"Sundowner bullets," explained Lady Maccon. "You're in no mortal danger from a mere shoulder injury, my lord, but I shouldn't leave the bullet in there if I were you."

Gingerly, the vampire settled back against the plush velvet seat. Alexia had always thought Lord Ambrose the pinnacle of what a vampire ought to look like. He had a full head of glossy dark hair, a cleft chin, and, currently, a certain air of childish petulance.

Lady Maccon, never one for shilly-shallying even when her life wasn't in danger, got straight to the point. "You can stop with all your uncouth attempts at execution. I have decided to give this child up for adoption."

"Oh? And why should that make any difference to us, Lady Maccon?"

"The lucky father is to be Lord Akeldama."

The vampire lost his sulky expression for one of genuine shock. He most certainly hadn't expected such a bizarre revelation. The surprise sat upon his face as precariously as a mouse on a bowl of boiled pudding.

"Lord Akeldama?"

Lady Maccon nodded, sharply, once.

The vampire raised one hand and fluttered it slightly from side to side in a highly illustrative gesture. "Lord Akeldama?"

Lady Maccon nodded again.

He seemed to recollect some of his much-vaunted vampire gravitas. "You would allow your progeny to be raised by a vampire?"

Alexia's hand, still clutching her gun, didn't waver one iota. Vampires were tricky, changeable creatures. No sense in relaxing her guard, for all Lord Ambrose seemed to have relaxed his. He still held the garrote in his other hand.

"The potentate, no less." Alexia reminded him of Lord Akeldama's relatively recent change in political status.

She watched his face closely. She was giving him an out and knew that he must *want* an out. Countess Nadasdy, Queen of the Westminster Hive, would want one. All the vampires had to be uncomfortable with this situation. It was probably why they kept bungling the assassination attempts; their little hearts simply weren't in it. Oh, not the killing—with vampires, that was but one step up from ordering a new pair of shoes. No, they would want to get out of having to kill an Alpha werewolf's mate. Lady Maccon's death at vampire hands, whether provable or not, would bring a whole mess of trouble down upon the hives. Trouble of the large, hairy, and angry variety. It was not that the bloodsuckers thought they would lose a war with werewolves; it was simply that they knew it would be bloody. Vampires hated to lose blood—it was troublesome to replace and always left a stain.

Lady Maccon pressed the point, figuring that Lord Ambrose had had enough time to cogitate her revelation. "Surely you can do nothing but approve so tidy a solution to our current predicament?"

The vampire pursed his full lips over his fangs. It was the very elegance of Alexia's proposal that had him seriously considering it. They both knew that. "You would not contemplate allowing Countess Nadasdy to be the infant's godmother, would you?"

Alexia placed a hand on her belly, taken aback. "Well," she hedged, trying for the most courteous response, "you know I should be delighted, but my husband, you must understand. He is already a little flustered by Lord Akeldama's parental undertaking. To add your hive into the mix might be more than he could stomach."

"Ah, yes, the sensitivities of werewolves must be taken into account. I always forget that. I can hardly countenance his approval of the scheme in the first place. He is amenable to this arrangement?"

"Unreservedly."

Lord Ambrose gave her a look of disbelief.

"Ah, well," Lady Maccon made light of the situation. "My dearest spouse has some reservations as to Lord Akeldama's ideas on schooling and, uh, proper dress, but he has approved the adoption."

"Remarkable powers of persuasion you possess, Lady Maccon."

Alexia was rather flattered he should think it all her idea, so she did not bother to correct him on the matter.

"You will make it fully legal, put the adoption in writing, file it with the Bureau?"

"Indeed. I understand Queen Victoria is agreeable. Woolsey is intending to lease the house adjacent to Lord Akeldama's to keep an eye on the child. You must allow me some level of motherly concern."

"Oh, yes, yes, entirely understandable. In writing, you said, Lady Maccon?"

"In writing, Lord Ambrose."

The vampire put his garrote away in a waistcoat pocket. "Given such a proposed arrangement, Lady Maccon, you will excuse me for the time being? I should return to Westminster at once. It is taxing to be so far away as it is, and my queen will want this new information as quickly as supernaturally possible."

"Ah, yes. I thought the hive's range extended only to parts of London proper."

"*Praetoriani* has some advantages."

With a gleam of pure mischief in her brown eyes, Lady Maccon remembered her manners. "You are certain you won't stay? Take a drop of port? My husband keeps a small stash in the carriage amenities compartment for emergencies."

"No, thank you kindly. Perhaps at some future date?"

"Not the whole killing thing, I hope? I should like to put that well behind us."

Lord Ambrose actually smiled. "No, Lady Maccon, the port. After all, you are taking a house in town. You will be in our territory now, won't you?"

Alexia blanched. Westminster Hive did hold sway over the most fashionable parts of London. "Why, yes, I suppose I will."

Lord Ambrose's smile became less friendly. "I will bid you good evening, then, Lady Maccon."

With that, he let himself out of the carriage, tossed her parasol in, and vanished into the night. Mere moments later, Lord Maccon, looking none the worse for his porcupine-herding activities, let himself back inside and unceremoniously swept Alexia into his arms. He was naked, of course, and Alexia had no time to reprimand him for not changing out of his clothing before he shifted form. Yet another jacket ruined.

"Where were we?" he rumbled into her ear before nibbling on it. He slid his arms about her, as far as they would reach, which admittedly wasn't far these days, and rubbed up and down her back.

Lady Maccon's increasing girth had rendered most bed sport impossible, but this did not stop them from what Conall affectionately referred to as *playing*. Despite Alexia's protestations that she was in perfect health, modern medical science banned connubial relations during the final months, and the earl refused to risk his wife's well-being. He had, Alexia discovered much to her distress, unanticipated powers of resistance.

She slid her gun out from between them and pushed it away along the bench. Time enough to tell her husband about Lord Ambrose later. If she told him now, he'd get all flustered and distracted. At the moment, *she* preferred to be the cause of both his flustering and his distraction.

"No lasting harm, my love?" She slid her hands along his sides, enjoying the silkiness of his skin just there and the way he writhed under her touch.

"Never." He kissed her mouth in a heated embrace.

Alexia wondered that even after so many months of marriage she still could get utterly lost in kissing her husband. It never became unexciting. It was like a rich milky tea—comforting, revitalizing, and delicious. Though she wasn't certain how he would take such an analogy, Alexia Maccon was *very* fond of tea.

She touched his chin with both hands, encouraging him to kiss deeper.

*   *   *

Moving house, thought Lady Maccon, *must be the world's most incommodious undertaking.*

She, of course, was not being allowed to physically help, although she did toddle about pointing at objects and indicating where they should go. She was enjoying herself immensely. Her husband and coconspirators having sallied off about their own business several days ago, she felt much like a chubby general in sole possession of a field of glittery battle, directing a mass invasion of foreign soil. Although, after having to mediate a head-to-head between Boots and Biffy over the efficaciousness of velvet decorative pillows, she suspected generals had it easier. Conall and Professor Lyall had arranged for her dominion over the relocation operation in order to distract her, but as she was well aware of the manipulation and, as they were well aware that she was well aware, she might as well have fun.

What made it particularly pleasant was that it had to be covert. They didn't want it known that Lord and Lady Maccon were actually taking up residence *inside* Lord Akeldama's house. The vampires had only reluctantly agreed to the Maccons moving in *next door,* frightened that a werewolf and a preternatural might unduly influence the rearing of a child, even one under Lord Akeldama's care. Further intimacy was strongly discouraged. Thus, they had made it look as though Lady Maccon were seeking refuge from the chaos by taking tea at Lord Akeldama's, while her belongings were moved into the rented accommodations adjacent. Alexia's personal effects were taken up one flight of stairs, down a hall, and out onto a balcony. They were then tossed over to Lord Akeldama's balcony—the balconies being a short distance apart and conveniently hidden by a large holly tree. Her private possessions were then carried down another hall, up another flight of stairs, and eventually into her new residential closet. This involved a good deal of ruckus, especially when it was furniture being tossed. *Thank goodness,* reflected Alexia, watching Biffy catch her favorite armoire with ease, *for supernatural strength.*

Lady Maccon's minions in this elaborate charade were three younger members of Woolsey's pack: Biffy, Rafe, and Phelan (Biffy as catcher and the other two as porter and chucker, respectively); the ever-efficient Floote; and a positive bevy of Lord Akeldama's drones scuttling about arranging everything *just so.*

After overseeing the tossing, Alexia repaired to monitor the arrangement of her new sleeping chamber. Lord Akeldama's third closet was quite spacious, almost the size of her bedchamber back at Woolsey. Admittedly, there were no windows, and there were gratuitous hooks, shelves, and rails covering the walls. But there was also enough room for a large bed (specially commissioned by Lord Akeldama to accommodate Lord Maccon's frame), a dressing table, and several other bits and bobs. Conall would have to make do without his dressing chamber, but since he was prone to wandering around underdressed, anyway, Alexia suspected this would not affect his habits detrimentally. The lack of a proper valet concerned her for about five seconds before she realized no drone of Lord Akeldama's would allow her husband passage through their hallways in anything less than tip-top, wrinkle-free condition.

Biffy was in his element, free to wander once more the luxurious, colorful, and somewhat effervescent corridors of his former master. Of all Alexia's acquaintances, Biffy was the most thrilled by the new cohabitation scheme. He was far more comfortable bustling about hanging Alexia's hats on hooks than he had been for the last five months at Woolsey Castle. One might even have described him as gay, no longer weighed down by the sport destiny had made of his afterlife.

The drones couldn't have been more excited if Queen Victoria were gracing them with her presence. A female in their midst, a baby in their future, and a room to decorate in the interim—pure heaven. After a brief scuffle over repapering the walls, it was decided, wholly without Alexia's say-so, that a new carpet and some additional lighting were sufficient to brighten up the closet.

Once Covert Operation Fling Furniture was concluded, the two other werewolves jumped easily from one balcony to the other and came to see if there was anything further their Alpha female wished of them. There was a good deal more, as she readily informed them. She desired the bed be moved slightly to the right and her armoire moved to the other side of the room, and then back again. Also the drones wished to inquire as to the werewolves' opinion on the matter of stacking Lady Maccon's hatboxes, and the correct order in which to hang Lord Maccon's cloaks.

By the end, Rafe wore the long-suffering look of an eagle being ordered about by a flock of excited pigeons.

Floote heralded completion by coming in with the last of
Lady Maccon's most prized possessions: her parasol, dispatch case, and jewelry box.

"What do you think, Floote?"

"It's rather glossy, madam."

"No, not that. What do you think about the whole
arrangement?"

They had been organizing and packing for several days,
and Floote had taken charge of leasing the house adjacent
to Lord Akeldama's (although not, much to the vampire's
disappointment, repainting it), but Alexia had not found
the time to consult with him on his opinion of the scheme
itself.

Floote looked grave and very much the butler. He was
ostensibly Lady Maccon's personal secretary and librarian
now but had never been one to let go of good training. "It is
a unique solution, madam."

"And?"

"You have always done things differently, madam."

"Will it work?"

"Anything is possible, madam," was Floote's noncommit-
tal answer. Very diplomatic was Floote.

It was well into the night and no longer quite the time
for social calls, even among the supernatural set, when Lord
Akeldama's doorbell sounded, interrupting Alexia's conversation and the drone's bustling.

Emmet Wilberforce Bootbottle-Fipps—whom everyone,
including Lady Maccon when she forgot herself, called

Boots—trotted off in a flutter of green velvet frock coat to see who would call at such an hour. Lord Akeldama didn't always keep a butler; he said his drones needed the practice. Whatever that meant.

Alexia thought of something she had better see dealt with before it slipped her mind and became inconvenient. "Floote, would you please see about some very discreet carpenters to build a bridge between the balconies?"

"Madam?"

"I realize that they are hardly more than a yard apart, but my stability is not what it once was. It seems likely we must persist in this charade of actually living in the one abode while sneaking into the other. I refuse to be hurled willy-nilly between houses, no matter how strong my husband or how diverting he would find the attempt. Clothing isn't always enough of a barrier to preternatural contact, and I should hate to be the victim of unreliable catching, if you take my meaning."

"Perfectly, madam. I shall see to the builders directly." Floote kept a remarkably straight face for a man having heard such a preposterous statement come out of the mouth of an overly pregnant aristocrat.

Boots reappeared wearing a look of mild shock under his sculpted topiary of muttonchops. "The caller is for you, Lady Maccon."

"Yes?" Alexia held out her hand for a card.

There was none forthcoming, only Boots's shocked statement. "It is a *lady,* what!"

"They do happen, Boots, much as you would prefer to deny it."

"Oh, no, sorry 'bout that. I mean to say, how'd she know you were here?"

"Well, if you told me which lady, I might be able to elucidate."

"It's a Miss Loontwill, Lady Maccon."

"Oh, fiddlesticks. Which one?"

Miss Felicity Loontwill sat in Lord Akeldama's drawing room in a dress of sensible heathered tweed with only one layer of trim and six buttons, a hat with minimal feathers, and a gray knit shawl with a ruffled collar.

"Oh, my heavens," exclaimed Lady Maccon upon seeing her sister in such a state. "Felicity, are you quite all right?"

Miss Loontwill looked up. "Why, yes, of course, sister. Why shouldn't I be?"

"Is there something amiss with the family?"

"You mean, aside from Mama's predilection for pink?"

Alexia, blinking in flabbergasted shock, lowered herself carefully onto a chair. "But, Felicity, you are wearing last season's dress!" She lowered her voice, in genuine fear that her sister might be deranged. "And *knitwear.*"

"Oh." Felicity wrapped the ghastly shawl tighter about her neck. "It was necessary."

Lady Maccon was only further shocked by such an unexpected statement. "Necessary? Necessary!"

"Well, yes, Alexia, do pay attention. Have you always been this frazzled, or is it your unfortunate condition?"

Felicity lowered her voice conspiratorially. "Necessary because I have been *fraternizing*."

"You have? With whom?" Alexia became suspicious. It was very late at night for an unmarried young lady of quality to be cavorting about unchaperoned, especially one who kept daylight hours and whose parents shunned association with the supernatural set.

"I am wearing *tweed*. With whom else? Some poor unfortunates of the middle class."

Lady Maccon would have none of it. "Oh, really, Felicity, you can hardly expect me to believe that you have had anything whatsoever to do with the lower orders."

"You may choose to believe it or not, sister."

Alexia wished for a return of her ability to stride about and loom threateningly. Sadly, striding was several months behind her, and should she attempt to loom, she would undoubtedly overbalance and pitch forward in graceless splendor. She settled for glaring daggers at her sibling. "Very well, then, what are you doing here? And how did you know to find me at Lord Akeldama's residence?"

"Mrs. Tunstell told me where to find you." Felicity looked with a critical eye at the golden magnificence surrounding her.

"Ivy? How did Ivy know?"

"Madame Lefoux told her."

"Oh, she did, did she? And how—"

"Apparently someone named Professor Lyall told Madame Lefoux your relocation was taking place this evening and that you would hole up at Lord Akeldama's, in case there were any orders pending delivery. Have you commissioned a new hat, sister? From that crass foreign female? Are you certain you should be patronizing her establishment after what happened in Scotland? And who is this Professor Lyall person? You haven't taken up with *academics,* have you? That cannot possibly be healthy. Education is terribly bad for the nerves, especially for a woman in your state."

Lady Maccon grappled for some appropriate response.

Felicity added, in a blatant attempt at distraction, "Speaking of which, you *have* gotten tremendously portly, haven't you? Is increasing supposed to cause you to swell quite so much as all that?"

Lady Maccon frowned. "I believe I have increased, as it were, to the maximum. You know me—I always insist on seeing a thing done as thoroughly as possible."

"Well, Mama says to make certain you don't get angry with anyone. The child will end up looking like him."

"Oh, really?"

"Yes, emotional mimicking they call it, and—"

"Well, that's no trouble. It will simply end up looking like my husband."

"But what if it is a female? Wouldn't that be horrible? She'd be all fuzzy and—"

Felicity would have continued but Lady Maccon lost her patience, a thing she was all too prone to misplacing. "Felicity, why are you visiting me?"

Miss Loontwill hedged. "This is quite the remarkable abode. I never did think I should ever see inside of a vam-

pire hive. And so charming and gleaming and full of exquisite collections. Almost up to my standards."

"This is not a hive—there is no queen. Not in the techni-
cal definition of the word. I will not be so easily detoured,
Felicity. Why have you shown up at such a time of night?
And why would you undertake such pains to discover my
whereabouts?"

Her sister shifted on the brocade settee, her blond head
tilted to one side and a small frown creasing her perfect forehead. She had not, Alexia noticed, modified her elaborately
styled ringlets to match her lowbrow outfit. A row of perfect
flat curls were gummed to her forehead in the very latest style.

"You have not paid the family much mind since your
return to London."

Lady Maccon considered this accusation. "You must
admit, I was made to feel rather unwelcome prior to my
departure." *And that is putting it mildly.* Her family had
always been a mite petty for her taste, even before they uni-
laterally decided to expel her from their midst at the most
inconvenient time. Since her ill-fated trip to Scotland and
subsequent dash across half the known world, she had simply elected to avoid the Loontwills as much as possible. As
Lady Maccon, denizen of the night, who fraternized with
werewolves; inventors; and, horror of horrors, actors, this
was a relatively easy undertaking.

"Yes, but it's been positively months, sister! I did not think
you the type to hold a grudge. Did you know Evylin has re-
newed her engagement to Captain Featherstonehaugh?"

Lady Maccon only stared at her sister, tapping one slipper lightly on the carpeted floor.

Miss Loontwill blushed, looking toward her and then away again. "I have become"—she paused as though searching for the correct way of phrasing it—"involved."

Alexia felt a tremor of real fear flutter through her breast. *Or is that indigestion?* "Oh, no, Felicity. Not with someone unsuitable? Not with someone middle class. Mama would never forgive you!"

Felicity stood and began to wander about the gilded room showing considerable agitation. "No, no, you misconstrue my meaning. I have become involved with my local chapter of the"—she lowered her voice dramatically—"National Society for Women's Suffrage."

If Lady Maccon hadn't already been sitting down, she would have had to sit at such a statement. "You want to vote? You? But you can't even decide which gloves to wear of a morning."

"I believe in the cause."

"Poppycock. You've never believed in anything in your whole life, except possibly the reliability of the French to predict next season's color palette."

"Well. Still."

"But, Felicity, really this is so very common. Couldn't you start up a ladies aid society or an embroidery social? *You?* Politically minded? I cannot deem such a thing feasible. It has only been five months since I met with you last, not five years, and even then you could not change your character so drastically. A feathered bonnet does not molt so easily as that."

At which juncture, and without any warning whatsoever, Lord Akeldama wafted into the room smelling of lemon and peppermint candy and sporting a playbill of some risqué comedy from the West End.

"Alexia, pudding, how *are* you faring this fine evening? Is moving house tragically unsettling? A relocation can be such a *trial* on one's finer feelings, I always find." He paused artfully on the threshold to put down his opera glasses, gloves, and top hat on a convenient sideboard. Then he raised his silver and sapphire monocle to one eye and regarded Felicity through it.

"Oh, dear me, pardon the intrusion." His keen eyes took in the dated dress and the effusive curls of Alexia's visitor. "Alexia, my dove, you have some sort of *company*?"

"Lord Akeldama. You remember my sister?"

The quizzing glass did not lower. "I do?"

"I believe you may have met one another at my wedding festivities?" Alexia was in no doubt that her esteemed host knew *exactly* who Felicity was from the very moment he entered the room—possibly before—but he did dearly love a performance, even if he had to put one on himself.

"I did?" The vampire was dressed to the height of fashion for an evening out. He wore a midnight-blue tailcoat and matched trousers, quite subdued for Lord Akeldama, or so it would seem at first glance. The careful observer soon noted that his satin waistcoat was silver, blue, and purple paisley in an excessively bold print, and he wore gloves and spats of the same material. Alexia had no idea how he thought to carry off such an outrageous ensemble. Whoever heard of patterned gloves, let alone spats? Then again, no ensemble had ever yet gotten the better of Lord Akeldama, nor was one likely to.

He certainly had the right to look askance at Felicity. "I did! Miss Loontwill? But you are so very much altered from when we last met. How has such a transformation been effected?"

Even Felicity had not the gumption to stand up to Lord Akeldama armed with a monocle. She crumbled in the face of the majestic authority of his perfectly tied and still fluffy—despite an evening's activities—cravat with its ostentatiously large sapphire pin. "Oh, well, you see, my lord, I've had a, ur, meeting and simply didn't have the time to change. I thought to catch my sister before she retired, on a matter of some delicacy."

Lord Akeldama did not take the hint. "Oh, yes?"

"Felicity has joined the National Society for Women's Suffrage," Alexia said placidly.

The vampire proved instantly helpful. "Oh, yes? I understand Lord Ambrose is a frequent contributor."

Alexia nodded her understanding at last. "Lord Ambrose, is it? Oh, Felicity, you do realize he is a vampire?"

Miss Loontwill tossed her curls. "Well, yes, but an *eligible* vampire." She glanced at Lord Akeldama from under her lashes. "And I am getting ever so old!"

He was instantly sympathetic. "Of course you are. You are already what? All of eighteen?"

Miss Loontwill sallied on. "But then I was quite taken with the rhetoric."

Alexia supposed a young lady so swayed by the Parisian fashion papers might be persuaded by a decent oratory display.

Felicity continued. "Why shouldn't we women vote? After all, it's not as though the gentlemen have done so wondrous a job of things with their stewardship. I do not intend to offend, my lord."

"No offense taken, my little *buttercup*."

Uh-oh, thought Alexia, *Felicity has been given an epithet. Lord Akeldama likes her.*

The vampire continued. "I find such struggles adorably commendable."

Felicity began pacing about in a manner Alexia had to admit not unlike her own good self when seized with a particularly inspired argument. "My point precisely. Don't you want the vote, Alexia? You cannot be content to allow that buffoonish husband of yours to speak for you in matters political. Not after the way he has behaved in the past."

Alexia declined to mention at this juncture that she already had the vote, and it was one of only three on Queen Victoria's Shadow Council. Such a vote as this counted a good deal more than any popular ballot might. Instead, she spoke a different truth. "I have never given the matter much thought. But this still does not explain how you have ended up on Lord Akeldama's doorstep."

"Yes, little snowdrop." Lord Akeldama took up a perch on the arm of the settee, watching Felicity as a parrot might watch a drab little sparrow that had strayed into his domain.

Miss Loontwill took a deep breath. "It is really not my

fault. Mama did not endorse my endeavors with regards to Lord Ambrose. So I have been liberating myself from the house after bedtime by means of the servant's entrance. You used to have some success with this approach, Alexia. Don't think I didn't know. I believed I could accomplish such a thing undetected."

Alexia was beginning to understand. "But you miscalculated. I had help. Floote's help. I cannot imagine Swilkins being sympathetic to the Ambrose cause."

Felicity grimaced in agreement. "No, you are perfectly correct. I did not realize how vital the approbation of one's butler is in allowing for nocturnal autonomy."

"So let us get to the crux of the matter. Has Mama tossed you out?"

Felicity got that look on her face that said whoever was at fault in this scenario it was probably Felicity. "Not exactly."

"Oh, Felicity, you didn't. You walked out?"

"I thought, since you were taking a house in town, perhaps I might come to stay with you for a little while. I understand the company will not be nearly so refined or elegant as that to which I am accustomed, but..."

Lord Akeldama's forehead creased ever so slightly at *that* statement.

Lady Maccon cogitated. She would like to encourage this new spirit of social-mindedness. If Felicity needed anything in her life, it was a cause. Then she might stop nitpicking everyone else. But if she stayed with them, she would have to be taken into their confidence regarding the living arrangements. And there was another thing to consider.

Should Felicity be exposed to a werewolf pack in all its ever-changing and overexposed glory while still unmarried? *This is the last thing I need right now. I can't even see my own feet anymore. How can I see that my sister is properly chaperoned?* Alexia had found pregnancy relatively manageable, up to a point. That point having been some three weeks ago, at which juncture her natural reserves of control gave way to sentimentality. Only yesterday she had ended breakfast sobbing over the fried eggs because they *looked at her funny.* The pack had spent a good half hour trying to find a way to pacify her. Her husband was so worried he looked to start crying himself.

Alexia copped out, embarrassed to have to do so in front of Lord Akeldama. "I shall have to consult my husband on the subject."

The vampire jumped in with alacrity. "You could stay here with me, little bluebell."

Felicity brightened. "Oh, why—"

Lady Maccon put her foot down. "Absolutely not." Of all the people Felicity should not be overexposed to, it was Lord Akeldama, on the basis of cattiness alone. If left together for too long, the two of them might actually take over the civilized world, through sheer application of snide remarks.

A tap sounded on the drawing room door.

"Now what?" wondered Alexia.

"Come in! We are unquestionably *at home,*" sung out Lord Akeldama.

The door opened and Boots and Biffy entered. Both were looking dapper and well put together as behooved a current

and former drone of Lord Akeldama's, although Biffy had
a certain aura that Boots lacked. Biffy was still the same
pleasant-mannered fellow with a partiality for modish attire
and the figure to show it off, but something had altered.
There was a slight smudge on his cheekbone that no drone
of Lord Akeldama's would ever show to his master. However, seeing the two stand together, Alexia didn't think
it was entirely the smudge's fault. There was no vampire
sophistication to Biffy anymore—no high-society shine, no
sharpened edge. Instead he sported a slight air of embarrassment that Alexia suspected all werewolves felt deep down.
It sprung from the certain knowledge that once a month he
would get naked and turn into a slavering beast whether he
liked it or not.

Lord Akeldama's inquisitive expression did not waver.
"Darlings!" he said to the two of them, as though he had
not seen them in years. "What exciting tidbits have you
brought me?"

Miss Loontwill looked with interest at the two young
men. "Oh," she said, "I remember you! You helped my sister plan her nuptials. You had that marvelous idea about a
groom's cake. Stylish, two cakes. Especially for my sister's
wedding—she is so very fond of food."

Biffy knew his duty and hurried forward to bow over
Felicity's proffered hand. "Sandalio de Rabiffano, at your
service, miss. How do you do?"

Alexia, who until that moment had never before heard
Biffy's real name, gave Lord Akeldama a startled look. The

vampire stood and wandered innocently over to her chair. "Spectacularly Spanish, wouldn't you say? Moorish blood some ways back."

She nodded sagely.

Biffy returned Felicity's hand. "I cannot take credit for the cake, miss. It's an odd little American custom."

Felicity flirted outrageously. "Oh, well, we won't tell anyone *that,* now, will we? Are you still in Lord Akeldama's employ?"

A brief flash of hurt passed over Biffy's pleasant face. "No, miss. I've been transferred to your sister's household."

Miss Loontwill clearly thought this a most beneficial arrangement. "Oh, have you, *indeed?*"

Alexia interrupted any continued flirtation. "Felicity, go next door and wait for me in the front parlor. Order tea if you must. When my husband returns, I'll discuss your request with him."

Felicity opened her mouth again.

"Now, Felicity." Lady Maccon was at her most dictatorial.

Much to everyone's surprise, including Felicity's, Felicity went.

Lord Akeldama tilted his head at Boots and gave a little nod after the retreating girl. With no verbal exchange required, Boots trotted obediently after Felicity. Biffy looked on wistfully. Alexia surmised that he was not yearning for Felicity's continued company but was regretting the fact that he could no longer obey Lord Akeldama's commands.

She brought him back around sharply. No sense in letting him dwell. "Biffy, did you have something to tell me or Lord Akeldama?"

"You, my lady. I am pleased to report that you have been successfully moved. The new house awaits your perusal and, hopefully, approval."

"Excellent! I should—Oh wait. Lord Akeldama, I keep meaning to ask. And while I'm in your company, if I may?"

"Yes, my little *syllabub*?"

"Do you recall, I was describing those porcupines to you? Or overgrown hedgehogs, or whatever their species inclination, from several nights ago? I was thinking, they were also ever so slightly vampiric in propensity. Their speed and their old dark blood and their susceptibility to the lapis solaris. Is that possible, do you think—vampire porcupines?"

Lord Akeldama's eyes lit with amusement. "Oh, my dearest girl, what *will* you think of next? Weregoats? Be on your guard, for at full moon they shall creep into your coat closet and eat up all your shoes!"

Biffy hid a smile.

Alexia was not in the mood to be mocked.

Lord Akeldama recovered his much-vaunted poise. "My darling *toffee button,* you can be quite the widgeon upon occasion. Animals do not have souls. How could they possibly? Next thing you know, I'll be petitioning Countess Nadasdy to bite old fatty there so I can have company into my dotage." He gestured to his cat. The chubby creature had delusions of being a vicious hunter but could never master anything more taxing than a pillow tassel. Or, on one recent and memorable occasion, one of Ivy's hats. Lady Maccon shuddered at the recollection. Why had she thought she could bring Ivy to tea with a vampire? Her dearest friend may have taken to the stage of late, but she was still not ready for intimate exposure to Lord Akeldama's brand of drama. Nor was Lord Akeldama entirely capable of withstanding intimate exposure to one of Ivy's hats. After that tea, Alexia had been forced to admit that Lord Akeldama and Ivy Tunstell were like plaid and brocade, utterly incompatible even in complementary colors.

At which juncture someone else came into Lord Akeldama's drawing room, only this time without announcement of any kind save a minor bellow.

"Good gracious me," said Lord Akeldama, sounding like some dowager countess of old Georgian inclination. "What has my house become? Charing Cross Station?"

Biffy looked to Lady Maccon, resplendent in her tentlike gown of eyelet lace and blue satin bows. "More akin to a dirigible landing green, I should think, my lord."

Alexia, who found her condition even more ridiculous than anyone else, was moved to smile at such a comparison. She had, of late, been feeling inflated.

Lord Akeldama chuckled softly. "Ah, Biffy, I have missed you, my dove."

The individual who had entered, unannounced and unbidden, observed this exchange with a frown.

Lord Akeldama turned upon him with mild censure in

his sharp blue eyes. "Lord Maccon, if you are to stay here, and I believe *that* is settled for the moment, we really must train you in the fine art of knocking before entering a room."

The earl was gruff in his embarrassment. "Oh, yes. Upon occasion, I find it hard to remember details of etiquette." He swirled his cloak off. It landed on the back of a side chair before sliding off and falling to the floor.

Lord Akeldama shuddered.

"Lord Akeldama. Wife. Pup." Lord Maccon nodded. His tawny eyes concerned, he moved to bend over Alexia. "Everything still corked up?" he asked her in one ear.

"Yes, yes, don't fuss, Conall." Alexia would have none of it.

"Everything else squared away?"

"I was just about to perform the inspection. Hoist me up, would you, please?"

The earl grinned, braced himself, and offered her one massive hand. Alexia grasped it in both of hers and he levered. At her preternatural touch, he lost supernatural strength, but he was still powerful enough to handle Alexia—even in her inflated dirigible state.

"We will have to be *seen* going next door, I suppose. And we will have to determine a way to sneak back into this house later tonight."

"Such skulking and folderol, all for the sake of appearances," grumbled Lord Maccon.

Alexia bristled. She'd been through quite a hellish time when her husband had booted her from his bed and company. Society had ostracized her all because she *appeared* to have been indiscreet. "Appearances are everything!"

"Hear, *hear*," agreed Lord Akeldama.

"Very well, wife. We must determine how to get you from our balcony to Lord Akeldama's."

He wore an expression Alexia suspected greatly. She glared at him. "You will find me a gangplank, thank you very much. I will not be flung, husband."

Lord Maccon looked a tad surprised at that. "Did I indicate I intended any such activity?"

"No, but I *know* how you get."

Conall was nonplussed by such an unwarranted accusation.

Alexia continued. "Oh, yes, and I should warn you. There's a surprise waiting for us in our new front parlor."

Lord Maccon grinned wolfishly. "Is it a nice surprise?"

"Only if you're in a very good mood," hedged his wife.

*   *   *

The ghost was in that space again, that insubstantial void. She thought she might float there forever if she could simply stay still. Still as death.

But reality intruded. Reality from her own mind, however little of it was left. "You have to tell someone. You have to tell them. This is wrong. You are mad and yet even you know this is wrong. Put a stop to it. You have to tell."

Oh, how inconvenient, when one's own brain starts issuing instructions.

"Who can I tell? Who can I tell? I am only a hen in a chicken coop."

"Tell someone who can do something. Tell the soulless girl."

"Her? But I don't even like her."

"That's no excuse. You don't like anyone."

The ghost hated it when she was sensible with herself.

CHAPTER THREE

Matters Ghostly

O h, really, must you?" was Lord Maccon's considered opinion, expressed to his wife upon seeing her sister in residence, as if Felicity were some sort of unfortunate digestive complaint Alexia had recently developed.

Lady Maccon ignored her sister, who sat waiting patiently in the parlor, and instead took in her new surroundings. The drones and the werewolves had done Woolsey Pack proud. Their new town house was quite filled to bursting with tasteful furniture, pleasingly arranged and minimally decorated. As the abode was intended to serve as a way station for those of the pack who had business in town, most personal items and vital survival necessities such as dungeons and clavigers were left back at Woolsey Castle. The result was that the new house had the look of a gentleman's club, rather than a private residence (but a nicely up-market gentleman's club). Lord Maccon muttered that it reminded him of one of the sitting rooms in the House of Lords. But he was muttering for the sake of it, and everyone knew it. Thick curtains kept harmful sunlight out, and thick, plush rugs kept heavy footfalls and claw scrapes to a minimum.

For the time being, Floote was to resume the post of butler to the secondary residence. He had not even batted an eye at this temporary demotion back to domestic staff. Alexia suspected that he had missed his former authority over the household and accompanying ability to monitor all business occurring within it. Personal secretary might be a higher position, but it did not carry with it quite the range of a butler's command over gossip.

The front parlor, where Felicity sat, was decked out in rich chocolate brown leather and cream twill, with only a small touch of brass here and there for accent—the filigree of a gas lamp, the fringe on a tablecloth, a large Oriental floor vase to hold Alexia's parasols, and a periscopic shoe-drying stand in front of the fireplace.

It was exactly the opposite of Lord Akeldama's brocade-and-gilt splendor.

Lady Maccon was impressed. "Floote, where did you find such lovely furnishings at such short notice?"

Floote looked at Alexia as though she had asked him the secrets of his daily ablutions.

"Now, now, wife. If Floote prefers to be thought a conjurer, who are we to inquire as to his sleight of hand? We must preserve a sense of wonder and faith, eh, Floote?"

Lord Maccon slapped the dignified gentleman amiably on the back.

Floote sniffed. "If you say so, sir."

Lord Maccon turned to his wife's sister, sitting in demure silence and drab gray, both so utterly out of character as to garner even Lord Maccon's notice.

"Miss Felicity, has somebody died?"

Felicity stood and bobbed a curtsy at the earl. "Not that I am aware, my lord. Thank you for inquiring. How do you do?"

"There's something rather singular about your appearance this evening, isn't there? Have you done something different with your hair?"

"No, my lord. I'm simply a tad underdressed for visiting. Only, I had a favor to ask my sister and it couldn't possibly wait."

"Oh, did you?" The earl turned his tawny eyes on his wife.

Alexia tipped her chin up and to one side. "She wants to come stay with us."

"Oh, she does, does she?"

"Here."

"Here?" Conall took his wife's point exactly. They could hardly have Felicity stay in their new town house and not actually be living there themselves. What if that information got out? Felicity would be known to have resided with a pack of werewolves and no chaperone.

"Why not at Woolsey? Bit of country air? Looks like she could do with it." Lord Maccon grappled for a better solution.

"Felicity has involved herself in some"—Alexia paused—
"questionable charitable work here in town. She seems to
believe she may require our protection."

Lord Maccon looked confused. As well he might. "Protection... protection from whom?"

"My mother," replied his wife, with meaning.

Lord Maccon could understand *that* and was about to
demand additional details when a ghost materialized up
through the plush carpet next to him.

Under ordinary circumstances, ghosts were too polite to
simply appear in the middle of a conversation. The better-
behaved specters took pains to drift into front hallways at
the very least, where a footman might notice and inquire as
to their business. In a startling fashion, this one wafted into
existence out of the center of the new rug, directly through
the bouquet of flowers depicted there.

Lord Maccon exclaimed. Lady Maccon let out a little
gasp and firmed her grip on her parasol. Floote raised one
eyebrow. Felicity fainted.

Alexia and Conall looked at each other for a moment and
then left Felicity slumped over in her chair by mutual and
silent agreement. Alexia's parasol did have a small bottle of
smelling salts among its many secret accoutrements, but this
ghost required immediate attention with no time to revive
troublesome sisters. The Maccons turned the full force of
their collective attention onto the specter before them.

"Floote," asked Lady Maccon slowly, so as not to startle
the creature, "did we know this house came with a ghost?
Was that in the leasing documentation?"

"I don't believe so, madam. Let me ascertain the particulars." Floote glided off to find the deeds.

The ghost in question was rather fuzzy around the edges and not entirely cohesive in the middle either. She must be close to poltergeist state. When she began speaking, it became abundantly clear that this was indeed the case, for the ghost's mental faculties were degenerated and her voice was high and breathy, sounding as though it emanated from some distance away.

"Maccon? Or was it bacon? I used to like bacon. Very salty." The ghost paused and twirled about, trailing misty tendrils through the air. These eddied in Lady Maccon's direction, pulled by the preternatural's attraction for ambient aether. "Message. Missive. Mutton. Didn't like mutton—chewy. Wait! Urgent. Or was that pungent? Important. Impossible. Information."

Lady Maccon looked at her husband curiously. "One of BUR's?"

The Bureau of Unnatural Registry kept a number of mobile ghost agents—exhumed and preserved bodies with tethered specters that could be placed in select locales or near key public institutions for information-gathering purposes. They took pains to have a noncorporeal communication network in place, where each ghost's tether crossed over the limits of at least one other's. This stretched the length and breadth of London, although it was not able to cover the city in its entirety. Of course, it had to be updated as its members went insane, but such maintenance was practically second nature to BUR's spectral custodians.

The werewolf shook his shaggy head. "Not that I know of, my dear. I'd have to look at the registry to be certain. I've met most of our noncorporeal recruits at least once. Don't think this one is under contract at all, or someone would be taking far better care of the body." He braced himself in front of the ghost, arms stiff by his side. "Hallo? Listen up. Where are you tethered? This house? Where is your corpse? It needs looking to. You are drifting, young lady. Drifting."

The ghost looked at him in puzzled annoyance and floated up and down. "Not important. Not important at all. Message, that's what's important. What was it? Accents, accents, everywhere these days. London's full of foreigners. And curry. Who let in the curry?"

"That's the message?" Lady Maccon didn't like to be out of the loop, even if the loop was inside some nonsensical ghost's head.

The ghost whirled to face Alexia. "No, no, no. Now, no, what? Oh, yes. Are you Alexia Macaroon?"

Alexia didn't know how to respond to *that,* so she nodded.

Conall, useless beast, started laughing. "Macaroon? I love it!"

Both Alexia and the ghost ignored him. All of the ghost's wavering attention was now focused on Lady Maccon. "Tarabitty? Tarabotti. Daughter of? Dead. Soulless. Problem? Pudding!"

Alexia wondered whether all this verbal rigmarole was related to her father or to herself, but she supposed in either context it was accurate enough. "The same."

The ghost twirled about in midair, pleased with herself.

"Message for you." She paused, worried and confused. "Custard. No. Conscription. No. Conspiracy. To kill, to kill…"

"Me?" Alexia hazarded a guess. She thought it might be a safe bet: someone was usually trying to kill her.

The ghost became agitated, straining at her invisible tether and vibrating slightly. "No, no, no. Not you. But someone. Something?" She brightened suddenly. "The queen. Kill the queen." The specter began to sing. "Kill the queen! Kill the queen! Kill the quee-een!"

Lord Maccon stopped smiling. "Ah, that's torn it."

"Good. Yes? That's all. Bye-bye, living people." The ghost then sank down through the floor of their new parlor and vanished, presumably back the way she had come.

Floote returned to the room at that juncture to find a silently shocked Lord and Lady Maccon staring at each other.

"No documented apparitions come tethered to this house, madam."

"Thank you, Floote. I suppose we should see to…?" Alexia did not need to continue. The ever-resourceful Floote was already tending to Felicity with a scented handkerchief.

Lady Maccon turned to her husband. "And you should—"

He was already clapping his top hat to his head. "On my way, wife. She has to be within tether radius of this house. There should be a record of her somewhere in BUR's files. I'm taking Professor Lyall and Biffy with me."

Alexia nodded. "Don't be out too late. Someone needs to help get me back into Lord Akeldama's house before morning, and you know all I seem to do these days is sleep."

Her husband swept over in the manner of some Gothic hero, cloak flapping, and administered a loud kiss both to her and then, to her utter embarrassment, to her protruding stomach before dashing off. Luckily, Floote was still seeing to Felicity, so neither witnessed the excessive display of affection.

"I suppose that makes Felicity the least of our concerns."

The sun had just set, and the Maccons were awake, across the temporary gangplank from Lord Akeldama's house, and downstairs in their own dining room. The conversation had not changed from that of the night before; it had only paused for Conall to conduct some slapdash investigations and then catch half a day's sleep.

Lord Maccon glanced up from his repast. "We must take any threat against the queen seriously, my dear. Even if my efforts so far have proved unproductive, that does not mean we can treat the ravings of a ghost with flippancy."

"You believe I am not concerned? I've alerted the Shadow Council. We have a special meeting called for this very evening."

Lord Maccon looked disgruntled. "Now, Alexia, should you be involving yourself in this matter at such a late stage?"

"What? The rumor has only just been reported! I understand you and Lyall got lengths ahead yesterday after I went to bed, but I hardly think—"

"No, wife. I mean to say, you are not exactly up to your usual galavanting about London with parasol at the ready, now, are you?"

Alexia glanced down at her overstuffed belly and then got *that* look on her face. "I am entirely capable."

"Of what, waddling up to someone and ruthlessly bumping into them?"

Lady Maccon glared. "I assure you, *husband,* that while the rest of me may be moving more slowly than has previously been my custom, there is nothing whatsoever wrong with my mental capacities. I can manage!"

"Now, Alexia, *please* be reasonable."

Lady Maccon was willing to concede somewhat due to the nature of her state. "I promise that I will not take any unnecessary risks."

Her husband did not miss the fact that this statement would have to bow to his wife's definition of the term *necessary.* He was, therefore, not at all reassured. "At least take one of the pups with you on your investigations."

Lady Maccon narrowed her eyes.

The earl wheedled. "I should feel much better knowing someone had care of your physical safety. Even if the vampires are abstaining—and we've no guarantee yet that they are—you do tend to get yourself into certain predicaments. Now, it's not that I think you are incapable, my dear, simply that you are currently much less mobile."

Alexia did have to admit his reasoning. "Very well. But if I am to troll about with a companion, I want it to be Biffy."

The earl did not approve this selection at all. "Biffy! He's a new pup. He can't even control the change. What good could he possibly be?"

"It's Biffy or nobody." *Typical of my husband to see only*

Biffy's limitations as a werewolf and not his admirable abilities as a human.

For the young dandy was, indeed, quite accomplished. Much to Lord Maccon's disgust, he had taken over many of the duties of lady's maid to his new mistress. Alexia had never bothered to hire a replacement for Angelique. Biffy's taste was impeccable, and he had a real eye for which hairstyles and fabrics would suit her best—better than Angelique, who had been good but rather more daringly French than Lady Maccon liked. Biffy, for all his audacious inclinations when it came to his own apparel, knew how to be sensible when it came to a lady who scurried around whacking at automatons and climbing into ornithopters.

"It isn't a wise choice." Lord Maccon's jaw was set.

No one else had yet joined them at the dining table. It was a rare thing in a pack to enjoy any privacy outside the bedroom. Alexia took advantage of their seclusion. She scooted toward her husband and rested her hand atop his on the fine lace tablecloth.

"Biffy has had Lord Akeldama's training. That is a skill set that branches away from being merely a dab hand with the curling tongs."

The earl snorted.

"I am not only thinking of my own comfort in this matter. He needs some kind of distraction, Conall. Haven't you noticed? Five months and he's still not settled."

The earl twisted his lips slightly to one side. He had noticed. Of course he had. He noticed everything about his wolves. It was part of his most essential being, to hold the pack together as a single cohesive entity. Alexia had read the papers; scientists called it the soul's intrinsic cross-linking of the essential humors, the enmatterment of aether. But she could also guess the truth of it: that just as vampires and ghosts became tethered to a place, so werewolves became tethered to a pack. Biffy's all too frequent melancholy must hurt Conall terribly.

"How will allowing him to accompany you help?"

"Am I not also part of this pack?"

"Ah." The earl turned his hand over to grip his wife's in a compliant caress.

"If you ask me, it is not so much Biffy who cannot find his place as Woolsey not giving him the right place to find. You are all thinking of him as you would any new werewolf. He's not, you understand? He's different."

Conall, remarkably, did not jump immediately to the defensive. "Yes, I'm aware. Randolph and I were recently discussing this very thing. But it cannot simply be a matter of Biffy's preferences. We werewolves are as experimental in our tastes as the vampires, if a little more reserved about the expression of them. And there's always Adelphus. He's willing."

Alexia made a disgusted noise. "Adelphus is always willing. Biffy does not need a lover, husband—he needs a purpose. This is a matter of culture. Biffy has come to you out of vampire culture. *Lord Akeldama's* vampire culture."

"So what do you recommend?"

"Woolsey has managed to accept me into its midst and I am by no means standard werewolf fare." Alexia played with her husband's fingers, threading and unthreading them with her own.

"But you are female."

"Exactly!"

"You are suggesting we treat Biffy as if he were a woman?"

"I am suggesting that you think about him as if he had married in from the outside."

Lord Maccon gave this due consideration and then nodded slowly.

Lady Maccon realized he must be very troubled by Biffy's unhappiness to listen to her suggestions with so few protestations.

Alexia squeezed his hand once more and then let go, returning to her meal of apple fritter and boiled arrowroot pudding with melted butter and currant jelly. Of late, her taste in comestibles had leaned ever more in the saccharine direction. Now she ate almost exclusively of the pudding course at any meal. "You think there's a chance you might lose him, don't you?"

Her husband did not answer her, which was an admission in and of itself. Instead he busily began tackling a veritable heap of fried veal cutlets.

Lady Maccon chose her next words with care. "How quickly can loner status be established?" She did not want to be perceived as doubting her husband's Alpha abilities. Men, even immortal ones, had fragile egos on certain subjects. Such egos could be as delicate and as messy as puff pastry. Though rather less palatable with tea. *Ooh, tea.*

"Wolves can go solitary at any time, but it is usually for a specific reason and occurs within the first few years of metamorphosis. Howlers say it has something to do with early bonding to the Alpha. Often it means the unbonded is too much Alpha himself. I don't believe Biffy falls into this category, but that is the only thing currently in our favor."

Alexia thought she spotted the real source of her husband's concern. "If Biffy becomes a loner, you don't believe he would survive. Do you?"

"Loners are unstable. They brawl constantly. Our new pup is not a fighter, not like that." Her husband's lovely eyes were pained and guilty. This mess with Biffy was his fault. Unintentionally his fault, but Lord Conall Maccon was not the kind of gentleman who shifted blame merely because they were all victims of circumstance.

Alexia took a breath and then dove for the kill. "Then you really should give him to me for a while. I'll see what I can do. Remember, I can tame him if I have to, if he loses control and goes to wolf." She wiggled ungloved fingers at her husband.

"Very well, wife. But you are to check in with either me or Randolph as to his progress."

As the earl said this, Professor Lyall wandered into the dining room. The Beta was his usual unassuming self—his sandy hair neatly combed; his angular features arranged into a nonthreatening expression; his demeanor quiet, self-effacing, and utterly forgettable. It was an aura that Alexia was beginning to suspect Professor Lyall had cultivated for decades.

"Good evening, my lady, my lord." The Beta assumed his seat.

A maid appeared at his elbow with fresh tea and the evening's paper. Professor Lyall was the type of man to have *that* kind of relationship with the domestic staff. Even newly hired and after only a day's residence, they were already providing exactly what he required without need for any time-wasting orders. Between him, Floote, and Biffy, there would never be a single upset in the running of the Maccon household. It was a good thing, too, for the indomitable Lady Maccon had other things to occupy her time and attention. The running of her household was best left to the gentlemen. Although, she did indicate to the maid that she, too, required tea.

"Professor Lyall, how are you this evening?" Alexia saw no reason why familiarity with an individual ought to breed familiarity of manner, except with her husband, of course. Even though she had been living, off and on, among the Woolsey Pack for almost a year, she never relaxed on courtesy.

"Tolerably well, my lady, tolerably well." Nor, indeed, did Professor Lyall, who was remarkably civilized for a werewolf and seemed particularly respectful of all codes of politeness and gracefulness of manner.

Now that she had both of them at her table, Lady Maccon directed the two werewolves back onto the weighty matter of the queen's life. "So, gentlemen, anything come out of BUR on the threat?"

"Not an aetheric sausage," complained the earl.

Professor Lyall shook his head.

"Must be the vampires," said Lord Maccon.

"Now, husband, why would you say that?"

"Isn't it always the vampires?"

"No, sometimes it's the scientists." Lady Maccon was referring obliquely to the disbanded Hypocras Club. "And sometimes it's the church." Now she was thinking of the Templars. "And sometimes it's the werewolves."

"Well, I say!" Lord Maccon stuffed another cutlet into his mouth. "I can't imagine you actually defending the vampires. They've been trying to kill you for months."

"Oh, Conall, do swallow first. Then speak. What kind of example is that for our child?"

The earl looked around as though trying to see if the little being had somehow been born without his notice and was now staring at him with an eye toward modeling its behavior upon his.

Lady Maccon continued. "Simply because the vampires are perennially trying to murder me doesn't mean they are trying to murder the queen as well, now, does it? One would think their resources would be somewhat taxed, if nothing else. Besides, what could possibly be their motive? The queen is a progressive." She was moved to defend her stance further. "I thought your lot was supposed to have long memories. Correct me if I'm wrong, Professor Lyall, but didn't the last major threat to Queen Victoria's life emanate from the Kingair Pack?"

"Really, Lady Maccon, couldn't it wait until I've at least finished my first cup of tea?" The Beta looked put upon.

Alexia said nothing.

Professor Lyall put down his tea pointedly. "There was that overeager Pate fellow with the walking stick some twenty years ago or so. Completely mutilated Her Majesty's favorite bonnet. Shocking behavior. And there was that disgruntled Irishman with the unloaded pistol before that." He helped himself to a small serving of smoked kipper but paused before digging in. "And the reputed incident a few years back with John Brown." The Beta considered his kipper as though it held all the answers. "Come to think on it, they've all been remarkably ineffective."

Her husband snorted. "Notoriety mongers, the lot of them."

Alexia puffed out her cheeks. "You know what I mean. Those were all isolated incidents. I mean planned cohesive plots backed by serious intent."

The maid reappeared with more tea and an extra cup for Lord Maccon. Who sneered at it.

Professor Lyall's face sobered. "Then, no, Kingair was the last."

A delicate subject, indeed, as Kingair was Lord Maccon's former pack, and they had betrayed him in order to attempt the ghastly deed. He had killed his Beta and moved to London to challenge for Woolsey as a result. Like politics, or personal dressing habits, this was not proper meal-time conversation.

Professor Lyall, a man of much delicacy, seemed to find the subject particularly uncomfortable. After all, Woolsey had ultimately benefited from the assassination attempt.

Their previous Alpha was reputed to be a man of petty disposition and profound temper, and Lord Maccon was considered one of the better werewolf leaders. The best, if Alexia had anything to say on the subject. Which she did. Often.

The bell sounded in the front entranceway, and Professor Lyall glanced up gratefully. There came a rumble of voices as Floote answered the door. Alexia couldn't make out who it was, but her husband and his Beta had werewolf hearing and their reactions—a slight smile from Lyall and a disgusted frown from Conall—gave her a pretty decent idea.

"Peaches!" Lord Akeldama wafted in on a wave of Bond Street's best pomade and a lemon-scented eau de toilette. Alexia's pregnancy had had a strange effect on her sense of smell, rendering it far more acute. She imagined she was getting some limited idea of how werewolves felt with their supernatural abilities in that arena.

The vampire, resplendent in a silver tailcoat and bright yellow waistcoat only one or two shades darker than his hair, paused in the doorway. "Isn't this delightfully *cozy*? How perfectly *splendid* that I can simply pop next door and visit you all à la table!"

"And how nice that you are not a hive queen to be so entirely confined to your own home," replied Alexia. She gestured for the vampire to draw up a chair. He did so with a flourish, shaking out his napkin and placing it in his lap, although he would, everyone knew, take no food.

Professor Lyall tilted his head at the teapot. When Lord Akeldama nodded, the Beta poured him out a cup. "Milk?"

"Lemon, if you would be so kind."

Lyall raised his eyebrows in shock but signaled one of the maids to run and see to this odd request. "I thought most vampires didn't tolerate citrus."

"Dolly, my pet, I am most assuredly not *most vampires*."

Professor Lyall did not pursue this, as he had a more pressing question in mind. "It has occurred to me to worry about this scheme of ours. I understand it is a delicate subject, but this last winter you did swarm, did you not? Because of that spot of bother with Biffy being stuck under the Thames."

"Yes, poppet, what of it?"

"That swarming isn't going to hinder the effectiveness of your residency now, is it? You understand I ask only with a mind toward the safety of the child and because I've no records pertaining to the consequences of a rove swarming. No insult is intended."

Lord Akeldama grinned. "Dolly, such a *careful* little creature, aren't you? But fret not—my house isn't technically a hive. I'm not bound by the same kinds of instincts. I can return to my previous residence without psychological upset. Besides, that was half a year ago. I'm well recovered from the experience by now."

Lyall did not look entirely convinced.

Lord Akeldama changed the subject. "So what say you, all my *lupine darlings,* to this new threat?"

Lord Maccon looked with shock at his Beta. "Randolph, you didn't!"

Professor Lyall did not flinch. "Of course not."

"Wife?"

Alexia swallowed her bit of pudding. "He knows because, well, this *is* Lord Akeldama. You are going to have to get accustomed to it, my dear."

"Thank you, darling *plum nubbin,* for your faith in my meager resources."

"Of course, my lord. So?"

"Ah, *dandelion fluff,* I regret that I have not yet formed a ready opinion as to the nature and origin of these latest twitterings."

A footman appeared with the lemon, and Lyall poured the vampire a cup of tea. Lord Akeldama sipped it delicately.

Lord Maccon snorted. "You haven't lacked for a ready opinion in the whole of your very long life."

The vampire tittered at that. "True, but those expressed traditionally concern matters of dress, not politics."

Floote came in with Alexia's dispatch case. "You're due at the palace shortly, madam."

"Oh, my, yes, look at the time. Thank you, Floote. My parasol?"

"Here, madam."

"And perhaps a bite to take along?"

Floote handed her a sausage roll wrapped in checked cloth, having anticipated just such a request.

"Oh, thank you, Floote."

The earl looked up hopefully. Wordlessly Floote handed him another sausage roll. The earl downed it in two satisfied bites, even though he had just finished a rather large meal. Floote and

Lyall exchanged knowing looks. It had become quite the task to keep both Lord and Lady Maccon fed these days.

Lady Maccon leaned forward onto the table, bracing against it with both hands, pleased to live in a household that did not favor the spindly furniture so in vogue with ladies of quality. By dint of some sizable effort, she managed to almost hoist herself to her feet before losing her balance and lurching back down.

"Oh, for goodness' sake," she cried out in abject frustration. The gentlemen all leaped to her assistance. Lord Maccon made it to her first. Which was probably a good thing. With her preternatural touch, none of the others present would have been of any use. They were all too slight in their mortal forms to handle her clumsiness.

Having gained her feet and some measure of her dignity, Alexia said, "I really must say, I am finding my own proportions quite vulgar."

Lord Maccon hid his smile. "Not all that much longer, my dear."

Alexia hated it when he called her his dear. "Really, it can't occur soon enough." She waved off Floote's offer of a cloak and accepted a light shawl instead. It was plenty warm enough even without the wrap, but formalities must be observed. Then she gathered up her case and parasol.

Biffy appeared at her elbow, bloodred tailcoat in place, pure white cravat emphasizing his pleasant features, and matched red top hat on his head. He may have had to sacrifice a good many things to take up his new role as a werewolf, but he had refused to sacrifice his tailor.

"I am to act as escort this evening, my lady?"

"Oh, yes, Biffy dear. How did you know?"

Biffy gave her a look remarkably similar to the one always worn by Lord Akeldama when he was asked such a question.

Alexia nodded her understanding and then looked to the vampire. "Share a carriage, my lord potentate?"

"Why not?" Lord Akeldama sucked down the last of his tea, stood, performed an exaggerated bow to the two werewolves still at the dining table, and offered his arm to Alexia. She took it and they swept from the room, Biffy trailing faithfully after.

As they left, Lady Maccon heard her husband say to Lyall, "How long do you imagine we are going to have to keep up this place of residence?"

"Until the child is grown, I suppose," responded the Beta.

"God's teeth, it's going to be a long sixteen years."

"I imagine you'll survive it relatively unscathed, my lord."

"Randolph, you and I both know there are things far worse than death."

Alexia and Lord Akeldama exchanged smiles.

*   *   *

"Did you tell her?" asked the first ghost, stretched as far as she could, shimmering in and out of existence with the strain of her extended tether.

"I told her." The second ghost bobbed up and down in the air above the street. She was a little more substantial,

a little closer to home. "I told her what I could remember. I told her to put a stop to it. Are we done now?"

They were both lucid, strangely lucid, for two so near the end of enmatterment. It was as though the afterlife were giving them this one chance to fix things.

"We're done," said the first ghost. Both of them knew she wasn't referring to their plan or to their relationship but to their inevitable demise. "Now only I must wait."

CHAPTER FOUR

―――――

Where Tethered Specters Meet

L ady Maccon, muhjah, and Lord Akeldama, potentate, were allowed through the entrance to Buckingham Palace with very little ceremony. It was not one of their scheduled visits, but Lord Akeldama and Lady Maccon were regulars and, as such, required only minimal perusal. They were also favorites, or Lady Maccon was. Lord Akeldama was generally regarded by members of both the military and the constabulary with whom he had congress as *challenging in large doses*. However, the castle guards were diligent, hardworking lads with a care to their royal duties. Lady Maccon's neck was checked for bite marks and her dispatch case for illegal steam devices. She yielded up her parasol without question. Alexia would rather have them confiscate it than have to explain how it worked. Lord

Akeldama's clothing was far too tight for any hidden weaponry, but the guards did check his top hat before allowing him to proceed.

Biffy was not permitted entrance, despite the extraordinarily royal color of his jacket. He was pronounced, with much forcefulness, as being *not on the register*. However, Biffy was of such a pleasant disposition that he was content to remain behind at the entrance for the duration of the council. Alexia distinctly heard him say, in lilting tones, "Such a big hat you have, Lieutenant Funtington!" to one of the stoic-faced palace guards.

"Incorrigible child," she said to Lord Akeldama with a smile of affection.

"I would say I taught him everything he knows, but Biffy's a natural." Lord Akeldama nodded his approval.

They made their way into the meeting chamber to find the dewan already pacing about in a tizzy. Queen Victoria was not there. The queen did not attend most Shadow Councils. She expected to be informed of anything significant but otherwise was uninterested in the minutiae.

"Threat to the queen, I hear." The dewan was a large gruff individual who reminded Alexia of her husband, in character if not in appearance or manner. Not that she would ever tell this to either of them. He held state as the Earl of Upper Slaughter but no longer boasted the country seat to accompany the title. Similarly, he had the demeanor of a leader without a pack. This freedom from responsibility both as lord and Alpha made the dewan the most powerful autonomous werewolf in all England. And, even though he was not

quite as big as Conall Maccon, it was generally acknowledged by all—including said Conall Maccon—that Lord
Slaughter could give even that most feared of Alphas a fight
for his fur. Thus, the dewan and Lord Maccon tended to
circle each other, both in and out of polite company, rather
like two tugboats drawing freight—widely and with much
tooting.

"Indeed." Alexia's practical side was pleased at the two
Alphas' respective similarities, because constant exposure
to her husband had given her the necessary skills for handling the dewan.

She and Lord Akeldama wafted—or, in Alexia's case,
toddled—in and took seats at the long mahogany table,
leaving the dewan to continue his pacing unmolested.

Lady Maccon snapped open the lid of her dispatch case
and extracted her harmonic auditory resonance disruptor. The spiky little apparatus looked like two tuning forks
sticking out of a bit of crystal. While Alexia rummaged
about for further necessities, Lord Akeldama tapped one
fork with his finger, waited a moment, and then tapped the
other. This resulted in a discordant, low-pitched humming,
amplified by the crystal. It would prevent their conversation
from being overheard.

"Serious, do you think? This threat? One to be taken seriously?"

The dewan ought to have been handsome with his dark
hair and deep-set eyes, but his mouth was a little too full,
the cleft in his chin a little too pronounced, and his mustache and muttonchops excessively aggressive. This facial

hair had initially given Alexia much distress. Why? was the question. Most gentlemen went clean-shaven into immortality's long night. Poor Biffy had had to wait in scruffy purgatory until Alexia returned home from her European tour and turned him mortal long enough to shave. Professor Lyall had reportedly been kind and sympathetic during that most trying of times.

Lady Maccon took out her notes on the ghostly event and closed her dispatch case. She had attempted to remember and transcribe everything the specter said to her. "The threat came to me via a ghost messenger. I think we must treat it with slightly greater significance than we would some blundering daylight opportunist with a taste to become the next darling of the anarchist press."

Lord Akeldama added, "And, my *sweetlings,* if a supernatural told of the threat to a preternatural, it is likely that something or someone equally unnatural is involved."

The dewan sucked at his teeth. "Very serious."

Lord Akeldama sat back and rested the tips of his long white fingers on the table before him. It was a gesture oddly reminiscent of his predecessor.

Alexia continued. "Greatly mysterious as well. My husband says that BUR records show nothing on this ghost. We've been unable to locate either her or her corpse since she delivered the message." Alexia had no compunction about involving the two disparate arms of Her Majesty's supernatural supervisory operations, nor tapping into the advantages afforded by her position as wife to BUR's chief officer. So far as she was concerned, bureaucratic restrictions were all very well in their place, but they couldn't be allowed to limit efficiency. So while BUR was supposed to handle enforcement and the Shadow Council deal with legislative issues, Alexia was actively causing the two to become ever more entangled.

This was largely held to be one of the reasons Queen Victoria had appointed her muhjah in the first place.

The dewan was suspicious. "Why was the message delivered to *you*? And why use a ghost? Most are instinctively afraid of you because of what you are and what you can do."

Lady Maccon nodded. Even when she was properly introduced to ghosts, they treated her with decided wariness. "Valid points. I don't know. If anyone, it should have been brought to the attention of my husband. He's the official channel."

"The fact that you are the muhjah is not well known around town except by the hives. A standard ghost would not have had access to information divulging your state and position and would not have known that you have the queen's ear. So, there is even less reason to tell you under such circumstances."

Alexia looked over her notes. "Perhaps it has something to do with my father."

The dewan paused in his pacing. "God's teeth, why should it?"

"The ghost muttered something about 'daughter of Tarabotti.' As though she were specifically driven to find me because of my name."

"Perhaps the ghost knew Alessandro Tarabotti in life, my little *dipped biscuit*."

Alexia nodded. "Perhaps. Regardless, if the threat is coming from the supernatural element, who do we like as suspects?"

Lord Akeldama immediately said, "I know one or two darling little lone werewolves who've been getting restless." He tilted his head and snapped his teeth together a couple times.

The dewan countered with, "There are some rove vampires with sharp fangs."

Lady Maccon was having none of this kind of scapegoat prejudice. "I think we ought to take everything into consideration and assume that it could also be a hive or a pack that is involved."

Lord Akeldama looked cagey and the dewan uncomfortable.

The dewan said, "Oh, very well, but what kind of lead do we have?"

"Only the ghost. I have to find her, and soon, for she was getting rather unsubstantial."

"Why you?" demanded the dewan.

"Clearly it has to be me. I was the one she was looking for, so I am the one she will converse with. Either one of you might do more harm than good. I'm already concerned that my husband is blundering about without my supervision."

Lord Akeldama laughed. "Thank heavens he never hears you talk like that, *petunia*."

"What makes you think he doesn't?" Alexia continued her line of reasoning. "A ghost left untended, no preservation enacted, in the dead of summer. How long would the specter remain sane under such conditions?"

The dewan answered, "Only a few days."

"And if she were given regular formaldehyde treatments?"

"Several weeks."

Alexia pursed her lips. "That is a rather broad window."

Lord Akeldama smoothed his fingertips over the tabletop. "Did she have any kind of accent, my petal?"

"You mean was she foreign?"

"No, snowdrop. I mean, could you make out her *place* in society?"

Lady Maccon considered this. "Good but not particularly well educated. I should say perhaps upstairs staff? Which could explain why she did not get proper preservation, burial...or registry with BUR." Alexia was smart enough to carry the line of reasoning full unto its undignified potential. "So I am looking for a shopgirl or perhaps a housekeeper or cook. One who has died within the past two weeks. Few or no family members. And within a tethering radius of the potentate's town house."

Lord Akeldama shook his head in distress. "You have my deepest sympathies."

Alexia knew this for the sham that it was. Lord Akeldama liked to pretend he attended only the best parties and fraternized with only the right kind of people. His drones were certainly drawn from the highest society had to offer. But Biffy, in his day, had unexpectedly turned up in more unsavory locales than a housekeeper would ever frequent, and Lord Akeldama would never make his drones go anywhere in London he had not vetted first himself.

The dewan kept the conversation on course. "But, Muh-jah, that's hundreds of houses, not to mention shops, private clubs, and other places of interest."

Lady Maccon considered Madame Lefoux's underground contrivance chamber, just outside the radius of inquiry. "In addition, it does not take into account cellars or attics built with subterfuge in mind. And it assumes strangers will tell me if someone within their household has recently died. Nevertheless, can you think of a better approach?"

Neither Lord Akeldama nor the dewan could.

The infant-inconvenience kicked out in apparent punc-tuation to this statement. Lady Maccon made an *oof* noise, glared down at her stomach, then cleared her throat when the others looked at her inquiringly.

"Do we inform the queen in the meantime?" Now that they had some kind of plan, the dewan seemed to feel that pacing about was no longer necessary. He came to sit at the table.

Lord Akeldama took a stand at that. He always took a stand over control of information. "Not just yet, I think, fluffy. Not until we have more concrete evidence. All we have now are the mutterings of a mad ghost."

Lady Maccon, a mite suspicious of his motives, neverthe-less had to agree with his point. "Very well, I'll investigate those residences that look to be nighttime inclined, as soon as we have finished here. I'll sleep tomorrow morning and continue in the afternoon with the daylight households."

Lord Akeldama winced and then took a deep breath. "This may be distressing to hear, my flower, but I'm afraid it simply *must* be said. I am loath to advocate such an *oner-*

ous thing, but as you are searching for someone beneath you, you might want to dress down accordingly."

Lady Maccon winced, thinking of Felicity and her knitwear. "Are you suggesting that I pretend to be a *servant*?"

"I am so very sorry, *dumpling,* but you might have greater success with subterfuge." The vampire's eyes welled with tears at the necessity of having to recommend such a horror.

Alexia took a deep breath to firm her resolve. "Oh, the actions I must undertake for my country."

So it was that Lady Maccon, dressed in some menial rags of ill design and shapeless cut, accompanied by Biffy in the guise of husband, became far more familiar with her new neighborhood than she had previously imagined possible. Biffy looked more uncomfortable in his baggy, lower-class Sunday best than Alexia had ever seen him in evening garb, no matter how tight the breeches or how high the collar. Nevertheless, he threw himself wholeheartedly into the role of out-of-work butler with pregnant housekeeper wife. At each new door, they asked politely after places recently vacated. At each they were treated with a modicum of compassion by the respective butlers—partly due to Alexia's condition but mostly due to the excellent references they were able to provide from one Lady Maccon of Woolsey Castle.

Still, after the eleventh cup of tea, they turned reluctantly back toward Lord Akeldama's street, none the wiser as to any recent deaths that might have gone to ghost. Although, they had received, much to Alexia's surprise, the offer of positions in the respectable town house of a minor baronet.

The infant-inconvenience, normally a fan of tea in any form, objected to such a quantity as was consumed upon visiting a succession of possible employers who treated prospective staff in accordance with all standards of common decency. Alexia positively sloshed as she walked. She gripped Biffy's arm, partly from necessity and partly from the need to keep him human should the rising sun beat their return home. She was moved to ask him something that had been somewhat troubling her of late. "Lord Akeldama takes his tea with lemon?"

Biffy nodded, looking down at her, curious as to where she was going with the conversation.

"It never occurred to me until Professor Lyall brought it up, but this is rather peculiar a preference in a vampire. I was under the impression there were problems with fangs and citrus."

Biffy smiled but said nothing.

Lady Maccon persisted. "Need I remind you where your loyalties now lie, young Biffy?"

"As if I could forget?" Biffy checked the lay of his collar in a nervous gesture. "Ah, well, it's no particular secret of the commonwealth. He spent several decades, as I understand it, building up a tolerance."

"Good gracious me, why?"

"Simply something to do, I suppose."

"That sounds more like the Lord Akeldama of the fashion rags than the Lord Akeldama you and I know."

"Of course, my lady. Truth?"

Alexia nodded.

"He likes to use lemon on his hair—says it adds brightness and shine. He's terribly vain." Biffy's smile was tinged with longing.

"Oh, I know." Alexia looked once more to her companion and then, with Lord Akeldama's colorful town house in sight, pretended exhaustion and slowed their walk even further.

"Biffy, my dear, I am worried about you."

"My lady?"

"I had a recent delivery of new fashion plates from Paris, and you hardly glanced at the hairstyles. My husband tells me you are still having difficulty controlling the change. And your cravat has been tied very simply of late, even for evening events."

"I miss him, my lady."

"Well, he is now living adjacent. You can hardly miss him all that much."

"True. But we are no longer compatible—I am a werewolf; he is a vampire."

"So?"

"So we cannot dance the same dance we used to." Biffy was so sweet when he tried to be circumspect.

Alexia shook her head at him. "Biffy, and I mean this in the kindest way possible: then you should *change the music.*"

"Very good, my lady."

Lady Maccon got very little sleep that day, partly due to the physical repercussions of too much tea and partly due to an unexpected visit from Ivy Tunstell early in the afternoon. Floote woke her with a gentle touch, a sincere apology, and the deeply troubling information that Miss Loontwill had taken it upon herself to entertain Mrs. Tunstell in the front parlor. They were awaiting Lady Maccon's pleasure. Alexia half fell, half rolled out of bed, leaving her poor husband, equally disturbed by her now-chronic restlessness, to sleep.

It being daylight, Biffy was still abed, so she had to ask Floote to assist in buttoning her dress. The butler paled in horror at the very idea and went to corral one of Lord Akeldama's drones in his stead. Boots proved willing to undertake the distasteful task. Although it seemed to leave him unexpectedly breathless. Lady Maccon was beginning to learn that Boots was ever willing to undertake anything she asked of him.

Floote then managed to balance her, by sheer strength of will, across the short gangplank between balconies.

Downstairs, Felicity was looking more herself, having sent for her things that morning on the assumption that no objections could be found to her assuming permanent residence in her sister's house. She wore a dress of modern cut with a shirtwaist-style top in turquoise satin trimmed in lace and complemented by matching turquoise rosettes on a white muslin skirt. A demure black bow was tied about her neck à la cravat, and black trim peeked forth between the flounces of the sleeves and at the center of the rosettes. The dress was new, expensive, and very stylish.

Mrs. Ivy Tunstell, by contrast, wore a visiting gown from two summers prior, its bustle a little too large and its design a little too bold. Unfortunate Ivy, having married a common theatrical, had to make over her existing gowns rather than order new ones.

For once, however, she did not seem to mind but was weathering Felicity's conversation, which could be nothing but barb-tipped under the circumstances of an overbustled dress, with complacent demeanor and atypical presence of mind. Either Ivy did not realize she was being insulted, or she had some more interesting matters occupying her thoughts.

Lady Maccon took a deep breath and entered the parlor.

"Oh, sister, you do keep such peculiar hours in this household of yours," commented Felicity, noticing her first.

Ivy hopped to her feet and tripped over to blow kisses at Alexia's face. It was a repulsively Continental habit that she had adopted since her marriage. Lady Maccon blamed overexposure to the stage, or possibly her sometime employment in Madame Lefoux's hat shop where the French propensity for familiar mannerisms, particularly between ladies, was encouraged beyond the pale.

"My dearest Ivy, how do you do? What an unexpected visit."

"Oh, Alexia, how perfectly splendid of you to be in residence. I was so afraid"—Ivy lowered her voice dramatically—"that you might be in your confinement. Your silhouette is alarmingly advanced. I am not intruding, am I? No, you would be abed. Even you would not receive callers at such a time. Have you been drinking enough tea? Very good for ladies in your condition, is tea."

Lady Maccon took a moment to allow the wash of Ivy's chatter to cascade over her much in the manner that dandelion seeds fly on the winds of inconsequentiality. "Pray, do not trouble yourself on my behalf, Ivy. As you see, I am still ambulatory. Although, I will admit that it is a little problematic getting *into* motion these days. I do apologize for keeping you waiting."

"Oh, pray, do not concern yourself. Felicity was quite proficient a substitute."

Lady Maccon raised her eyebrows.

Ivy nodded in a conspiratorial way to indicate she was being entirely sincere. Her copious dark ringlets bobbed about. Her marriage had had little effect on her girlish preferences in hairstyles. It was probably just as well she had made a less-than-favorable match, for the wives of actors were rather expected to be eccentric in the matter of appearance.

At this juncture Felicity rose. "If you will excuse me, ladies, I have a meeting to attend."

Lady Maccon looked after her sister in shock as she left with neither a remark as to Alexia's corpulence nor one to Ivy's substandard attire. "I wonder if she will change her dress again."

Ivy swished back over to the settee and collapsed onto it dramatically. "Change? Why should she? That was a perfectly splendid day gown."

"Ivy, did you not notice something peculiar about Felicity's demeanor?"

"Should I have?"

"She was awfully nice, wasn't she?"

"Yes."

"To you."

"Yes."

"And to me."

"Yes, why"—a pause—"come to think on it, that *is* peculiar."

"Isn't it just?"

"Is she in poor health?"

"My dear sister has *joined a society*." Lady Maccon pursed her lips and pretended coyness.

This was lost on Mrs. Tunstell, who said only, "Well, there you have it. Constructive occupation and attention to good works can have just such a beneficial effect on peevish young ladies. Either that or she has fallen in love."

Alexia could hardly find the words to explain in a manner that Ivy would comprehend. "It is a feminine-advocacy association."

Ivy gasped and clutched at her bosom. "Oh, Alexia, what a thing to say out loud!"

Lady Maccon realized that Ivy might be right—they were heading into highly indecorous, not to say dangerous, territory. "Well, of course"—Alexia cleared her throat ostentatiously—"do tell me, what business is it that has brought you to call this afternoon, my dear Ivy?"

"Oh, Alexia, I do have quite the surfeit of delightful news to relate. I hardly know where to start."

"The beginning, I find, is usually the best place."

"Oh, but, Alexia, that's the most overwhelming part. It is all happening at once."

Lady Maccon took a firm stance at this juncture—she rang for Floote. "Tea is obviously necessary."

"Oh, my, yes," agreed Ivy fervently.

Floote, having anticipated just such a request, came in with tea, treacle tart, and a bunch of grapes imported at prodigious expense from Portugal.

Lady Maccon poured the tea while Ivy waited, fairly vibrating with her news but unwilling to begin recitation until her friend had finished handling the hot liquid.

Alexia placed the teapot carefully back on the tray and handed Ivy her cup. "Well?"

"Have you noticed anything singular about my appearance?" Ivy immediately put the cup down without taking a sip.

Lady Maccon regarded her friend. If a brown dress could be called glaring, Ivy's could be so described. It boasted an overdress and bustle of chocolate satin with a pure white skirt striped, like a circus tent, in the same shade. The accompanying hat was, of course, ridiculous: almost conical in shape but covered with what looked to be the feathers of at least three pheasants mixed in with a good deal of blue and yellow silk flowers. However, none of these extremes of dress were unusual for Mrs. Tunstell. "Not as such."

Ivy blushed beet red, apparently mortified by what she must now relate given Alexia's failed powers of observation. She lowered her voice. "I am very eager for the tea." This garnered no response from the confused Alexia, as Ivy wasn't drinking it. So Ivy soldiered bravely on. "I am—oh, dear, how to put this delicately?—anticipating a familial increase."

"Why, Ivy, I didn't know you expected any kind of inheritance."

"Oh, no." Ivy's blush deepened. "Not that kind of increase." She nodded significantly toward Alexia's portly form.

"Ivy! You are pregnant!"

"Oh, Alexia, really, must you say it so loudly?"

"Felicitations, indeed. How delightful."

Ivy moved the conversation hurriedly onward. "And Tunny and I have decided to form our own dramatic association."

Lady Maccon paused to reinterpret this confession. "Ivy, are you saying you intend to establish an acting troupe?"

Mrs. Tunstell nodded, her curls bouncing. "Tunny thinks it a good plan to start a new family of players as well as a new family, as he is keen on saying."

A family, indeed, Alexia thought. Having left the werewolf pack, Tunstell must be trying, in his own way, to build a new pack for himself. "Well," she said, "I do wish you all the best luck in the world. However, Ivy—and I do not mean to be crude—how have you managed to gather the means to fund such an undertaking?"

Ivy blushed and lowered her eyes. "I was dispatched to consult you on just such a subject. I understand Woolsey is quite enthusiastic in its patronage of artistic endeavors. Tunny implied you even had some capital invested in a circus!"

"Indeed, but, Ivy, for obvious reasons, those are in the interest of furthering the pack. Claviger recruitment and so forth. Tunstell has voluntarily severed any such connection."

Ivy nodded glumly. "I thought you would say as much."

"Now, wait just a moment. I'm not so feeble a friend as to abandon anyone, especially you, my dear, when in need." Lady Maccon frowned in thought. "Perhaps I could dip into my own coffers. You may not be aware, but my father left me rather well set up, and Conall is quite generous with a weekly allowance. We have never discussed my personal income, but he seems disinterested in my financial affairs. I am convinced he shouldn't object if I were to become a patron of the arts. Why should Woolsey have all the fun?"

"Oh, Alexia, really? I couldn't ask such a thing of you!" protested Ivy in a tone that suggested this had been her objective in calling all along.

"No, no." Alexia was becoming rather entranced with the proposal. "I think it a capital idea. I wonder if I might ask a rather odd favor in return?"

Ivy looked amenable to anything that might further her husband's goal. "Oh, please do."

Alexia grappled with how exactly to phrase this next question without exposing too much of her nature to her dear friend. She had never told Ivy of her preternatural state, nor of her post as muhjah and the general investigative endeavors that resulted.

"I find myself curious as to the activities of the lower orders. No insult intended, my dear Ivy, but even as the mistress of your own troupe, and clientele notwithstanding, you will have a certain amount of contact with less savory elements of London society. I would appreciate...information...with regards to these elements on occasion."

Mrs. Tunstell was overcome with such joy upon hearing this that she was moved to dab at one eye with an embroidered handkerchief. "Why, Alexia, my dear, have you undertaken an interest in *scandal mongering* at last? Oh, it is too much. Too wonderful."

Even prior to her marriage, Miss Ivy Hisselpenny's social position had prevented her from attending events of high standing, while Miss Alexia Tarabotti had suffered under the yoke of just such events. As far as Ivy was concerned, this yielded up a poor quality and quantity of gossip. The Alexia of her girlhood had not been curious about the interpersonal relationships of others, let alone their dress and manners.

The handkerchief lowered and Ivy's face became suffused with a naive cunning. "Is there anything in particular you wish me to look out for?"

"Why, Ivy!"

Mrs. Tunstell sipped her tea coquettishly.

Lady Maccon took the plunge. "As a matter of fact, there have been rumors of late with regards to a threat upon a certain peer of the realm. I cannot say more, but if you wouldn't mind?"

"Well, I did hear Lord Blingchester's carriage was to be decommissioned."

"No, Ivy, not that kind of threat."

"And the Duchess of Snodgrove's chambermaid was so incensed recently that she indicated she might actually not affix her hat properly for the midsummer ball."

"No, not quite that either. But this is all intriguing

information. I should appreciate your continued conversation and company even after your evolved circumstances."

Ivy closed her eyes and took a small breath. "Oh, Alexia, how kind of you. I did fear..." She flipped open a fan and fluttered it in an excess of sentimental feeling. "I did fear that once Tunny and I launched this endeavor, you would be unwilling to continue the association. After all, I intend to perhaps take on some small roles myself. Tunny thinks I may have dramatic talent. Being seen to take tea with the wife of an actor is one thing, but taking tea with the actress herself is quite another."

Lady Maccon shifted forward as much as possible and stretched out a hand to rest softly atop Mrs. Tunstell's. "Ivy, I would never even consider it. Let us say no more on the subject."

Ivy seemed to feel the time had come to move on to yet another pertinent bit of news. "I did have one other thing to relate to you, my dear Alexia. As you may have surmised, I have had to give over my position as assistant to Madame Lefoux. Of course, I shall miss the society of all those lovely hats, but I was there just the other evening when a very peculiar event occurred. Given your husband's state, I immediately thought of you."

"How very perspicacious." Much to her own amazement, Lady Maccon had found that Mrs. Tunstell, a lady of little society and less apparent sense, often had the most surprising things to relate. Knowing well that the best encouragement was to say nothing, Alexia drank her tea and gave Ivy a dark-eyed look of interest.

"Well, you should never believe it, but I ran into a scepter in the street."

"A scepter...what, like the queen's?"

"Oh, no, you know what I mean. A ghost. Me, can you imagine? Right through it I went, all la-di-da. I could hardly countenance it. I was completely unnerved. After I had recovered my capacities, I realized the poor thing was a tad absent of good sense. Subsequent to much inane burbling, she did manage to articulate some information. She seemed peculiarly attracted to my parasol, which I was carrying at night only because my business with Madame Lefoux had taken longer than expected. Otherwise, you understand, I have always found your habit of toting daytime accessories at all hours *highly* esoteric. Never mind that. This ghost seemed peculiarly interested in my parasol. Kept asking about it. Wanted to know if it *did* anything, apart from shield me from the sun, of course. I informed her flat out that the only person I knew who boasted a parasol that extruded things was my dear friend Lady Maccon. You remember I saw yours emit when we were traveling in the north? Well, I told this to the ghost in no unceremonious terms, at which point she got most stimulated and asked as to your current whereabouts. Well, since she was a ghost and, as such, tethered within a shortened area of the location, I saw no reason not to relay your new address to her. It was all very odd. And she kept repeating the most peculiar turn of phrase, regarding a cephalopod."

"Oh, indeed? What exactly did she say, Ivy?"

" 'The octopus is inequitable,' or some such drivel." Ivy

looked as though she might continue her discussion, except at that moment she caught sight of Felicity through the open parlor door.

"Alexia, your sister appears to be most unbalanced. I am quite convinced I just observed her wearing a lemon-yellow knit shawl. With a fringe. Going out into public. I cannot countenance it."

Lady Maccon closed her eyes and shook her head. "Never mind that now, Ivy."

"Convinced, I tell you. How remarkable."

"Anything more about the ghost, Ivy?"

"I think it might have had something to do with the OBO."

This comment brought Alexia up short. *"What did you just say?"*

"The Order of the Brass Octopus—you must have heard of it."

Lady Maccon blinked in shock and put her hand to her stomach where the infant-inconvenience kicked out in surprise as well. "Of course I have heard of it, Ivy. The question is, how have *you*?"

"Oh, Alexia, I have been working for Madame Lefoux for positively ages. She has been traveling overmuch of late, and her appearance can be very distracting, but I am not so unobservant as *all that*. I am well aware that when she is in town, she undertakes fewer hat-orientated activities than hat-focused ones. She runs an underground contrivance chamber as I understand it."

"She told you?"

"Not exactly. If Madame Lefoux prefers to keep things a

secret, who am I to gainsay her? But I did look inside some of those hatboxes of hers, and they do not always contain hats. I did inquire as to the specifics, and Madame Lefoux assured me it was better if I not become involved. However, Alexia, I wouldn't want you to think me ignorant. Tunny and I do talk about such things, and I have eyes enough in my head to observe, even if I do not always understand."

"I apologize for doubting you, Ivy."

Ivy looked wistful. "Perhaps one day you, too, will take me into your confidence."

"Oh, Ivy, I—"

Ivy held up a hand. "When you are quite ready, of course."

Alexia sighed. "Speaking of which, you must excuse me. This news about the ghost, it is of no little importance. I must consult my husband's Beta immediately."

Ivy looked about. "But it is daylight."

"Sometimes even werewolves are awake during the day. When the situation demands it. Conall is asleep, so Professor Lyall is probably awake and at his duties."

"Is a cephalopod so dire as all that?"

"I am afraid it might be. If you would excuse me, Ivy?"

"Of course."

"I shall inform Floote about the little matter of my patronage. He will set you up right and proper with the necessary pecuniary advance."

Ivy grabbed at Lady Maccon's hand as she passed. "Oh, thank you, Alexia."

Alexia was as good as her word, going immediately to Floote and issuing him with instructions. Then, in the interest of economy and perhaps saving herself a trip to BUR, she casually asked, "Is there a local OBO chapter in this area? I understand it is quite the secret society but thought perhaps you might know."

Floote gave her a meditative look. "Yes, madam, a block over. I noticed the marking just after you began visiting with Lord Akeldama."

"Marking, Floote?"

"Yes, madam. There is a brass octopus on the door handle. Number eighty-eight."

CHAPTER FIVE

———

The Lair of the Octopus

Number 88 was not a very impressive domicile. In fact, it was one of the least elegant in the neighborhood. While its immediate neighbors were nothing when compared to Lord Akeldama's abode, they still put their very best brick forward. They acknowledged, in an entirely unspoken way, that they were denizens of the most fashionable residential area in London and that architecture and grounds should earn this accolade. Number eighty-eight was altogether shabby by comparison. Its paint was not exactly peeling, but it was faded, and its garden was overgrown with herbs gone to seed and lettuces that had bolted.

Scientists, thought Alexia as she made her way up the front steps and pulled the bell rope. She wore her worst dress, altered to compensate for her stomach and made of a worsted fabric somewhere between dishwater brown and green.

She couldn't remember why she'd originally purchased the poor sad thing—probably to upset her mother. She had even borrowed one of Felicity's ugly shawls, despite the fact that the day was too warm for such a conceit. With the addition of a full white mob cap and a very humble expression, she looked every inch the housekeeper she wished to portray.

The butler who answered her knock seemed to feel the same, for he did not even question her status. His demeanor was one of pedantic pleasantness, exacerbated by a round jolliness customarily encountered among bakers or butchers, not butlers. He sported a stout neck and a head of wildly bushy white hair that called to mind nothing so much as a cauliflower.

"Good afternoon," said Alexia, bobbing a curtsy. "I heard your establishment was in need of new staff, and I have come to inquire about the position."

The butler looked her up and down, pursing his lips. "We did lose our cook several weeks ago. We have been doing fine with a temporary, and we certainly don't wish to take on someone in your condition. You can understand that." It was said kindly, but most firmly, and meant to discourage.

Alexia stiffened her spine. "Oh, yes, sir. My lying-in shouldn't be a day over a fortnight, and I do make the best calf's-feet jelly you will ever taste." Alexia took a gamble with that. The butler looked like the kind of man who liked jelly, his shape being of the jelly inclination already.

She was right. His squinty eyes lit with pleasure. "Oh, well, if that is the case. Have you references?"

"The very best, from Lady Maccon herself, sir."

"Indeed? How comprehensive is your knowledge of herbs and spices? Our gentlemen residents, you understand, are mostly bachelors. Their table requirements are simple, but their extracurricular requests can be a tad esoteric."

Alexia pretended shock.

The butler made haste to correct any miscommunication. "Oh, no, no, nothing like that. They simply may ask for quantities of dried herbs for their experiments. They are all men of intellect."

"Ah. As to that, my knowledge is unequaled by any I have ever met before or since." Alexia was rather enjoying bragging about things about which she knew absolutely nothing.

"I should find that very hard to believe. Our previous cook was a renowned expert in the medicinal arts. However, do come in, Mrs....?"

Alexia scrabbled for a name, then came up with the best she could at short notice. "Floote. Mrs. Floote."

This butler didn't seem to know *her* butler, for his expression did not alter at the improbability of such a pairing as Floote and Alexia. He merely ushered her inside and led her down and into the kitchen.

It was like no kitchen Alexia had ever seen. Not that she had spent much time in kitchens, but she felt she was at least familiar with the general expectations of such a utilitarian room. This one was pristinely clean and boasted not only the requisite number of pots and pans, but also steam devices, one or two massive measuring buckets, and what looked like glass jars filled with specimen samples lining the counters. It resembled the combination of a bottling factory, a brewery, and Madame Lefoux's contrivance chamber.

Alexia made no attempt to disguise her astonishment—any normal housekeeper would be as surprised as she upon seeing such a strange cooking arena. "My goodness, what a peculiar arrangement of furnishings and utensils."

They were alone in the kitchen, and it was just that time of the afternoon when most household staff had a brief moment to satisfy their own concerns before the tea was called for.

"Ah, yes, our previous cook had some interest in other endeavors apart from meal preparation. She was a kind of intellectual herself, if you would allow such a thing in a female. My employers sometimes encourage aberrant behavior."

Alexia, having spent a goodly number of years immersed in books and having attended many Royal Society presentations, not to mention her intimacy with Madame Lefoux, could indeed allow such things in females, but in her current guise forbore to say so. Instead, she looked around in silence. Only to notice a prevalence of octopuses. They were positively everywhere, stamped onto jar lids and labels, etched into the handles of iron skillets, engraved onto the sides of copper pots, and even pressed into the top of a vat of soap set out to harden on a sideboard.

"My, someone certainly has an affection for cephalopods." Alexia waddled over, all casualness, to examine a row of very small bottles of dark brown glass and mysterious content. They were corked up, each cork boasting a small glass octopus pressed into it in a range of colors. Otherwise, there was no mention made of the content.

She reached to pick one up only to find that the butler, in the silent manner customary to the breed, had sidled up next to her. "I should not, Mrs. Floote, if I were you. Our previous cook had an interest in rather more hazardous forms of distillery and preservation as well."

"What happened to the good lady, sir?" Alexia asked with a forced lightness in tone.

"She stopped. If I were you, I should take particular care with that yellow octopus there."

Alexia moved hurriedly away from the whole row of little bottles, suddenly feeling that they were precariously placed on their shelf.

The butler looked her up and down. "There are many stairs in this house, you understand, Mrs. Floote? You will not be able to remain in only the kitchen. How am I to be convinced you are capable of your duties?"

Alexia seized upon this as a perfect opportunity to further her investigations. "Well, I am interested in seeing the accommodations, should you choose to engage my services. If you would be so kind as to show me to the staff quarters, I can demonstrate my mobility."

The butler nodded and gestured her toward a back staircase that wound up through the house to the attic apartments. The room he eventually shepherded her into was a tiny, cramped cell that still contained some remnants of its previous occupant, just as Alexia had hoped. More small brown bottles and a few curious-looking vials lay about. A handkerchief was spread across the windowsill, upon which bunches of herbs lay drying.

"Of course, we will clear out these quarters prior to new occupation." The butler curled his lip as he looked around.

Small cloth-bound notebooks were scattered here and there; several were quite dusty with neglect. There were also bits of scrap paper and even what looked to be some kind of ledger.

"Your previous cook was literate, sir?"

"I warned you she was peculiar."

Alexia took another look around and then, thinking rapidly, maneuvered toward the small bed. "Oh, dear, perhaps those stairs were a tad much given my present condition. I seem to be feeling rather overstimulated." She collapsed onto the bed, leaning back dramatically and almost overbalancing. It was a paltry performance.

Nevertheless, the butler seemed convinced. "Oh, I say, Mrs. Floote. This simply isn't on. Really, we can't consider anyone who—"

Alexia cut him off by groaning and clutching at her stomach significantly.

The man blanched.

"Perhaps if I could have a little moment to recover, sir?"

The butler looked like he would prefer to be anywhere else but there. "I shall fetch you a glass of water, shall I? Perhaps some, er, jelly?"

"Oh, yes, capital idea. Do take your time."

At which he hurried out.

Immediately, Alexia lurched upright, an exercise that made up in efficiency what it lacked in dignity, and began searching the room. She found very little memorabilia with regards to the occupant's personality, but there were even more notebooks and mysterious bottles tucked away in the bedside drawer and the wardrobe. She tucked anything that looked to be secret or significant into the stealth pockets of her parasol. Then, knowing she must limit herself, she took what seemed to be the most recent notebook and one that looked to be the oldest and most dusty, along with a neatly printed ledger, and bundled them up in Felicity's shawl. The parasol was clanking slightly and drooping from its excess load, and she thought the knitwear bundle must look very suspicious, but when the butler returned, he was so over-joyed to find her recovered he didn't notice either.

Alexia decided to make good her escape. Saying she felt weak and had best hurry home before nightfall, she moved toward the door. The butler led her downstairs, declining to offer her the position, despite her calf's-foot jelly, but suggesting she call round in several months when she had recovered from her inconvenience, jelly apparently being quite the alluring prospect.

He was just letting her out when a voice stopped them both in their tracks. "Well, gracious me. Miss Tarabotti?"

Alexia clutched her loot closer to her breast, closed her eyes, and took a deep breath. Then she looked upward.

The gentleman walking slowly down the staircase toward her was an iconic example of the scientific species. His gray muttonchops were untended, his eyes bespectacled, and his attire too far into tweed for midsummer and midtown. Unfortunately, Alexia was all too familiar with that face.

"Why, Dr. Neebs! I thought you were dead."

"Ah, not quite. Although Lord Maccon did do his level best." The man continued down the steps, moving with a pronounced limp probably sustained during that last battle in the Hypocras Club's exsanguination chamber. As he closed in upon her, Alexia noted his eyes were very hard behind those spectacles.

"In which case, shouldn't you be serving a sentence for intellectual misconduct?"

"I assure you, it has been served. Now, I think perhaps you should come with me, Miss Tarabotti."

"Oh, but I was just leaving."

"Yes, I am certain you were."

The butler, at a bit of a loss, was looking back and forth between them.

Alexia backed toward the open door, lifting up her parasol in a defensive position and pressing her thumb against the appropriate lotus petal in the handle, arming the tip with one of the numbing darts. She wished she had not left Ethel behind; guns, by and large, were far more threatening than parasols.

Nevertheless, Dr. Neebs looked at it with wary respect. "Madame Lefoux's work, isn't that?"

"You know Madame Lefoux?"

Dr. Neebs looked at her as though she were an idiot. *Of course,* thought Alexia, *this is a chapter of the Order of the*

Brass Octopus. Madame Lefoux is also a member. I did not realize the Order was reabsorbing the Hypocras Club. I must tell Conall.

The scientist tilted his head to one side. "What are you about, Miss Tarabotti?"

Alexia faltered. Dr. Neebs was not to be trusted, of that she was certain. Apparently, he felt much the same about her, for he issued a sharp instruction to the butler.

"Grab her!"

Luckily, the butler was confused by the proceedings and did not understand how his role had suddenly become one of ruffian. He was also holding a glass of water in one hand and a jar of calf's-foot jelly in the other.

"What? Sir?"

At which juncture Alexia shot the scientist with a numbing dart. Madame Lefoux had armed the darts with a high-quality, fast-acting poison that had some affiliation with laudanum. Dr. Neebs pitched forward with an expression of shock on his face and collapsed at the base of the staircase.

The butler recovered from his inertia and lunged at Alexia. Lady Maccon, clumsy at the best of times, lurched to the side, waving her parasol wildly in a wide arc and managing to strike the butler a glancing blow to the side of the head.

It was not a very accurate hit but it was violent, and the man, clearly unused to anything of the kind, reeled away looking at her with an expression of such disgruntlement that Alexia was moved to grin.

"Why, Mrs. Floote, such indecorous behavior!"

Alexia armed her parasol and shot him with a second numbing dart. His knees gave out and he crumpled to the floor of the foyer. "Yes, I know. I do apologize. It is a personal failing of mine."

With that, she let herself out into the street and lumbered off, clutching her plunder and feeling very furtive and rather proud of her afternoon's achievement.

Unfortunately for Lady Maccon, there was absolutely no one to appreciate her endeavors when she returned home. Any werewolves in town were abed, Felicity was still out (not that Alexia could confide in *her*), and Floote was off tending to some domestic duty or another. Disgruntled, Alexia set herself up in the back parlor to examine her misappropriated loot.

The back parlor was already her favorite room. It had been made over with quiet card parties in mind: cream and pale gold walls, ornate dark cherry furniture, and royal blue curtains and coverings. The several small tables were marble topped, and the large chandelier boasted the very latest in gas lighting. It was just that kind of soulful elegance that soulless Alexia could never hope to achieve on her own.

She set the bottles aside to give to BUR for analysis and picked up the ledger and journals with interest. Two hours later, stomach growling and tea cold and forgotten at her elbow, she put them back down again. They had been as absorbing as only the highly private musings of a complete stranger can be. They were illuminating as well, in their way, although not with regards to the current threat to the queen's life. Of that there was no mention at all, nor was there any concrete evidence to implicate the OBO.

The ledger proved to be a record of transactions, mainly sales the cook had made to various individuals, everything encoded with symbols, initials, abbreviations, and numbers. After reading the journals as well, Alexia surmised that the cook must have been an honorary OBO member. Her interests were focused on those concoctions that one could not purchase easily from apothecary or pharmacist. Such liquids, for example, as Madame Lefoux incorporated into Alexia's parasol and perhaps other potions even more deadly.

The most recent journal, unfinished and unhelpful, articulated only the increasingly disorientated views of an aging woman who seemed to be succumbing to a brew of her own fabrication, either involuntarily or out of a derangement of the spirit. There was no way to determine whether she was, indeed, the ghost who had come to warn Lady Maccon, but it was as good a lead as any.

However, it was the older journal that drew her attention. One particular entry was dated some twenty years ago. It mused with interest over a new order—for ingredients to be sent by post in separate allotments, for sake of security, to a werewolf pack in Scotland. The connection between time and location caused Alexia to ruminate over her husband's anguished retelling of a certain betrayal. The same betrayal that would cause him to abandon the Kingair Pack and then take over Woolsey. He had been so very cut up about it. "I

caught them mixing the poison," he had said. "Poison, mind
you! Poison has no place on pack grounds or in pack business. It isna an honest way to kill anyone, let alone a monarch." She realized there was no way to prove a connection,
but coincidence in date was good enough for her. This *must*
be an accounting of the order for the poison that long ago
was meant to kill Queen Victoria.

"Astonishing," she said into the empty room, rereading
the incriminating passage. Absentmindedly, she picked up
her teacup and sipped. The liquid being cold, she placed it
back down with a grimace. She quickly ascertained that the
remainder under the cozy was equally tepid and pulled the
bell rope.

Floote materialized. "Madam?"

"Fresh tea, please, Floote. There's a dear."

"Certainly, madam."

He vanished, reappearing in a miraculously short time
with a freshly brewed pot and, much to Lady Maccon's
delight, a small wedge of tempting-looking cake.

"Oh, thank you, Floote. Is that lemon sponge? Marvelous.
Tell me, are any of the men awake yet?"

"I believe Mr. Rabiffano and the professor are just rising."

"Mr. Rabiffano, who is...? Oh, Biffy! Not my husband,
then?"

"Difficult to tell, madam, him being in the other house."

"Ah, yes, of course, how silly of me." Lady Maccon went
back to her perusal of the little journal.

"Will there be anything else, madam?"

"The question is, Floote, why order the toxins from London? Why not patronize the baser elements who supply such pernicious needs closer to home?"

"Madam?"

"I mean, Floote, hypothetically, why special-order poison from one destination only to eventually transport it back to do the dastardly deed? Although, I suppose the queen might have been visiting Scotland at the time. But still, why all the way from town?"

"Everyone orders from London, madam," replied Floote most decidedly, even though he had no idea as to the specifics of her question. "It is the fashion."

"Yes, but if one were afraid of being caught?"

Floote seemed to feel he might participate in the discussion even without full possession of the necessary facts. "Perhaps one wanted to be caught, madam."

Lady Maccon frowned. "Oh, no, I hardly think—" She was cut off by the arrival of Professor Lyall, who looked his normal unremarkably dapper self, despite having just arisen.

He stuck his head around the corner of the door in some surprise, evidently unsure of what to make of his mistress's encampment.

"Lady Maccon, good evening. How are you?"

"Professor Lyall. Oh, Floote, do carry on."

Floote wafted away, giving Lyall a very significant look, as though to say, *She is in one of her moods—tread with caution.*

Heeding the unspoken advice, the werewolf let himself in hesitantly. "You are in the back parlor, Lady Maccon?"

"Just as you see. "

"Not the front?"

"I like the wallpaper. I have had a most illuminating day, Professor Lyall."

"Oh, dear. Have you, indeed?" The gentleman settled down into a chair near his Alpha female. At a nod from Lady Maccon, he helped himself to tea. Floote, being Floote, had thought to provide more than one cup. "I have not yet read the evening papers. Is that going to signify, my lady?"

Lady Maccon frowned. "I doubt it. I don't think the constabulary were alerted to my activities."

Professor Lyall forbore to mention that this indicated there might have been a need for such action. "Well?"

In as flattering a manner as possible, Lady Maccon detailed her afternoon's shenanigans. As she did so, Professor Lyall's face creased with worry.

"On your own? In your state?"

"I'm perfectly capable."

"Yes, indeed. You even managed to use your condition to your advantage. But I thought you were meant to take Biffy with you on these jaunts. Himself ordered it."

"Well, yes, but this couldn't wait for evening. And such interesting evidence I have uncovered. Now where did I put my pen?" She began patting about her lap—what there was left of it—in annoyance.

Professor Lyall produced a stylographic pen from his waistcoat and passed it to her. Alexia nodded her thanks.

"You really believe that this new threat has some connection to the old Kingair attempt?" he asked while she made a note in the margin of one of the journals.

"It seems likely."

"Your evidence appears to be circumstantial at best."

"Never discount serendipity. Would you be so kind as to have some of these potions analyzed? Also, I should like to see BUR's report regarding the Kingair failed assassination and my husband's subsequent challenge for Woolsey Alpha, plus any corresponding postings in the popular press."

Professor Lyall looked rather pained. "If you insist, my lady."

"I do."

"Give me a few hours to organize everything? The laboratory will take some time with those samples—several days, at least—but I shall bring the other items you requested back with me."

"Oh, no need. I shall jaunt to BUR after I call on Madame Lefoux and file the appropriate requisition forms myself."

"Ah, had you intended—?"

"Not until I traced this OBO connection. Of course, Genevieve would have had nothing to do with OBO operations twenty years ago, being only a small child, but still it is worth making inquiries. She knows *things*. Not to mention the fact that Ivy ran into a ghost in that area the other night. Can't possibly be the same ghost—no tether stretches so far—but there must be a connection to our mysterious messenger."

"If you must, my lady. But this time do please take Biffy with you."

"Of course. I shall be glad of the company. Shall we go in to supper?"

Professor Lyall nodded gratefully and they arose to make their way to the dining room.

"What ho, wife?"

Conall Maccon thumped down the stairs looking far more pulled together than Alexia had ever seen him in all their acquaintance. His cravat, a becoming ethereal azure that perfectly complemented his tawny eyes, was tied Nabog style over unusually high collar points. His shirt was tucked to perfection, his waistcoat seamless, and the sleeves of his jacket just so. As a direct result, he was also looking rather uncomfortable.

"My goodness, husband. How handsome you are this evening! Did the drones get hold of you?"

The earl give his wife a very telling stare before sweeping down upon her and planting a kiss on her lips right in front of the embarrassed gazes of Lyall, Floote, and a small number of household staff.

Alexia's limited mobility prevented her from any evasive maneuvers. Like some wanton hussy, she could do nothing but endure his amorous attentions with blushes and sputterings of delighted horror.

He pulled back finally. "Excellent, best way to start one's evening. Wouldn't you agree, gentlemen?"

Professor Lyall rolled his eyes at his Alpha's antics, and Floote bustled quickly off about his business.

They entered the dining room. During the course of Alexia's conversation with Professor Lyall, most of the rest of the current town residents—two werewolves and a few assorted clavigers—had arisen and assembled around the table. They all stood politely as Lady Maccon seated herself before returning to prior conversation or consumption, depending upon personality. Biffy, seated slightly apart from the others, was pretending deep absorption in the latest issue of *Le Beaux Assemblée,* otherwise known as *Beau's Court and Fashionable Magazine Addressed Particularly to the Gentleman of Leisure.* Lord Maccon frowned at him, but the dandy didn't seem to notice.

Alexia helped herself to a bowl of stewed fruit, plum pudding, and custard. After some conversation with her husband on domestic matters, she turned his attention to her own recent investigations.

"You didn't!"

"I most assuredly did. And now I have need of the carriage. I should like to visit Madame Lefoux before calling at BUR for the documentation Professor Lyall promised me."

Lord Maccon gave his Beta a repressive look.

Professor Lyall shrugged, as though to say, *You married her.*

"Alexia," Lord Maccon said in a drawn-out growl, "you know I am not comfortable with that particular incident resurfacing. I shouldn't like you to be stirring up trouble over an event well and truly settled."

Lady Maccon, perfectly understanding that the nature of his growl was not one of anger but of distress, put down her fork and placed her hand over his. "But you must acknowledge that if there is a connection, we should pursue all avenues of investigation. I promise to keep my attention focused on the relevant details and not be distracted by personal curiosity."

Lord Maccon sighed.

Lady Maccon lowered her voice, although she was perfectly well aware that she was surrounded by beings with supernatural hearing who could discern every word she said. "I know this is a subject that pains you, my love, but if we are to get to the root of this matter, you must see that there may indeed be a correlation."

He nodded. "But have a care, please, my heart? I fear you are messing with matters best left undisturbed."

A stillness in the crinkling of Professor Lyall's evening paper seemed to indicate the Beta was entirely in agreement with his Alpha on this point.

Alexia nodded and let go of her husband. She glanced up and across the table. "Biffy, would you be amenable to accompanying me this evening as I make my rounds? I should appreciate the companionship of one more mobile than myself."

"Of course, my lady, delighted. What hat should I wear?"

"Oh, your town topper should suit us well enough. We shan't be going into society."

His face fell slightly at that. "Very good, my lady. Should I retrieve it now?"

"Oh, no, please finish your meal. No sense in wasting food in the pursuit of information. The one is far more vital than the other, despite what Lord Akeldama may think."

Biffy smiled slightly and continued on with the consumption of his raw steak and fried egg.

Madame Genevieve Lefoux was a woman of style and understanding. If that style leaned toward gentlemen's dress and mannerisms and if that understanding leaned toward scientific theory and practice, Lady Maccon was certainly not the kind of person so in want of sensibility that she would critique a friend for such eccentricities. Some considerable intimacy had left Alexia with the distinct feeling that Madame Lefoux liked her and that she liked Madame Lefoux, but not a great deal more. Trust, for example, seemed still in question. Between them existed a friendship quite different from the one she shared with Ivy Tunstell. There was no discussion of the latest fashions or societal events. If asked, Alexia might say that she could not recall precisely what it was she and the French inventor did discuss, but whatever it was, it always left Alexia feeling intellectually stretched and vaguely exhausted—rather like visiting a museum.

Madame Lefoux had a new, pretty, young shopgirl behind the counter when they arrived at Chapeau de Poupe. Madame Lefoux's shopgirls were always young and pretty. This one seemed overset by the unexpected arrival of the grand Lady Maccon and was mightily relieved when her mistress, elegant and refined in gray tails and top hat, appeared to take over the management of such an august personage.

"My dear Lady Maccon!"

"Madame Lefoux, how do you do?"

The Frenchwoman grasped both of Alexia's hands and kissed first one and then the other of Alexia's cheeks. No air was left between lips and flesh, as was the custom among women of fashion, nor was this an extravagant gesture for fashion's sake. No, for Madame Lefoux, such a greeting was as natural as a handshake among American businessmen. Her actions were tender and her smile dimpled with genuine affection.

"What an unexpected pleasure! But are you certain you should be in public in your condition?"

"My dear Genevieve, you have been so long away I began to suspect you might never return to us. Then what should London do when in need of a new hat?"

Madame Lefoux acknowledged both the compliment and rebuke of Alexia's statement with a tilt of her dark head.

Lady Maccon noted, with some concern, that her friend was looking practically gaunt. Mostly composed of sharp angles, Madame Lefoux could never be described as full figured, but during her most recent travels, she had lost flesh she could not afford to lose. The inventor always had been more concerned with the pursuits of the mind than the body, but never before had her lovely green eyes sported such dark circles.

"Are you well?" asked Alexia. "Is it Quesnel? He is supposed to be home for the month, is he not? Is he being perfectly beastly?"

Madame Lefoux's son was a cheerful towheaded creature with an unfortunate nose for mischief. There was no malice to his actions, but his mere presence resulted in a kind of microcosmic chaos that kept his mother on edge whenever he was in residence.

Madame Lefoux flinched slightly and shook her head. "He did not make it home this time."

"Oh, dear! But then if not Quesnel, what could possibly be the matter? Truly, you do not look at all well."

"Oh, pray, do not concern yourself, Alexia. Some trouble sleeping, nothing more. How are you? I understand you have taken a residence in town. You certainly look amplified. Have you been maintaining a tranquil environment? I read recently that it is terribly important for the baby to be surrounded by peace. Knowing your disposition, this has me worried."

Alexia blinked at her.

Perceiving that her solicitude was unwelcome, the Frenchwoman moved hastily on. "Did you come to pick up Woolsey's new glassical order, or is this merely a social call?"

Lady Maccon accepted the conversational redirection. She respected her friend's need for privacy and her expertly cultivated aura of mystery. She also did not want to appear nosy. "Oh, is there an order? I suppose I could collect it. But, in actuality, there is a matter I should very much like to discuss with you." Alexia noticed the curiosity in the eyes of the new shopgirl. "In seclusion, perhaps?" And then, as she was not certain as to the extent of the shopgirl's knowledge, she confined her voice to a whisper. "Below?"

Madame Lefoux lowered her eyelashes and nodded gravely. "Of course, of course."

Alexia looked to her escort. "Biffy, will you find yourself entertainment enough here for a quarter of an hour, or
should you prefer to run along to the Lottapiggle Tea Shop
on Cavendish Square?"

"Oh, I can abide a while among such loveliness as this."
The young werewolf waved a graceful gloved hand at the
forest of dangling hats displayed all about him. He brushed
his fingers along an exaggerated ostrich feather, much as
a young girl would trail her fingertips through a fountain.
"Beautiful brim rolling."

"I shan't be very long," replied his mistress before following her friend toward the back of the shop, where a door in
the wall led to an ascension room that took them down to a
passageway, underneath Regent Street, and into the inventor's much-vaunted contrivance chamber.

Madame Lefoux's laboratory might have been a great
wonder of the world, if only because it was a wonder the
Frenchwoman could ever find anything inside it. The massive, cavelike laboratory was not only messy, but it was also
noisy. Alexia often thought that the only reason it could not
be heard in the street above was that Regent was one of the
busiest thoroughfares in London. Then she wondered if that
was why Madame Lefoux had chosen this particular spot.

As ever, Lady Maccon took in her surroundings with a
kind of reverence that was part appreciation, part horror.
There were engines and mysterious constructs galore, some
of them running, many of them disassembled into component parts. There were diagrams and sketches of larger
projects strewn about, mostly aeronautical devices such as

ornithopters, as aetheric travel was one of Madame Lefoux's specialties. It smelled of oil.

"Oh, my, is that a new commission?" Alexia picked her way slowly through the clutter, holding her skirts well out of the way of any possible grease stains.

Dominating the chamber was a partly assembled transport contraption. Or Alexia assumed it was a transport—as yet, it had no apparent wheels, rails, or legs. It was shaped like a massive bowler hat without a brim, so she supposed it might be an underwater conveyance. Inside were levers and pull cords, an operator's seat, and two small slits at the front for visibility. It was almost buglike and well outside of the Frenchwoman's ordinary principles of subtlety. Alexia's parasol with all its secret pockets and component parts was far more to Genevieve's taste. Traditionally, she did not go in for big and flashy.

"Something I've been working on of late."

"Is it armored?" Lady Maccon had an embarrassingly unladylike interest in modern technology.

"In part." Something in Madame Lefoux's tone warned Alexia off.

"Oh, dear, is it under contract from the War Office? I'm probably not supposed to know. I do apologize for asking. We shall say no more about it."

"Thank you." Madame Lefoux smiled in tired gratitude. Her dimples barely showed.

Government defense commissions were lucrative but not something one could speak of openly, even to the queen's muhjah. The inventor moved to take Alexia's hand, her own work-hardened by decades of tool use. Alexia could feel the roughness even through her gloves, along with a companion thrill she had grown to accept was part of the price of intimacy with this woman. Genevieve was so very *intriguing.*

"Was there something specific you wanted, my dear Alexia?"

Alexia hesitated and then, without subtlety, jumped right to the point. "Genevieve, do you know anything about the Kingair assassination attempt on Queen Victoria of twenty years ago? I mean, anything from the Order of the Brass Octopus?"

Madame Lefoux started in genuine surprise. "My goodness, what has brought you back around to that?"

"Let us say I made a contact recently who has led me into explorations of the past."

Madame Lefoux crossed her arms and leaned back against a coiled roll of brass plating. "Hmm. I personally know nothing. I would have been no more than thirteen at the time, but we could ask my aunt. I'm not certain how useful she might be but the attempt can't hurt."

"Your aunt? Oh you mean...?"

Madame Lefoux nodded, her face sad. "She's finally undergoing diminished spectral cohesion. Even with all my preservation techniques and chemical expertise, it was inevitable. However, she does have her lucid moments."

Alexia realized this must be the true source of Genevieve's distress. She was losing a treasured family member. The woman who had raised her. Genevieve may have a well-developed mystique, but she was not emotionally reserved and she loved deeply. Alexia moved to her friend and stroked her upper arm where the muscles tensed. "Oh, Genevieve, I am so very sorry."

The inventor's face crumpled slightly at the sympathy. "I cannot help but think that this is to be my fate, too. First Angelique and now Beatrice."

"Oh, surely not! You cannot be so confident you have excess soul." Alexia would have offered to ensure exorcism, but Genevieve had been so angry when she performed the service for Angelique.

"No, you are correct. I have been traveling, researching, studying, trying to find a way to extend my aunt's afterlife. But there is *nothing*." Her tone was anguished, that of a scientist who sees a problem but no solution.

"Oh, but you have done your level best! You have given her *years,* far longer than any ghost has a right to expect."

"Years for what? Humiliation and madness?" Genevieve took a breath, then placed her hand over Alexia's where it stroked her arm, stilling the movement. "I do apologize, my lovely Alexia. This is not your burden. You still wish to speak to her?"

"Would she talk to me, do you think?"

"We can but try."

Lady Maccon nodded and attempted to shrug herself out of her normally regal posture, trying to be less overbearing and physically threatening. She didn't want to scare the ghost. Not that a woman in her corpulent condition boasted so fearsome a visage.

Madame Lefoux yelled, her normally melodious voice sharp, "Aunt, where are you? Aunt!"

Several moments later, a ghostly form shimmered into existence out of the side of a conveyer belt spool, looking grumpy.

"Yes, Niece, you summoned me?" Formerly Beatrice Lefoux had been in life an angular spinster of severe attitude and limited affection. She might once have been pretty but obviously never allowed herself, nor others, to enjoy that fact. There was much of her in Madame Lefoux, tempered by a level of good humor and mischief that the aunt had never bothered to cultivate. The specter was beginning to go fuzzy, not so badly as Alexia's ghostly messenger but enough for it to be clear she wasn't long for this world.

As soon as she spotted Lady Maccon, the ghost drew herself inward, appearing to wrap the drifting threads of her noncorporeal self closer, as a werewolf wraps his cloak around after shifting.

"Why, you have the soulless visiting you, Niece. Honestly, I don't know why you persist in such an association." The ghost's voice was bitter, but more out of habit than any real offense. Then she seemed to lose track of what she was saying. "Where? What? Where am I? Genevieve, why, you are so old. Where is my little girl?" She swirled in a circle. "You have built an octomaton? I said never again. What could possibly be so dire?" As she spoke, the ghost shifted between French and heavily accented English. Luckily, Alexia was tolerably competent in both.

Madame Lefoux, her expression stiff in an attempt to hide

distress, snapped her fingers in front of her deceased aunt's face. "Now, Aunt, please pay attention. Lady Maccon here has something very serious to ask of you. Go on, Alexia."

"Formerly Lefoux, are you familiar with the attempt on Queen Victoria's life that took place in the winter of 1853? A Scottish werewolf pack was implicated. It was a matter of poison."

The ghost bobbled up and down in surprise, losing some small measure of control over bits of herself. An eyebrow detached from her forehead. "Oh, why, yes. Although not intimately, of course. Not from the actual assassination perspective but more from the sidelines. I lost one of my students because of it."

"Oh?"

"Why, yes. Lost her to the mist of the moor. Lost her to duty. So promising, so strong, so…wait. What were you asking? What are we discussing? Why must I forget things all the time?"

"The Kingair assassination attempt," Alexia prompted.

"Silly dogfight. Poor girl. Imagine having to take on that kind of responsibility. At sixteen! And over werewolves. Werewolves who planned a poisoning. So many things wrong with the very idea. So many things out of character. Out of the supernatural order. Was it ever put right, I wonder?"

Alexia pulled a measure of this rambling together. "Sidheag Maccon was your student?"

The ghost's head tilted. "Sidheag. That name is familiar. Oh, why, yes. So hard to finish in one way, so easy to finish in another. A strong girl, good at finishing. But then again, strength in girls is not so much valued as it ought to be."

Lady Maccon, as interested as she was in anything to do with her husband's great-great-great-granddaughter, now one of the only female werewolves in England and Alpha of the Kingair Pack, felt she must still steer the ghost back onto more relevant matters. "Did you happen to hear, at the time, whether there was a connection between the assassination attempt and the Order of the Brass Octopus?"

"Connection? Connection? Of course not."

Alexia was taken aback by the firm confidence in the ghost's voice. "How can you be so certain?"

"How can I not? Imagine such a thing. No, no, not against the queen. Never against Queen Victoria. We would have known. I would have known. Someone would have told me." Formerly Beatrice Lefoux swirled about in her distress, once more catching sight of Madame Lefoux's latest project. She paused as though hypnotized by the imposing thing. "Oh, Genevieve, I can't believe you would. I can't. Not for anything. Why, child, why? I must tell. I must convince..." She ended up facing Alexia once more and, as though seeing her for the first time, said, "You! Soulless. You will stop everything in the end, won't you? Even me."

Madame Lefoux pressed her lips together, closed her eyes, and gave a sad sigh. "There she goes. We won't get any more sense out of her this evening. I'm sorry, Alexia."

"Oh, no, that's quite all right. It wasn't precisely what I was hoping for, but it has convinced me that I must contact Lady Kingair as soon as possible. I must convince my husband's old pack to reveal the details of the original plot. Only they can fully unravel this mystery. I can't believe that the OBO was not involved, but if your aunt says so with such conviction, only the source of the threat itself can reveal the truth of the matter."

"And, of course, my aunt was never a member of the Order."

"She wasn't?" Alexia was genuinely surprised.

"Absolutely not. Women weren't allowed to join back in her day. It's difficult enough now." The French inventor, one of the smartest people Alexia had ever met, reached behind her neck to finger the octopus tattoo that lay hidden there, just under the curls of her scandalously short hair. Alexia tried to imagine Genevieve without her secret underground world. Impossible.

Alexia said, "I shall have to send someone to Scotland. I don't suppose...?"

Madame Lefoux looked even more unhappy. "Oh, no. I am sorry, my dearest Alexia, but I cannot afford the time. Not right now. I have this"—she waved a hand at the monstrous thing she was building—"to finish. And my aunt to think of. I should be with her, now that the end is near."

Lady Maccon turned to the inventor and, because she seemed to need it more than anything else, embraced her gently. It was awkward given Alexia's belly but worth it for the slight lessening Alexia could feel in Genevieve's stiffened shoulders. "Would you like me to send her on?" she asked in a hushed voice.

"No, thank you. I am not yet ready to let her go. You understand?"

Alexia sighed and released her friend. "Well, worry not on this particular matter. I will get to the bottom of it. Even if I have to send Ivy Tunstell to Scotland for me!"

Fated words that, as is often the case with frivolous speech, Alexia was going to come to regret.

CHAPTER SIX

In Which Mrs. Tunstell Proves Useful

Were they not recently moved into new accommodations, Lady Maccon might have made a different choice—one of Woolsey's older clavigers, perhaps. But the pack was in chaos over the relocation. They were nowhere near as tethered to a place as vampires, but werewolves were, in simple terms, tethered to each other and were creatures of profound habit. Such arbitrary reorganization ruffled the fur. Solidarity and proximity became ever more necessary for the pack's continued cohesion. Were BUR not occupied with its own investigation as to the current threat against Queen Victoria, Alexia might have tapped Haverbink or another experienced investigator. And, finally, were the Shadow Council supplied with its own agents, the muhjah would have had manpower to call upon. However, with none of these options readily available, Lady Maccon cast about herself and found that she had only one possible choice—as unlikely and as addlepated as that choice might be.

Mrs. Tunstell ran a tight household, despite overseeing her rented accommodations with a floppy hand and absent-minded disposition. Her abode was clean and neat, and callers could be assured of a decent cup of tea or candy dish of raw meat, depending upon taste and inclination. Despite an interior resplendent in every shade of pastel, Ivy's home was a popular watering hole. As a result, the Tunstells had developed a name for themselves among the more esoteric members of the West End as agreeable hosts interested in a wide range of topics and ever willing to open their door to the friendly visitor. This meant that, at any given time, one was practically guaranteed to find some breed of indifferent poet or insipid sculptor in residence.

So it was that when Lady Maccon called around teatime that summer afternoon, a delighted Mrs. Tunstell welcomed her inside with assurances that while they had indeed adopted a stray poet, that versifier was quite firmly asleep and had been for the better part of three days.

Ivy's good-humored little face fell. "He drinks, poor man, to forget the pain of the embittered universe that subsumes his soul. Or do I mean sublimes his soul? Anyhoo, we've had to remove the tea quite forcibly from his grasp on more than one occasion. Barley water, says Tunny, is the only thing one should take when suffering such ailments of the emotional humors."

"Oh, dear," commiserated Alexia. "I suppose one might

recover one's spirits out of desperation if all one had to drink was barley water."

"Exactly so!" Ivy nodded over her husband's evident sagacity on the application of revolting beverages to despondent poets. She motioned her friend into her front parlor, a diminutive room that boasted all the elegance of iced Nesselrode pudding.

Lady Maccon deposited her parasol into the small umbrella stand and made her way gingerly toward a wingback chair, careful not to upset any of the decorative objects strewn about. Her visiting dress was of flowing blue paisley with a stiffened quilted skirt. Designed to accommodate her increasing girth, it was much wider—and thus more dangerous to Ivy's receiving room—than the current trends dictated.

She sat heavily in the chair, sighing at the relief of getting the weight off her poor feet, which seemed to have swollen to near twice their original proportions. "Ivy, my dear, I was wondering if I might prevail upon you for a very great favor."

"Oh, Alexia, of course. You have only to ask and I shall do whatever."

Lady Maccon hesitated, wondering exactly how much to reveal. Ivy was a dear little soul, but was she reliable? She decided to buck up and take the plunge. "Ivy, have you ever wondered if there might, just possibly, be something slightly unusual about me?"

"Well, Alexia my dear, I never liked to say, but I have

always wondered about your hat preferences. They have struck me as mighty plain."

Lady Maccon shook her head. The long blue ostrich feather of her not-at-all-plain hat wafted back and forth behind her. "No, not that, I mean... Well, dash it, Ivy, there's nothing for it."

Mrs. Tunstell gasped in enchanted shock at Lady Maccon's lowbrow language. "Alexia, you have been fraternizing with werewolves overmuch! Military men can be terribly bad for one's verbal concatenation."

Alexia took a deep breath and then blurted out, "I'm preternatural."

Ivy's dark eyes widened. "*Oh, no!* Is it catching?"

Alexia blinked at her.

Ivy donned a sympathetic expression. "Is it a terribly painful condition?"

Lady Maccon continued to blink.

Ivy put a hand to her throat. "Is it the baby? Will you both be well? Should I send for barley water?"

Alexia finally found her voice. "No, *preternatural.* You might know the term, as in *soulless*? Or curse-breaker. I have no soul. None at all. As a matter of fact, I can cancel it out in supernatural creatures given half a chance."

Ivy relaxed. "Oh, *that.* Yes, I knew. I shouldn't let it concern you, my dear. I doubt anybody minds."

"Yes, but... Wait, you knew?"

Ivy tut-tutted and shook dark ringlets at her friend in mock amusement. "Of course I knew—have done for simply ages."

"But you never mentioned a thing to me on the subject."

Alexia was not often flummoxed. She found it an usual sensation and wondered if this was what Ivy felt like most of the time. Her friend's revelation did, however, give her some degree of confidence in her next move. Despite all her frivolities, Ivy could clearly keep a secret and, it turned out, was more observant than Alexia had previously given her credit for.

"Now, Alexia, I thought you were embarrassed about it. I didn't want to bring up an uncomfortable personal disability. I have more sensitivity and care for the feelings of others than that!"

"Ah, oh, well. Of course you do. Regardless, as a preternatural, I am currently engaged in some investigations. I was hoping to enlist your aid. It has to do with my husband's work." Alexia didn't want to tell Ivy absolutely everything, but she didn't want to fib outright either.

"For BUR? Espionage! Oh, really? How terribly glamorous." Ivy clasped yellow-gloved hands together in delight.

"To which end I was hoping to, well, induct you into a kind of secret society."

Ivy looked as though she had not heard anything so thrilling in all her life. "Me?" she squeaked. "Really? How *marvelous*. What's it called, this secret society?"

Alexia hesitated and then, recalling a phrase her husband had once offered up in the heat of annoyance, suggested tentatively, "The Parasol Protectorate?"

"Oooh, what a perfectly splendid name. So full of ornamentation!" Ivy practically bounced up and down on the lavender settee in her excitement. "Must I make a pledge, or memorize a sacred code of conduct, or engage in some pagan ritual or other?" Ivy had an expectant look on her face that suggested she would be very disappointed if this were not the case.

"Well, yes, of course." Lady Maccon floundered, trying to come up with something appropriate to the occasion. She couldn't make Ivy kneel, not in that dress—a periwinkle muslin day gown with an extremely long, tight bodice of the style favored by actresses.

After a moment's thought, Alexia stood laboriously and waddled over to the umbrella stand to retrieve her parasol. This she opened and placed point downward in the center of the room. Since the room was so very small, this did manage to take up most of the free space. Motioning Ivy to stand, Alexia handed her the handle and said, "Spin the parasol three times and repeat after me: I shield in the name of fashion. I accessorize for one and all. Pursuit of truth is my passion. This I vow by the great parasol."

Ivy did as she was told, face serious and concentrated. "I shield in the name of fashion. I accessorize for one and all. Pursuit of truth is my passion. This I vow by the great parasol."

"Now pick the parasol up and raise it, open, to the ceiling. Yes, just like that."

"Is that all? Shouldn't the vow be sealed in blood or something like?"

"Oh, do you think?"

Ivy nodded enthusiastically.

Alexia shrugged. "If you insist." She took back her parasol, snapped it closed, and twisted the handle. Two wickedly sharp spikes projected out of the tip, one of silver, the other of wood.

Ivy inhaled in appreciation.

Lady Maccon flipped the parasol about. Then she took off one of her gloves. After a moment's hesitation, Ivy did the same. Alexia nicked the pad of her thumb with the silver spike and then did the same for Ivy, who gave a little squeak of alarm. Then Alexia pressed their two thumbs together.

"May the blood of the soulless keep your own soul safe," intoned Alexia, feeling appallingly melodramatic but knowing Ivy would love this better than anything.

Ivy did. "Oh, Alexia, this is so very stirring! It should be part of a play."

"I shall have a special parasol made up for you, similar to mine."

"Oh, no, but thank you for the thought, Alexia. I couldn't possibly carry an accessory that emitted things all willy-nilly like that. Really, I'm much obliged, but I simply couldn't bear it. You, of course, manage to carry it off with aplomb, but it would be too vulgar on someone like me."

Lady Maccon frowned, but knowing her friend's true weakness, she made another suggestion. "A special hat, perhaps?"

Ivy hesitated.

"Madame Lefoux designed my parasol."

"Well, perhaps a small hat. One that isn't too oozy?"

Alexia smiled. "I am convinced that could be arranged."

Ivy bit her lip on a smile. "Oh, Alexia, a secret society.

How marvelous of you. Who else is a member? Do we have regular meetings? Is there a covert signal so we should know one another at social gatherings?"

"Um, well, as to that, so far you are my first inductee, so to speak. I anticipate future members, though."

Ivy looked quite crestfallen.

Lady Maccon continued on hastily. "But you will have to operate and report in under a cipher, of course—for aethero-grams and other secret messages."

Ivy brightened at that. "Oh, of course. What shall my cipher be? Something romantic yet subtle, I hope?"

Lady Maccon contemplated her friend while a series of rather silly names suggested themselves. Finally, she settled on one she knew Ivy would like, because it represented a style of headdress to which she was rather devoted but that Alexia might remember because it struck her as particularly Ivyish. "How about Puff Bonnet?"

Ivy's pretty face glowed with pleasure. "Oh, fabulous. Perfectly modish. And what's yours?"

Again, Alexia was ill prepared for the question. She cast about helplessly. "Uh. Oh, let me think." She grappled, running through her mind several of Lord Akeldama's epithets and some of her husband's more affectionate endearments. Nothing quite suited a secret society, at least not that she could admit openly to Ivy. Finally, she settled on the simplest she could think of. "You may refer to me as the Ruffled Parasol. That should do well enough."

Ivy clapped her hands. "Oh, excellent. Alexia, this is superb fun."

Lady Maccon sat back down. "Do you think we might have tea now?" she asked plaintively.

Ivy immediately rang the bell rope, and in short order a nervous young maid brought in a laden tea tray.

"Marvelous," said Lady Maccon in evident relief.

Ivy poured. "And now that I have been properly inducted into the Protectorate, what is my first assignment?"

"Ah, yes, the reason I came to visit in the first place. You see, there is a matter of national delicacy concerning an assassination attempt on Queen Victoria. Some twenty years ago, members of the Kingair Pack tried to eliminate Her Majesty."

"Oh, no, really? Not those nice Scotsmen? They couldn't possibly do anything so treasonous. Well, except trot around displaying their knees for all to see, but nothing so calamitous as attempted regicide."

"I assure you, Ivy, this is the honest truth, universally acknowledged by those in a position to know such details." Lady Maccon sipped her tea and then nodded wisely. "Fact—my husband's previous pack tried to kill Queen Victoria by means of a poison. I need *you* to float back to Castle Kingair and ascertain the particulars."

Ivy grinned. She had developed, since her first trip with Alexia to Scotland, a most unladylike fondness for dirigible travel. Her current position in life did not allow her to indulge, but now ...

Lady Maccon grinned back. "All I know is that the previous Beta spearheaded the plot and was killed. My husband left the pack as a result. Any further information could be invaluable to my current investigation. Do you think you are up to this task, even in your present condition?"

Ivy blushed at the very mention. "I am barely along, and you *certainly* cannot go."

Alexia patted her belly. "My difficulty exactly."

"Can I take Tunny with me?"

"I should hope you would. And you may tell him of your mission, although not your new position."

Ivy nodded. More pleased, Alexia suspected, by the need to keep one secret from her husband than by permission to reveal another.

"Now, Ivy, please pay particular attention to any information on the poison that was going to be used. I believe that may be key. I shall give you a crystalline valve frequensor for aetheric transmission to my personal transponder at Woolsey. At sunset you are to report in, even if you have uncovered nothing of interest. I should like to know you are safe."

"Oh, but, Alexia, you know how clumsy I am with gadgetry."

"You will do fine, Ivy. How soon can you leave? Naturally your expenses will be covered."

Ivy blushed at the mention of such unseemly matters as fiscal settlements.

Alexia brushed her friend's embarrassment aside. "I know one doesn't ordinarily talk of such matters, but you are operating under the umbrella of the Parasol Protectorate now, and you must be free to act in accordance with the needs of the organization, regardless of expense. Is that clear, Ivy?"

Mrs. Tunstell nodded, cheeks still hot. "Yes, of course, Alexia, but—"

"It is a good thing I am to be patroness of your acting troupe, as it is the perfect way to hide pecuniary advancements."

"Oh, yes, indeed, Alexia. But I wish you didn't insist on mentioning such things while we are eating—"

"We shall say nothing more on the subject. Can you leave directly?"

"Tunny has no performances on at the moment."

"Then I shall send Floote tomorrow with the necessary papers." Lady Maccon finished the last of her tea and stood. She was suddenly tired. It was as though she had been out and about most of the night, sorting out the problems of the entire empire. Which, in her way, she had.

Mrs. Tunstell stood as well. "To Scotland I go, investigating assignation attempts of the past!"

"Assassination," corrected Lady Maccon.

"Yes, that. I must find my extra special hairmuffs for dirigible travel. I had them made to match my own curls. They are rather stunning, if I do say so myself."

"Of that, I have no doubt."

Lady Maccon returned to her new house and then made her way across to Lord Akeldama's. Floote's builders produced exemplary work. They had constructed a small secret drawbridge between the two balconies that operated by way of a hydraulic lever. It flipped downward. At the same time an elaborate spring mechanism caused the railing on each balcony to fold away. This allowed Alexia to easily traverse from one building to the next despite encumbrances.

She retired to her closet with alacrity. She had been keeping remarkably odd hours recently, what with having to consult daylight folk yet living with the supernatural set. It was of little consequence, as the infant-inconvenience was making it increasingly arduous to sleep for any length of time without some part of her body going numb or some unmentionable function driving her out of bed. Really, pregnancy was the most undignified thing she had ever had to endure in all her life, and for several years Alexia Tarabotti had been a confirmed spinster living with the Loontwills—a most undignified state—so that was saying something.

She slept restlessly, shifting aside when her husband joined her only to be awakened fully just after sunset by someone banging on the closet door.

"Conall, there is someone at the door to our *bedroom*!" She shook her massive husband where he lay in a boneless pile next to her.

He snuffled softly and rolled over, trying to gather her in closer. He had to settle for patting her belly absently and burrowing into her neck.

Alexia arched against him as much as she was able, enjoying the affection and the movement of his lips against her skin. For such a scruffy man, he had very soft lips.

"Darling, light of my life, lord of my heart, there is someone at the door to our closet, seeking entrance. And I don't believe Lord Akeldama and his boys are awake yet."

The earl merely burrowed in against her with greater

interest, apparently finding the flavor of her neck most intriguing.

The door shook and rattled as whoever it was seemed to be trying to physically force it open. But for all Lord Akeldama's frolicsome decorative choices, his town house was built with the supernatural in mind, the protection of his clothing being paramount. The door barely budged. Someone on the other side yelled, but a door so massive that it could withstand shoe thieves could also muffle even the loudest commentary on the subject.

Lady Maccon was becoming concerned. "Conall, get up and answer the door, do! Really, it sounds most pressing."

"I, too, have matters that are pressing and must needs be taken into hand."

Alexia giggled at the terribleness of both pun and innuendo. She was pleased her husband still thought her attractive, despite her beached-whale state, but was finding it increasingly awkward to accommodate him. The spirit was willing but the flesh was swollen. Still, she enjoyed the compliment and understood that there was no real demand behind the caresses. The earl knew her well enough to realize she valued his desire almost as much as his love. After a lifetime of feeling ugly and unworthy, Alexia was now tolerably assured that Conall genuinely did want her, even if they could do nothing about it at present. She also understood that he was expressing his conjugal interest partly out of knowledge of her own need for such assurances. A werewolf and a buffoon, her husband, but wonderfully caring once he'd blundered into the way of it.

And yet, someone was still torturing their poor door. Conall blinked awake, his tawny eyes wide and direct. He kissed the tip of his wife's long nose and, with a massive sigh, rolled out of bed and lumbered over to the door.

Alexia, sleepy lidded, admired his backside, then shrieked, "Conall, robe! For goodness' sake."

Her husband ignored her, throwing open the door and crossing his arms over a wide, hairy chest. He was wearing not one stitch of clothing. Alexia sank down under the covers in mortification.

She need not have worried; it was only Professor Lyall.

"Randolph," grumbled her husband, "what's all the ruckus about?"

"It's Biffy, my lord. Best come quickly. You're needed."

"Already?" Lord Maccon swore a blue streak, his blistering language the result of military service combined with a creative imagination. After a glance about the room, he seemed to decide that changing his form would be faster than getting dressed. He began to shift, the musculature underneath his skin rearranging, the hair on his head migrating downward and turning into fur. Quick enough, he dropped to all fours. Then he dashed out and down the hall, presumably to leap the gap between houses and see to whatever had gone wrong. Alexia caught sight of the brindled tip of his fluffy tail as he skidded out of sight without even a nod in her direction.

"What is it, Professor?" she demanded imperiously before her husband's Beta could follow in his Alpha's wake. It was rather unlike Professor Lyall to disturb them with such forcefulness. It was equally rare for there to be any issue so in need of the earl's attention that his second could not delay the matter or handle the preliminaries himself.

Professor Lyall turned back to the dim interior with a reluctant droop to his posture. "It's Biffy, my lady. He really is not handling the curse well this month. He fights it too much, and the more he fights it, the more painful it is."

"But it's over a week until full moon! How long will he suffer such bouts of early physiological disjunction?" *Poor Biffy. It is so embarrassing—premature transfluctuation.*

"Difficult to say. Could be years, could be decades of losing nights around full moon until he has better control. All new pups are like this, although they are not often taken so suddenly or so badly as Biffy. Usually it is only a few days before the moon. Biffy's cycle is off."

Alexia winced. "And you could not...?"

Backlit by the expensively bright gas lighting of Lord Akeldama's hallway, it was impossible to make out the werewolf's expression. Even if she could, knowing Professor Lyall, his face would not reveal much.

"In the end, I am only a Beta, Lady Maccon. When a werewolf is in wolf form, moonstruck and rampaging, there is nothing that can calm or control him except an Alpha. You must have realized by now that there is much more to Alpha than being simply big and strong. There is power of restraint and wolf-form intelligence as well."

"But, Professor Lyall, you are very restrained all the time."

"Thank you, Lady Maccon. There can be no higher

compliment to a werewolf, but mine is a matter of self-control only. That does others little good."

"Except that you lead by example."

"Except that. And now I should leave you to get dressed. I believe we may expect your results from BUR shortly."

"My results?"

"Those little OBO bottles of mysterious liquid."

"Ah, yes, fantastic! Will you please arrange for Floote and I to have the carriage after supper? I must visit Woolsey's library as soon as possible."

The Beta nodded. "I have a feeling it will already be commissioned. We'll have to take Biffy to the countryside for his confinement. His most recent inabilities have resulted in some rather disastrous redecoration of your back parlor."

"Oh, no, really? And after the drones did such a lovely job with it."

"We had to lock him somewhere, and that room has no windows."

"I understand. But claw marks are murder on wallpaper."

"Too true, Lady Maccon."

Professor Lyall drifted away and, because he was Professor Lyall, managed to corral one of Lord Akeldama's drones, just awakened, to help Lady Maccon dress.

Boots stuck his head in before catching sight of Lady Maccon still abed. The head instantly retreated and a back was presented in the doorway.

"Oh, dear me, most sorry, Lady M. Can't be me. Couldn't handle it a second time. Not that noble. I'll go rustle up someone a little more suitable to assist you. Shall I? Be back in a jiff."

Mystified, Alexia began the laborious process of squirming herself around and lurching by stages out of bed. She was just standing when Lord Akeldama came traipsing merrily into the room. "Top of the evening to you, my *blooming* marigold! My lovelorn little Boots said you could use a bit of twisting up, and I thought since I was awake I might avail myself of your *delicious* company and provide much-needed assistance simultaneously."

Lord Akeldama himself was not yet properly dressed for the evening. His affected monocle was absent, as were the obligatory spots of rouge on his alabaster cheeks and the ridiculous spats about his ankles. Nevertheless, even in his least formal attire, Lord Akeldama excelled.

"But, my dear friend, your knees!"

He was wearing royal blue breeches of watered silk, a damask waistcoat of white and gold, and a quilted velvet smoking jacket ornamented with brandenbourgs. His trousers were of such very fine quality, Alexia was quite aghast that the vampire should even consider playing at lady's maid, for he might have to kneel—on the floor!

"Oh, phooey, you know me, darling—always open to an adventure *à la toilette*."

Lord Akeldama was a man who Lady Maccon very much doubted had had much to do with dressing—or undressing—ladies on a regular basis, yet he seemed more than equal to the task. In the early days of her pregnancy, Alexia might have managed it herself, rejecting her corset and selecting a carriage dress or some other gown that fastened up the front. However, at this point, she couldn't even see her own feet, let alone touch them. So she acquiesced to this very strange new form of servant.

"I suppose it was courteous of Professor Lyall to think to send someone in. But really, if a gentleman who is not my husband is to see me bare, why not him?"

Lord Akeldama sashayed over to her, scooping up her underthings along the way. He tittered at the very idea. "Oh, my darling *pea blossom,* your professor might enjoy it a little too much. Like my poor Boots. And they are both gentlemen of principle." His hands began nimbly dealing with ties and buttons.

"What could you possibly be implying, my lord?" Lady Maccon asked this from within a chemise partly stuck over her head.

The vampire pulled the fine muslin down and smoothed it out over her belly with a little pat. His other hand was on her naked arm, and the contact turned him human in that moment. His fine, sharp fangs vanished, his pale white skin flushed slightly peach, and his lustrous blond hair lost a mote of its brilliance. He grinned at her, his face more effeminate than ethereal. "La, *honeysuckle,* you are well aware that we *here* are all, in our own special way, *deviants* in our penchants."

Lady Maccon thought about Lord Akeldama's drawing room with all its gilt and tassels. Even knowing this was not the vampire's point of reference, she nodded. "Oh, yes, I noticed."

Lord Akeldama rarely shrugged, for this upset the fall of his jacket, but he looked as though he would have at this juncture. Instead, he flounced over to the side of the room where Alexia's clothing hung on a long rack and began perusing various gowns, eyeing each with a discerning eye.

"Not that one," said Alexia when he paused overlong, considering a green and gold stripe.

"No?"

"The décolletage is too low."

"My dearest girl, this is a good design point, not a bad one. You should accentuate your best *features*."

"No, honestly, my lord, these days I—how to put this?—overflow. It's terribly incommodious." Alexia made a kind of flip-forward gesture with both hands at her bosom area. Always substantial, that particular region had expanded to near scenic proportions over the last few months. Lord Maccon was delighted. Lady Maccon found it ridiculous. *As if I weren't well enough endowed to start with!*

"Ah, yes. I do see your point, *periwinkle*." He moved on.

"You were saying, about Professor Lyall?"

"What I mean to articulate, *honey bee,* is that there are *levels* of deviation. Some of us are, shall we say, more *experimental* than others in our tastes. In some, I believe it is a matter of boredom, in others it is nature, and for still others it is indifference." The vampire's tone of voice was filled with the usual airy flippancy, but Alexia had a feeling this was something he had studied much over the centuries. Also, Lord Akeldama never doled out information without good reason.

The vampire continued to prattle on as he sorted through her wardrobe without looking up at her, as though he were having a conversation with the dresses. "So few are lucky enough to love where they will. Or unlucky, I suppose." Finally, he selected a walking outfit comprised of a ruffled purple skirt, cream blouse, and square cropped Spanish jacket in mauve. Despite the fact that there was very little trim, something about it clearly appealed to him. Alexia was delighted with this choice, as the outfit coordinated with one of her favorite hats, a little mauve bowler with a purple ostrich feather.

He brought it over to her and held it up, nodding. "Excellent palette for your coloring, my *little Italian pastry*. Did our Biffy help you order this?" Without waiting for confirmation, he continued his previous discussion with studied casualness. "Your Professor Lyall is one of those."

"One of the indifferent ones?"

"Ah, no, petal, one of those who has no particular preferences."

"And Boots?" Alexia held very still as the vampire moved around behind her, very much like a real maid, and began lacing up the back of the skirt.

"Boots is another one."

Lady Maccon thought she understood what he was trying to say but was determined to ensure things were as clear as possible. Lord Akeldama may enjoy prevarications and euphemisms, but no one had ever accused Alexia of being coy. "Are you telling me, my lord, that Boots enjoys the *company* of both men and women?"

The vampire came back around to the front and cocked his head to one side, as though more interested in the fit of the jacket than their conversation. "I know, peculiar of him, isn't it, my little *pigeon*? But I and mine, possibly more than anyone else in London, do not presume to judge the predilections of others." He bent forward to tidy the fall of the bow at Alexia's neck. Then he had her sit while he fussed with stockings.

"Well, I should never venture to question your assessment of Boots's taste, but really, you must be mistaken in Professor Lyall's nature. He's in the military, for goodness' sake!"

"I take it you have heard very little on the subject of Her Majesty's Royal Navy?" The vampire moved on to her shoes. Her feet were so swollen she no longer fit into any of her boots, much to his disgust. "Imagine wearing a walking dress with dancing slippers!"

"Well, it's not as though I *walk* all that much anymore. But, my dear lord, I can't believe it. Not Professor Lyall. You must misconstrue."

Lord Akeldama became motionless, his head bent over one of her kid slippers. "Oh, little lilac bush, I *know* I do not."

Lady Maccon stilled herself, frowning down at the blond head bent so diligently at her feet. "I have never seen him favor anyone of either sex. I had thought it was a part of being Beta, to love the pack at the expense of every other romance. Not that I have met many Betas. It is not a personality trait, then? Has he not always been so reticent?"

Lord Akeldama stood and came back behind her, beginning to toy with her hair.

"You arrange a lady's ensemble rather well, for an aristocrat. Don't you, my lord?"

"We all came from somewhere originally, *buttercup,* even us vampires. Of course, your Professor Lyall and I have never run in the same circles, and until you came into our lives, I must admit I never paid him much mind." The vampire frowned and a look of genuine disfavor crossed his beautiful face. "This may yet prove to be a rather catastrophic oversight. As bad as that brief period wherein I became enamored of a lime-green overcoat." He shuddered at the unpleasantness of the memory.

"Surely it cannot be so awful as all that. It is *only* Professor Lyall of whom we speak."

"*Exactly,* my plum puff. So few of us can be so easily dismissed as an *only.* I've done some inquiring. They say he never quite recovered from a broken heart."

Alexia frowned. "Oh, do *they?*"

"An embarrassing affliction in an immortal, brokenheartedness, wouldn't you say? Least of all in a man of sense and dignity."

Lady Maccon gave her friend a sharp look through the looking glass as he pinned one of her curls into place. "No, I should say instead *poor Professor Lyall.*"

Lord Akeldama finished with her hair. "There!" he pronounced with a flourish. He held up a hand mirror for her to look at the back. "I haven't our lovely Biffy's skill with the curling tongs, so a simple updo will have to suffice. I apologize for such ineptitude. I should add one or two rosettes or a fresh flower, just here."

"Oh, simple is absolutely splendid, and anything is better than what I could do for myself. I shall take your advice about the flower, of course."

The vampire nodded, took the mirror back, and placed it on the armoire. "And...how is Biffy?" The very flatness in the vampire's words alerted Alexia to the importance of this oh-so-casual question.

"He is still upset at having to give up snuff." Lord Akeldama smiled only slightly at her attempted lightheartedness, so Alexia adopted his serious tone. "Not as well as he could be. My husband thinks, and I am inclined to agree with him, there is something holding him back. Pitiable, for Biffy did not ask for the lupine afterlife, but he must learn to accept it."

Lord Akeldama's perfect mouth twisted slightly.

"I am given to understand there is a matter of control. He must learn to master the shift rather than allow it to master him. Until he does, there are all sorts of restrictions. He cannot go out during the day or he may be permanently damaged, he must be kept near silver for simply ages around the moon, and no sweet basil within smelling distance. It's all quite tragic."

Lord Akeldama stepped back and then spoke as though she had never answered his question. "Ah, well, I must bid you adieu, *my dearest girl.* I have my own toilette to see to. There is a most licentious music hall show opening this *very* evening, and I have a mind to attend in full regalia." He made his way toward the door in the sweeping manner much favored by an operatic villain when exiting stage left.

Lady Maccon was not fooled.

"My lord." Alexia's voice was soft and gentle, or as soft and as gentle as she could make it, being not a woman generally in command of such feminine wiles. "On our subject of brokenheartedness, should I now be saying *poor Lord Akeldama?*"

The vampire left without dignifying that with a reply.

Lady Maccon lowered the balcony drawbridge and made her way into Woolsey's town home and down the stairs. Walking a gangplank when one cannot see one's feet was a tad nerve-racking, but Alexia Maccon was a woman of forthright character and firm principle, not to be defeated by a mere fat belly. She encountered Felicity, obviously recently returned from one of her unmentionable jaunts, for she was once more attired in knitwear. They had no chance for idle conversation, thank goodness, for the house was in a veritable uproar.

Still, Felicity would not allow Alexia to pass without some commentary. "Sister! What is that tremendous ruckus in the back parlor?"

"Felicity, you did know, when you prevailed upon my hospitality, that this was the den of werewolves, did you not?"

"Yes, but to behave like animals? Surely that's not polite."

Lady Maccon narrowed her eyes, tilted her head, and gave her sister a look and the time to contemplate what she had just said.

Felicity sputtered. "You mean to say? Changed! Here!

In town? How unspeakably shameful!" She turned to walk with her sister back down the stairs. "May I see?"

Lady Maccon wondered if she did not prefer the cuttingly nasty Felicity of previous incarnations.

"No, you most certainly may not! Really, what has gotten into you of late? You are not at all yourself."

"Is it so unlikely that I should wish to improve myself?"

Alexia fingered the dull gray shawl draped over her sister's faded dress. "Yes. Yes, it is."

Felicity huffed in annoyance. "I must go change for supper."

Lady Maccon looked her up and down, emitting a lip curl that was, quite frankly, remarkably Felicity-like. Sometimes, although not too often, there came an indication that they were, indeed, related. "Yes, I do believe you must."

Felicity wiggled her shoulders and emitted the "Oh, la," of an insult being shaken off, and proceeded back up to the best bedroom, which she had, naturally, commandeered as her own.

Lady Maccon waddled on down, one careful stair at a time. The urgency of the noises below made her increasingly annoyed by her own inability to move with any kind of alacrity. *Really, this is simply too ridiculous! I'm trapped by my own body.* She attained the main hall only to find that the door to the back parlor was locked and shaking. Professor Lyall and two clavigers were milling about unhappily, crowding the passageway with masculine concern.

"Why aren't you at supper?" demanded Lady Maccon

imperiously. "I am certain Floote and the staff have gone to substantial lengths to provide."

Everyone stilled and looked at her.

"Go on, go eat," she said to them, as though they were small children or pet dogs.

Professor Lyall raised a quizzical brow at her.

Lady Maccon lowered her voice. "Biffy wouldn't want anyone to see."

"Ah." Then the Beta, obedient to his mistress's will, followed his fellows into the dining room, shutting the door behind him.

Lady Maccon let herself into the back parlor. Which was an absolute mess. Lord Maccon, now a massive brindled wolf—quite handsome, Alexia always thought, even in lupine form—was squared off against a younger, lankier animal. Biffy's fur was a deep chocolate color, much the same as his hair, except for his stomach and up to the ruff, which was oxblood. His eyes were yellow and crazed.

Lord Maccon barked at his wife authoritatively. Lord Maccon was always barking at his wife, the form of his body mattering not one jot.

Alexia dismissed the commanding tone. "Yes, yes, but you must admit I can be quite useful under such circumstances as these, even in my less-than-nimble state."

Lord Maccon growled in evident annoyance.

Biffy caught Lady Maccon's scent and turned instinctively to hurl himself at her, a new threat. The earl twisted to place his own body in the way. The slighter wolf charged full tilt into his Alpha. Biffy reeled, shaking his head and whining. Lord Maccon feinted toward him, teeth nipping, backing him flush against the now mostly destroyed chaise.

"Oh, Conall, look at this room!" Lady Maccon was displeased. The place was in chaos—furniture overturned, drapes shredded, and one of the cook's precious journals had been bitten into and slobbered all over.

"Oh, doesn't that just take the biscuit! That's evidence, that is." Alexia's hand was to her breast in distress. "Oh, dear, I suppose I ought to have kept it with me." She couldn't really blame Biffy, of course, but it was vexing. She toddled her way toward him, stripping off her gloves.

Biffy continued to snap and slather in her direction, growling in uncontrollable rage, the cursed monster of folklore made flesh and fur before her.

Alexia tsked at him. "Really, Biffy, must you?" Then she used her best Lady Maccon voice. "Behave! What kind of conduct is this for a gentleman!"

Alexia was Alpha, too, and the commanding tone sunk in. Biffy mellowed his snapping frenzy. Some measure of sense entered his yellow eyes. Lord Maccon seized the opportunity and charged, clamping down hard on the other wolf's neck, bearing him down to the floor by sheer superiority of mass.

Lady Maccon approached and looked down at the tableau. "It's no good, Conall. I can't bend down to touch him without falling over."

Her husband let out a snort of amusement. Then, with a casual flick of his head, he hurled the young wolf upward. A surprised Biffy landed on his back on the chaise lounge, scrambling to right himself and attack once more.

Lady Maccon grabbed his tail. He jerked in surprise, enough to overbalance her so that she fell with an *oof* onto the chaise next to him. In that same instant, the power of her preternatural touch forced him back into human form. Even as Biffy's tail retreated, Alexia reached for a paw with her other hand.

In very short order, a naked Biffy lay sprawled in a most undignified way upon the chaise lounge with his foot firmly grasped by his mistress. Since contact with Alexia made him mortal, with all the physical responses such a state entailed, it was not unsurprising to find him blushing crimson in humiliation.

Alexia, while sympathetic to his plight, maintained her grasp and noted, with scientific detachment, that his blush went *all the way* down. *Remarkable.*

Her husband's growl drew her attention back to him. He, too, was back in his human form and naked.

"What?"

"Stop looking at him. He's bare."

"So are you, husband."

"Yes, well, you can look at me all you like."

"Yes, well. Oh." Lady Maccon clutched suddenly at her stomach with her free hand.

Conall's mild jealousy translated instantly to overbearing solicitude. "Alexia! Are you ailing? Oh, you shouldna hae come in here! It's too dangerous. You fell."

Biffy sat up, also concerned. He tried to extract his ankle, but Lady Maccon refused to let go. "My lady, what is wrong?"

"Oh, stop it! Both of you. The infant is simply kicking up a fuss over such sudden activity. No, Biffy dear, we must stay in contact, however indecorous you find it." Biffy offered her his hand instead of his foot. Alexia accepted the exchange of prisoners.

"Shall I ring for Floote?" suggested Biffy, blushing slightly less now that he had something to be worried about that wasn't his own shame.

Alexia hid a smile. "You should find that rather difficult, as you seem to have chewed up the bell rope."

Biffy looked around, blushing again. He covered his face with one hand, peeking through open fingers as though he couldn't stand to look, yet was unable to drag his eyes away. "Oh my ruffled bacon! What have I done? Your poor parlor. My lord, my lady, *please* forgive me. I was not myself. I was in thrall to the curse."

Lord Maccon was having none of it. "That's the problem, pup. You were yourself. You continue to refuse to accept that."

Lady Maccon understood her husband's meaning and tried to phrase it in a more sympathetic manner. "You must begin to accustom yourself to being a werewolf, Biffy dear. Even attempt to enjoy it. This continued resistance is unhealthy." She looked around. "Mainly to my furniture."

Biffy looked down and nodded. "Yes, I know. But, my lady, it's so undignified. I mean to say, one must strip before shifting. And then after…" He looked down at himself, attempting to cross his legs. Lord Maccon took sympathy on him and tossed him a velvet throw pillow. Biffy placed it into his lap gratefully. Alexia noted her husband took no such pains himself.

Biffy's blue eyes were wide. "Thank you, my lady, for bringing me back. It hurts, but it is worth anything to be human again."

"Yes, but the question is, how are we to get you dressed while I maintain contact?" Alexia wanted to know, ever practical.

Lord Maccon grinned. "Something can be arranged. I shall call Floote in, shall I? He will know how to manage." In the absence of the bellpull, Conall strode out into the hall, yelling for the butler.

Mere moments later, Floote appeared. He took in the wretched condition of the room, furniture everywhere, and the entirely unfurnished condition of two of its occupants without even the flicker of an eyelid.

"Sirs. Madam."

"Floote, my man," said the earl jovially. "We will need someone to see to this room. It's a wee bit messy. A re-covering of the chaise, I think; repairs to the wallpaper and curtains; and a new bell rope. Oh, and Biffy here needs to be dressed without letting go of my wife's paw."

"Yes, sir." Floote turned to see to the matter.

Lady Maccon cleared her throat and looked meaningfully at her husband, up and down and then up again.

"What? Oh, yes, and send one of the clavigers next door for some kit for me as well. Deuced inconvenient, but I suppose I may need garments at some point tonight."

Floote vanished and then reappeared in due time carry-

ing a stack of clothing for Biffy. The young werewolf looked
as though he would like to object to the butler's selection
but didn't want to cause any more of a fuss. It did seem that
Floote had chosen the most somber attire possible out of all
of the dandy's peacocklike closet. Biffy's bottom half was
seen to rather simply. After which Floote suggested the
young man kneel at the edge of the chaise lounge and Lady
Maccon touch the back of his head while shirt, waistcoat,
jacket, and cravat were summarily dealt with. Floote han-
dled everything with consummate skill, an ability Alexia
attributed to his many years as valet to her father. Alessandro Tarabotti, by all accounts, had been a bit of a dandy
himself.

While Floote, Alexia, and Biffy performed their complicated game of knotted parts on the chaise, a claviger arrived
with apparel for Lord Maccon. The earl threw it on in an
arbitrary way, showing all the attention to detail a ferret
might employ if called upon to decorate a hat. Lord Maccon
believed that if his trousers were on his legs, and something
else was on his torso, he was dressed. The less done after
that, the better. His wife had been startled to find that in
the summertime, he actually went around their room bare-
foot! Once—and only once, mind you—he even attempted
to join her for tea in such a state. *Impossible man.* Alexia put
a stop to *that* posthaste.

Professor Lyall stuck his head in to see if everything was
sorted.

"Ah, good. You've managed matters."

"Doesn't she always?" grumbled her husband.

"Yes, Professor Lyall?" asked Alexia.

"I thought you should know, my lady, those results you wanted came in from our laboratory at BUR."

"Yes?"

"On those little vials you, uh, found?"

"Yes?"

"Poison. All of them. Different kinds, different effectiveness levels. Some detectable, some not as such. Mostly for mortals but one or two that might put even a supernatural under the weather for some time. Nasty stuff."

CHAPTER SEVEN

The Werewolves of Woolsey Castle

Having to keep Biffy mortal made for a pretty incommodious several hours. Ordinarily, Lady Maccon, even pregnant, could manage a meal and a carriage ride with aplomb, but when one must stay attached in some manner to a dandy, even the most mundane tasks become an exercise in complexity.

"It's a good thing I enjoy your company, Biffy. I can't imagine having to handle daily tasks with someone less agreeable affixed. Like my husband, for example." Alexia shuddered at the very idea. She enjoyed having Conall affixed to her, but only for a limited amount of time.

The husband in question looked up at his lady with a grumbled, "Oh, thank you verra much, wife."

They were sitting in the carriage together. Woolsey Castle loomed on the horizon—a sizable blob in the moonlight.

Lady Maccon, being a woman of little artistic preference, regarded her domain with an eye toward its practicality as an abode for werewolves rather than an architectural endeavor. Which was good, as it was rather more of an architectural tragedy. Those unfortunate enough to happen upon it during daylight could tender only one compliment—that it was pleasingly situated. And it was, atop rising ground in extensive, if slightly unkempt, grounds with a cobbled courtyard and decent stables.

"Oh, you know perfectly well what I mean, husband. We've had to stay attached before, but customarily only when violence was imminent."

"And sometimes for other reasons." He gave her his version of a seductive look.

She smiled. "Yes, dear, exactly."

Biffy said, being on his best behavior, "Thank you for the compliment, my lady, and I do apologize for the inconvenience."

"So long as there are no more zombie porcupines, we should do very well."

"Shouldn't be," said her husband. "Seems the hives have officially declared a cease-fire. Hard to tell truth with vampires but they appear to be pleased with the idea of Lord Akeldama adopting our child."

"Well, at least someone is."

Woolsey Castle was no castle at all but a large Georgian manor house augmented by mismatched Gothic-style flying buttresses. On her most recent trip to Italy, Lady Maccon had encountered a bug—a creature larger than her thumb that flew upright, like an angel, with a nose like an elephant, horns like a bull, and multiple wings. It stayed aloft in an erratic up-and-down manner as though it were remembering, occasionally, that a bug of its size and shape ought not to be able to fly. Woolsey Castle was built, in principle, upon much the same lines as that bug: improbably constructed, exceedingly ugly, and impossible to determine how it continued to stay upright or, indeed, why it bothered to do so.

Since Lord and Lady Maccon had set forth to their country seat with no warning, their unanticipated arrival at Woolsey threw the residents into a tizzy. Lord Maccon swept into the bevy of sprightly young men who'd congregated in the courtyard, taller than most by a head, and carved a path before him, scythelike.

Major Channing, Woolsey's Gamma, strode down from his sanctum and out the front door to greet them, still knotting his cravat and looking as though he had only just arisen, despite the lateness of the hour. "My lord, you were not expected until full moon."

"Emergency trip. Have to stick certain persons down the dungeon sooner than anticipated." There were rumors as to the original owner's use of Woolsey's dungeon, but regardless of initial intent it had proved ideal for a werewolf pack. In fact, the whole house was well suited. In addition to a well-fortified holding area and brick walls, there were no less than fourteen bedrooms, a goodly number of receiving parlors, and several precarious-looking but fully functional towers, one of which Lord and Lady Maccon utilized as their boudoir.

Channing waved a hand at a gaggle of clavigers, directing

them to help with luggage and assist in extracting Lady Maccon from the carriage. The earl was already cocking an ear to a murmured report from one of his pack. He left his wife to see to Biffy, secure in the knowledge that if nothing else, Alexia was good at setting a gentleman in his proper place, even if that place be a dungeon.

Lady Maccon, happy to lean upon Biffy, for exhaustion was beginning to take its toll once more, made her way down into the dungeon and saw the young dandy safely into one of the smaller cells. Two clavigers accompanied them, carrying the requisite amount of silver-tipped and silver-edged weaponry, just in case Lady Maccon lost her grip.

Alexia did not want to let go, for Biffy's face was pale with the imminent terror of transformation. It was an agonizing process for all werewolves to endure, but the new ones had it the worst, for they were not yet accustomed to the sensation, and they were forced into it more frequently by their own lack of control.

Biffy clearly did not care to leave contact with the safe haven of her preternatural skin, but he was too much the gentleman to say. He would be more mortified to impose upon her for the duration of an entire night than to transform into a rampaging monster.

Alexia averted her eyes and kept her hand to the back of his head, her fingers buried in his thick chocolate brown hair, while the clavigers stripped him and clapped silver manacles about his elegant wrists. Conscious of his fading dignity, she kept a stream of irreverent chatter mostly concerning matters fashionable and decorative.

"We are ready, my lady," said one of the clavigers, arms full of clothing, as he exited the prison cell. The other stood outside the silver-plated bars, ready to slam the door as soon as Lady Maccon came through.

"I am sorry," was all Alexia could think to say to the young man.

Biffy shook his head. "Oh, no, my lady, you have given me unexpected peace."

They stretched apart, fingertips just touching.

"Now," said Lady Maccon, and she broke contact, moving as fast as she could in her condition through the door and into the viewing hall.

Biffy, mindful of any damage he might do before she could touch him again, threw himself away in that same instant, using all his regained supernatural strength and speed, before the change descended upon him.

Alexia found the werewolf transformation an intellectually fascinating occurrence and enjoyed watching it, as one might enjoy dissecting a frog, but not in the younger werewolves. Her husband, Professor Lyall, and even Major Channing could manage shifting form with very little indication as to the pain accompanying the experience. Biffy could not. The moment they broke contact, he began to scream. Lady Maccon had learned over the past several months that there is no worse noise in the universe than a proud, kind young man suffering. His scream evolved into a howl as bones and organs broke and re-formed.

Swallowing down bile and wishing she had wax to stopper her ears, Alexia firmly took the arm of one of the clavigers and ushered him toward the stairs and up into the comforting hullabaloo of the pack, leaving the other to stand solitary vigil over a broken man.

"You really want that?" she asked her escort.

The claviger did not try to hedge. Everyone knew Lady Maccon to be direct in her conversation and intolerant of shilly-shallying. "Immortality, my lady, is nothing to treat lightly, no matter the package or the price."

"But at such a cost as that?"

"I would be choosing it, my lady. He did not."

"And you wouldn't prefer trying for vampire instead?"

"To suck blood for survival and never see the sun again? No, thank you, my lady. I'll take my chances with the pain and the curse, should I be so lucky as to have the choice."

"Brave lad." She patted his arm as they attained the top of the stair.

The hubbub resulting from the sudden arrival of Alphas in their midst had settled down into the pleasant boisterous hum of pack in full play. There was some discussion of going hunting, others thought a game of dice was in order, and a few were advocating a light wrestling match. "Outside," grumbled Lady Maccon mildly upon hearing *that*.

At first, Alexia had thought she would never acclimatize to living with over a dozen grown men—she, who had been reared with only sisters. But she rather enjoyed it. At least with men, one always knew where they were located, great yelling, galumphing creatures that they were.

She flagged down Rumpet, the pack butler. "Tea in the library when you have a moment, please, Rumpet? I have some research to undertake. And, would you be so kind as to ask my husband to attend me when he has the time? No hurry."

"Right away, my lady."

The library was Alexia's favorite room and personal sanctuary. However, this evening she intended to use it for its actual purpose—research. She headed toward the far corner, where behind a massive armchair she had carved out some space on the shelves for her father's collection. He had favored tiny leather-covered journals of the type used by schoolboys to keep accounts—navy blue with plain covers dated in the upper left corner.

From what his daughter had gleaned, Alessandro Tarabotti had not been a very nice person. Practical, as all preternaturals are, but without the ethical grounding Alexia had managed to cultivate. Perhaps this was because he was male, or perhaps it was the result of a childhood spent in the wilds of Italy far from the progressive posturing of England. His journals began the autumn of his sixteenth year, during his first term at Oxford, and ended shortly after his marriage to Alexia's mother. They were sporadic at best, constant for weeks and then absent of a single word for months or years. They were mainly concerned with sexual exploits, violent encounters, and long descriptions of new jackets and top hats. Nevertheless, Alexia turned toward them hopefully, hunting out any possible mention of an assassination attempt. Sadly, the journals stopped some ten years before the Kingair plot. She allowed herself only a brief time to get lost in her father's tidy handwriting—amazed, as always, to note how similar that writing was to her own—before pulling herself back and turning her attention to other books. She whiled away the rest of the night thus occupied. Her reverie was disturbed only by Rumpet bringing in an endless supply of fresh tea and, at one point, by Channing, of all people.

"Why, Lady Maccon," he said, unconvincingly. "I was simply looking for—"

"A book?"

Major Channing Channing of the Chesterfield Channings and Lady Alexia Maccon had gotten off on the wrong foot and never managed to stabilize their relationship—despite the fact that he had, on more than one occasion, saved her life. As far as Alexia was concerned, Major Channing was uncomfortably good-looking—a strapping blond with icy-blue eyes, marked cheekbones, and imperiously arched brows. He was a true soldier to the bone, which might not have been so bad a thing had not his nobility of profession been augmented by an arrogance of manner and toothiness of accent so extreme only the bluest of the blue-blooded individuals ought to foist such upon others. As to Channing's opinion of his mistress, the less said on the subject the better, and even *he* was wise enough to understand *that*.

"What are you researching, my lady?"

Alexia saw no reason to hide. "The old Kingair assassination attempt on Queen Victoria. Do you remember any of it?" Her tone was sharp.

The Gamma could not quite disguise the look of concern that suffused his face. Or was that guilt? "No. Why?"

"I think it might be relevant to our current situation."

"I hardly think *that* likely."

"Are you certain you remember nothing?"

Channing evaded the question. "Any success?"

"None. Dash it."

"Well"—Channing shrugged and made his way nonchalantly back out of the library, without a book—"I think you're on the wrong track. No good can come of meddling in the past, my lady." Only Channing could put on such an air of dismissive disgust.

"Meddling! I like that."

"Yes, you do," said the Gamma, closing the door behind him.

After that, no one else intruded upon Alexia's investigations until some few hours before dawn, when her husband came thumping in.

She looked up to see Conall watching her fondly, propping up a bookshelf with one massive shoulder.

"Ah, finally remembered me, have you?" She smiled, her eyes soft and dark.

He strode over and kissed her gently. "Never forgot. Simply misplaced while handling matters of pack and protocol." He tugged playfully at a dark curl that had escaped to lie against her neck in a loose whorl.

"Anything of import?"

"Nothing that should concern you." He had learned enough to add, "Although I'm happy to relay the inconsequential details, should you wish to hear them."

"Oh, no thank you. Do restrain yourself. How is Biffy?"

"Not so good. Not so good."

"I'm afraid your brand of roughness is not working as it ought to pull him into the pack."

"You may be right. I am troubled, my love. I have never faced the problem of a reluctant werewolf before. Of course, in the Dark Ages they had to deal with this kind of thing all the time. Lord knows how they managed it. But our Biffy is such a unique case in this modern time of enlightenment that even I canna fix..." He paused, struggling for the right words, almost stuttering. "I canna fix his unhappiness."

He cleared himself some space among the piles of books and manuscripts around his wife and settled next to her, flush against her side.

Alexia took his big hand in both of hers, stroking the palm with her thumbs. Her husband was a gorgeous lout of a man, and she could not but admit she adored both his size and his temperament, but it was his caring mother-henishness she loved best of all. "I hold them both in the highest of esteem, but Biffy has become overly Byronic. He really must endeavor to fall out of love with Lord Akeldama."

"Oh? And how does one fall out of love?"

"Unfortunately, I have absolutely no idea."

The earl was learning to have a good deal of faith in his capable wife. "You will think of something. And how is my delicious wife? No ill effects from your tumble earlier this evening?"

"What? Oh, onto the chaise? No, none at all. But, husband, I am having very little success on the matter of this threat to the queen."

"Perhaps the ghost was mistaken or misheard. We have not considered that. She was close to poltergeist phase."

"That's possible. And it might be possible that there is no connection to the Kingair attempt."

Lord Maccon growled in irritation.

"Yes, I am well aware that you hate to be reminded."

"Every man hates remembering failure. But we werewolves are the worst of the lot on the subject. I cannot believe there is a connection."

"It is my only avenue of inquiry."

"Perhaps you can leave it for the moment. I require your presence."

Alexia bristled at the commanding tone. "Oh, yes?"

"In bed."

"Oh. Yes." Alexia relaxed and smiled, allowing her husband to help her to her feet.

Alexia slept on the far side of the bed from Conall. This was not because he was a restless sleeper. In fact, he was as still as any supernatural creature, though not quite so dead-looking as a vampire, and he snored softly. And, though Lady Maccon would never admit it to anyone, not even to Ivy, she was a bit of a cuddler. She simply didn't want him vulnerable while he slept. Also, given his irreverence for physical appearance, she was in constant fear that should she touch him all night long, he would grow a beard and then neglect to shave.

On this particular day's rest, the infant-inconvenience allowed Lady Maccon to doze only fitfully on her side, facing the tower window. Which was why she was partly awake when the burglar entered.

There were many things wrong with a thief breaking into Woolsey Castle in the middle of the day. First, what thief in his right mind travels all the way to Barking to perform a break-in? Prospects were much better in London. Second, why bother with Woolsey Castle, a den of werewolves? Just down the road was a small but wealthy ducal estate. And third, why aim for one of the challenging tower windows and not a downstairs parlor?

Nevertheless, the masked form clambered over the sill with graceful economy of movement and stood, light and balanced on his feet, silhouetted against the thick curtains that could not entirely block out the full afternoon sun. He inhaled sharply upon seeing Lady Maccon up on one elbow staring at him. Clearly, he expected to find the room abandoned.

Lady Maccon was far less reticent. She let out a scream that might have raised the dead, and in this case did.

Her husband was no pup who, required by recent metamorphosis and weak control, must sleep solid the entire day through. Oh, no, he *could* be awakened. It was simply that when he was very tired, it took a mighty loud noise. Not much of a screamer as a general rule, Alexia's lung capacity was nevertheless sufficient to the task and produced a trumpeting kind of yell. Once emitted, however, it did not, as one might expect, bring domestic staff and clavigers running. It had taken only one or two highly embarrassing incidents for the denizens of Woolsey Castle to ignore any and all strange noises produced by Lord and Lady Maccon during their slumbering hours.

Still, one angry husband was sufficient to meet Lady Maccon's needs.

The burglar darted to one side of the room, running for Alexia's armoire. There he opened several drawers, finally extracting a sheaf of papers. These he stuffed into a sack. Alexia rolled from the bed, cursing her own lack of mobility, and charged toward him at the same time as her husband. Conall, made clumsy by the full sun, deep sleep, and the unexpectedness of the event, got his feet caught in the bedclothes and pinwheeled widely in a circle like some large and eccentric ballet dancer, before righting himself and lurching at the intruder. *That'll teach him to steal the coverlet,* thought his wife in satisfaction.

Choosing wisely, the burglar went for Alexia, the weaker link, pushing her aside. She kicked out. Her foot met flesh, but not hard enough. All that resulted was Alexia losing her balance and tumbling backward onto the floor, twisting her ankle in the process.

The intruder dove for the open window. Literally dove right through, for he managed to unfold some kind of metal reinforced cape that became a parachute. This carried him gently down the five stories to the ground. Without registering his wife's predicament, floundering about on the floor, Lord Maccon leaped after.

"Oh, no, Conall, don't you dare—" But Alexia's admonishment met only empty air, for he had already jumped out of the window. A werewolf could take such a fall and survive, of course, but not without substantial damage, especially during daylight.

Greatly concerned, Alexia crawled and squirmed her way across the floor, then used a stool and the windowsill to haul herself upright, balancing precariously on her good foot. Her husband had angled his leap to land on the rooftop of the castle keep; he then lowered himself some three stories to the ground and dashed after the culprit. Naked. The wrongdoer, however, was equipped to escape at speed. He had a mono-wheel cycle, rigged up with a small steam propeller, that carried him away across the landscape at a remarkably rapid pace.

The sun was full in the sky, so Lord Maccon was unable to change into his wolf form, and even as fast as a werewolf could be after sunset, it was probably not sufficient to catch up to that wheel. Alexia watched Conall run a goodly distance before coming to this realization and stopping. Sometimes his hunter instinct took a while to defuse.

She tsked in annoyance and turned to glare at her armoire, a mile away and impossible to get at without crawling, trying to determine what exactly had been stolen. What on earth had she stashed in that drawer? She certainly hadn't looked at whatever it was since she unpacked after her wedding. So far as she could remember, it had been full of old letters, personal correspondences, party invitations, and visiting cards. Why on earth would anyone want to steal *that*?

"Really, husband," she said from her post by the window when he got around to climbing back up the many flights of stairs to their sleeping chamber, "how you manage to jump about like some deranged jackrabbit without any permanent damage is a mystery to me."

Lord Maccon snorted at her and went to sniff suspiciously at her armoire. "So, what was in that drawer?"

"I can't readily recall. Some society missives from before we were married, I believe. Can't imagine what anyone would want with those." She frowned, trying to dig her way through the mire of pregnancy-addled wits.

"You'd think they'd be after your dispatch case if it was classified paperwork they wanted."

"Exactly so. What did you smell?"

"A bit of grease, probably from that parachute contraption. Nothing else significant. And you, of course—the whole armoire smells of you."

"Mmm, and how do I smell?"

"Vanilla and cinnamon baked puff pastry," he answered promptly. "Always. Delicious."

Alexia grinned.

"But not of child. I've never been able to smell the bairn. Neither has Randolph. Odd that."

Alexia's grin faded.

Her husband returned to his examination of the drawer. "I suppose the constabulary will have to be called."

"I don't see why. It was only the odd bit of paperwork."

"But you kept them." The earl was confused.

"Yes, but that doesn't mean they were important."

"Ah." He nodded his understanding. "Like all your many pairs of shoes."

Alexia chose to ignore this. "It must be someone I know who stole it. Or arranged for the theft."

"Hmm?" Lord Maccon slumped thoughtfully onto the bed.

"I saw him enter. He was after that drawer in particular. I don't think he was expecting us to be here—he seemed more than usually startled to see me. He must be intimate with our family, or acquainted with some member of Woolsey staff, to know where our room is located and that we were not supposed to be in residence."

"Or it is meant to throw us off the scent. Perhaps he stole something else or did something that has nothing to do with those papers."

Alexia pondered, still standing on one foot, like an egret, propped back against the windowsill. "Or he is after some important item to use for blackmail. Or something to give to the popular press. There has been remarkably little scandal since you and I reconciled. I wouldn't put that kind of thing past old Twittergaddle and the *Chirrup*."

"Well, idle speculation is getting us nowhere. Perhaps he got the wrong room or the wrong drawer. Now, why are we not both back in bed?"

"Ah, yes, there is some difficultly there. My ankle, you see, no longer appears to be functioning as designed." Alexia gave Conall a weak smile, and he noticed, for the first time, her awkward stance.

"God's teeth, why?" The earl strode over to his wife and offered his own substantial form instead of the windowsill. Alexia transferred her weight gratefully.

"Well, I did take a little bit of a tumble just now. Seems I have twisted my ankle."

"You never...? Wife!" He half carried her to the bed before bending over to examine her foot and lower leg carefully. His hands were impossibly gentle, but still Alexia winced. The joint was already starting to swell. "I shall call for a surgeon immediately! And the constabulary."

"Oh, now, Conall, I scarcely think that necessary. The surgeon, I mean. You may, of course, summon the police if you think it best, but I hardly require the services of a physician for a twisted ankle."

Lord Maccon entirely ignored this and marched from the room, already yelling at the top of his considerable lungs for Rumpet and any claviger who might be awake.

Lady Maccon, ankle throbbing dreadfully, tried to go back to sleep, knowing that in very short order her room would be swarming with surgeons and policemen and that her dozing time would be drastically curtailed.

As predicted, Alexia got very little respite that day, which barely made much difference, as she was forced to rest that night after the surgeon pronounced her unfit to walk. She was confined to her bed with a splint and barley water and told that on no account was she to move for an entire week. Worse, she was also told that she was to lay off tea for the next twenty-four hours, as imbibing any hot liquid was bound to increase the swelling. Alexia called the doctor a quack and threw her bed cap at him. He retreated, but she knew perfectly well that Conall and the rest of Woolsey would see that his instructions were obeyed to the letter.

Lady Maccon was not the kind of woman who could be easily confined to bed for seven hours, let alone seven days. Those who knew her well were already dreading her confinement, and this, so close to that fated time, was seen as a preliminary test as to both her behavior and everyone else's ability to cope with it. It was pronounced, by Rumpet and Floote much later in some private butler musings, to be an abject failure on all counts. No one survived it intact, least of all Alexia.

By the second day, she was chafing, to put it politely. "Queen Victoria could be in imminent danger and here I lie, confined to my bed by that fool of a physician because of an *ankle*. It is not to be borne!"

"Certainly not with any grace," muttered her husband.

Lady Maccon ignored this and continued with her ranting. "And Felicity—who is keeping an eye on Felicity?"

"Professor Lyall has her well in hand, I assure you."

"Oh, well, if it's Professor Lyall. He can handle you—I have every confidence in his ability to restrain my sister." Her tone was petulant, for which she wasn't entirely to be blamed, being grimy, sore, and stationary. Nor was her lying-in translating to actual rest. She was too far along for the infant-inconvenience to permit anything more than a few fitful minutes of shut-eye at a time.

"Who says he can handle me?" The earl looked most offended by this blight on his independence.

His lady wife arched an eyebrow at him as if to say,

Oh, now, Conall, really. She continued on to a new worry, without further disparagement of such frivolous masculine dignity. "Have you had the lads check the aethographic transmitter every evening at sunset? You remember, I'm expecting some very important information."

"Yes, dear."

Alexia twisted her lips together in contemplation, trying to come up with something else to gripe about. "Oh, I do hate being cooped up." She picked at the blanket draped over her belly.

"Now you know how Biffy feels."

Lady Maccon's temper softened at the mention of the dandy. "How is he?"

"Well. I have taken your suggestion under advisement, my dear, and I am trying a gentler approach—less firmness of manner."

"Now *that* I should like to see."

"I have been sitting and talking him through the change at sunset. Rumpet suggested some light music might help as well. So I have Burbleson—you remember Catogan Burbleson, that new musically minded claviger we recruited last month?—playing violin all the while. A nice soothing piece of European fluff. Hard to tell if any of this is helping, but my efforts don't seem to be making the poor boy feel any worse."

Alexia was suspicious. "Is young Catogan any good on the violin?"

"Rather."

"Well, perhaps he could come play a bit for me, then? I must say, Conall, it is exceedingly dull being bedridden."

Her husband grunted at that—his version of a sympathetic murmur.

Eventually, the earl resorted to pulling Floote back from London in order to cater to Alexia's whims. No one could manage Lady Maccon quite so well as Floote. As a result, most of Woolsey's library and a goodly number of newspapers and Royal Society pamphlets took up residence about Alexia's bed, and her imperious bell ringing and strident demands ebbed slightly. She began receiving hourly reassurances that Queen Victoria was under guard. Her Majesty's Growlers, special werewolf bodyguards, were on high alert, and in deference to the muhjah's conviction that werewolves might be a risk factor, there was also a rove vampire and four Swiss guards in attendance at all times.

Lord Akeldama sent Boots around with not only inquiries as to Lady Maccon's health, but also a small spate of useful information. The ghosts around London seemed to be in turmoil, for they were appearing and disappearing and wafting here and there, whispering dire threats concerning imminent danger. If queried directly, none of them seemed to know exactly what was going on, but the ghostly community was certainly all aflutter about something.

Alexia went nearly spare at this information combined with the fact that she was unable to rush off to London at *that very moment* in order to continue inquiries. She turned from demanding to positively imperious and made life rather unbearable for those unfortunate enough to be at Woolsey. As full moon was just around the corner, older members of the pack were out running, hunting, or working in the moonlight hours and the youngsters were now locked in with Biffy. This meant only the household staff really had to suffer the yoke of Lady Maccon's impatience, and Floote, ever saintly, undertook the bulk of her amusement.

No one was particularly surprised when on the evening of the fifth day, even Floote's powers failed and Lady Maccon threw off her covers, put weight upon her ankle, which seemed perfectly functional, if a tad achy, and pronounced herself fit enough for a carriage ride into London. No, what surprised everyone was that she had lasted that long.

She had just persuaded a blushing claviger to help her dress when Floote appeared in the doorway clutching several pieces of paper and looking thoughtful. So thoughtful that he did not, initially, attempt to prevent her from her planned departure.

"Madam, the most interesting series of aetherograms have just come in through the transmitter. I believe they are intended for you."

Alexia looked up with interest. "You believe?"

"They are directed to the Ruffled Parasol. I doubt someone would actually attempt to communicate with an accessory."

"Indeed."

"From someone calling himself Puff Bonnet."

"Herself. Yes, go on."

"From Scotland."

"Yes, yes, Floote, what does she *say*?"

Floote cleared his throat and began to read. " 'To Ruffled Parasol. Vital information regarding super-secret subject of confabulation.' " He moved on to the next bit of paper. " 'Past persons of Scottishness in contact with mastermind of supernatural persuasion in London, aka Agent Doom.' " Floote moved on to the third bit of paper. " 'Lady K says Agent Doom assisted depraved Plan of Action. May have all been his idea.' " Moving on to the last one, he read out, " 'Summer permits Scots to expose more knee than lady of refinement should have to withstand. Hairmuffs much admired. Yours etc., Puff Bonnet.' "

Lady Maccon put out her hand for Ivy's correspondence. "Fascinating. Floote, send a message back thanking her and telling her she can return to London. Would you, please? And call up the carriage. My husband is at BUR tonight? I must consult with him immediately on the subject."

"But, madam!"

"It's no good, Floote. The fate of the nation may be at stake."

Floote, who knew well when he had no chance of winning an argument, turned to do as ordered.

CHAPTER EIGHT

Death by Teapot

W hy, Lady Maccon, I understood you to be confined to the countryside for two more days at the very least." Professor Lyall was the first to notice Alexia as she let herself into BUR's head office. The building was situated just off of Fleet Street and was a mite grimy and bureaucratic for Alexia's taste. Lyall and her husband shared a large front office, crammed with two desks, a changing closet, a settee, four chairs, multiple hat stands, and a wardrobe full of clothing for visiting werewolves. Since the Bureau was always untangling some significant supernatural crisis or another and didn't seem to employ a decent cleaning staff, it was also crammed with paperwork, metal aethographic slates, dirty teacups, and, for some strange reason, a large number of stuffed ducks.

Lord Maccon looked up from a pile of antiquated parchment

rolls. His tawny eyes were narrowed. "She bloody well was. What are you doing here, wife?"

"I'm perfectly fine," protested Alexia, trying not to look as though she were leaning on her parasol for assistance in walking. Although, truth be told, she was grateful for its support, as her waddle had evolved into a lurching hobble.

Her husband, with a long-suffering sigh, came out from behind his desk and loomed over her. Alexia expected recriminations, but instead the big man administered an enthusiastic embrace by which masterful tactic he managed to maneuver her backward and down onto a chair in one corner of the room.

Bemused, Lady Maccon found herself firmly off her feet. "Well," she sputtered, "I say."

The earl took that as an excuse to give her a blistering kiss. Presumably to stop her from saying anything further.

Professor Lyall chuckled at their antics and then returned to quietly going about official business, papers rustling softly as he calculated and correlated some complex mathematical matter of state.

"I have just come by the most interesting bit of information," was Lady Maccon's opening gambit.

This statement effectively distracted her husband from any further admonishments. "Well?"

"I sent Ivy to Scotland to find out from Lady Kingair what *really* happened with that previous assassination attempt."

"Ivy? As in Mrs. Tunstell? What a very peculiar choice."

"I shouldn't underestimate Ivy if I were you, husband. She has discovered something."

Conall ruminated a brief moment on this absurd statement and then said, "Yes?"

"It wasn't simply that the poison was to come from London; there was a London agent involved, a *mastermind* if you would believe it. Ivy seems to think that this man orchestrated the whole attempt."

Lord Maccon stilled. "What?"

"Here you thought you had put the matter to rest." Alexia was feeling justifiably smug.

The earl's face became still—the quiet before the storm. "Did she provide any details concerning the identity of this agent?"

"Only that he was supernatural."

Behind them, Professor Lyall's paper rustling stopped. He looked over at them, his vulpine face sharpened further by inquisitiveness. Randolph Lyall's position at BUR was not held because he was Beta to Lord Maccon, but because of his innate investigative abilities. He had an astute mind and a nose for trouble—literally, being a werewolf.

Lord Maccon's temper frothed over. "I knew the vampires had to be involved somehow! The vampires are always involved."

Alexia stilled. "How do you know it was vampires? It could have been a ghost, or even a werewolf."

Professor Lyall came over to participate in the conversation. "This is grave news."

The earl continued to expound. "Well, if a ghost, she would have long since disanimated, so we're well out of luck there. And if a werewolf, he must have been a loner of some kind. Most of those were killed off by the Hypocras Club last year. Damned scientists. So I suggest we start with the vampires."

"I had already reached a similar conclusion myself, husband."

"I'll go to the hives," suggested Professor Lyall, already heading for a hat rack.

Lord Maccon looked as though he would like to protest.

His wife put a hand to his arm. "No, that's a good idea. He is far more politic than you. Even if he isn't strictly gentry."

Professor Lyall hid a smile, clapped his top hat to his head, and walked briskly out into the night without another word, merely touching the brim in Lady Maccon's direction before departing.

"Very well," grumbled the earl. "I'll go after the local roves. There's always a chance it could be one of them. And you—you stay right here and keep off that foot."

"*That* is about as likely as a vampire going sunbathing. I am going to call upon Lord Akeldama. As potentate, he must be consulted on this matter. The dewan as well, I suppose. Could you send a man to inquire if Lord Slaughter could attend me this evening?"

Figuring that Lord Akeldama would at least ensure that his wife remain seated for some length of time in pursuit of gossip if for no other reason, the earl made no further protest. He cursed without much rancor and acquiesced to her request, sending Special Agent Haverbink off to alert the dewan. Lord Maccon did, however, insist upon seeing her to Lord Akeldama's abode himself before pursuing his own investigations.

"Alexia, my *poppadom,* what are you doing in London this fine evening? Aren't you supposed to be abed reveling in the romanticism of a weakened condition?"

Lady Maccon was, for once, not in the humor to entertain Lord Akeldama's flowery ways. "Yes, but something highly untoward has occurred."

"My dear, how *perfectly splendid*! Do sit and tell old Uncle Akeldama all about it! Tea?"

"Of course. Oh, and I should warn you, I have invited the dewan over. This is a matter for the Commonwealth."

"Well, if you insist. But, my *dearest flower,* how ghastly to consider that such a mustache must shadow the clean-shaven grandeur of my domicile." Lord Akeldama was rumored to insist that all his drones go without the dreaded lip skirt. The vampire had once had the vapors upon encountering an unexpected mustache around a corner of his hallway. Muttonchops were permitted in moderation, and only because they were currently all the rage among the most fashionable of London's gentlemen-about-town. Even so, they must be as well tended as the topiary of Hampton Court.

With a sigh, Alexia settled herself into one of Lord Akeldama's magnificent wingback chairs. The ever-considerate Boots rushed over with a pouf on which to rest her throbbing ankle.

Lord Akeldama noticed him and thus the fact that they

were not alone. "Ah, Boots, my *lovely* boy, clear the room, would you, please? Oh, and bring me my harmonic auditory resonance disruptor. It's on my dressing table next to the French verbena hand cream. There's a dear."

Boots, resplendent in his favorite forest-green velvet frock coat, nodded and vanished from the room. He reappeared shortly thereafter pushing in a laden tea trolley upon which lay the expected assortment of delicacies and a small spiky device.

"Will there be anything else, my lord?"

"No, thank you, Boots."

Boots turned his attention eagerly onto Lady Maccon. "My lady?"

"No, thank you, Mr. Bootbottle-Fipps."

Remarkably, her use of his proper name seemed to cause the young dandy some embarrassment, for he blushed and backed hurriedly out of the room, leaving them alone save for a plethora of gold-tasseled throw pillows and the fat calico cat purring placidly in a corner.

Lord Akeldama flicked the forks of the auditory disruptor, and the low-pitched humming sound commenced, the sound of two different kinds of bees arguing. He situated the device carefully in the center of the trolley. The cat, who had been lying on her back in a highly undignified sprawl, rolled over, stretched languidly, and ambled toward the drawing room door, disgruntled by the noise. When her lashing tail and obviously presented backside were ignored, she yowled imperiously.

Lord Akeldama rose. "Your servant, Madam Pudgemuffin," he said, letting her out of the room.

Lady Maccon calculated that she and her host were on familiar enough terms for her to pour her own tea. She did so while he dealt with the demanding feline.

The vampire resumed his seat, crossing one silken leg over the other and rocking the crossed foot back and forth slightly. This was a gesture of impatience when exhibited by any ordinary human, but with Lord Akeldama it seemed to express suppressed energy rather than any particular emotional state. "I used to love pets, my dove, did you know? When I was mortal."

"Did you?" Alexia encouraged cautiously. Lord Akeldama rarely spoke of his life *before*. She was afraid of saying more and thus forestalling further confidences.

"Yes. It is greatly troubling that I am now left with only a cat for company."

Alexia refrained from mentioning the plethora of fashionable gentlemen who seemed to be ever in, out, and about Lord Akeldama's domicile. "I suppose you might consider keeping more than one cat."

"Oh, dear me, *no*. Then I should be known as *that vampire with all the cats*."

"I hardly think that ever likely to become your defining characteristic, my lord." Alexia took in her host's evening garb—black tails and silver trousers, coupled with a corseted black and silver paisley waistcoat and silver cravat. The neckwear was pinned with a massive silver filigree pin, and the monocle dangling idly from one gloved hand was silver and diamond to match. Lord Akeldama's golden hair was brushed to shiny butter yellow glory, fastened back in such a way that one long lock was allowed to artfully escape.

"Oh, *clementine,* what a splendid thing to say!"

Lady Maccon took a sip of tea and firmed up her resolve. "My lord, I do hate to ask this of you especially, but will you be completely serious with me for a moment?"

Lord Akeldama's foot stopped rocking and his pleasant expression tightened. "My darling girl, we have known each other many years now, but such a request breaches even the bonds of *our* friendship."

"I meant no offense, I assure you. But you remember this matter I have been investigating? How the current threat on the queen's life has led me to dredge up a certain uncomfortable assassination attempt of the past?"

"Of course. As a matter of interest, I have some rather *noteworthy* information to relay to you on the subject. But, please, ladies first."

Alexia was intrigued but spoke on as etiquette demanded. "I have heard from Scotland. It seems that there was an agent here in London who apparently concocted the whole dismal plot. A supernatural agent. You wouldn't know anything of this, would you by any chance?"

"My dearest girl, you cannot possibly think that I—"

"No, actually, I don't. You enjoy gathering information, Lord Akeldama, but very rarely seem to put it to any active use, aside from furthering your own curiosity. I fail to see how a botched assassination attempt could have anything to do with your unremitting inquisitiveness."

"Quite logical of you, *buttercup.*" Lord Akeldama smiled,

showing his fangs. They glistened silver in the bright gas lighting, matching his cravat.

"And, of course, you would never have botched it."

The vampire laughed—a sharp sparkling sound of unexpected delight. "So kind, my little crumpet, *so kind.*"

"So, what do you make of it?"

"That twenty years ago, some supernatural or other, in London, was trying to kill the queen?"

"My husband thinks it must be a vampire. I'm inclined to suspect a ghost, which would leave the trail cold, of course."

Lord Akeldama tapped one fang with the edge of his monocle. "I dare say your last option is best."

"Werewolves?" Alexia looked into her teacup.

"*A werewolf,* yes, my gherkin."

Alexia put down her cup and then flicked the two sounding rods on the harmonic device to encourage greater auditory disruption. "A loner I suppose, which leaves me in the same situation as a ghost. Most of the local loners were eliminated by the Hypocras Club's illegal experiments last year." She poured herself a second cup of tea, added a small dollop of milk, and lifted it to her lips.

Lord Akeldama shook his head, looking unusually pensive. The monocle stopped tapping. "You are missing a piece in this game, I think, *butterball.* My instincts are inclined to say pack, not loner. You don't know what the local pack was like at that time. But I remember. Oh, yes. There were rumors all over town. Nothing proven, of course. The last Alpha wasn't right in the head. A fact kept well away from public and press, and from daylight musings for that matter, but a *fact,* nonetheless. What he was doing to earn that reputation, well..."

"But even twenty years ago, the local pack was..." Alexia sat back, sentence unfinished, hand instinctively and protectively pressed upon her belly.

"Woolsey."

Alexia mentally catalogued the Woolsey Pack members. Aside from her husband and Biffy, *all of them* were holdovers from the previous Alpha. "Channing," she said finally. "I'll wager it was Channing. He certainly didn't like the idea of my investigating the past. Interrupted me in the library just the other day. I'll need to check the military records, of course, find out who was in England at the time and who was billeted overseas."

"Good girl," approved the vampire. "Nice and thorough, but I have something more for you. That cook who worked for the OBO who you were investigating? The little poisoner?"

"Oh, yes. How did you know about her?"

"*Please,* darling." He gestured with the monocle toward himself, as if pointing a finger.

"Oh, of course. I apologize. Do go on."

"She preferred a tannin-activated dosing mechanism. Very hard to detect, you understand. Her preferred brand of poison at the time was stimulated by the application of hot water and a chemical component most commonly found in tea."

Alexia put down her teacup with a clatter.

Lord Akeldama continued, eyes twinkling. "It requires a specialized automechanical nickel-lined teapot. The teapot was to arrive as a gift for Queen Victoria, and the first time she drank from it—death." The vampire made a gesture with two slim, perfectly manicured fingers curving down toward his own neck, like fangs. "Your little ghost may have supplied the poison, but teapots of that type were made by only one specialty manufacturer."

Lady Maccon narrowed her eyes. Coincidence was a fateful thing. "Let me guess, Beatrice Lefoux?"

"Indeed."

Alexia stood, slowly and cautiously by degrees but with evident firmness of intent, leaning upon her parasol. "Well, this has been most edifying, Lord Akeldama. Most edifying. Thank you. I must be on my way."

Right at that moment, there was a scuffle in the hallway and the door to the drawing room burst open to reveal the dewan.

"What is the meaning of such a summons as I just received?" He barreled into the room all loud bluster, bringing along an odor of London night air and raw meat.

Lady Maccon waddled past him as though the summons had nothing whatsoever to do with her. "Oh, hello, Dewan. The potentate will be happy to explain everything. Please excuse me, my lords. Important business." She paused, searching for an excuse. "Shopping. I'm certain you understand. Hats. Very critical hats."

"What?" said the werewolf. "But you directed me to attend you! Here, Lady Maccon! At the house of a *vampire*!"

Lord Akeldama stood up from his consciously relaxed posture as though he might try to waylay Lady Maccon.

Alexia waved at them both cheerily from the doorway before hobbling out and into her waiting carriage. "Regent Street, please, posthaste. Chapeau de Poupe."

Lady Maccon barely glanced at the hats. She headed straight through the shop past the sputtering attendant in a, it must be said, very grand *Lady* Maccon–like manner. "I shall make my own way," she said to the fretful girl, and then, "*She* is expecting me." Which was, of course, an outfight fib but served to mollify the chit. Luckily, for all concerned, the shopgirl had the presence of mind to flip the CLOSED sign and shut the door before anyone could observe Lady Maccon's disappearance into the wall.

Madame Lefoux was in her contrivance chamber, looking, if possible, even more gaunt and unwell than when Alexia had seen her last.

"My dear, Genevieve! I thought I was the one meant to be laid up. You look as though you could use a week's rest. Surely this new project cannot be so vital you must damage your health over its completion."

The inventor smiled wanly but barely glanced up from her work, concentrating on some engine schematic rolled out on a metal crate before her. The massive bowler-hat contraption she was still building loomed behind her, looking more of-a-piece. It was at least three times Lord Maccon's height, with its podlike driving chamber now seated atop multiple tentacle-like supports.

Alexia thought perhaps her friend's intense focus on work was a necessary distraction from her aunt's terminal condition. "Goodness me, quite a fearsome thing, is it not? How do you intend to get it out of the chamber, Genevieve? It will never fit through that passageway of yours."

"Oh, it's only loosely assembled. I shall take it out in pieces. I have an arrangement with the Pantechnicon to utilize a warehouse for the final stage of construction." The Frenchwoman stood, stretched, and turned to face Lady Maccon full-on for the first time. She scrubbed her grease-covered hands with a rag and then came over to greet her guest properly. A soft kiss was pressed lovingly against Alexia's cheek, and Alexia was reminded of her friend's consistently solicitous care in the past.

"Are you certain there is nothing you wish to talk about? I assure you I am the soul of discretion; it should go no further. Is there nothing I can do to help?"

"Oh, my dearest lady, I wish there were." Madame Lefoux moved away, elegant shoulders hunched.

Alexia wondered if there might not be some other component to her friend's unhappiness. "Has Quesnel been asking about his real mother again?"

Genevieve and she had discussed such matters in the past. Angelique's violent death was deemed too much for an impressionable young boy. As was the former maid's identity as his biological mother.

Madame Lefoux's soft chin firmed. "*I* am his real mother."

Lady Maccon understood such defensiveness. "It must be hard, though, not telling him about Angelique."

Genevieve dimpled wanly. "Oh, Quesnel knows."

"Oh, oh, dear. How did he...?"

"I should prefer not to talk about it just now." The inventor's face, always tricky to read, shut down completely, her dimples vanishing as surely as poodles after a water rat.

Alexia, saddened by such icy reticence, nevertheless respected her friend's wishes. "I actually have a matter of business to consult you on. I recently learned something of your aunt's past activities. She undertook the manufacture of special automated teapots, I understand, very special ones. Nickel plated?"

"Oh, yes? When was this?"

"Twenty years ago."

"Well, I should hardly remember that myself, I'm afraid. You may be correct, of course. We can attempt to converse with my aunt on the subject or look through her records. I warn you, she is difficult." She switched to her perfect musical French. "Aunt Beatrice?"

A ghostly body shimmered out of a wall nearby. The specter was looking worse than last time, her form barely recognizable as human, misty with lack of cohesion. "Do I hear my name? Do I hear bells? Silver bells!"

"She has gone to poltergeist?" Alexia's voice was soft in sympathy.

"Unfortunately, almost entirely. She has some lucid moments. So not yet completely lost to me. Go ahead, try." Genevieve's voice was drawn with unhappiness.

"Pardon me, Formerly Lefoux, but do you recall a special order for a teapot, twenty years ago. Nickel plated?" Alexia relayed some of the other details.

The ghost ignored her, drifting up toward the high ceiling, floating about the head of her niece's massive project, extending herself so that she became a crude kind of tiara.

Genevieve's face fell. "Let me go check her old records. I think I may have kept them when we moved."

While Madame Lefoux fussed about a far corner of her massive laboratory, Formerly Lefoux drifted back down to Alexia, as if drawn against her will. She was definitely beginning to lose control over noncorporeal cohesion, the end stages before involuntary disanimus. As her mental faculties failed, she was forgetting she was human, forgetting what her own body once looked like. Or that was what the scientists hypothesized. Mental control over the physical was a popular theory.

The ambient aether feathered hazy tendrils off the ghostly form, carrying them toward Lady Maccon. Alexia's preternatural state fractured some of the remaining tether of the ghost's body, pulling it apart. It was an eerie thing to watch, likes soap suds in water curling down a sink.

The ghost seemed to be observing the phenomenon of her own destruction with interest. Until she remembered her selfhood and tugged back, gathering herself inward. "Preternatural!" she hissed. "Preternatural female! What are you—Oh, oh, yes. You are the one who will stop it. Stop it all. You are."

Then she became distracted by something unseen. She swirled about, drifting away from Alexia, still muttering to herself. Behind her murmuring voice, Alexia could make out the high keening wail that all her vocalizations would eventually dissolve into—the death shriek of a dying soul.

Alexia shook her head. "Poor thing. What a way to end. So embarrassing."

"Wrong track. Wrong track!" Formerly Lefoux garbled.

Madame Lefoux returned, walking right through her aunt she was so lost in thought. "Oh, oops, sorry, Aunt. I do apologize, Alexia. I can't seem to locate the crate where I stashed those records. Allow me some time and I'll see what I can find later tonight. Would that do?"

"Of course, thank you for the attempt."

"And now, if you will excuse me? I really must return to work."

"Oh, certainly."

"And you must return to your husband. He's looking for you."

"Oh? He is? How did you know?"

"Please, Alexia, you are wandering around out of bed, with a limp, grossly pregnant. Knowing you, I'm quite certain you are not meant to be. Ergo, he must be looking for you."

"How well you know us both, Genevieve."

Lord Maccon was indeed looking for his errant wife. The moment her carriage drew up before their new town residence, he was out the front door, down the steps, and scooping her up into his arms.

Alexia withstood his solicitous attentions with much

forbearance. "Must you make a scene here in the public street?" was all she said after he had kissed her ardently.

"I was worried. You were gone much longer than I expected."

"You thought to catch me at Lord Akeldama's?"

"Well, yes, and instead I caught the dewan, for my pains." This was growled out in a very wolfish manner for a man whose husbandly duties rendered him not a werewolf at that precise moment.

The earl carried his wife into their back parlor, which five days' absence had seen adequately refurbished, if not quite up to Biffy's exacting standards. Alexia was convinced that once recovered from this month's bone-bender, the dandy would see to it the room was brought back up to snuff.

Lord Maccon deposited his wife into a chair and then knelt next to her, clutching one of her hands. "Tell me truthfully—how are you feeling?"

Alexia took a breath. "Truthfully? I sometimes wonder if I, like Madame Lefoux, should affect masculine dress."

"Gracious me, why?"

"You mean aside from the issue of greater mobility?"

"My love, I don't think that's currently the result of your clothing."

"Indeed, well, I mean *after* the baby."

"I still don't see why you should want to."

"Oh, no? I dare you to spend a week in a corset, long skirts, and a bustle."

"How do you know I haven't?"

"Oh, ho!"

"Now stop playing games, woman. How are you really feeling?"

Alexia sighed. "A little tired, a lot frustrated, but well in body if not spirit. My ankle is paining me only a little, and the infant-inconvenience has been remarkably patient with all my carriage rides and poodling about." She contemplated how to raise the subject of Lord Akeldama's thoughts on the matter of the queen. Finally, knowing she had little inherent delicacy of speech and that her husband had none at all, she decided he would probably appreciate directness.

"Lord Akeldama thinks the London mastermind of your Kingair plot was a Woolsey Pack member."

"Does he, by George?"

"Now, stay calm, my dear. Think logically. I know that is difficult for you. But wouldn't someone like Channing take—"

Lord Maccon shook his head. "No, not Channing. He would never—"

"But Lord Akeldama said that the previous Alpha was not right in the head. Couldn't that have had something to do with it? If he ordered Channing to—"

Lord Maccon's voice was sharp. "No. But Lord Woolsey himself? That *is* an idea. Much as I hate to admit it. The man was mad, my dear. Utterly mad. It can happen that way, especially to Alphas when we get too old. There's a reason, you know, that we werewolves fight amongst ourselves. I mean aside from the etiquette of the duel. Especially Alphas. We shouldn't be allowed to live forever—we go all funny in the brain. Or that's what the howlers sing of.

Vampires do, too, if you ask me. I mean, you only have to look at Lord Akeldama to realize he's...but I digress."

His wife reminded him of where they were in the conversation. "Lord Woolsey, you were saying?"

Lord Maccon looked down at their joined hands. "It can take on many forms, the madness—sometimes quite harmless little esoteric inclinations and sometimes not. Lord Woolsey, as I understand it, became deviant. Even brutal in his"—he paused, looking for the right word that might not shock even his indomitable wife—"tastes."

Alexia contemplated this. Conall was an aggressive lover, demanding, although he could be quite gentle. Of course, with her, he had no real teeth to do damage beyond a nibble or two. But there had been one or two times, early on in their courtship, when she had wondered if he might not actually think of her as food. She had also read overmuch of her father's journals.

"You mean, conjugally violent?"

"Not precisely, but from what I have been told, he was inclined to derive pleasure from sadistic activities." Lord Maccon actually blushed. He could do that while touching her. Alexia found it little-boy endearing. With the fingers of her free hand, she stroked through his thick dark hair.

"Gracious. And how did the pack manage to keep such a thing secret?"

"Oh, you'd be surprised. Such proclivities are not confined to werewolves alone. There are even brothels that—"

Alexia held up a hand. "No, thank you, my dear. I should prefer not to know any additional details."

"Of course, my love, of course."

"I am glad you killed him."

Lord Maccon nodded, letting go of his wife's hand, then standing and turning away, lost to his memories. He fiddled with a little cluster of daguerreotypes arranged on the mantelpiece. That quick, feral quality was back to his movements, a supernatural facet of his werewolf self. "As am I, wife, as am I. I have killed many people in my day, for queen and country, for pack and challenge; rarely do I get to say I am proud of that part of my afterlife. He was a brute, and I was fortunate indeed that I was just strong enough to see him eliminated, and he was just mad enough to make bad choices during the passion of battle. He allowed himself to enjoy it too much."

Lord Maccon's head suddenly cocked—supernatural hearing making out some new sound that Alexia could not discern.

"There is someone at the door." He put down the image he had been toying with and turned to face the entrance, crossing his arms.

His wife picked up her parasol.

*   *   *

The ghost was confused. She spent a good deal of her time confused these nights. She was also alone. Everyone had gone, to the very last, so that she floated in her madness, losing her afterlife into silence and aether. Threads of her true self were drifting away. And there was no friendly face to sit with her while she died a second time.

She remembered that there was something unfinished. Was it her life?

She remembered there was something she still needed to do. Was it die?

She remembered that there was something wrong. She had tried to fix it, hadn't she? What should she care for the living?

Wrong, it was all wrong. She was wrong. And soon she wouldn't be. That was wrong, too.

CHAPTER NINE

_____

In Which the Past Complicates
the Present

A knock came at the back parlor door, and Floote stuck his debonair head around the side. "Madame Lefoux to see you, madam."

Lady Maccon placed her parasol carefully to one side, pretending her husband had not just given her due warning. "Ah, yes, show her into the front parlor, would you, please, Floote? I'll be in shortly. We simply can't have company in this room yet—it's not decent."

"Very good, madam."

Alexia turned back to her husband, beckoning with one hand to get him to come help her stand. He did, bracing himself.

"Oomph," she said, attaining her feet. "Very well, I shall add Lord Woolsey to our ever-growing list of suspects who are now dead and thus useless. Death can be jolly well inconvenient, if you ask me. We can't possibly prove his involvement."

"Or what bearing it might have on this new threat to the queen." The earl placed a casual arm about his wife, assistance couched in a more Alexia-acceptable act of affection. Nearly a year of marriage and he was finally learning.

"True, true." His wife leaned against him.

Another knock sounded at the back parlor door.

"What now!" growled Lord Maccon.

Professor Lyall's sandy head popped in this time. "You're wanted, my lord, on a matter of pack business."

"Oh, very well." The earl helped his wife waddle down the hallway. He abandoned her at the door to the front parlor and then followed his Beta out into the night.

"Hat, my lord," came Professor Lyall's mild rebuke, a disembodied voice from the darkness.

Conall came back inside, scooped a convenient top hat off of the hall stand, and disappeared outside again.

Alexia paused at the door to the front parlor. Floote had left it slightly ajar, and she overheard conversation drifting from within, Madame Lefoux's mellow voice and that of another, clear and erudite, confident with age and authority.

"Mr. Tarabotti had significant romantic success. I often wondered if the soulless weren't dangerously attractive to those with too much soul. You, for example, probably have excess. You like her, don't you?"

"Oh, really, Mr. Floote, why this sudden interest in my romantic inclinations?"

Lady Maccon started at that. She might have recognized Floote's voice, of course, except that she had never heard him string so many words together at once. It must be admitted, she had privately doubted his ability to formulate a complete sentence. Or at least his willingness to do so.

"Be careful, madam." The butler's voice was stiff with rebuke.

Alexia flushed slightly at the very idea of her staff taking such a tone with a *guest*!

"Is it my care you are concerned with or Alexia's?" Madame Lefoux seemed well able to withstand such a grave breach in domestic protocol.

"Both."

"Very well. Now, would you be so kind as to check up on Her Highness? I am in a bit of a rush and the evening isn't getting any longer."

At this juncture, Lady Maccon made a great blundering noise and entered the room.

Floote, unflappable, backed away from his intimate proximity to the French inventor as though it were the most natural thing in the world.

"Madame Lefoux, to what do I owe the pleasure of your company? I seem to have just left you." Alexia made her way laboriously across the room.

"I have that information you were looking for. About the teapots." The inventor handed over a sheaf of old parchment paper, yellowed about the edges, thick and ridged, marked by hand and the assistance of a straight edge into some sort of ledger. "It's in my aunt's code, which I am certain you could decipher if you wished. But essentially it indicates that she had only one order for the teapot invention that year, but it was a big one. It didn't come through any suspicious channels. That's the intriguing part. It was a government order, out of London, with funds originating in the Bureau of Unnatural Registry."

Lady Maccon's mouth opened slightly, then snapped shut. "Ivy's Agent Doom was at BUR?" She sighed. "Well, I suppose that puts Lord Woolsey to the top of my suspect list. He would have held my husband's position at the time."

Floote, in the act of shutting the door behind himself, paused on the threshold. "Lord Woolsey, madam?"

Alexia looked at him, all big-eyed and innocuous. "Yes. I'm beginning to think he must have had a hand in the Kingair assassination attempt."

Madame Lefoux looked entirely uninterested at this. Her present concerns must be outweighing any curiosity over the past. "I do hope the information will be of some use, Alexia. When you're finished, could I please have those records back? I like to keep these things in proper order. You understand, don't you?"

"Of course."

"And now, I hate to be so abrupt, but I must get back to it."

"Of course, of course. Do try to get some rest, please, Genevieve?"

"I'll rest when the souls do," quipped the inventor with a shrug. Then she left the room, only to return a moment later. "Have you seen my top hat?"

"The gray one out in the hall?" Lady Maccon's stomach

fell in a way that had nothing whatsoever to do with the child.

"Yes."

"I believe my husband may have accidentally absconded with it. Was it *special*?"

"Only in that it was my favorite hat. I can't imagine it fit him. Must be several sizes too small."

Lady Maccon closed her eyes at the very idea. "Oh, he must look quite a picture. I do apologize, Genevieve. He is so very bad about these things. I'll have it sent over as soon as he returns."

"Oh, no trouble. I do, after all, own a hat shop." The inventor flashed a dimpled smile, and Alexia felt a strange bump of pleasure at the sight. It had been so long since Genevieve had smiled fully.

Floote saw the Frenchwoman to the door, but before he could even attempt to resume his regular duties, Lady Maccon called him back into her presence.

"Floote, a moment of your time."

Floote came to stand before her, wary. His face, as always, was impassive, but Alexia had learned over the years to watch the set of his shoulders for clues as to his real feelings.

"Floote, I wouldn't wish to be an eavesdropper, not on my friends or my staff—that is, by rights, your provenance. However, I couldn't help but overhear some bit of your conversation with Madame Lefoux before I entered this room. Really, I didn't know you had it in you. Several sentences in a row. And some of them quite sharp."

"Madam?" The shoulders twitched.

Floote really didn't have much of a sense of humor, poor man. Lady Maccon stopped teasing him and moved on to the meat of the matter. "You were discussing my father, weren't you?"

"In a manner, madam."

"And?"

"Madame Lefoux pays you a good deal of conspicuous attention."

"Yes. I always figured it was her *way*. If you take my meaning."

"I do, madam."

"But you think it is something more?"

His shoulders tensed and Floote looked, if such a thing were to be conceived, uncomfortable. "I have made observations over the years."

"Yes?" Having a conversation with Floote was about as easy as explaining the formulation of the counterbalance theorem to a bowl of macaroni pudding.

"On the nature of preternatural interactions, if you would, madam."

"Yes, I would. Go on."

Floote spoke slowly, choosing his words with care. "I have arrived at certain conclusions."

"Concerning what, exactly?" *Coaxing, coaxing,* thought Alexia. Never her strong point in a conversation, letting others take their time getting to a point. Still, the company of Lord Akeldama had taught her much in the way of it.

"There may be attraction between those who have excess soul and those who have none at all, madam."

"You mean preternatural and supernatural?"

"Or preternatural and natural folk with supernatural potential."

"What kind of attraction?" asked Lady Maccon rather injudiciously.

Floote raised an eloquent eyebrow.

"Did my father—" Alexia stopped, trying to come up with the correct phrasing. This was a strange sensation for her, thinking before she spoke. Her husband was much the same way or they might never have tolerated each other. Floote was notoriously reluctant to talk about his former employer, citing classified protection of international relations and the safety of the empire. Lady Maccon tried again. "Did my father exercise this appeal on purpose?"

"Not to my knowledge." Suddenly Floote switched topics, volunteering information in a most unexpected and un-Floote-like manner. "Do you know why the Templars gave up their preternatural breeding program, madam?"

Alexia's brain tried to change gears, a steam engine caught on the wrong track. "Uh, no."

"They never could entirely control preternaturals. It's your pragmatism. Your kind cannot be persuaded by faith; pure logic must be applied."

Alexia's very pragmatic nature was confused as to why normally taciturn Floote was telling her this, and right now. "Is that what happened to my father? Did he lose faith?"

"Not exactly faith, madam."

"What do you mean, precisely, Floote? Enough shilly-shallying."

"He engaged in an exchange of loyalties."

Alexia frowned. She was beginning to suspect there were far fewer coincidences in life than she had previously believed. "Let me guess. This occurred about twenty years ago?"

"Nearer to thirty, but if you are asking if the three events are linked, the answer is yes."

"My father rejecting the Templars, his death, and the Kingair assassination attempt? But when the Kingair Pack tried to kill the queen, he was already dead."

"My point exactly, madam."

A loud crashing and banging came at the front door. Lady Maccon would have liked to query Floote further, but pressing noises seemed to be calling on his butler attentions.

Floote glided out, all calmness and dignity, to see what the fuss was about. Whoever it was, however, pushed past him and came rushing into the front parlor, crying, "Lady Maccon! Lady Maccon, you are needed most urgently!"

The intrusion resolved itself into the form of two of Lord Akeldama's boys, Boots and a young viscount by the name of Trizdale. They were overwrought and disheveled— conditions highly out of character for any of Lord Akeldama's drones. One sleeve of Boots's favorite green jacket was torn, and Tizzy's boots actually looked to be scuffed in places. *Scuffed, indeed!*

"My goodness me, gentlemen, has there been an *incident?*"

"Oh, my lady, I can hardly bear to say it. But we are being assaulted!"

"Oh, my." Lady Maccon signaled them to come closer. "Don't stand there gawping—help me to rise. What can I do?"

"Well, my lady, we are under attack from a werewolf!"

Alexia paled considerably. "In a vampire's abode? Deary me! What is this world coming to?"

Boots said, "That's just the thing, my lady. We thought it best to fetch you. The creature is on a bender."

Lady Maccon grabbed up her parasol and her reticule. "Of course, of course. I'll come directly. Lend me your arm, please, Mr. Bootbottle-Fipps."

As quickly as possible, the two young dandies helped Alexia to waddle out the front door and along the path past the lilac bushes into Lord Akeldama's house.

The arched and frescoed hallway was packed with concerned-looking young men, several of them worse off than Boots and Tizzy. Two were even missing their cravats. A truly startling thing to see. They were milling about and talking in obvious trepidation, at a loss but eager to do something.

"Gentlemen!" Lady Maccon's shrill feminine voice cut through the masculine hubbub. She raised her parasol on high as though about to conduct a concert. "Where is the beast?"

"Please, mum, it's our master."

Alexia paused in perplexity and lowered her parasol slightly. Lord Akeldama was a vampire, but no one would ever refer to him as a *beast*.

The dandies continued in a chorus of explanations and objections.

"He's gone and locked himself in the drawing room."

"With *that* monster."

"I should never wish to question our lord's choices, but *really!*"

"So ill-kempt. I'm convinced its fur had split ends."

"Said he could handle it."

"For our own good, he said. Not to let anyone in."

"I'm not *anyone*." Lady Maccon pushed her way through the throng of perfectly tailored jackets and high white collars, as one of those particularly chubby terriers might clear a path through a pack of poodles.

The young men gave way until she was faced with the gilt door, painted with white and lavender swirls, that led into Lord Akeldama's infamous drawing room. She took a deep breath and knocked loudly with the handle of her parasol.

"Lord Akeldama? It's Lady Maccon. May I enter?"

From behind the door came the sound of scuffling and possibly Lord Akeldama's voice. But no one actually bid her entrance.

She knocked again. Even under the most dire of circumstances, one didn't simply go bursting into a man's private drawing room without sufficient provocation.

A particularly loud crash was all the response she got.

Alexia decided that *this* could be considered sufficient provocation and slowly turned the knob. Parasol at the ready, she waddled in as quick as she could, closing the door firmly behind her. Just because she was disobeying Lord Akeldama's orders didn't mean the drones could as well.

Her fascinated gaze fell upon quite the tableau.

Lady Maccon had witnessed an altercation between a vampire and a werewolf once before, but it had been inside a moving carriage and had rather rapidly relocated from carriage to road. Also, back then, the two opponents had genuinely been trying to kill each other. This was different.

Lord Akeldama was locked in single combat with a werewolf. The wolf was definitely trying to kill him, jaws snapping and all his supernatural strength bent on the vampire's destruction. But Lord Akeldama, while fighting the wolf off, did not seem to be enthusiastic about killing him. For one thing, his favored weapon, a silver-edged glaive that masqueraded as a piece of gold plumbing, was still in its customary place above the mantelpiece. No, Lord Akeldama seemed to be employing mostly evasive strategies, which only served to frustrate and anger the wolf.

The beast lunged for the vampire's elegant white neck, and Lord Akeldama dodged to the side, flicking out one arm in a blasé manner, as if flapping a large handkerchief at a departing steamer. It was a gesture that, for all its casualness, still lifted the werewolf up and entirely over the vampire's blond head to land on his back near the fireplace.

Alexia had never had the chance to observe Lord Akeldama fight before. Of course, one knew Lord Akeldama must be *able* to fight. He was rumored to be quite old, and as such must be at least capable of combat. But this was akin to knowing, academically, that his chubby calico house cat was capable of hunting rats—the actual execution of the task always seemed highly improbable and possibly embarrassing for all concerned. Thus, she now found herself quite intrigued by the display before her. And soon discovered that she was wrong in her initial assumption.

Far from any discomfit or awkwardness, Lord Akeldama fought with a nonchalant lazy efficiency, as though he had all the time in the world on his side. Which Alexia supposed he did. His advantage was in speed, eyesight, and dexterity. The wolf had strength, smell, and sound to rely on, but he was inexperienced. The werewolf hadn't an Alpha's skill, either, which Lord Maccon had once described to his wife as fighting with soul. No, this wolf was moon mad. His jaws snapped and his claws speared surfaces without regard to logic or expense. The vampire's perfectly elegant drawing room was faring no better than Alexia's back parlor. He was also getting saliva all over the pretty throw cushions.

It would have been an entirely uneven match except that Lord Akeldama really was trying not to hurt Biffy.

Because that was who it was: Biffy, chocolate brown fur with an oxblood stomach.

"How on earth did you get out of the Woolsey dungeon?"

No one answered her, of course.

Biffy charged Lord Akeldama. The vampire seemed to flash spontaneously from one side of the room to the other, leaving the werewolf to complete his leap with no quarry at the end of it. Biffy landed on a gold brocade chair, overturning it so that its legs stuck up, shockingly bare, into the air.

The werewolf noticed Lady Maccon's presence first.

His nostrils flared. His hairy head swiveled around to cast a yellow-eyed glare in her direction. There was none of Biffy's soft blue gentleness in those eyes, only the need to maim, feast, and kill.

Lord Akeldama was only seconds behind noticing that they had company. "Why, Alexia, my *little cowslip*, how kind of you to call. Especially in your present condition."

Alexia played along. "Well, I had nothing better to do of an evening, and I did hear you needed help in entertaining an unexpected guest."

The vampire gave a little chuckle. "La so, my custard. As you see. Our company is a *tad* overwrought. Methinks he could use some good cheer."

"I do see. Is there any way in which I may provide assistance?"

While this conversation took place, Biffy charged at Alexia. She barely had time to arm her dart emitter before Lord Akeldama interposed, protecting her gallantly.

He took on the brunt of the attack. Biffy's claws scraped down the vampire's legs, tearing silk trousers to ribbons and gouging deep into the muscle. Old black blood seeped out. At the same time, the werewolf's jaws locked about Lord Akeldama's upper arm, biting clean through the meatiest part. The pain must have been phenomenal, but the vampire merely shook the wolf off, as a dog will shake off water. Even as Alexia watched, Lord Akeldama's wounds began to heal.

Biffy launched himself at the vampire once more, and together they grappled, Lord Akeldama always just that split second faster and a whole lot craftier so that even with all the predatory advantages afforded by the werewolf state, Biffy could not break the vampire's hold nor his will when both were set so firmly against him.

Alexia said, "I've been meaning to have this little chat with you, my lord. Some of your young gentlemen friends do seem to get overly clingy, don't you find?"

The vampire puffed out a breath of amusement. His hair was coming loose from its ribbon, and he appeared to have lost his cravat pin.

"My *darling pumpkin blossom,* it is not my intent to engender such gripping affection, I assure you. It is purely by accident."

"You are too charismatic for your own good."

"*You* said it, my dabble-duck, not I." Once more the vampire managed to use grip and speed to lever the wolf off of him and hurl the creature across the room, away from Alexia. Biffy landed full against the wall and slid down, taking several watercolors with him. He crashed to the floor, the paintings now lying amidst shards of glass and gilt frames. He shook himself and stumbled dizzily to his feet.

Alexia fired the parasol. Her dart struck home and the werewolf collapsed back. He seemed to wobble, losing control of bits of himself, but then, quicker than any vampire Alexia had ever shot, fought against the effects of the drug and regained his feet. She wondered if Madame Lefoux's last batch of numbing agent was up to snuff or if it was simply less effective on werewolves.

Lord Akeldama flitted to one side, catching the wolf's

attention and directing his next charge away from Lady Maccon.

Alexia said, deciding on a new tactic, "If you think you could hold him steady, my lord, I might be able to manage a calming touch. You know, some lads these days simply require a female to administer discipline."

"Of course, my plum, of course."

Biffy hit Lord Akeldama broadside, and in the same movement, the vampire turned all affectionate, instead of tossing him away. Wrapping both his arms and legs about the wolf, Lord Akeldama used the beast's own momentum to tumble them both to the lush carpet. In an amazing feat of wrestling, the vampire got one elbow about Biffy's muzzle, his hand closing firmly over the nose. With his other arm, he locked down the forelegs. With his legs, Lord Akeldama secured Biffy's hindquarters. It was a remarkable exhibition of agility and flexibility. Alexia was duly impressed, having wrestled a bit with her husband. Lord Akeldama was clearly very experienced in the matter of intimate tussling.

Alexia knew the vampire would not be able to pin the werewolf thus for very long. In the end, Biffy was stronger and would break free, but Lord Akeldama did have the beast momentarily confused.

She waddled up and, casting her own safety to the winds, leaned forward, not unexpectedly losing her balance. She landed fully atop both supernatural creatures, ensuring her bare hands were in contact with Biffy but turning both men mortal in her enthusiasm.

It was a very odd sensation, for in such a position, Alexia

was uncomfortably aware of Biffy's body changing from wolf to human. She could feel the slide of muscle and bone beneath her protruding belly as he shifted. It was eerily like the feel of her child kicking underneath her own skin.

Biffy howled with the pain of it, directly into Alexia's ear. A howl that turned to a scream of agony, then a whimper of remembered suffering, and finally little snuffles of acute embarrassment. Then, as he came to the horrific realization of what he had almost done, he turned to his former master.

"Oh, dear, oh, dear. Oh dear." It was a litany of distress. "My lord, are you well? Did I cause any permanent injury? Oh look at your trousers! Oh, mercy. I am so sorry."

Lord Akeldama's healing was paused midway so that the claw marks were still visible under the tattered ribbons of his silken britches.

"'Tis but a scratch, my pet. Do not trouble yourself so." He looked down at himself. "Well, several scratches, to be precise."

At this juncture, Alexia was forced into a realization that rather shook the foundations of her universe: there are some circumstances that even the very best manners could not possibly rectify. This was one such situation. For there she lay, pregnant and out of balance, atop a pile consisting of one overdressed vampire and one underdressed werewolf.

"Biffy," she said finally, "to what do we owe the pleasure of your visit? I was under the impression you were other-wise contained this evening." It was a valiant attempt, but even such talk as this could not mask the awkwardness.

Lord Akeldama attempted to unwind himself from Biffy

and extract himself from Alexia without the aid of supernatural strength. When this was finally accomplished, he stood, dashed to the door to reassure his drones of his undamaged state, and sent one of them to fetch clothing.

Biffy and Alexia helped each other to rise.

"Are you unharmed, my lady?"

Alexia did a quick internal check. "It would appear so. Remarkably resilient, this baby of mine. I could use a bit of a sit-down, though."

Biffy helped her to an ottoman—one of the few pieces of furniture in the room not overturned—her hand firmly clasped in his. They sat and stared off into space, grappling with how best to handle their predicament. Lord Maccon might be a blustering instrument of rudeness, but he did have his uses in dispersing awkward silences. Alexia handed Biffy a shawl, only slightly saliva-ridden. He set it gratefully in his lap.

She tried not to look, of course she did, but Biffy did have a rather nice physique. Not nearly so splendid as her husband's, but not everyone could be built like a steam engine, and the young dandy had kept himself well in hand before metamorphosis, for all his frivolous pursuits.

"Biffy, were you secretly a Corinthian?" Alexia wondered out loud before she could stop herself.

Biffy blushed. "No, my lady, although I did enjoy fencing rather more than some of my compatriots might consider healthy."

Lady Maccon nodded sagely.

Lord Akeldama returned, looking not a whit put out. His

brief sojourn among his drones had resulted in hair and neck cloth back to crisp and pristine order and a new pair of satin trousers. *How do they do it?* wondered Alexia.

"Biffy, *duckling,* what a surprise your visiting little old *me* at this time of moon." He handed his former drone a pair of sapphire-colored britches.

Biffy blushed, pulling them on with one hand. Alexia took polite interest in the opposite side of the room. "Yes, well, I wasn't entirely in my right faculties, my lord, when I made the decision to, uh, call. I think I simply, well, instinctively"—he glanced at Lady Maccon from under his lashes—"headed home."

Lord Akeldama nodded. "Yes, my *dove,* but you have missed the mark. Your home is next door. I know it's easy to be confused."

"Too easy. Especially in my altered state."

They were speaking about Biffy's werewolfness as one would an evening's inebriation. Alexia looked back and forth between the two of them. Lord Akeldama had taken a seat opposite his former drone, his eyes heavy-lidded, his posture informal, revealing nothing.

Biffy, too, was beginning to assume his old dapperness, as though this were actually a social call. As though he were not half naked in a vampire's drawing room. As though he had not just tried to kill them both.

Lady Maccon had always admired Lord Akeldama's ability to remain patently unruffled by the world about him. It was as commendable as his never-ending efforts to ensure that his own small corner of London was filled with nothing but beauty and pleasant conversation. But sometimes, and she should never say such a thing openly, it smacked of cowardice. She wondered if the immortal's avoidance of life's ugliness was a matter of survival or bigotry. Lord Akeldama did so love to know all the gossip about the mundane world, but it was in the manner of a cat amusing himself among the butterflies without a need to interfere should their wings get torn off. They were only butterflies, after all.

Lady Maccon felt it behooved her, just this once, to point out the wounded wingless insect before him. Soullessness may confer practicality, but it did not always confer caution. "Gentlemen, you may place my abruptness at the door of my current condition, but I am not in the mood to tolerate idiosyncrasies. Circumstances have placed us all in an untenable position. No, Biffy, I do not mean your unclothed state—I mean your werewolf one."

Both Lord Akeldama and Biffy looked at her, mouths slightly agape.

"The time has come to move onward. Both of you. Biffy, your choices were taken from you, and that is regrettable, but you are still an immortal—and not dead—which is more than most can say." She turned her baleful look upon the vampire. "And you, my lord, must let go. This is not some contest you have lost. This is life, or afterlife, I suppose. For goodness' sake, stop wallowing, both of you."

Biffy looked duly chastised.

Lord Akeldama sputtered.

Lady Maccon tilted her head in such a way as to dare him to deny the truth in her words. He was certainly old enough to know himself; whether he cared to admit such a fault out loud remained to be seen.

The two men looked at each other, their faces tight.

It was Biffy who closed his eyes a long moment and then nodded briefly.

Lord Akeldama lifted one white hand and trailed two fingers down the side of his former drone's face. "Ah, my boy. If it must be so."

Lady Maccon could be merciful, so she moved the conversation on. "Biffy, how did you get out of Woolsey's dungeon?"

Biffy shrugged. "I don't know. I can't remember much when I'm a wolf. Someone must have unbolted the cell door."

"Yes, but why? And who?" Alexia looked suspiciously at Lord Akeldama. Was he meddling?

The vampire shook his head. "Not me or mine, I *assure* you, blossom."

A loud knock sounded at the door to the drawing room, all the warning they got before it burst open and two men came stomping in.

"Well," said Alexia, "at least he knocked first. Perhaps he's learning."

The earl strode across the room and bent to kiss his wife's cheek. "Wife, thought I would find you here. And young Biffy, too—how are you, pup?"

Lady Maccon looked to her husband's Beta, gesturing at Biffy with her free hand. "The pack business that took you away?"

Professor Lyall nodded. "He led us a merry chase before
we traced him here." He tapped his nose, indicating the
method of tracking.

"How'd he get out?"

Professor Lyall tilted his head, which was as good as he
would get to admitting that he had no idea.

Alexia nudged her husband in Biffy's direction. He shot
her a brief glance out of resigned tawny eyes and then
crouched down in front of the half-naked dandy. It was a
very servile position for an Alpha. He lowered his voice to
a soft growl, of the kind meant to be comforting. It's terribly difficult for a werewolf to be comforting—especially an
Alpha dealing with a reluctant pack member. The instinct is
to subdue and discipline.

Alexia nodded at him encouragingly.

"My boy, why did you run here?"

Biffy looked up at the ceiling and then back down again.
He swallowed, nervous. "I don't know, my lord, some
instinct. I'm sorry, but this is still home to me."

Lord Maccon looked at Lord Akeldama, predator to
predator. Then he turned back to his pack member.

"It has been six months, many moons, and still you are not
settling. I know this was not the end you wanted, but it is the
end you have been given. Somehow we must make this work."

No one missed the *we*.

Alexia was extremely proud of her husband at that
moment. *He can be taught!*

He took a deep breath. "How can we make this easier for
you? How can I?"

Biffy looked utterly startled to be asked such a question by such a man. "Perhaps," he ventured, "perhaps I could be allowed to take up permanent residence here, in town?"

Lord Maccon frowned, glancing at Lord Akeldama. "Is that wise?"

Lord Akeldama stood as though totally disinterested in the entire conversation. He walked to the other side of the room and stared down at his torn watercolor paintings.

Professor Lyall stepped in to fill the breach. "Young Biffy might benefit from a distraction. Some form of employment, perhaps?"

Biffy started. He was a gentleman, born and bred; honest work was a little beyond his frame of reference. "I suppose I could try it. I've never had proper employment before." He spoke as though it were some kind of exotic cuisine he had not yet sampled.

Lord Maccon nodded. "At BUR? After all, you have contacts within society that might prove useful. I am in a position to see you well settled with the government."

Biffy looked somewhat intrigued.

Professor Lyall came around to stand before Alexia, next to her crouching husband. His normally passive face showed genuine concern for the new pack member, and it was clear that he had put thought into how Biffy might be better integrated.

"We could come up with a suitable range of duties. Regular occupation might help you acclimatize to your new position."

Lady Maccon looked, really looked, at her husband's second for the first time in their acquaintance. At the way he stood, shoulders not too straight, gaze not too direct. At the way he dressed, almost to the height of style but with a studied carelessness, the simple knot to his cravat, the reserved cut to his waistcoat. There was just enough not perfect about his appearance as to make him forgettable. Professor Lyall was the type of man who could stand in the center of a group and no one would remember he was there, except that the group would stay together because of him.

And then, right there, holding on to the hand of a half-naked dandy, Alexia discovered the piece of the puzzle she had been missing.

CHAPTER TEN

Ivy's Agent Doom

I t was you!"
It had taken well over two hours to configure the wine
cellar of the new house to hold Biffy for the remainder of
the evening without damage to either the wine, the cellar, or,
most importantly, Biffy. They would have to devise a better
long-term solution if he was to take up permanent residence
in town. They left Lord Maccon coaching him through
the change, arms wrapped about him, gruff voice keeping
him calm.

Alexia had pigeonholed Lyall and practically dragged
him into the back parlor, giving Floote very strict instructions that under no circumstances were they to be disturbed
by anyone. Now she was busy waving her parasol wildly in
his direction.

"You're Agent Doom! How ninnyhammered of me not to have seen it sooner! You rigged the whole thing back then. The whole Kingair attempt. And that was the point, of course, that it should be only an *attempt*. It was never meant to succeed. The queen was never meant to die. The point was to convince the Kingair Pack to turn against their Alpha, to give him a reason to leave. You needed Conall to come to London so he could challenge Lord Woolsey. The Alpha who had gone mad." The parasol inscribed ever increasing wiggles in the air in her enthusiasm.

Professor Lyall turned away, walking to the other side of the room, his soft brown boots making no noise on the carpet. His sandy head was bent only slightly. He spoke to the wall. "You have no idea what a blessing it is, to have a capable Alpha."

"And you are Beta. You would do whatever it took to keep your pack together. Even arrange to steal another pack's leader. Does my husband know what you did?"

Lyall stiffened.

Alexia answered her own question. "No, of course he doesn't know. He needs to trust you. He needs you to be his reliable second just as much as you need him as leader. Telling him would defeat the very action you took; it would disturb the cohesion of your pack."

Professor Lyall turned to face her. His hazel eyes were tired, for all they were set in that eternally young face. There was no pleading in them. "Are *you* going to tell him?"

"That you were a double agent? That you destroyed his relationship with his old pack, with his best friend, with his homeland, to steal him for Woolsey? I don't know." Alexia put a hand to her stomach, suddenly exhausted by the events of the past week. "It would destroy him, I think. Treachery from his Beta, his lynchpin. A second time."

She paused, looking him full in the face. "But to keep this information from Conall, to share in your deception? You must know that this puts me in an untenable position as his wife."

Professor Lyall avoided her direct gaze, wincing slightly. "I had no choice. You must see that? Lord Maccon was the only werewolf in Britain capable of taking on Lord Woolsey and winning. When Alphas go bad, my lady, it is sickening. All that concentrated attention to pack cohesion and all that protective energy turns rotten—no one is safe. As Beta, I could shield the others but only for so long. Eventually, I knew his psychosis would leak out, encompassing them as well. Such a thing can drive an entire pack to madness. We don't talk of it. The howlers don't sing of it. But it occurs. I am not trying to excuse myself, you understand, simply explain."

Alexia was still stuck on the horror of having such knowledge when her husband did not. "Who else knows? Who else knew?"

A knock sounded and then immediately the door crashed open.

"Oh, for goodness' sake, doesn't anyone wait to be bidden entrance anymore?" cried Alexia in vexation, whirling to face the intruder, parasol quite definitely at the ready. "I said *no one* was to disturb us!"

It was Major Channing Channing of the Chesterfield Channings.

"And what are you doing here?" Lady Maccon's tone was far from welcoming, but her parasol relaxed into a safer position.

"Biffy is missing!"

"Yes, yes, you're late. He turned up next door, got into a tussle with Lord Akeldama, and now Conall has him down in the wine cellar."

The Gamma paused. "You have a crazed werewolf in your wine cellar?"

"You can think of a better place to stash him?"

"What about the wine?"

Lady Maccon abruptly lost interest in dealing with her husband's Gamma. She turned back to Professor Lyall, who was looking cowed. "Does *he* know?"

"Me? Know what?" Channing's beautiful ice-blue eyes were the picture of innocence. But his eyelids flickered as he took in Alexia's militant attitude and Professor Lyall's intimidated demeanor, the latter as out of character as the former was standard. Everyone was accustomed to Professor Lyall skulking about in the background, but he did that with an air of quiet confidence, not shame.

The major looked back and forth between the two, but instead of leaving them to their private discourse, he turned, slammed the door, and wedged a seat under the handle.

"Lyall, your disruptor, if you would?"

Professor Lyall reached into his waistcoat and pulled out a harmonic auditory resonance disruptor. He tossed the small crystal device to Channing, who set it atop the chair in front of the door and then quickly flicked the two tuning forks, activating the discordant humming.

Only then did he approach Lady Maccon. *"What do I know?"* He asked it as though he could predict her answer.

Alexia looked at Lyall.

Channing cocked his head. "Is this about the past? I told you no good could come of your meddling."

Lyall raised his head, smelling the air. Then he turned to look at Channing.

For the first time, Alexia realized the two men were probably old friends. Sometime enemies, of course, but only in the manner of those who have been too long in each other's company, possibly centuries. These two had known each other far longer than either had known Lord Maccon.

"You know?" Lyall said to the Gamma.

Channing nodded, all patrician beauty and aristocratic superiority as compared to Professor Lyall's studied middle-class inoffensiveness.

The Beta looked at his hands. "Did you know all along?"

Channing sighed, his fine face becoming suffused with a brief paroxysm of agony. So brief Alexia thought she had imagined it. "What kind of Gamma do you take me for?"

Lyall laughed, a huff of pain. "A mostly absentee one." There was no bitterness to the statement, simply fact. Channing was often away fighting Queen Victoria's little wars. "I didn't think you realized."

"Realized what, exactly? That it was occurring? Or that you were taking the brunt of it so he'd stay off the rest of us?

Who do you think kept the others from finding out what was really going on? I didn't approve of you and Sandy—you know I didn't—but that doesn't mean I approved of what the Alpha was doing either."

Alexia's previous self-righteousness disintegrated under the implication of Channing's comments. There was more to Lyall's manipulations than she had realized. "Sandy? Who is Sandy?"

Professor Lyall twisted his lips into a little smile. Then he reached into his waistcoat—he always seemed to have everything he needed in that waistcoat of his—and pulled out a tiny leather-covered journal, navy blue with a very plain cover dated 1848 to 1850 in the upper left corner. It looked achingly familiar.

He walked softly across the room and handed it to Alexia. "I have the rest as well, from 1845 on. He left them to me on purpose. I wasn't keeping them intentionally away from you."

Alexia could think of nothing whatsoever to say. The silence stretched until finally she asked, "The ones from after he abandoned my mother?"

"And from when you were born." The Beta's face was a study in impassivity. "But this one was his last. I like to keep it with me. A reminder." A whisper of a smile crossed that deadpan face, the kind of smile one sees at funerals. "He didn't have an opportunity to finish it."

Alexia flipped the journal open, glancing over the scribbled text within. The little book was barely half full. Lines jumped out at her, details of a love affair that had altered everyone involved. Only as she read did the full scope of the ramifications come into focus. It was rather like being broadsided by a Christmas ham.

Winter 1848—for a while he walked with a limp but would not tell me why,

said one entry. Another, from the following spring, read:

There is talk of a theater trip on the morrow. He will not be permitted to attend, of that I am convinced. Yet we both pretended he would accompany me and that we should laugh together at the follies of society.

For all the tight control of the penmanship, Alexia could read the tension and the fear behind her father's words. As the entries progressed, some of his sentences turned her stomach with their brutal honesty.

The bruises are on his face now and so deep sometimes I wonder if they will ever heal, even with all his supernatural abilities.

She looked up at Lyall, attempting to appreciate all the implications. Trying to see bruises almost twenty-five years gone. From the stillness in his face, she supposed they might be there—well hidden, but there.

"Read the last entry," he suggested gently. "Go on."

```
June 23, 1850
  It is full moon tonight. He is not going
to come. Tonight all his wounds will be
self-inflicted. Time was once, he would
spend such nights with me. Now there is no
surety left for any of them except in his
presence. He is holding his whole world
together by merely enduring. He has asked
me to wait. Yet I do not have the patience
of an immortal, and I will do anything to
stop his suffering. Anything. In the end
it comes to one thing. I hunt. It is what I
am best at. I am better at hunting than I
am at loving.
```

Alexia closed the book. Her face was wet. "You're the one he's writing about. The one who was maltreated."

Professor Lyall said nothing. He didn't need to respond. Alexia was not asking a question.

She looked away from him, finding the brocade of a nearby curtain quite fascinating. "The previous Alpha really was insane."

Channing strode over to Professor Lyall and placed a hand on his arm. No more sympathy than that. It seemed sufficient. "Randolph didn't even tell Sandy the worst of it."

Professor Lyall said softly, "He was so old. Things go fuzzy with Alphas when they get old."

"Yes, but he—"

Lyall looked up. "Unnecessary, Channing. Lady Maccon is still a lady. Remember your manners."

Alexia turned the small slim volume over in her hand—the end of her father's life. "What really happened to him, at the last?"

"He went after our Alpha." Professor Lyall removed his spectacles as though to clean them, but then seemed to forget he had done so. The glasses dangled from his fingers, glinting in the gas lamplight.

Channing seemed to feel further explanation was necessary. "He was good, your father, very good. He'd been trained by the Templars for one purpose and one purpose only—to hunt down and kill supernatural creatures. But even he couldn't take on an Alpha. Even an insane, sadistic bastard like Lord Woolsey was still an Alpha with a pack at his back."

Professor Lyall put his spectacles down on a side table and rubbed a hand across his forehead. "I told him not to, of course. Such a waste. But he was always one to pick and choose listening to me. Sandy was too much an Alpha himself."

Alexia thought for the first time that Professor Lyall and Lord Akeldama shared some mannerisms. They were both good at hiding their emotions. To a certain extent, this was to be expected in vampires, but in werewolves...Lyall's reserve was practically flawless. Then she wondered if his very quiet stillness were not like that of a child climbing into hot water, afraid that every little movement would only make things hotter and more painful.

Professor Lyall said, "Your father's death taught me one thing. That something needed to be done about our Alpha. That if I had to bring down another pack to do it, so be it. At the time, there were only two wolves in England capable of killing Lord Woolsey. The dewan and—"

Alexia filled in the rest of his sentence. "Conall Maccon, Lord Kingair. So it wasn't simply a change of leadership you were after; it was self-preservation."

One corner of Lyall's mouth quirked upward. "It was revenge. Never forget, my lady, I'm still a werewolf. It took me nearly four years to plan. I'll admit that's a vampire's style. But it worked."

"You loved my father, didn't you, Professor?"

"He was not a very good man."

A pause. Alexia thumbed through the little journal. It was worn about the edges from countless readings and rereadings.

Professor Lyall let out a little sigh. "Do you know how old I am, my lady?"

Alexia shook her head.

"Old enough to know better. Things are never good when immortals fall in love. Mortals end up dead, one way or another, and we are left alone again. Why do you think the pack is so important? Or the hive, for that matter. It is not simply a vehicle for safety; it is a vehicle for sanity, to stave off the loneliness. Our mistrust of loners and roves is not only custom, it is based on this fact."

Alexia's brain buzzed with all these new revelations, but

finally the whirling settled on one thing. "Oh, lordy, Floote. Floote knew."

"Some, yes. He *was* Sandy's valet at the time."

"Is it you who are keeping him quiet?"

Professor Lyall shook his head. "Your butler has never taken his orders from me."

Alexia looked at the little journal again, stroking the cover, and then offered it back to Lyall. "Perhaps you will let me read it in its entirety sometime?"

The Beta's eyes crinkled up, wincing as though he might cry. Then he swallowed, nodded, and placed the book inside his waistcoat pocket.

Alexia took a deep breath. "So, back to the crisis at hand. I suppose neither of you is currently planning to kill Queen Victoria, even in jest?"

Two almost simultaneous head shakes met that question.

"Are you telling me I've been on the wrong track all this time?"

The werewolves looked at each other, neither of them willing to risk her wrath.

Alexia sighed and extracted the sheaf of paper Madame Lefoux had given her from her reticule. "So this is entirely useless? No connection between the last attempt and this one. Pure coincidence that the poisoner you were going to use, Professor, happened to die in service to the OBO. And that she possibly then became a ghost who delivered a warning to me."

"Looks like it must be, my lady."

"I don't like coincidences."

"Now that, my lady, I can't help you with."

Alexia sighed and stood, using her parasol as a crutch. "Back to the beginning, I suppose. Nothing for it. I shall have to return these papers to Madame Lefoux." The child inside her kicked mightily at the very idea. "Perhaps tomorrow night. Bed first."

"A very sensible idea, my lady."

"None of that from you, Professor, thank you very much. I'm still miffed. I understand why you did it, but I *am* miffed." Alexia began making her way painstakingly to the door, prepared to climb upstairs and across the balcony bridge into her closet boudoir.

Neither werewolf tried to help her. She was clearly not in the mood to be coddled. Lyall did touch her arm as she passed. The action turned him mortal for a moment. Alexia had never had an opportunity to see him mortal before. He looked much the same as he did when immortal—perhaps there were more lines about his mouth and at the corners of his eyes—but he was still a pale vulpine man with sandy hair—utterly unremarkable.

"*Are* you going to tell Conall?"

Alexia turned around slowly and leveled a decided glare in his direction. It told him, in no uncertain terms, exactly how she felt about this state of affairs. "No, no, I'm not. Damn you."

And then, with as much dignity as was possible given her condition, she waddled from the room, like some unbalanced galleon under full sail.

*   *   *

Only to run into Felicity in the hallway. It was like trundling full tilt into a pillar of molasses, the conversation likely to be sticky and the individual attractive only to creepy-crawlies. Alexia was never prepared to run into her sister, but on such a night as this when the chit should be fast asleep, it really was *beyond.*

Felicity, for her part, was bleary-eyed and wearing nothing but a highly ornamented nightgown, the excess material of which she clutched, with artful trembling hands, to her breast. Her hair was a tousle of golden curls that cascaded over one shoulder, a ridiculous pink bed cap perched precariously atop her head. The nightgown, too, was pink, a foulard with printed magenta flowers, replete with ruching, frillings, a quantity of lace trim, and a particularly large ruff about the neck. Alexia thought Felicity looked like a big pink Christmas tree.

"Sister," said the tree, "there is a most impressive rumpus emanating from the wine cellar."

"Oh, go back to bed, Felicity. It's only a werewolf. Really. You'd think people never had monsters in their cellars."

Felicity blinked.

Channing came up behind Alexia. "Lady Maccon, might I have a private word, before you seek your rest?"

Felicity's eyes widened and her breath caught.

Alexia turned around. "Yes, well, if you insist, Major Channing."

A sharp elbow met her protruding belly. "Introduce us," hissed Felicity. Her sister was looking at the Gamma with much the same expression as that which entered Ivy Tunstell's eyes when faced with a particularly hideous hat, which is to say, covetous and lacking in all elements of good judgment.

Alexia was taken well aback. "But you are in your night attire!" Felicity only gave her a big-eyed head shake. "Oh, very well, Felicity. This is Major Channing Channing of the Chesterfield Channings. He is a werewolf and my husband's Gamma. Major Channing, do please meet my sister, Felicity Loontwill. She is human, if you can believe such a thing after ten minutes' conversation."

Felicity tittered in a manner she probably thought was musical. "Oh, Alexia, you so like to have your little jokes." She offered her hand to the handsome man before her. "I do apologize for my informal state, Major."

Major Channing clasped it elegantly in both of his, bowing with evident interest, even daring to brush his lips across her wrist. "You are a picture, Miss Loontwill. A picture."

Felicity blushed and took back her hand more slowly than was proper. "I should never have thought *you* a werewolf, Major."

"Ah, Miss Loontwill, it was eternal life as a gallant soldier that called to me."

Felicity's eyelids fluttered. "Oh, a soldiering man through and through, are you, sir? How romantic."

"To the bone, Miss Loontwill."

Alexia felt she was about to be sick, and it had nothing to do with her pregnancy. "Really, Felicity, it is the middle of the night. Don't you have one of your meetings tomorrow?"

"Oh, yes, Alexia, but I should never wish to be rude in fine company."

Major Channing practically clicked his heels. "Miss Loontwill, I cannot deny you your beauty rest, however unnecessary I might feel it. Such loveliness as yours is already so near to perfection it can require no further assistance in that regard."

Alexia tilted her head, trying to determine if there was an insult buried in all that flowery talk.

Felicity tittered again. "Oh, really, Major Channing, we hardly know one another."

"Your meeting, Felicity. Rest." Alexia tapped her parasol pointedly.

"Oh, la, yes, I suppose I should."

Lady Maccon was tired and out of temper. She decided she had a right, under such circumstances, to be difficult. "My sister is an active member of the National Society for Women's Suffrage," she explained sweetly to Major Channing.

The Gamma was taken aback by this information. No doubt in all his long years he had never encountered a woman of Felicity's ilk—and her ilk was in very little doubt after even a few seconds of acquaintance—who would be involved in such a thing as politics.

"Really, Miss Loontwill? You must tell me more about this little club of yours. I can hardly believe a woman of your elegance need dabble in such trifles. Find yourself a nice gentleman to marry and he can do such fiddling things as voting for you."

Rather suddenly, Alexia felt like she might want to join the movement herself. Imagine such a man as Major Channing thinking he had any inkling of what a woman might want. *So condescending.*

Felicity's eyelashes fluttered as though doing battle with a very fierce wind. "No one has asked me yet."

Lady Maccon marshaled her displeasure. "Felicity, bed, now. I don't care one jot for your finer feelings, but I need my rest. Channing, help me up the stairs and we shall have our little confidence."

Felicity reluctantly undertook to do her sister's bidding.

Major Channing, even more reluctantly, took Alexia's arm. "So, my lady, I wanted to—"

"No, Major, wait until she is well away," cautioned Lady Maccon.

They waited, making their way slowly up to the next floor.

Alexia finally deemed it safe, but still she spoke in a very low voice. "Yes?"

"I wanted to say, about that business with our Beta. Randolph is different from the rest of us wolves, you do realize? Your father was the love of his life, and we immortals don't say such a thing lightly. Oh, there were others before Sandy—mostly women, I'll have you know." Channing seemed to be one of the few immortals Alexia had met who was concerned with such things. "But Sandy was the last. I worry. It was a quarter of a century ago."

Lady Maccon frowned. "I have other pressing concerns at the moment, Major, but I will give the matter my due attention as soon as possible."

Channing panicked. "Oh, now, I'm not asking you to matchmake, my lady. I'm simply pleading for leniency. I could not confide such fears to Lord Maccon, and you are also our Alpha."

Alexia pinched at the bridge of her nose. "Could we talk about this tomorrow evening, perhaps? I really am quite done in."

"No, my lady. Have you forgotten? Tomorrow is full moon."

"Oh, blast it, it is. What a mess. Later, then. I promise not to take any rash action with regards to the good professor without due consideration as to the consequences."

Channing clearly knew when to retreat from a battle. "Thank you very much, my lady. As to your sister, she is quite a peach, is she not? You have been hiding her from me."

Lady Maccon would not be goaded. "Really, Channing, she is practically"—she paused to do some calculations—"one-twentieth your age. Or worse. Don't you want some maturity in your life?"

"Good God, no!"

"Well, how about some human decency?"

"Now you're just being insulting."

Alexia huffed in amusement.

Channing raised blond eyebrows at her, handsome devil that he was. "Ah, but this is what I enjoy so much about immortality. The decades may pass for me, but the ladies, well, they will keep coming along all young and beautiful, now, won't they?"

"Channing, someone should lock you away."

"Now, Lady Maccon, that transpires tomorrow night, remember?"

Alexia did not bother to warn him off her sister. Such a man as Channing would only see that as a challenge. Best to pretend not to care. Felicity was on her own with this one. Lady Maccon was exhausted.

So exhausted, in fact, that she didn't awaken when her husband later crawled in next to her in their bed. Her big, strong husband who had spent the night holding on to a boy afraid of change. Who had coached that boy through a pain Conall could no longer remember. Who had forced Biffy to realize he must give up his love or he would lose all of his remaining choices. Her big, strong husband who curled up close against her back and cried, not because of what Biffy suffered but because he, Conall Maccon, had caused that suffering.

Alexia awoke early the next evening to an unfamiliar sense of peace. She was not, by and large, a restful person. This did not trouble her overmuch. But it did mean that peace was, ironically, a slightly uncomfortable sensation. It drove her fully awake, sharp and sudden, once she had recognized and identified it. Her husband had slept pressed against her the whole day through, and she had been so very tired even the inconvenience of pregnancy had awakened her only a few times. She luxuriated in the pleasure of Conall's broad, comforting presence. His scent was of open fields, even here in town. She reflected whimsically that he was the incarnation of a grassy hill. His face was rough with a full day's growth. It was a good thing they were now encamped in Lord Akeldama's house. If any household were to employ the services of an excellent barber, it was this one.

Alexia pushed aside the bedding, the better to examine her personal territory with greater thoroughness. She smoothed her hands along her husband's massive shoulders and chest, resting fingertips at the notch in the base of his throat. She petted him as though he were in wolf form. She rarely got to indulge in such a luxury; usually her preternatural touch turned him back to human before she even got in one good scratch. Sometimes, though, and no one had ever been able to tell her why, she could put on her gloves and pet his thick brindled coat, even tug on his velvety ears with no shifting. *Yet another mystery of my state,* she thought. It had happened once in Scotland, and then a few other times during the winter months. These days, however, her preternatural abilities seemed to be amplified. He went human simply by being close to her. *I wonder if it has something to do with the pregnancy. I should do some experiments and see if I can isolate the conditions.* Before her marriage, she'd never spent much time in the company of supernaturals, apart from Lord Akeldama, and she had never had the opportunity to really study her own abilities.

But in the interim, she would continue petting whatever form he presented her with. She trailed her hands back over his chest, threading fingers through the hair there, tugging slightly, and then down along his sides.

A rumbling snuffle of amusement met this action.

"That tickles." But Conall did not make any move to prevent her continued explorations. Instead, he picked up his own hand and began smoothing it over her protruding belly.

The infant-inconvenience kicked in response, and Conall twitched at the sensation.

"Active little pup, isn't he?"

"She," corrected his wife. "As if any child of mine would dare be a boy."

It was a long-standing argument.

"Boy," replied Conall. "Any child as difficult as this one has been from the start must, perforce, be male."

Alexia snorted. "As if *my* daughter would be calm and biddable."

Conall grinned, catching one of her hands and bringing it in for a kiss, all prickly whiskers and soft lips. "Very good point, wife. Very good point."

Alexia snuggled against him. "Did you manage to settle Biffy?"

Conall shrugged, an up and down of muscle under her ear. "I spent the remainder of last night with him. I think that helped mitigate the trauma. It is hard to tell. Regardless, by this point, I should be able to sense him."

"Sense, what do you mean, sense?"

"Difficult to articulate. Do you know that sensation you get when there is someone else in the room, even if you cannot see them? For us Alphas, pack members are a little like that. Whether we are in the same room or not, we simply know the pack is there. Biffy, he isn't a part of that yet. So he isn't part of my pack."

Alexia was struck with a moment of inspiration. "You should encourage him and Lyall to spend more time together."

"Now, Alexia, are you trying to matchmake?"

"Maybe."

"I thought you said Biffy did not need to be in love, he needed to find his place."

"Perhaps, in this matter, Biffy is not the half of the equation who needs to be in love."

"Ah. How did you know Randolph might favor...? Never mind, I don't want to know. It would never work. Not those two."

Alexia took mild offense. Biffy and Lyall were both such good men, so personable and kindly. "Oh, I don't know about that. They seem eminently suited."

Lord Maccon looked up at the ceiling. Clearly he was trying to come up with a delicate way to phrase this. "They are both, uh, too much the Beta, if you take my meaning."

Alexia didn't. "I don't see how that can be an objection."

Lord Maccon obviously felt he could not go into the matter any further without spoiling what little was left of his wife's feminine delicacy, so he grappled for a means of changing the subject. Only to recall exactly what night this was.

"Oh, bugger it. It's full moon, isna it?"

"Indeed it is. Good thing we're all cozied up together, isn't it, my dear?"

Lord Maccon pursed his lips, trying to decide what to do. He had not intended to sleep the whole day through but had wanted to be on his way back to the dungeons before moonrise. "I left orders for Lyall and Channing to transport Biffy back to Woolsey before sunset, but I really should get there myself."

"Too late now—the moon is up."

He grunted, annoyed with himself. "Would you mind terribly taking the journey with me? The wine cellar here might hold a new pup, but it won't hold me. And I should be with him, tonight of all nights. Even moonstruck myself, my presence will soothe him. Besides, I can't imagine you want to stay attached to me all night."

Alexia blinked at him flirtatiously. "You know, under more slender circumstances, I wouldn't mind spending an evening thus occupied, but I really must be getting on with this investigation. I need to return some paperwork to Madame Lefoux, and I'm back to square one questioning the ghosts. I do wish this pregnancy didn't make me so abstracted. I keep missing things, and I shouldn't have allowed myself to be so easily sidetracked by history."

Lord Maccon didn't bother trying to argue. Given her ankle and her pregnancy, his wife was in no condition to do any such thing as continue an active inquiry. It was full moon. What could he do to see her safe except have her tailed? Which, naturally, he'd been doing for the past five weeks. For one moment, he did consider coming up with some kind of excuse to keep her at Woolsey even while he, himself, was incapacitated.

Instead, he growled out, "Very well. But, please, take some precautionary measures?"

Lady Maccon grinned. "Oh, my love, but that is so very boring."

Lord Maccon growled again.

Alexia kissed the tip of his nose. "I'll be good, I promise."

"Why is it that I am always at my most terrified when you say that?"

*   *   *

Above the ghost, under a full moon, the living celebrated being alive.

Mortals trotted about in shoes and corsets made to limit movement, fashion for prey. They drank (becoming pickled as any gherkin) and puffed at cigars (becoming smoked as any kipper), behaving like the food they were. Silly, thought the ghost, that they couldn't see such simple comparisons.

Immortals saluted the full moon with blood, some in crystal glasses, others by tearing into meat and howling. Aside from the ancient Greeks and their long-ago offerings, there was no blood for ghosts. Not anymore.

The ghost could hear herself crying. Not the herself that still remembered what being herself meant. Some other part of her, the part that was fading into aether.

She wished she had studied more on the nature of the supernatural and less on the nature of the technological world. She wished her passions had taken her into a learning that would allow her to tolerate the sensation of disanimus with dignity. But there was no dignity in death.

And she was alone. Perhaps that was not so bad, under such ignominious circumstances?

Still, where were the scientific pamphlets that taught a woman how to listen to herself die?

CHAPTER ELEVEN

Wherein Hairmuffs Become
All the Rage

L ady Maccon accompanied her husband home to Woolsey Castle and saw him safely locked away in its well-fortified dungeons. He shared a cell with Biffy, both of them tearing into the walls of their impenetrable prison—and into each other. They would do no permanent damage, but still Alexia could not watch. As with most things in life, Lady Maccon preferred the civilized exterior to the dark underbelly (with the exception of pork products, of course).

"This is an odd world I have become part of, Rumpet." The Woolsey butler was helping her back to the carriage to return to town. Woolsey's formal coach was fitted out with full-moon regalia: ribbons tied to the top rails, crest newly polished, a matched set of parade bays hitched to the front. Lady Maccon gave the nose of one a pat. She liked the bays; they were steady, sensible horses with high prances and the general temperaments of gormless newts. "And I used to think werewolves were such simple, basic creatures."

"In some ways, madam, but they are also immortal. Dealing with eternity requires a certain complexity of spirit." The butler handed her up into the carriage.

"Why, Rumpet, have you been hiding the soul of a philosopher under that efficacious exterior?"

"What butler isn't, madam?"

"Good point." Lady Maccon signaled the coachman to drive on.

London at full moon was a different city entirely from any other time of the month. For this one night, out of default or desire, the vampires ruled. Hives throughout England hosted parties, but the biggest occurred in London proper. Roves were at liberty to roam undisciplined and unmonitored. It wasn't that the werewolves necessarily kept vampire largess in check, just that with guaranteed werewolf absence, the vampires had the autonomy to be that little bit more toothsome than normal.

It was also an excuse for the daylight folk to dance the night away. Or, in the case of the conservatives who wanted nothing to do with immortals and their ilk, to dirigible the night away. Most of the Giffard fleet was afloat at full moon, running short-haul tourist jaunts above the city. Some were rented out for private parties; others simply took advantage of the moonlight and the festivities to run special offers at high expense for the fashionable to display their latest floating attire. A few airships were outfitted with firework display apparatuses, shooting off colorful explosions of red and yellow sparkles, like hundreds of shooting stars, into the sky.

It was always a challenging night for BUR. Several core staff were werewolves—three from Woolsey, two from HM Growlers, and one new loner. A number of clavigers also held commissions. All were conspicuous by their absence. Top that off with the vampire agents away enjoying the revels, and full moon left the Bureau understaffed and unhappy about it. There were a few contract ghosts paying very close attention to what went on during the extravagances, but they couldn't exactly provide physical enforcement if such became necessary. That left the mortal agents at the fore during moon time, spearheaded by the likes of Haverbink— capable, tough, working-class men with a taste for danger and an ear for trouble. Of course, the potentate's drones were also out and about, but they couldn't be trusted to report their findings to BUR, even if the rumors were true and Lord Maccon was sleeping in Lord Akeldama's closet.

Lady Maccon liked full moon. There was something irrepressibly celebratory about it. London came alive with excitement and dark ancient mysteries. Admittedly, there were fangs and blood and equally acrimonious things, but full moon also brought with it blood-sausage pies, candy sugar wolves, and other tasty treats. Lady Maccon was easily ruled by her stomach into approval of any event. It was the poor quality of the comestibles, not the company, that caused her to continually refuse invitation to most public assembly rooms. The rest of the ton thought this snobbish and approved. They did not realize it was solely based on the shabbiness of the provisions.

Apart from the food and the pleasant aspect of dirigibles silhouetted against the moon, Alexia also enjoyed the fact that a night ruled by vampires meant everyone was in their best looks and tip-top manners. While her own taste was, frankly, pedestrian, Lady Maccon did enjoy seeing what all the peacocks had arranged to drape themselves with. In the better parts of London, one could run into almost anything: the latest evening gowns from Paris, floating dresses to the extremes of practicality from the Americas, and the fullest, most complex cravat ties imaginable. One could witness a veritable cornucopia of visual delights merely by driving through the crowded streets.

If Alexia had not been so enthralled, with her face pressed firmly to the carriage window, she would have missed the porcupine. But she was and so she didn't.

She banged on the roof of the carriage with her parasol, sharp and loud. "Halt!"

The coachman pulled the bays up, right there in the middle of the busy thoroughfare—aristocracy had its privileges and Woolsey's carriage was crested.

Lady Maccon lifted up the speaking tube she'd recently had installed and belled through to the box.

The coachman picked up his receiver. "Yes, madam?"

"Follow that porcupine!"

"Certainly, madam." In his years of service to Lord Maccon, the poor man had received far more ludicrous requests.

The carriage lurched to the side, causing Alexia to drop her end of the tube, which swung from its heavy metal cord and whacked her in the arm. There was no high-speed chase— for which Alexia was grateful, as she'd had quite enough of those to last a lifetime, thank you very much!—because the porcupine, which happened to be on a lead like a little dog, was moving at a sedate pace often interrupted by curious bystanders. The creature was obviously out for a stroll for that purpose, to attract interest and attention on a night practically designed for such displays of eccentricity and ostentation.

Eventually, traffic allowed the carriage to pull a little ahead of the porcupine and stop. The coachman came around and let Lady Maccon down in time for her to accost the owner.

"Ah, pardon me, madam," said Lady Maccon to the young lady in charge of the porcupine before realizing that they were already acquainted. "Why, Miss Dair!"

"Goodness me, Lady Maccon? Should you be in public in your condition? You are looking most encumbered." The vampire drone seemed genuinely surprised to see her.

"But it is a lovely evening to be out, as you obviously realize, Miss Dair."

"Indeed, the moon has got his cravat on."

"If you don't mind my asking, what on earth are you doing strolling the streets of London with a zombie porcupine?"

"Why shouldn't I be enjoying the company of my new pet?" Miss Mabel Dair, renowned actress, was exactly the type of original female to elect to keep a pet porcupine, but Lady Maccon would have none of it.

"New pet, indeed! A whole herd of those nasty creatures attacked me and my husband only recently."

The actress paused, a look of defensiveness suffusing her pretty face. "Perhaps the inside of your carriage, Lady Maccon, might be a better place for this conversation?"

Mabel Dair boasted a stylish figure, if a little round, with an arrangement of curves that cemented her appeal firmly among a specific class of fashionable gentlemen. And, if the rumors were to be believed, one very fashionable woman, Countess Nadasdy. Miss Dair had risen to prominence and become the reigning darling of the West End via the Westminster Hive's unflagging support. She'd engaged in no less than three continental tours and garnered a considerable amount of popularity in the colonies as well. She had copious blond curls done up in high piled coques of the very latest style, and her face was pleasingly sweet. She gave off an entirely unwarranted air of innocence, for Miss Dair was a woman of strong character—an excellent rider, a dab hand at cards, and a personal friend to the countess as well as being her drone. She also had very good taste in evening dresses. A woman not to be taken lightly, porcupine or no.

She and her pet climbed inside the Woolsey carriage, leaving her escort to shadow them on the street. Lady Maccon turned her attention from the actress to the porcupine. It looked very like those that had attacked her husband, which is to say, not exactly alive.

"An undead porcupine," insisted Lady Maccon with conviction.

"Ah, yes, I see how you might make that kind of assessment, but no. That is not possible, as it was never alive." The actress settled herself in the facing seat next to Alexia, smoothing out the silk skirts of her green gown as she did so.

"It can't be mechanical. I tried a magnetic disruption emission on them and nothing resulted."

"Oh, did you? Well, it's worth knowing Albert here has been field tested against one of the best. I should like to see the emitter you used."

"Yes, I wager you would." Alexia made no move to show her anything whatsoever about her parasol or its armament. She gestured at the porcupine, which had settled into a kind of crouch at the actress's feet. "May I?"

Mabel Dair considered the request. "If you must." Then she bent and lifted the little creature up to the bench between them so that Lady Maccon could examine it at her leisure.

At such close range, it became clear rather quickly that there was no way it had been, or ever would be, alive. It was a construct of some kind, its inner workings covered over in skin, fur, and spines that made it *look* like a porcupine.

"I thought mechanimals were outlawed."

"This is not a mechanimal."

"It has been made without any ferric parts? Inspired, indeed." Lady Maccon was duly impressed. She was no Madame Lefoux, to be able to understand the construct's makeup fully in the space of only a few minutes' examination, but she was well enough versed in scientific literature to know she held some very advanced technology in her grasp.

"But why use such skill merely to create a pet?"

Mabel Dair shrugged, an elegant little movement, refined so as not to disturb the fall of her gown. "The extermination mandate has been retracted. Your relocation and adoption agreement was quite a masterly maneuver in the great game. My mistress was impressed. Not that I am admitting to anything, of course, but those first porcupines were highly experimental. They were not as effective as we had hoped, so she has let me make a pet of one of the few we have left."

"Ingenious technology." Lady Maccon continued her examination of the little creature. There were small clips behind each of its ears that, when pressed, popped open to reveal some of the inner workings in the brain area.

"I supposed it would have been far more dangerous had it been a real African zombie." She tapped at one of the faux bones. "Remarkable. I take it the hive has filed all the appropriate licensing with the patent office? Must be one of the countess's pet scientists, since I haven't read anything from the Royal Society on the subject. Is it designed specifically to withstand a magnetic disruption?" Then she noticed that the porcupine had ceramic and wooden moving parts held together with string and sinew, greased with some kind of dark waxy liquid. Alexia had misinterpreted this as blood, but closer inspection revealed it to be of exactly the same type as that found in the Hypocras Club's automaton. "Oh, dear. Did you get hold of some of the Hypocras Club's reports? I thought BUR put a lockdown on those."

"Only you, Lady Maccon, would draw such a connection." Miss Dair was beginning to look a little nervous.

At that juncture, it occurred to Lady Maccon to ask, "Why are you in my carriage, Miss Dair?"

The actress recovered her poise. "Ah, yes, well, Lady Maccon, there has been a breach in social etiquette, and it was only when you accosted me in the street that I realized it. I know the countess would want me to rectify the situation. You must believe, we understood that on full-moon nights you were otherwise occupied or we should never have neglected you."

"What *are* you on about?"

"This." Miss Dair handed Alexia an embossed invitation to a full-moon party taking place later that night.

The Maccons and the Nadasdys always invited each other to their respective festivities. The Westminster vampires, out of tether and hive bounds, had never been able to visit Woolsey Castle, and the countess herself, of course, could not leave her house. But Lord and Lady Maccon had visited her on several occasions, always staying exactly as long as was polite and no longer. Vampire hives were not comfortable places for werewolves to be, particularly Alpha werewolves, but the social niceties must be observed.

Alexia took the invitation reluctantly. "Well, thank you, but I have a busy schedule, and at such late notice, please understand I will try to put in an appearance but—"

Miss Dair continued making the excuses for her. "In your current condition, that would be difficult. I understand perfectly and the countess will as well. But I didn't want you to think we were slighting you in any way. Case in point, I have been instructed by my mistress to inform you, should we encounter each other, that we are officially delighted with your new living arrangements and wish it to be known outright that there are no hard feelings. Or"—she paused delicately, her actress training becoming apparent—"consequences."

As if they were not the ones who had been actively trying to kill me! Lady Maccon, in a huff, said pointedly, "Likewise. Perhaps next time if your lot told me why they were trying to exterminate me from the start, much unnecessary chaos could be avoided. Not to mention loss of porcupine life."

"Yes, indeed. What did happen to them?"

"Lime pit."

"Oh. Oh! Very good, Lady Maccon. I should never have thought of that."

"Is this little creature still armed with the projectile spines? Some kind of numbing agent, I assume."

"Yes, but not to worry—he's quite tame. And it is for my protection and not any ulterior motive."

"I am very glad to hear it. Well, Miss Dair, can I take you to your destination, or would you prefer to walk? I can see you might wish to display your pet to advantage. Your mistress is looking to profit by the new technology, isn't she?"

"You know vampires."

Normally polite company wouldn't mention pecuniary matters, but Miss Dair was only an actress, so Alexia said, "You'd think owning half the known world would be enough for them."

Mabel Dair smiled. "Control, Muhjah, comes in many different forms."

"Indeed it does, indeed it does. Well...," Lady Maccon picked up the speaking tube and addressed her coachman. "Pull up here, please. My companion wishes to alight."

"Very good, my lady," came the tinny reply.

The carriage pulled to the side, allowing Miss Dair and her porcupine to disgorge themselves and continue their promenade.

"Perhaps we will enjoy the pleasure of your company later tonight, Lady Maccon."

"Perhaps. Thank you for your scintillating conversation, Miss Dair. Good night."

"Good night."

They parted, many a reveler now curious as to the relationship between a werewolf's wife and a vampire drone. The rumors were out concerning Biffy. Was Lady Maccon trying to poach yet another key player from the vampire's camp? New gossip was set in motion. And that, too, Alexia realized, might have been all part of Miss Dair's scheme in visiting with her.

She spoke once more into the tube. "Chapeau de Poupe, if you please."

It was early still, so far as the night's festivities were concerned. No establishment of worth in all of London would dare be closed on such an evening. Thus Lady Maccon was unsurprised to find Madame Lefoux's hat shop not only open but also occupied by multiple ladies of worth and their respective escorts. The hats, suspended on their long cords from the ceiling, swayed to and fro, but without imparting their usual aura of undersea calm. There was too much clatter and bustle (in both senses of the word) for that. Alexia was surprised to find that Madame Lefoux herself was not in residence. For all her more atypical pursuits, the inventor normally made a point of putting in an appearance in her shop on busy nights. Half the reason the ladies chose to frequent Chapeau de Poupe was on the off chance they might encounter the scandalous proprietress in all her top-hatted glory.

In her absence, Lady Maccon trundled in and stood, confused. How was she to make her way to the contrivance chamber without someone seeing her? She respected Madame Lefoux's wish to keep the chamber, its activities, and its entrance a secret from the general public. But with what seemed to be at least half said general public milling about in the shop, how was Alexia to return the papers and consult the inventor on the nature of the porcupines without being observed? Alexia Maccon was many things, but stealthy was not one of them.

She made her way to the counter—an attractive high table painted white to add to the modern atmosphere that was a hallmark of Madame Lefoux's refined taste.

"Pardon me?" Lady Maccon used her best, most imperious tone.

"I'll be right with you, madam," chirruped the girl who stood there. She was all bright chatter and false friendliness, but her back remained quite firmly presented. She was busy rustling through stacks of hatboxes.

"I don't mean to interrupt your work, young lady, but this is an urgent matter."

"Yes, madam, I am certain it is. I do apologize for the delay, but as you can see, we are a little understaffed this evening. If you wouldn't mind waiting just one more moment."

"I must see Madame Lefoux."

"Yes, yes, madam, I know. *Everyone* wishes the personal attention of the madame, but she is unavailable this particular evening. Perhaps one of the other ladies might be of assistance?"

"No, really, it must be Madame Lefoux. I have some important paperwork to return to her."

"Return? Oh, did the hat not suit madam's needs? I *am* sorry."

"Not a hat. Nothing to do with hats." Lady Maccon was getting impatient.

"Yes, certainly, if madam would simply wait. I shall be at your service momentarily."

Alexia sighed. This was getting her nowhere. She moved away from the counter and took a slow turn about the room, utilizing her parasol as a kind of cane and exaggerating her limp so that sympathy drove those ladies out of her way who did not already know her face and rank. This maneuver garnered her more attention, rather than less, and she was left with a distinct feeling of inertia.

Madame Lefoux's hats were of the latest style, a number of them too daring for any save Ivy and her ilk. Cabinets displayed other accessories as well—mob caps, sleeping caps, hair pins, and bands all decorated beautifully. There were reticules of varying shapes and sizes; gloves; and dirigible accessories such as velvet ear protectors, skirt ties, weighted hem inserts, and the finest in color-tinted glass goggles. There was even a line of masquerade goggles trimmed with feathers and flowers. And, last but not least, a rack displaying Ivy Tunstell's hairmuffs, designed for the fashionable young lady who wished to keep her hair untangled and her ears warm while still sporting the latest ringlets. They had gone somewhat out of favor recently, having enjoyed a brief spate of popularity during the winter months, but were still on display in deference to Mrs. Tunstell's finer feelings.

Alexia completed her circuit of the shop and came to a decision. Given that any kind of stealth was out of the question, she must opt for her only alternative—making a fuss.

"Pardon me, miss."

The same shopgirl was still rummaging behind the counter. Really, how long did it take to find a hatbox?

"*Yes,* madam, I will be right with you."

Lady Maccon reached down inside herself for her most regal, difficult, aristocratic nature. "I will *not be ignored,* young lady!"

That got the girl's attention. She actually turned around to see who this interfering female was.

"Do you know who I am?"

The young woman gave her the full once-over. "Lady Maccon?" she hazarded a guess.

"Indeed."

"I had been warned to keep an eye out for you."

"Warned? Warned! Were you, indeed? Well, now I am here and...and..." She floundered. It was terribly hard to be angry when one wasn't. "I have a very grave matter to discuss with your patroness."

"I told you, madam, and I do apologize, but she is not available this evening, even for you."

"Unacceptable!" Alexia was rather pleased with both the word choice and her execution. Very commanding, indeed! *That's what living with werewolves will do for a girl. Now where to go from here?* "I'll have you know I have been swindled! Absolutely swindled. I will have none of it. I shall call on the constabulary. You see if I don't."

By this time, Lady Maccon and the now-trembling shopgirl had attracted the attention of the entire establishment, both patrons and hire.

"I came here looking for hairmuffs. I hear they are *the thing* for dirigible travel, and I desire a set that matches my hair, and what do I find? Not a single pair of the appropriate shade. Where are they all?"

"Well, you see, madam, we are currently out of the darker colors. If madam would like to put in an order—"

"No, madam would *not* like! Madam would like a set of the hairmuffs right this very moment!" At this juncture, Alexia contemplated stamping her foot, but that was probably excessively dramatic, even for this audience.

Instead, she waddled over to the muff display stand near the shop window. She grabbed a cluster of her own curls, artfully arranged over the shoulder of her blue and green plaid visiting dress, and waved them at the stand. Then she backed off as though physically repulsed by the mismatch.

"You see?" She stood away and pointed with the tip of her parasol at the offending hairmuffs.

The shopgirl did see. So, in fact, did all the other ladies present. What they saw was that Lady Maccon, only a few days from her confinement, had still extricated herself from bed and the bosom of her husband's affection in order to come to this very shop to buy hairmuffs. They must, perforce, be *back en mode*. Lady Maccon, wife to the Earl of Woolsey, was known to fraternize with the trendsetters and fashion leaders of the ton. She herself might prefer more practical garb, especially in her present state, but if she was buying hairmuffs, then Lord Akeldama approved the accessory. If Lord Akeldama approved, then the vampires approved, and if the vampires approved, well, that was simply it: hairmuffs must be *the living end*.

Suddenly, every lady in that shop had to have a set of Mrs. Tunstell's *Hairmuffs for the Elevated Lady Traveler.* They all stopped admiring whatever hat they were fawning over and swarmed the little stand. Even those who had absolutely no intention of ever setting foot on board a dirigible suddenly were in a mad passion to own hairmuffs. For what became fashionable for floating descended to the ground— witness the craze for decorative goggles.

Lady Maccon was swarmed by a gaggle of bustled and trussed ladies, all grabbing for the muffs, squealing at each other while they tried desperately to snatch the colors that

matched their own coiffures. There was even a little pushing and some shortness of breath. It was practically a rout.

The shopgirls obligingly descended into the milieu as well,
notepads out, trying to convince the ladies not to purchase
right away but to place an order for the appropriate color and
perhaps multiple styles and different-size ringlets as well.

In the resulting chaos, Lady Maccon extracted herself
and lurched, as stealthily as was within her limited capacity, to the very back of the shop. Here, in a shadowed corner under an attractive display of gloves, was the handle to
the entrance to the ascension chamber. She activated it, the
hidden door swinging quietly open. Alexia noted with relief
that the chamber was already at the upper level waiting for
her. She clambered inside, drawing the door to the shop
closed behind her.

After many months of friendship, not to mention parasol maintenance and aethographor repairs, Alexia was more
than familiar with the operation of Madame Lefoux's ascension chamber. What once had upset her stomach and frightened her was now standard procedure on her visiting rounds.
She flipped the lever that operated the windlass machine
and did not even stumble when the contraption landed with
a jarring thud.

Lady Maccon waddled down the passageway and thumped
loudly at the contrivance chamber door.

Silence.

Figuring that Madame Lefoux probably could not hear
her knock, for inside the chamber was always a cacophony
of mechanical noises, she let herself in.

It took her a long moment of scanning over all the piles of machinery, but she eventually became convinced that Madame Lefoux really was not in residence. Nor was her new contraption. The shopgirl had not lied in the interest of social niceties. Madame Lefoux was definitely unavailable. Alexia pursed her lips. Genevieve had said something about relocating in order to put the finishing touches to the latest invention. Alexia debated trying to remember where and following her there or simply leaving the papers behind. *They'll probably be safe enough.* She placed them on a nearby metal tabletop and was about to depart when she heard something.

Alexia had no werewolf's hearing to be able to note some strange noise among the rattling, humming, hissing clatter. Even without the Frenchwoman in residence, some machines never ceased their activity. But she definitely heard another sound, an underlying keen to the rattles that might, or might not, be human in origin.

It might also be a very excited mouse.

Lady Maccon contemplated not getting involved. She also contemplated not using her parasol—after all, some of the machines in that chamber might be engaged in some delicate feat of manufacturing that could not afford to be paused midclatter. In Alexia's case, contemplation was never signified by more than a pause before performing the action she would have taken, contemplation or no.

She took her parasol firmly in hand, raised it high above her head, and activated the magnetic disruption emitter by pulling down on the appropriate lotus leaf in the handle with her thumb.

Silence descended—the unnatural silence of work stilled midmotion. If Alexia had been a fanciful girl, she would have said it was like time freezing, but she wasn't, so she didn't. She merely listened for the one sound that didn't stop.

It came, a low keening wail, and Alexia realized that she was familiar with just such a noise. Not a sound made by the living, but still a sound *made* rather than a sound *manufactured*. It was the intermittent sharp cry of second-death, and Alexia had a pretty good guess as to who was suffering it.

CHAPTER TWELVE

Formerly Beatrice Lefoux

F ormerly Lefoux. Formerly Lefoux, is that you?" Alexia
tried to make her voice gentle.

The silence stretched and then the faraway screaming
came again.

There was something inexorably sad about the sound,
as though it were that much worse to die a second time. It
moved even Lady Maccon's practical heart. "Formerly
Lefoux, please, I will not harm you. I promise. I can bring
you peace, if you would like, or simply be here with you. I
promise, no soulless touch unless you request it. Don't be
afraid. There's nothing I could do. I don't even know where
your body is kept."

The magnetic disruption wore off at that juncture, and
the contrivance chamber sprang back into humming, clanking motion. Right next to Alexia's head, a contraption that

looked like a tuba, a sleigh, and a mustache trimmer cobbled together let out the most amazing sound of reverberating flatulence. Lady Maccon started in disgust and moved hurriedly away.

"Please, Formerly Lefoux, I should very much like to ask you something. I need your help."

The ghost materialized into existence out of a massive glass valve to Alexia's left. Or, more properly, she materialized as much as she was able into existence, which wasn't all that much anymore. Bits of her were now drifting off in spiraling fuzzy tendrils. Her shape was no longer human, but more cloudlike, as little wisps of her noncorporeal form fought against the aether currents. Many of those currents were now centered in on Lady Maccon, so the ghostly parts were carried toward Alexia. The vampires called preternaturals *soul-suckers,* but science was coming around to thinking of them more as aether absorbers. This particular phenomenon of her physiology was only really visible when she shared the room with a dying ghost.

"Soulless!" screamed Formerly Lefoux once she had found her voice, or possibly, found her voice box. She spoke in French. "Why are you here? Where is my niece? What has she done? What have you done? Where is the octomaton? What. What? Who is that screaming? Is that me? How can that be me *and* this be me, talking to you? You. Soulless? What are you doing here? Where is my niece?"

It was like some broken symphony destined to repeat the same few lines of music over and over again. The ghost was caught up in a loop of reasoning. Periodically, Formerly

Lefoux interrupted herself to cry out, a long low moan of agony to accompany the wail of second-death. Whether it was pain of the spirit or pain in truth was difficult to tell, but it sounded to Alexia not unlike poor Biffy being forced into werewolf shift.

Alexia straightened her spine. Before her lay her preternatural duty, staring her in the face. That didn't occur very often. Under ordinary circumstances, she would have asked Genevieve for permission, but the inventor was gone. She had abandoned her poor aunt in this state. The ghost was suffering.

"Formerly Lefoux," she said politely, "I am in the unique position to offer you...that is, I could...Oh, dash it, would you like an exorcism?"

"Death? Death! Are you asking me if I want death, soulless? To not exist at all." The ghost twirled like a child's toy, spiraling all the way up to the beams of the contrivance chamber ceiling. The tendrils of her fleshless body swirled around like the feathers of one of Ivy's more excitable hats. Floating far above, the ghost became contemplative. "I have served my time. I have taught. Not many get to say that. I have touched lives. I have finished them all. And I have done it after I died as well." She paused and drifted back down. "Not that I like children all that much. What can a ghost do? When my niece, my lovely intelligent girl, became enamored of that awful woman. All I taught her was gone. Then the boy. Just like his mother. Devious. Who thought I should end up teaching a boy child? And now. Look what it has all come to. Death. My death, and a soulless offering me succor. Unnatural. All of it. Preternatural girl, what good are you to me?"

"I can give you serenity." Lady Maccon's eyebrow was quirked. Really, ghosts in near poltergeist phase did ramble most awfully.

"I don't want peace. I want hope. Can you give me that?"

Sympathy, so far as Alexia was concerned, only went so far. "Very well, then, this is getting disturbingly philosophical. Formerly Lefoux, if you'd rather not have my aid in the matter of your existence, or lack thereof, I should probably be on my way. Do try not to wail so loudly. They will hear you in the street above, and then BUR will be called. Frankly, the Bureau really doesn't need this kind of additional work on full moon."

The ghost floated back down. For a moment, she recollected herself, switching from French to heavily accented English. "No, wait. I will...What will I? Oh, yez, I will show you. Follow me."

She began bobbing slowly across the room. She had no concern for obstacles or pathways through the devices, instruments, and tools of Madame Lefoux's collection, merely floating in a straight line. Alexia, who was more substantial in every understanding of the word, made her cumbersome way after. She lost sight of the ghost on more than one occasion, but eventually they ended up in a corner of the massive room, next to a large barrel that rested on its side and was marked with the logo of a well-respected pickled onion manufacturer.

As Formerly Lefoux neared the barrel, she became more

and more substantial, until she was almost her old self—
the ghost Alexia had first met nearly half a year ago. A tall,
gaunt, severe-looking older woman, in clothing years out of
date and small spectacles, who bore a marked resemblance
to Madame Lefoux. There might even once have been
dimples.

The keening wail was much louder here, although it still
seemed to be coming from some distance away, with an
echo as though emanating from the bottom of a mine.

"I do apologize. I can't stop that," said the ghost at Alexia's wince.

"No, you wouldn't be able to. Your time has come."

The ghost nodded, an action that was visible now that she
had managed to gather herself into better order. "Genevieve
gave me a long afterlife. Few ghosts are so fortunate. They
usually have only months. I had years."

"Years?"

"Years."

"She is a truly brilliant woman." Alexia was properly
impressed.

"Yet she loves too frequently and too easily. I couldn't
teach her that lesson. So much like her father. She loves you,
I think, a little. More, if you had given her the opportunity."

The discussion had gotten away from Alexia again. This
was often the case with ghosts—no more control over conversation than of their own forms. "But I'm married!"

"All the best ones are. And that son of hers."

Lady Maccon looked down at her own belly. "Everyone
should love their child."

"Even if he is a wild creature born to another woman?"

"Especially then."

The ghost let out a dry laugh. "I can see why you two are friends."

It was in thinking about Genevieve's love life (a thing, Alexia must admit, she tried desperately not to do, as it was so preposterously captivating) that Alexia put everything together. Not fast enough, of course, because the wails were getting louder, and nearer. Even a ghost such as Formerly Lefoux, with such strength of character and mental fitness, could not resist her own demise when it was fated.

Alexia asked, "Is there something wrong with Genevieve?"

"Yes." It was said on a hiss. The ghost was shaking, shivering in the air before her, as though riding atop an ill-balanced steam engine.

"That machine, the one she was building, it wasn't a government commission, was it?"

"No." The ghost began spinning as she vibrated. The tendrils were back, drifting away, floating into the air—puffs of selfhood carried away. Her feet were almost entirely disintegrated. While Alexia watched, one of Formerly Lefoux's hands detached and began drifting toward her.

Lady Maccon tried to dodge the hand, but it followed her. "It's the kind of contraption that could break into a house, isn't it? Or a palace?"

"Yes. So unlike her, to build something brutish. But sometimes we women get desperate." The screaming was getting louder. "Right question, soulless. *You aren't asking me the right question.* And we are almost out of time." Her other hand detached and wafted toward Alexia. "Soulless? What are you? Why are you here? Where is my niece?"

"It was *you* who activated the ghost communication network, wasn't it? Did *you* send me the message, Formerly Lefoux? The one about killing the queen?"

"Yessss," hissed the ghost.

"But why would Genevieve want to kill the—"

Alexia was cut off midquestion as Formerly Lefoux burst apart, like a rotten tomato thrown against a tree. The ghost exploded noiselessly. Parts of her drifted off in all directions at once, a spread of white mist wafting all around and through the machinery of the contrivance chamber. Then, showily, all those bits began drifting in Alexia's direction— eyes, eyebrows, hair, a limb or two.

Alexia couldn't help herself; she let out a scream of shock. There was no going back now. Formerly Beatrice Lefoux had gone to full poltergeist. It was time for Lady Maccon to fulfill her duty to queen and country and perform the required exorcism.

She approached the barrel of pickled onions. It lay on its side, and it was a very big barrel. She checked around the back where multiple coils and tubes were coming out, hooked into some interesting-looking lidded metal buckets. Either Madame Lefoux was particularly interested in the quality of her pickled onions or...

Alexia knew well her friend's style and design aesthetic, so she looked for any small protrusion or unusual sculptural addition to the barrel, something that might be pressed or pulled. On the end of the barrel facing the wall, she found a small brass octopus. She pushed against it. With a faint clunking noise, the wood of the pickle barrel slid away, like that of a rolltop desk, revealing that there were, unsurprisingly, no onions inside. Instead it housed a coffin-sized fish tank filled with a bubbling yellow liquid and the preserved body of Beatrice Lefoux.

The formaldehyde, for that is what the liquid must be, had done its job. There was also clearly some way in which the bubbling injections of gas were allowing the ghost to still form a noncorporeal self while not losing too much flesh to decomposition. Alexia was caught by the genius of the invention. It was one of the great trials of ghostly employment, that specters would stay sane only so long as their bodies could be preserved, but that they could not form a tether and apparition if that body was immersed fully in a preservation liquid. Madame Lefoux had invented a way around this conundrum by having air bubbling through the formaldehyde in enough quantity to permit a tether, while allowing the flesh to stay submerged and preserved. No wonder Formerly Lefoux had enjoyed such a long afterlife.

But even such ingeniousness as this, the height of scientific breakthrough, could not save a ghost in the end. Eventually the body would decay enough so that it could no longer hold the tether; the ghost would lose cohesion and succumb to second-death.

Alexia thought she might mention this tank to BUR. They would probably want to order a few for their more valuable spectral agents. She wondered if the gas injections had something to do with the explosive nature of Formerly Lefoux's poltergeist state. In any event, the tank's work was completed. Alexia had to devise a way inside.

The screams were now deafening. Formerly Lefoux's misty body parts were centering on Alexia, attaching themselves to the exposed skin of her arms, face, and neck, like body part burrs. It was repulsive. Alexia tried to brush them off, but they merely transferred to her wrist.

There seemed no way into the tank. Madame Lefoux had never intended to open it once it was built.

Lady Maccon was getting frantic to stop the screaming. She was also becoming increasingly aware of time wasted. She must get out of the contrivance chamber and stop Madame Lefoux's mad scheme to build a monster to kill the queen. Why would Genevieve, of all people, want to do such a thing?

Desperate, she flipped her parasol, hefted it as far behind her back as her condition would allow, and swung it around with all her might. She hit the side of the glass tank with the hard pineapple-looking handle. The tank cracked and then broke, spilling the yellow fluid and with it a strong, suffocating scent. Lady Maccon backed away hurriedly, lifting her ruffled skirts out of the toxic liquid. Her eyes began burning and watering. She coughed as the sensation moved to her throat, and she tried to breathe in shallow gasps. Luckily, most of the liquid was absorbed quickly by the hard, compact dirt of the contrivance chamber floor.

The body inside flopped over and against the cracked side of the tank, one hand dangling out through the broken glass.

Quickly, Alexia tugged off her glove and stepped up to it. She touched the cold dead hand once, flesh to flesh, and just like that, it was over.

The wailing stopped. The body part wisps vanished— mist gone to aether. All that remained was the clanking sound of Madame Lefoux's machines in motion and the empty air.

"May you find your stillness, Formerly Lefoux," said Alexia.

She looked ruefully at the mess before her: broken glass, fractured tank, dead body. She abhorred such untidiness, but she had no time to see to the cleanup. Best to contact Floote on the matter as soon as she found some time.

With that, she turned away and waddled back out of the chamber and into the passageway. She hoped the clientele above her was still arguing over hairmuffs, for she had no time to scheme her way around exposing Madame Lefoux's secret entrance this time. She must stop her friend from imprudent action. And, more importantly, she desperately needed to find out why. Why Madame Lefoux, such an intelligent woman, would try to do something so dull-witted as mount a frontal attack on Buckingham Palace in order to kill the Queen of England.

Fortunately, the hairmuff obsession was still in full sway. Almost no one noticed Lady Maccon scuttle, like some kind of gimpy goose, out of the door in the wall. She then made her way through the myriad of dangling hats and out of the shop. A few remarked upon the smell of formaldehyde, and one or two noted her ladyship's undignified ascension into the depths of her fancy carriage, but few thought to connect the two. However, the head shopgirl did, and made a note to tell the mistress everything, before returning to the sudden increase in hairmuff orders.

Lady Maccon remembered what Madame Lefoux had said about relocation. She'd arranged to utilize space in the Pantechnicon. Alexia was unaware of the location of the warehouse consortium. Being a matter of *trade,* it was not something Lady Maccon *ought* to know. Sometimes Madame Lefoux's engineering interests led her into the most peculiar parts of London. Alexia had, of course, heard of the Pantechnicon but had never had occasion to visit such a thing as the facility in which Giffard's Incorporated housed and maintained its dirigible fleet. The Pantechnicon stored and distributed a good deal of furniture as well. The very idea of a lady of good breeding visiting such a place. There would be tables lying about, on their sides, naked! Not to mention *flaccid* dirigibles! Alexia shuddered at the very idea. However, sometimes the muhjah had to go where Lady Maccon would not, and so she gave the order and trusted her driver to know the location, which turned out to be Belgravia, a deeply suspect part of London.

After clattering for some time down one cobbled street after another, having passed through the worst and most raucous crowds of the West End and moving toward Chelsea, the carriage drew to a stop. Lady Maccon's speaking tube rang imperiously.

She picked up the listening trumpet. "Yes?"

"Motcomb Street, madam."

"Thank you." *Never heard of it.* She looked suspiciously out the carriage window. What Lady Maccon had never quite fathomed was how extraordinarily large the Pantechnicon had to be in order to accommodate both flaccid dirigibles and naked tables. She was in front of a massive caterpillar of warehouses. Each one resembled a barn, only bigger, being several stories high with arched metal roofs. Alexia assumed these must somehow open or come off in order to accommodate the dirigibles. The street was dimly lit by the flickering yellow glow of torchlight rather than by the steady white of gas, and the area was bereft of humanity. This was a part of the city that catered to day dealers, workers of transport and industry who loaded and unloaded their contraptions and carriers under the light of the sun. It was not a place for the likes of Lady Maccon to be traipsing about on full moon.

But Alexia was not going to let a little thing like the dark emptiness of an alleyway prevent her from proceeding with her intent to assist a friend in dire need of sensible council. So she alighted from the carriage, Ethel in one hand and her parasol in the other. She waddled slowly along the row of gigantic structures, listening at the door of each, standing on tiptoe to peer in at small dingy windows—the only means of viewing the interior. She rubbed the grimy coating on leaded glass with her soiled glove. The Pantechnicon appeared to be as abandoned as the street. There was no sign of Madame Lefoux or her contraption.

Then, finally, inside the last building in the row, Alexia

caught sight of a spark of light. Inside, Madame Lefoux, or the person she assumed must be Madame Lefoux, wore a glass and metal bucket over her head, like the offspring of a medieval knight's helmet and a fishbowl. She was also wearing the most hideous pair of coveralls and was busy with a flaming torch, welding great slabs of metal together. Her giant mechanical construct had taken its final form, and Alexia could not help but emit a little gasp of amazement at the sight of the monstrous thing.

It was colossal, at least two stories high. The brimless bowler-hat portion now rested atop eight articulated metal tentacles that hung down like pillars, but if Lady Maccon knew Madame Lefoux, each would be able to move independently of the others. A remarkable creature, indeed. It looked like nothing so much as a massive upright octopus on tiptoe. Alexia wondered what it said about her current state that this comparison made her hungry. *Ah, pregnancy.*

She banged on the window to attract Madame Lefoux's attention, but the French woman clearly could not hear, for she did not pause in her activities.

Lady Maccon circumnavigated the building, looking for an entrance. It had massive loading doors street-side, but these were bolted firmly shut. There must be a smaller, more convenient, one-person door somewhere about the place.

Finally, she found it. It, too, was locked. She whacked at it with her parasol in frustration, but brute force was also ineffectual. Not for the first time, Alexia wished she knew how to pick a lock. Conall had frowned most severely upon that

particular request and on her proposed venture into New-
gate Prison in order to hire the necessary criminally minded
individual as instructor.

She went back round to the front and considered breaking one of the lower windows; while it was too small to
climb through, even if she were not eight months pregnant,
she could at least yell. A massive noise interrupted her right
before she was about to swing the parasol.

The building began shaking slightly, the metal roof
creaking most terribly, and the two great loading bay doors
clattered against their hinges. Gouts of steam billowed from
beneath the doors and around the edges. Metal screeched
and the trundling thrumming sound of a steam engine in
full operation emanated from within. Alexia backed away
from the door. The sounds began to get louder and louder
and the doors shook with more vigor. More steam puffed
forth.

It was getting closer.

Lady Maccon waddled as fast as she could away from the
doors, and just in the nick of time, too, for they burst open,
crashing against the sides of the building in a great splinter-
ing of wood, left to hang askew on their hinges.

A gigantic tiptoeing octopus came through, looking
almost as though it floated atop the cloud of steam that
gushed forth from under its mantle to swirl about its tentacles. The doors were not quite tall enough to permit an
easy exit, but this didn't seem to trouble the creature. It simply took a chunk of the roof off with its head. Tiles fell and

splintered, dust wafted up, and steam wafted down as the world's biggest automated cephalopod tentacled its way into the London street.

"The octomaton, I presume. I see Genevieve didn't quite get the size measurements right," said Alexia to no one in particular.

The octomaton didn't notice Lady Maccon, a rotund little being far below in the shadows, but it spotted her carriage. It raised up one tentacle and took careful aim. A burst of fire came pouring out the tip. The beautifully matched horses (chosen for appearance and docility around werewolves rather than for bravery) panicked, as did the stunned coach-man (chosen for precisely the same reasons). All three took off at high speed. The carriage careened wildly around a street corner, ribbons trailing merrily behind it, and disap-peared into the night.

"Wait!" cried Lady Maccon. "Come back!" But the con-veyance was long gone. "Oh, bother. Now what?"

The octomaton, untroubled by Alexia's cry or predica-ment, began to make its way up the street away from her, following the carriage. Lady Maccon raised her parasol and pulled at the special lotus leaf in the handle, activat-ing the magnetic disruption emitter. Even aimed directly at the massive creature, it had absolutely no effect. Either Madame Lefoux also had access to the vampire's porcu-pine technology, or she had installed some kind of defen-sive shield to protect her creation from Alexia's armament. Alexia was not surprised; after all, the Frenchwoman was not so thickheaded as to build one weapon that could so easily be defeated by another of her own design. Especially if she knew Alexia was on the case and might very well find her out.

Alexia switched to Ethel, raising and firing the gun. The bullet bounced harmlessly off the octomaton's metal exterior. It left behind a dent, but once again, the massive creature did not register her tiny efforts against it.

It proceeded down the street in a not-very-dignified manner. Madame Lefoux had not gotten the en pointe tentacle balance quite right. Windows rattled as it passed, and periodically it staggered slightly to one side, crashing into and partly destroying the sides of buildings. At last, rounding the corner away from the Pantechnicon, it lurched into one of the streetlamps, an old-fashioned brassier-style torch, tipping it onto the thatched roof of a storage shed. Almost immediately the shed caught fire, and the flames began to spread. Metal roof notwithstanding, it presently became apparent that even the Pantechnicon could not resist the blaze.

Alexia was at a loss. None of her parasol's special abilities were designed to deal with fire. In her current state, she reckoned her best option was to beat an undignified retreat to safety. After all, she was practical enough to know when there was little even she could do to rectify such a situation. She turned south, toward the river.

As she limped along, Alexia's mind whirled with confusion. Why would Madame Lefoux build such a creature? She was, by and large, a woman of subtlety in both life and art. Why was she heading north and not due east to Buckingham? Queen Victoria never left the safety of her palace on full moon—it was simply too wild a night for her staid sensibilities. If Madame Lefoux had designs on the queen, she was going in the wrong direction. Alexia frowned. *I am clearly missing something. Either something Genevieve said, or did not say, or something Formerly Lefoux said or did not say. Or…*

Lady Alexia Maccon stopped in her very solid tracks and hit her forehead with the butt of her hand. Fortunately, it was the hand that held Ethel, not the hand that held her parasol, or she might have done herself damage.

"Of course! How could I be so silly? I have *the wrong queen.*"

Then she started walking again, her mind now calculating in a steel-traplike fashion—that is, if the trap were of the spring-loaded, not-very-sensitive variety. Lady Maccon was not one to do too many things at once, especially not right now, but she was tolerably convinced she could handle bipedal motion and thought at the same time.

The original ghostly messenger had never specified Queen Victoria, and neither had Formerly Lefoux. Genevieve Lefoux and her octomaton weren't after the monarch of the empire; oh, no, they were after a hive queen. That made far more sense. Genevieve had never liked the vampires, not since they corrupted Angelique (although she was always content enough to take their money). Given their rocky history, again over that troublesome violet-eyed French maid, Alexia would wager good money Genevieve was after Countess Nadasdy. This made sense given the northward direction of her tentacleing, toward Mayfair. Somehow, Madame Lefoux had deduced the whereabouts of the Westminster Hive.

Another mystery. The location of a hive was a guarded secret. Lady Maccon herself knew of it, of course, but that was only because...

"Oh, Alexia, you idiot!" *The burglary at Woolsey!* Madame Lefoux must have been the thief, stealing those old missives because among them was Alexia's original invitation from Countess Nadasdy to visit the hive. It had been delivered to her by Mabel Dair in Hyde Park the afternoon after Alexia killed her first vampire. It contained the address of the hive house, and Alexia had foolishly never thought to destroy it. *When did I tell Genevieve that story?*

Lady Maccon cast desperately about the empty street. She had to reach the Westminster Hive, and fast. Never before had she resented the infant-inconvenience more than at this moment, not to mention her dependence on horse-drawn transport. She even had an invitation that would get her in the door, but no way to get there in time to warn them of imminent tentacled doom. She was stranded in the wilds of Belgravia!

She waddled faster.

The fire was spreading and whooshing behind her. The once-dim alley was alight with a flickering orange and yellow glow. The din of collapsing buildings and roaring flames was added to by the loud clanging bell of an approaching fire engine. One of the dirigibles must have spotted the blaze and drop-messaged the appropriate authorities. If anything, this made Alexia move faster. The last thing she needed was to be detained trying to explain her presence at the Pantechnicon. It also reminded her to look up to see if she could spot a dirigible.

Sure enough, there were several headed sedately in her direction, having caught sight of the fire and redirected their lazy circling toward an intriguing new attraction. They were safely above the conflagration, not yet in the aether but high enough to avoid any risk associated with even the most massive of ground fires.

Lady Maccon waved her parasol commandingly and yelled, but she was a mere speck far below, unless someone had a pair of Shersky and Droop's latest long-distance binoculars. Since her marriage, Alexia had adopted a more respectable and somber color palette than that of the pastel-inclined unattached young lady. This made her even less visible in the flickering shadows of Motcomb Street.

It was then that Alexia noticed that the Giffard symbol (a shaping of the name that turned the G into a massive red and black balloon) on a nearby warehouse was modified with a kind of starburst pattern at its end and a phrase underneath that read PYROTECHNIC DIVISION LTD. She stopped, turned on her heel, and headed for a nearby lamppost. With barely a pause for consideration, she hauled off, took careful aim, and threw her parasol hard at the torch section. The parasol, spearlike, crashed into the lamp and brought both it and the hot coals inside down to the ground with a clang.

Lady Maccon huffed her way over to the coals, retrieved her now-slightly-scorched and sooty accessory by its tip, and, holding it like a mallet, used the chubby handle to hit one particularly nice-looking coal along the street toward the Giffard pyrotechnic warehouse. It was an excellent thing, reflected Alexia at that juncture, that she was good at croquet. At a nice distance, she took careful aim and, with a kind of scooping action, struck the wedge of coal hard. It arced splendidly upward, crashing through the window of the warehouse in a most satisfactory manner.

Then she waited, long, slow counts, hoping the coal had managed to hit upon something reliably explosive.

It had. A popping, cracking noise came first, then some whizzing and whirling sounds, and finally a series of loud gunshots. The doors and windows of the warehouse exploded outward, pushing Alexia backward. Instinctively, she popped open her parasol to shield herself as the world around her turned into a smoking cornucopia of brightly flashing lights and loud noises. The entire stockpile of what she imagined must be a very expensive collection of gunpowder display sparkles and sky-lighters exploded, shimmering and flashing in an ever-increasing series of flares.

Lady Maccon cowered in the road—there was really no other way of putting it—behind her open parasol, trusting in the durability of Madame Lefoux's design to protect her from the worst of it.

Eventually, the popping detonations slowed, and she began to register the heat of the real fire as it crept down

Motcomb Street toward her. She coughed and waved her parasol. The moonlight made the residual smoke silvery white, as if a thousand ghosts were collected around her.

Alexia, eyes watering, blinked and tried to take shallow, steady breaths. Then, through the dispersing smoke, a massive upside-down shepherdess-style bonnet appeared, hovering some two stories above the ground and heading toward her. As the smoke vanished, the cumbersome form of a small private dirigible bobbed into view above the bonnet, proving that it was, in fact, not a hat at all but the gondola portion of the air conveyance. The pilot, some miracle worker of the first order, navigated the small craft down toward Lady Maccon, lowering it carefully between the rows of buildings while battling to keep it away from the flames of the burning Pantechnicon.

CHAPTER THIRTEEN

———

The Octopus Stalks at Moonlight

It was Giffard's smallest craft, short-range and generally hired only for classified recognizance or personal pleasure jaunting. The gondola portion, even more strongly resembling a shepherdess's hat upon close inspection, was big enough for only five people. The model was based off of Blanchard's original balloon. It had four dragonfly-like wing rudders, sprouting below the passenger section. There was a small steam engine and propeller at the back, but the captain had to steer by means of multiple levers and tillers, making him perform a frantic dance. In usefulness, it resembled those small Thames crossing barges so favored by the criminally minded. Giffard had come out with a whole fleet recently, at luxury prices, so the affluent could invest in private air transport. Alexia found them undignified, not the least because there was no door. One had to actually clamber over the edge of the gondola to get inside. Imagine that, fully grown adults clambering! But when one was stranded in an alley with a burning Pantechnicon and a rampaging octomaton, one really couldn't afford to be picky.

Two of the figures inside the hat leaned over the edge, pointing at her.

"Yoo-hoo!" yodeled one of them jovially.

"Over here! Quickly, gentlemen, please, this way!" replied Alexia at full volume, waving her parasol madly.

One of the gentlemen touched the brim of his top hat at her (no tipping was possible with a hat tied down for air travel). "Lady Maccon."

"By George, Boots! How the deuce can you possibly tell that there is Lady Maccon?" queried the other top-hatted gentleman.

"Who else would be standing in the middle of a street on full-moon night with a raging ruddy fire behind her, waving a parasol about?"

"Good point, good point."

"Lady Maccon," came the yell. "Would you like a lift?"

"Mr. Bootbottle-Fipps," said Alexia in exasperation, "ask a silly question…"

The dirigible gondola bumped softly down, and she toddled over to it.

Boots and the second young dandy, who proved to be Viscount Trizdale, hopped nimbly out and came to assist her. Tizzy was a slight, effete young blond with an aristocratic nose and a partiality for the color yellow. Boots had a bit more substance in physicality and taste, but not much.

Lady Maccon looked from one to the other of the two gentlemen and then at the side of the gondola that she must now scale. With great reluctance and knowing she had no other choice, she put herself into their well-manicured hands.

No one, later that evening, nor ever again so long as any of them lived, mentioned what had to be done in order to get a very pregnant Lady Maccon into that passenger basket. There was some heaving, and a good deal of squeaking (both from Alexia and Tizzy), and hands might have had to be placed upon portions of the anatomy pleasing to neither Alexia nor her rescuers. Suffice it to say that Lady Maccon had cause to be grateful Lord Akeldama insisted that his drones undertake some sporting activity, for all their fashionable proclivities.

Alexia landed upon her bustle, legs slightly in the air. Gravity being even more forthright than Lady Maccon, she flailed about before managing to roll to one side and climb laboriously to her feet. She had a rather severe stitch in her side, a few bruises on her nether regions, and she was flushed with heat and exertion, but everything else, including the child, seemed to be in working order. The two young men jumped back inside after her.

"What are you doing here?" Lady Maccon demanded, still in shock that her plan to signal for help had actually worked. "Did my husband put a tail on me? What is it with werewolves and tails?"

Tizzy and Boots looked at each other.

Finally Boots said, "It wasn't entirely the earl, Lady Maccon. Our lord asked us to keep an eye on you this evening as well. He indicated things might come to pass on full moon that required additional recognizance in this part of London, if you take my meaning."

"How on earth would he know to do a thing like that? Oh, forget I asked. How does Lord Akeldama know anything?" Logic returned along with dignity, and Alexia took stock of her change in circumstances.

Boots shrugged. "Things _always_ come to pass on full moon."

Without having to be directed, the pilot was already taking the small craft back up, away from fire and smoke. He was a diminutive man, clean-shaven, with a snubbed nose and a mercurial expression. His cravat was very well tied and it coordinated perfectly with his waistcoat.

"Don't tell me." Alexia looked him up and down. "This dirigible happens to be owned by Lord Akeldama?"

"If that's what you desire, my lady, we won't tell you." Boots looked guilty, as though he were somehow failing her in this request.

Lady Maccon twisted her lips together in thought. The infant-inconvenience kicked at her mightily, and she clutched reflexively at her stomach. "I hate to do this to you, gentlemen, but I find myself in desperate need to call upon Westminster Hive, as quickly as possible. How fast does this contraption go?"

The pilot gave her a cheeky grin. "Oh, you'd be surprised, my lady. Very surprised. Lord Akeldama had this little beauty retrofitted by Madame Lefoux. That he did."

"I didn't know they had professional dealings with each other." Lady Maccon arched an eyebrow.

"I understand this was a first commission. The very first. Lord Akeldama was delighted with her work. Quite delighted. As, indeed, am I. Can't try floating himself, poor man." The pilot looked as though he really felt genuinely sorry for the vampire's inability. "But he's had this beauty put through her paces around the green, and I assure you, that Frenchwoman is a miracle worker. A miracle worker, I say. The things she can do with aeronautics."

"She did comment once that it was her specialty at university. And, of course, there's always Monsieur Trouvé and the ornithopter."

The pilot looked up from his activities with a gleam of interest. "Ornithopter you say? I'd heard the French were branching out. My goodness, what a sight that must be."

"Yes." Lady Maccon's voice was low. "Better to see in action than to use oneself, if you ask me." She raised her voice. "About this dirigible going faster? It's very important that I put in an appearance within the next few minutes. Why don't you show me the full extent of this lovely craft's paces?"

Another grin met that request. "Just point me in the appropriate direction, my lady!"

Alexia did so, gesturing north. They were already above the rooftops, the fire well behind them. She toddled to the edge and looked down: Hyde Park was to their left and a little ahead, while Green Park and the Palace Garden lay spread behind them and to the right. Even so high, she could hear the howling of Queen Victoria's personal werewolf guard, the Growlers, locked away in one special wing of Buckingham below.

She indicated a point ahead and slightly to the right, between the two parks—the center of Mayfair. The pilot pulled down hard on a doorknob-ended lever, and the craft lurched in that direction, faster than Alexia had thought dirigibles could go. Madame Lefoux's touch, indeed.

"Does she have a name, Captain?" she yelled into the rushing air.

Both the interest and the title earned Lady Maccon a great deal of loyalty from the young pilot. " 'Course she does, my lady. Himself calls her *Buffety,* for the rocking motion, I suspect. She's on the registry as *Dandelion Fluff Upon a Spoon.* Don't know as I can rightly explain that one."

Tizzy tittered knowingly. Lady Maccon and the pilot looked at him, but the young lordling seemed disinclined to elaborate.

Lady Maccon shrugged. "I suppose Lord Akeldama names in mysterious ways."

Boots, his eyes on Alexia's other hand, which was still wrapped protectively about her swollen belly, inquired solicitously, "Is it the child, Lady Maccon?"

"The reason for our urgency? Oh, no. I have an invitation to attend Countess Nadasdy's full-moon party, and I am late."

Boots and Tizzy nodded their full understanding of this grave social necessity. All speed was indeed called for.

"We shall make haste, then, my lady. We wouldn't want you to arrive beyond the fashionable hour."

"Thank you for your understanding, Mr. Bootbottle-Fipps."

"And the fire, my lady?" Boots's muttonchops fluffed up in the breeze.

Alexia batted her eyelashes. "Fire? What fire?"

"Ah, is that how it is?"

Lady Maccon turned to look once more out of the gondola. She could make out the massive form of the octomaton, careening through the corner of Hyde Park behind Apsley House directly below them. But with another pull on that lever, *Dandelion Fluff Upon a Spoon* surged ahead and on into Mayfair, leaving the rampaging octopus far behind. The drones, having noticed the great crashing beast, made little warbling noises of distress before insisting Alexia tell them *all about it.*

The Westminster Hive house was one of many similar fashionable residences. It stood at the end of the block and a little apart from the row, but nothing else distinguished it as special or supernaturally inclined. Perhaps the grounds were a little too well tended and the exterior a little too clean and freshly painted, but no more or less than that customarily afforded by the very wealthy. It was a good-enough address, but not too good, and it was large enough to accommodate the countess, the primary members of her hive, and their drones, but not too large.

On this particular full moon, it was busier than usual,

with a number of carriages pulling in at the front and disgorging some of the ton's very highest and most progressive politicians, aristocrats, and artists. Alexia, as muhjah, knew (although others might not) that the assembled were all in the vampire's enclave, or employ, or service, or all three. They were attired in their very best, collars starched high, dresses cut low, britches tight, and bustles shapely. It was a parade of consequence—Countess Nadasdy would allow nothing less.

High floating was assuredly a fashionable way to arrive at a party, the latest and greatest, some might say. But it was not at all convenient for a street already clogged with private carriages and hired hansoms. As the dirigible neared, a few of the horses spooked, rearing and neighing. Ground conveyances crashed into one another in their efforts to clear space, which resulted in a good deal of yelling.

"Who do they think they are, arriving like that?" wondered one elderly gentleman.

Vampires enjoyed investing in the latest inventions, and they did have trade concerns, most notably with the East India Company, but they were traditionalists at heart. So, too, were their guests. For no matter how modish the private pleasure dirigible might be in principle, no one approved of it disturbing their own dignified arrival with its puffed-up sense of novelty. Dignity aside, the dirigible was going to land whether they liked it or not, and consequently, space was eventually made. The gondola bumped down in front of the hive house's wrought-iron fence.

Lady Maccon was left in a quandary. She now had to get out over the side of the passenger basket. She could conceive of no possible way her exit would be any less humiliating than her entry. She did not want to go through such a process again, let alone in front of such august bodies as those now glaring at her. But she could swear she heard the crashing sound of the octomaton, and she really had no time to spare for anyone's decorum, even her own.

"Mr. Bootbottle-Fipps, Viscount, if you would be so kind?" She puffed out her cheeks and prepared herself for mortification.

"Of course, my lady." The ever-eager Boots stepped over to assist her. Tizzy, it must be admitted, moved with less alacrity. As they prepared to boost her (there really was no other way of putting it) over the edge of the gondola (at which juncture she foresaw landing on her much-abused bustle yet again), a savior appeared.

No doubt alerted by the disapproving cries and exacerbation of activity in the street, Miss Mabel Dair emerged from the hive house, dramatically silhouetted against the crowded, well-lit interior. She paused, center stage, on the front stoop. She wore an evening gown the color of old gold with a low square neckline, trimmed with loops of black lace and pink silk roses. There were fresh roses in her hair and her bustle was full—the more risqué trends out of Paris with the smaller bustle and form-fitting bodice were not for her. No, here, under her mistress's guarded eye, even an actress like Miss Dair dressed demurely.

Lady Alexia Maccon, at the side of a dirigible passenger basket, looked as though she was in imminent danger of not playing by the rules.

Miss Dair yelled from the step, using her stage voice to cut through the noise of the crowded street. "Why, Lady Maccon, how delightful. We did not expect you. Especially not in so elaborate a transport."

"Good evening, Miss Dair. It is rather smart, isn't it? Unfortunately, I seem to be having difficulty getting out."

Miss Dair bit her lower lip, hiding a smile. "Let me fetch some help."

"Ah, yes, thank you, Miss Dair, but I *am* in a wee bit of a hurry."

"Of course you are, Lady Maccon." The actress turned back into the house, signaling with a sharp gesticulation of a satin-gloved hand. Mere moments later, she turned and traipsed down the steps followed by a veritable herd of dignified-looking footmen, all of whom took to the lifting and depositing of Lady Maccon as they would any household task, with gravely serious faces and not one flicker of amusement.

Once Alexia had attained her freedom, Boots touched his hat brim with one gray-gloved hand. "A very good evening to you, Lady Maccon."

"You won't be joining me?"

Boots exchanged a telling look with Mabel Dair. "Not at this particular party, my lady. We would make things"—he paused delicately—"prickly."

Lady Maccon nodded her understanding and gave the

matter no further thought. There are some places where, despite their universal skills at being ubiquitous, even Lord Akeldama's drones could not go.

Mabel Dair offered Lady Maccon her arm. Alexia took it gratefully, although she firmed her grip on her parasol with her free hand. She was, after all, entering a hive house, and despite the strictures of polite society, vampires had never looked upon her, and her soullessness, with any degree of acceptance. On every prior occasion but one, Lady Maccon had visited this hive with her husband. Tonight she was going in alone. Miss Mabel Dair may have her arm, but Alexia knew very well that the actress did *not* have her back.

Together the two women entered the party.

The house itself had not changed from when Alexia visited it that first time. Inside, it was far more luxurious than its exterior suggested, although all displays of prosperity were tasteful, without a hint of vulgarity. Persian carpets still lay thick and soft, in coordinating shades of deep red, their patterns subtle, but they were difficult to see as so many top boots and evening slippers trod over them. Striking paintings still hung on the walls, masterworks ranging from contemporary abstract pieces to one relaxed, porcelain-skinned lady that could only be by Titian. But Alexia only knew they were there because she had seen them before; this time as she wended her way through the throng, coiffured comb-outs and flowered headdresses obscured her view. The lavish mahogany furniture was actually being sat upon, and the many stone statues of Roman senators and Egyptian gods had become nothing more than stony members of the milling throng.

"My goodness me," yelled Alexia at her escort over the loud chatter. "This is quite the crush."

The actress nodded enthusiastically. "The countess is supposed to make a very important announcement this evening. Everyone, and I do mean *everyone,* accepted her invitation."

"Announcement, what kind of...?"

But Miss Dair's attention was back to pushing their way through the throng.

One or two people recognized Alexia—heads tilted in her direction, faces perplexed. "Lady Maccon?" came the confused acknowledgment of her presence, accompanied by small nods. She could hear the gossipmongers whirling away like so many steam engines gearing up to explode. *What was the wife of an Alpha werewolf doing there? And so far along in her pregnancy. And alone! On full moon!*

As they pressed on, Alexia became aware of a presence shadowing them through the crowd. Just as a tall, thin man accosted Miss Dair from the front, a person behind them cleared his throat.

Lady Maccon turned to find herself face-to-face with a nondescript gentleman, so nondescript in countenance as to be challenging to describe. His hair was just this side of brown, and his eyes just that side of blue, combined with an arrangement of other features neither striking nor interesting. He wore unremarkable but stylish clothing, all of which suggested a level of premeditated obscurity that reminded her irresistibly of Professor Lyall.

"Your Grace," she said warily in greeting.

The Duke of Hematol did not smile, but that might have

been because he did not wish to show her his fangs just yet. "Lady Maccon, what an unexpected pleasure."

Alexia glanced at Miss Dair, who was engaging in a hushed and rather forceful conversation with Dr. Caedes, another member of Countess Nadasdy's inner circle. He was a tall, thin vampire who Alexia always thought looked like a parasol without its fabric cover, all points and sharp angles. He *unfolded* rather than walked. He did not look pleased.

The duke was more subtle and better able to hide his feelings over Lady Maccon's unanticipated presence. Alexia wondered where Lord Ambrose, the last member of this little band, was stashed. Probably near the countess, as he acted as her *praetoriani*. At a party as crowded as this, the queen would want her pet bodyguard as close as possible.

"We did not expect you on this particular night, Lady Maccon. We had assumed you would be assisting your husband with his"—a calculated pause—"disability."

Alexia narrowed her eyes and fished about in her reticule, coming up with the required card. "I have *an invitation*."

"Of course you do."

"It is most urgent I speak with your mistress immediately. I have some vital information to impart."

"Tell it to me."

Alexia put on her most superior Lady Macconish expression and looked him up and down. "I think *not*."

The vampire stood his ground.

He was not a very large man. Alexia figured if push came to shove, she could probably take him on even in her current state. Being soulless had its uses. She removed her gloves.

He watched this movement with concerned interest.

"No need for that, Lady Maccon." If he was as much like Professor Lyall as Alexia believed, physical conflict would not be his preferred solution to any given confrontation. He looked up toward the storklike doctor and gestured sharply with his chin. The other vampire reacted with supernatural swiftness, grabbing Miss Dair's arm and melting away into the crowd, leaving Lady Maccon with a new, far less attractive, escort.

"It really is most vital that I see her as soon as possible. She may be in grave danger." Alexia left her gloves off and tried to impress upon the vampire her urgency without being too threatening.

The duke smiled. His fangs were small and sharp, barely present, as subtle as the rest of his projected image. "You mortals are always in a hurry."

Lady Maccon gritted her teeth. "This time it is in *your* best interest—really, it is."

The duke looked at her closely. "Very well, come with me."

He led her through the crowd, which thinned as they left the main hallway that serviced the drawing room, parlors, dining hall, and receiving area. They rounded a corner into a part of the house Alexia loved, the museum of machinery, where the history of human innovation was displayed with as much care as the marble statuary and oil paintings of the public areas. The duke moved at a sedate pace, too sedate for Alexia, who, even pregnant and knowing she was going beyond the bounds of proper etiquette, pushed past him. She scuttled by the very first steam engine ever built and then past the model of the Babbage Engine with barely a glance to spare for either feat of human ingenuity.

The vampire hurried to catch up, pushing past her in turn when they reached the stairs, leading the way up rather than, as had occurred on previous occasions, into the back parlor that was the countess's preferred sanctuary. This was a special evening, indeed. Lady Maccon was being let into the high sanctum of the hive. She had never before been allowed *upstairs.*

There were drones strategically placed on the staircase, all attractive and perfectly dressed, looking like they might be guests at the party, but Alexia knew from the way they watched her that they were as much fixtures in the house as its Persian rugs. Only more deadly than the rugs, one supposed. They did nothing, however, as Lady Maccon was in the company of the duke. But they did watch her carefully.

They arrived at a closed door. The Duke of Hematol knocked, a pattern of taps. It opened to reveal Lord Ambrose, as tall, as dark, and as handsome as any milkwater miss might wish her own personal vampire to be.

"Lady Maccon! How unexpected."

"So everyone keeps pointing out." Alexia tried to barge past him.

"You can't come in here."

"Oh, for goodness' sake, I mean her no harm. Truth be told, quite the opposite."

An exchange of glances occurred between Lord Ambrose and the duke.

"She is part of this new order. I think we must believe her."

"You used to think Walsingham was right!" Lord Ambrose accused his compatriot.

"I still do. But in character, she is no more her father's daughter than Lord Maccon is Lord Woolsey's successor or Lord Akeldama is Walsingham's."

Lady Maccon glared. "If you mean that I think for myself and make my own choices, then you are spot-on. Now, I must see the countess immediately. I have—"

Lord Ambrose didn't budge. "I must take possession of your parasol."

"Absolutely not. We may need it shortly, especially if you don't let me in. I tell you I have—"

"I must insist."

"Let her in, Ambrose dear." Countess Nadasdy had a voice as warm as butter and just as greasy. She could fry people with that voice, if she wanted to.

Immediately, Lord Ambrose moved out of Alexia's direct line of sight, revealing the interior of the chamber. It was a very-well-appointed boudoir, complete with not only a massive canopied bed, but also a full sitting area and other highly desirable accoutrements. There was the latest and most sophisticated in exsanguination warmers, an overlarge teapot for storing blood with multiple spouts and tubing attached. Both the pot and the tubes wore knitted tea cozies, and there was a warming brazier underneath to keep the vital liquid moving through the tubes.

The countess was indeed *at tea*. Her version being a lavish affair, complete with lace-covered tea trolley set out with teacups and matched teapot of fine china painted with little pink roses and edged in silver. There were pink and white petits fours that no one was eating and cups of tea that no one was drinking. A three-tiered serving dish of silver held a tempting display of finger sandwiches and sugared rose petals, and there was even a small platter of...could it be? *Treacle tart!*

Lady Maccon was excessively fond of treacle tart.

The assembled drones and guests were all dressed in shades of white, pale green, and pink to accessorize the decor. Elegant Greek urns held massive arrangements of flowers—pale cream roses with pink edges and long leaf ferns. It was all very well coordinated, perhaps too well, as a scientific etching of an animal compares to the real thing.

A second tea trolley was also prominently displayed, similarly draped in a fine lace cloth. It was one of the lower styles meant for front parlors and afternoon visiting hours. Upon it lay the supine form of a young lady, dressed to match the china in a white damask evening gown with pink flowers. Her throat was bare and exposed, and her fine blond hair was piled high and off of her neck.

The countess, it would appear, had a very particular definition of high tea.

"Oh, dear. I do hate to interrupt you at mealtime," said Lady Maccon, not at all apologetically. "But I have the most important information to impart."

She waddled forward, only to have her way blocked yet again by Lord Ambrose. "My Queen, I must protest, a soulless in your inner sanctum. While you are at table!"

Countess Nadasdy looked up from the young girl's fine white neck. "Ambrose. We have been over this before." Alexia had never thought the Westminster queen entirely suited the role of vampire. Not that Lady Maccon's opinion mattered much. If the rumors were to be believed, Countess Nadasdy had been suiting the role for over a thousand years. Possibly two. But, unlike Lord Ambrose, she simply didn't look the part. She was a cozy little woman—short and on the plump side. Her cheeks were round and rosy, and her big eyes sparked. True, the blush was mercuric and the eyes sparkled with belladonna and calculation, not humor, but it was hard to feel threatened by a woman who looked like the living incarnation of one of Lord Akeldama's shepherdess seduction paintings.

"She is a hunter," protested Lord Ambrose.

"She is a *lady*. Aren't you, Lady Maccon?"

Alexia looked down at her protruding belly. "So the evidence would seem to suggest." The baby inside of her moved around as though to punctuate the statement. *Yes,* said Alexia to it internally, *I don't like Lord Ambrose either. But now is not the time for histrionics.*

"Ah, yes, felicitations on the imminent event."

"Let us hope not all *that* imminent. Incidentally, my apologies, venerable ones. Until recently, you seem to have found the advent of my progeny discombobulating."

"Exactly, My Queen, we cannot have that—"

Lady Maccon interrupted Lord Ambrose by the simple expedient of prodding his ribs with her parasol. She aimed

exactly for that point in the rib cage that the ticklish find
most discomposing. Not that vampires got ticklish, so far as
Alexia was aware, but it was the principle of the thing. "Yes,
yes, I know you still would prefer it if I were dead, Lord
Ambrose, but never mind that now. Countess, listen to me.
You have to get away."

Lord Ambrose moved and Lady Maccon proceeded
toward the hive queen.

The countess dabbed at a bit of blood on the side of her
mouth with a white linen handkerchief. Alexia barely caught
a hint of fang before they were tucked away behind perfect
cupid's bow–shaped lips. The countess never showed fang
unless she meant it. "My dear Lady Maccon, what *are* you
wearing? Is that a *visiting* gown?"

"What? Oh, yes, sorry. I hadn't intended to come to your
lovely gathering, or I would be more appropriately dressed.
But, please listen, you must leave now!"

"Leave this room? Whatever for? It is one of my particular favorites."

"No, no, leave the house."

"Abandon my hive? Never! Don't be foolish, child."

"But, Countess, there is an octomaton heading in this
direction. It wants to kill you and it knows the location."

"Preposterous. There hasn't been an octomaton in a dog's
age. And how would it know where to find me?"

"Ah, yes, well, as to that. There was this break-in, you see—"

Lord Ambrose bristled. "Soul-sucker! What have you
done?"

"How was I to remember one little invitation from way back?"

The countess went momentarily still, like a wasp atop a slice of melon. "Lady Maccon, who is it that wants to kill me?"

"Oh, too many to choose from? I am similarly blessed."

"Lady Maccon!"

Alexia had hoped not to reveal the identity of the culprit. It was one thing to warn the hive of imminent attack; it was quite another to expose Madame Lefoux without first understanding her motives. *Well, perhaps if my friend had let me in on her reasoning, I might not now be forced into this situation. But in the end, I am muhjah, and I must remember that my duty is to maintain the solidarity of the peace between humans and supernatural folk. No matter Madame Lefoux's grounds, we cannot have a hive arbitrarily attacked by an inventor. It is not only impolitic, it is impolite.*

So, Lady Maccon took a deep breath and told the truth. "Madame Lefoux has built the octomaton. She intends to kill you with it."

The countess's big cornflower-blue eyes narrowed.

"What!" That was Lord Ambrose.

The Duke of Hematol made his way over toward his queen. "I told you no good would come of taking in that French maid."

The countess held up a hand. "She's after the boy."

"Of course she is after the boy!" The duke's voice was harsh with annoyance. "Dabble in the affairs of mortal women and this is what transpires. Octomaton at your doorstep. I warned you."

"Your complaint was recorded by the edict keeper at the time."

Lady Maccon blinked. "Quesnel? What has he to do with any of this? Wait." She tilted her head and gave the countess a look. "Did you kidnap Madame Lefoux's son?"

Alexia often felt it wasn't possible for a vampire to look guilty. But the countess was giving the expression a fair facsimile.

"Why? I mean, for goodness' sake." Lady Maccon shook her finger at the hive queen as though the ancient vampire were a very naughty schoolgirl caught with her hand in the jam jar. "Shame on you! Bad vampire."

The countess tsked dismissively. "Oh, really. There's no cause for condescension, soul-sucker. The boy was promised to us. In her will, Angelique named the hive guardian to her child. We didn't even know he existed until that moment. Madame Lefoux wouldn't hear of it, of course. But he *is ours*. And we never let go of what is rightfully ours. We didn't kidnap him. We *retrieved* him."

Lady Maccon thought of her own child, now promised away to Lord Akeldama in order to keep them both safe from fang interference and assassination attempts. "Oh, really, Countess. *I mean to say!* What is it with you vampires? Don't you ever relax your machinations? No wonder Genevieve wants to kill you. Kidnapping. That's very low. Very low, indeed. What could you possibly want with the boy anyway? He's a terrible scamp."

The countess's round, pleasant face went very hard. "We want him because he is *ours*! What more reason do we need? The law is on our side in this. We have copies of the will."

Lady Maccon demanded details. "Does it name the hive, or you specifically, Countess?"

"Me alone, I believe."

Lady Maccon cast her hands heavenward, although there was no one up there for her to appeal to. It was an accepted fact that preternaturals had no spiritual recourse, only pragmatism. Alexia didn't mind; the latter had often gotten her out of sticky situations, whereas the former seemed highly unreliable when one was in a bind. "Well, there you have it. With no legal recourse, Genevieve only has to see you dead in order to get her child back. Plus, she has the added pleasure of killing the woman who corrupted her lover."

The countess looked as though she had not thought of matters in such a way.

"You cannot be serious."

Alexia shrugged. "Consider her perspective."

The countess stood. "Good point. And she is French. They get terribly emotional, don't they? Ambrose, arm the defenses. Hematol, send out runners. If it really is an octomaton, we are going to need additional military support. Get me my personal physician. Oh, and bring out the aethertronic Gatling gun."

Lady Maccon could not help but admire the countess's command of the situation. Alexia herself was sometimes known, among members of the pack, as *the general*. Of course, the gentlemen in question believed their mistress unaware of this moniker. Alexia preferred it that way and would periodically go into fits of autocratic demands simply to ascertain if she could get them to grumble about it when they thought she couldn't hear. Werewolves tended to believe all mortals slightly deaf.

As the countess set about putting her people in order, her meal, left to lie on the tea table in soporific languor, stirred. The young blonde raised herself slowly up onto her elbows and looked about foggily.

"Felicity!"

"Oh, dear, Alexia? What on earth are *you* doing here?"

"Me! Me?" Lady Maccon was reduced to sputtering. "What about you? I'll have you know, sister mine, that I came here because I had an invitation to the party!"

Felicity wiped delicately at the side of her neck with a tea cloth. "I didn't know you ran in the countess's circles."

"You mean, supernatural circles? My husband is a werewolf, for goodness' sake! Must you keep forgetting that tiny little detail?"

"Yes, but on full-moon night, shouldn't you be with him? And aren't you terribly far along to be out in public?"

Lady Maccon practically growled. "Felicity. My presence here is not of concern. But yours most certainly is! What on earth are you doing allowing a vampire—and not just any vampire, mind you, but the ruddy Westminster queen herself—to feed on you? You're...you're...not even chaperoned!" she sputtered.

Felicity's expression became hard and calculating. Alexia

had seen that look before but had never given it much cre-
dence beyond smallness of mind. However, this time she
had the upsetting realization that she might have underesti-
mated her sister. "Felicity, *what have you done?*"

Felicity gave a humorless little smile.

"How long has this relationship been going on?" Alexia
tried to think back. When had her sister first started wearing
high-necked dresses and lace collars?

"Oh, Alexia, you can be so dim-witted. Since I met Lord
Ambrose at your wedding, of course. He very kindly said
that I looked like just the type of creative and ambitious
young lady who would have excess soul. He asked if I would
like to live forever. I thought to myself, well, *of course* I
have excess soul. Mama is always saying what a good art-
ist I would be, should I ever try, and what a good musician
I would be, should I ever learn to play. And, most assuredly, I should like to live forever! Not to mention be courted
by Lord Ambrose! Then what should the other ladies have
to say?"

Lady Maccon ground her teeth together. "Felicity! What
have you done? Oh, gracious me, it was you who stole my
journal on the dirigible to Scotland, wasn't it?"

Felicity looked archly up at the ceiling.

"You leaked my pregnancy to the press intentionally,
didn't you?"

Felicity gave a delicate little shrug.

Alexia was quite disgusted with her sister. To be stupid
was one thing; to be stupid and evil yielded up untidy consequences. "Why, you conniving bit of baggage! How could

you? To your own flesh and blood!" She was also scandal-ized. "Do pull your dress up. What a neckline!" Alexia was so out of temper, in fact, she nearly forgot that they were all in danger from a rampaging two-story octopus. "And?"

Felicity pursed her lips and looked at the ceiling.

"Go on!"

"Oh, really, sister, there is no need to take that tone of voice with me. All Lord Ambrose wanted was a few reports on your activities and health now and again. Well, and the journal. Until this recent change of address—then we thought if I were to take up residence with you, well, you know... And I've been visiting with the countess only now and again, let her have a little nibble, relay some informa-tion. No harm done. She's perfectly lovely, isn't she? Quite the motherly sort."

"Aside from the neck biting?" Sarcasm was, of course, the lowest form of discourse, but sometimes Alexia couldn't resist such temptation as her sister offered. That was prob-ably how Countess Nadasdy felt. *Which explains those ugly shawls Felicity's been wearing. She's been hiding her neck.*

They both turned to watch the countess as she conferred with two of her drones. She was moving lightning fast from one task to the next, preparing to defend her territory with both might and cunning and, if Alexia's eyes were to be believed, a tin of what looked to be pickled herring. The vampire queen had the demeanor and appearance of some sort of small, quick hedge bird—a tit, perhaps. If a tit could kill you with a mere nod of its little feathered head.

"Felicity. What did you tell her about me?"

"Well, anything I could think of, of course. But really, Alexia, your activities are very dull. I fail to see why anyone should be interested in you or that child of yours."

"You would."

With her hive busy mustering up troops, the countess flitted back over, sat down, and looked as though she intended to return to tea.

Lady Maccon narrowed her eyes, marched the last few feet to the beautiful cream brocade settee, and placed a very firm and very bare hand on the vampire queen's forearm. Alexia was a good deal stronger than a proper English lady ought to be, and the countess was suddenly ill equipped to shake off such a grip.

"No more tea." Alexia was quite decided on this point.

The countess looked from her to her sister. "Remarkable, isn't it? Sisterhood, I mean. One would never guess it to look at you."

Alexia rolled her eyes, let go of the countess's arm, and gave her a look of mild reproach. "My sister cannot possibly have been an effective spy."

The vampire queen shrugged and reached for her tea—the ordinary kind. She sipped at the bone china cup delicately, taking no pleasure or sustenance from the beverage.

Waste of perfectly good tea, thought Alexia. She looked at Felicity. But, then, the countess probably thought Felicity was a waste of perfectly good blood.

Her sister assumed a dramatically relaxed pose atop the tea trolley, her face petulant.

Alexia reached for a treacle tartlet and popped it into her own mouth.

"You have been conducting some interesting investigations recently, Lady Maccon," said the vampire queen slyly. "Something to do with your father's past, if what your sister has relayed is true. And a ghost. I know you are adverse to my advice, but trust me, Lady Maccon, it would be best not to delve too deeply into Alessandro Tarabotti's records."

Alexia thought about Floote, who always seemed to know more about her father than he was willing to tell her. Or was allowed to tell her.

"Did you vampires somehow have my father classified? Do you have my butler under a gag order? And now you are corrupting my sister. Really, Countess Nadasdy, why go to such lengths?" Lady Maccon put her hand back onto the vampire queen's arm, turning her mortal once more.

The countess flinched but did not pull away. "Really, Lady Maccon, must you? It's a most unsettling sensation."

At which juncture Lord Ambrose turned and saw what was occurring on the couch.

"Let go of her, you soul-sucking bitch!" He charged across the room.

Alexia let go and raised her parasol.

"Now, Ambrose, no harm done." The countess sounded placid but her fangs were showing slightly.

Felicity was looking back and forth between the players around her with increasing befuddlement on her pretty face. Since Felicity often wore such a look whenever attempting to understand any conversation not directly concerning herself, Alexia saw no reason to explain. The last thing Felicity needed to know was that her older sister was anything more than a bother. *That is, assuming Felicity still doesn't know I'm preternatural. Right now it's difficult to put anything past her.*

Lord Ambrose looked as though he would very much like to strike Lady Maccon.

Still holding the parasol at the defensive, Alexia reached inside her reticule and withdrew Ethel. She then lowered the parasol to reveal the gun now pointed at the vampire.

"Back away a little, if you would, Lord Ambrose. You are making me feel most unwelcome."

Lord Ambrose did as he was told with a snorted, "You *are* unwelcome."

"Do I have to keep reminding everyone? I had an invitation!"

"Alexia, you have a gun!" exclaimed Felicity, horrified.

"Yes." Lady Maccon relaxed back into the settee and allowed the gun to waver slightly over toward the countess. "I should warn you, Lord Ambrose, my aim is not very accurate."

"And is that gun loaded with...?" He did not finish the sentence. He did not need to.

"I should never, of course, admit to the fact that Ethel here is equipped with sundowner bullets. But a few may have *accidentally* made it from my husband's stock into my own. Can't imagine how."

Lord Ambrose backed farther away.

Alexia looked with annoyance at her sister. "Get off the tea trolley, Felicity, do. What a place for a young lady to be sitting. Do you have any idea what kind of trouble you are in?"

Felicity sniffed. "You sound just like Mama."

"Yes, well, *you* are beginning to *act* like Mama!"

Felicity gasped.

Lord Ambrose made a move forward, thinking Lady Maccon's attention distracted.

Ethel swung once more toward the countess. Alexia's hand was remarkably steady. "Ah, ah, ah."

The vampire backed away again.

"Now," said Alexia, "I do so hate to do this to you all. But really, our safest bet would be to get out of here. And quickly."

The countess shook her head. "You may leave, of course, Lady Maccon, but—"

"No, no, both of us, I insist."

"Foolish child," said the Duke of Hematol, coming back into the room. "How can anyone know so little of vampire edict and sit the Shadow Council? Our queen cannot leave this house. It is not a matter of choice—it is a matter of physiology."

"She could swarm." Lady Maccon swung her gun once more toward the vampire queen.

Lord Ambrose hissed.

Lady Maccon said, "Go on, Countess, swarm. There's a good vampire."

The duke let out an annoyed sigh. "Save us all from the

practicality of soul-suckers. She can't swarm on command, woman. Queens don't just up and swarm when told they have to. Swarming is a biological imperative. You might as well tell someone to spontaneously combust."

Alexia looked at Lord Ambrose. "Really? Would that work on him?"

At which juncture the most tremendous crash reverberated through the house, and guests at the party below started screaming.

The octomaton had arrived.

Lady Maccon gestured with her gun in an arbitrary manner. "*Now* will you swarm?"

CHAPTER FOURTEEN

In Which Lady Maccon Mislays
Her Parasol

The countess jumped to her feet. So, too, did Felicity. Lord Ambrose decided Lady Maccon was no longer the greatest threat in his world and turned toward the racket.

"Now would be an excellent time," prodded Alexia.

The countess shook her head in exasperation. "Swarming is not something one chooses. I know this is difficult for you to understand, soul-sucker, but not everything is the result of conscious thought. Swarming is instinct. I have to know, deep down in my soul on a supernatural level, that my hive is no longer safe. Then I would have to source a new hive, never to return to this one. Now is not that time."

The house fairly rattled on its foundations as another mighty crash rent the air.

"Are you convinced of that?" wondered Alexia.

Something was literally tearing its way through the

building, as a child will rip paper twists to get at the sugar candy inside. *Tasty vampire candy. Mmm.*

Felicity started to scream.

"Where did you stash Quesnel, Countess Nadasdy?" Lady Maccon raised her voice to carry over the din.

The countess was distracted by the commotion. "What?"

"I was simply suggesting you might want to retrieve him. Have him with you, and soon."

"Oh, yes, excellent plan. Hematol, would you fetch the boy?"

"Yes, my queen." The duke, having only just appeared, looked reluctant to obey; no vampire wishes to leave the side of his queen when she is in danger. But a direct order was a direct order, so he bowed perfunctorily and scurried off.

Yet another crash sounded. The door burst open. Dr. Caedes, a number of the footman-drones, and several other hive vampires ran into the room. Mabel Dair was the last inside, slamming the door behind her. The actress's beautiful gold gown was ripped, and her hair had fallen down about her face. She looked as though she were just about to perform Ophelia's death scene to a packed audience.

"My queen, you would not believe the monster down there! It is horrible! It ripped right through the wall, the one with the Titian. And it broke the bust of Demeter."

The countess was obligingly sympathetic to the trauma. "Come to me, my dear."

Mabel Dair ran to her mistress, knelt at her feet, and buried her face in the vampire's full skirts. Her hands were trembling where they gripped the fine taffeta material.

Alexia was tempted to clap. *Spectacular performance!*

The queen set one perfect white hand atop Miss Dair's cascading blond curls and looked to her hive. "Dr. Caedes, report! What is the octomaton's armament? Is it standard to the earlier model?"

"No, my queen, it seems to have been modified."

"Fire?"

"Yes, but only one tentacle. And the customary wooden blades. But a third seems to be able to shoot stakes. And the fourth has bullets."

"Go on. That's only four."

"It hasn't yet used any of the others yet."

"If this is Madame Lefoux we are dealing with, she'll have armed every single tentacle with something deadly. That's how she thinks."

Alexia couldn't help but agree. Genevieve was like that about her gadgets—the more uses the better.

The wall on the opposite side of the room shook. They heard a horrible, wrenching, tearing, crashing noise. It was the sound of metal and wood and brick colliding. The entire wall before them was ripped asunder. Once the dust settled, the domed head of the octomaton became visible, balanced atop its many tentacles. The creature scrabbled for purchase within the rubble of what had once been one of London's most stylish residences. The silver light of the moon and the bright gas of the streetlamps lit up the gleaming metal hide of the mechanical creature. Alexia could just see the fleeing forms of the countess's party guests in the street below.

Alexia raised her parasol and stood. She pointed the frilly

accessory at the octomaton accusingly. "Genevieve, I do hope you didn't kill anyone."

But if Madame Lefoux was in there, guiding the creature, she did not acknowledge Lady Maccon. She had one intended target and one target only—Countess Nadasdy.

A gigantic tentacle wormed its way up into the room and hit out at the vampire queen, trying to crush her. Alexia preferred to lead with an airborne offensive, but Madame Lefoux was opting for hand-to-hand—or was that hand-to-tentacle?—combat. Possibly to protect as many innocents as she could.

The queen, supernatural in speed and cunning, simply dodged out of the way of the massive metal thing. But she was well and truly trapped, for there were no other doors out of that room, and half of her house was now destroyed.

Felicity let out another scream and then did the most sensible thing she could do under the circumstances—she fainted. At which point, everyone else did an equally sensible thing and ignored her.

Lord Ambrose charged. Alexia had no idea what he intended to do or how he intended to do it, but he seemed bent on something. He leaped, impossibly fast and high, landing atop the head of the creature, where he began trying to scrabble for a way inside. *Ah, going for the brains of the operation.*

Lady Maccon figured that was a pretty intelligent plan, but the vampire was thwarted in his attempts to pull off the hatch of the dome. He tried to punch through the helmet-like mantle, but Madame Lefoux was a master worker in such matters. The head was practically seamless, with no possible way of getting in from the outside, not even for a vampire. She had given herself slits to see out of, but those slits were just big enough to peer through; they were not sufficiently large for a vampire to get his fingers inside and pry open the casing.

A tentacle whipped around and with a casual gesture brushed Lord Ambrose off as if he were a crumb. The vampire fell past the edge of the floor where the wall once had stood, grabbing wildly and missing, and disappeared out of sight. Only to reappear moments later, simply leaping up from one story to the next until he was back inside.

This time Lord Ambrose dove for the root of one of the tentacles, trying to tear it off the body. Relying on all his strength, he attempted to forcibly rip away the ball bearings and pulleys that directed the thing's movements. Nothing. Madame Lefoux always thought in terms of supernatural strength and designed her devices accordingly.

While Lord Ambrose was thus occupied with a direct attack, several of the more courageous drones also charged the octomaton. These were swept aside with little more than the perfunctory wave of a free tentacle. Others made their way to their queen, standing in a protective huddle between her and the mechanical beast. One of the vampires was loading the pickled herring, which seemed to actually be some kind of ammunition, into an aethertronic Gatling gun. He cranked the belt through, and the machine spat the shiny fish at the octomaton in a *rat-tat-tat* of automated fire. The fish sizzled and stuck where they hit, eating angry holes into the octomaton's protective plating.

Another tentacle crept into the room, which now seemed to be filled with writhing metal octopus arms. This one raised up slowly, like a snake. Its tip opened with a snap, and it shot a blast of fire at the group surrounding Countess Nadasdy.

Drones screamed, and the countess, fleet and fast, leaped to the side, carrying two of them with her. She would try to rescue any she could from the flames, much as Conall would do with his clavigers under similar circumstances.

Knowing it was probably futile, Alexia put her gun back in her reticule and activated the magnetic disruption emitter in her parasol, aiming it at the octopus. As before, there was no reaction to the invisible blast, although the Gatling gun seized up. The tentacle swung around, spraying fire over the boudoir. The canopy over the handsome four-poster bed caught and flamed up to the ceiling. Alexia popped open her parasol and raised it before her like a shield, protecting herself from the blast.

Upon lowering it, she found that all was chaos and dust, with the smell of burning and the sound of screaming around her. Yet another tentacle slithered into the room. She had a sinking feeling that this one might actually be a real threat. Madame Lefoux was done playing. Alexia knew what her parasol was capable of where vampires were concerned, and this particular tentacle dripped an ominous liquid out of its tip—a liquid that sizzled when it hit the carpet and burned a hole where it landed.

Lapis solaris, unless Alexia missed her guess. It was one

of the most deadly weapons in her parasol, and a favorite among those who opposed vampires. The danger was that it had to be diluted in sulfuric acid, and that could kill most anyone else as well as damage a vampire.

"Genevieve, don't! You could injure innocents!" Alexia was scared, not just for the hive but also for the drones and her sister, who all seemed to be in the line of squirt.

"Countess, please, you must draw her away. People will die." Lady Maccon turned her plea on the endangered vampire queen.

But Countess Nadasdy was beyond reason. All her efforts were now focused on protecting herself and her people from annihilation.

The Duke of Hematol reappeared, carrying an undersized grubby boy child in his supernaturally strong arms. If possible, the duke moved even faster than the queen had, coming to a stop before her and thrusting Quesnel's kicking form into her grasp. Everything stilled.

Quesnel was hollering and thrashing, but upon seeing the octomaton, he seemed more afraid of it than the vampires. He squealed and clutched reflexively at Countess Nadasdy's neck with one skinny, smudged arm.

The octomaton could not fire without risk of injury to the boy. No modern science had yet devised a weapon, apart from sunlight, that could harm a vampire without also harming a human. One of the tentacles, already falling with deadly force toward the vampire queen, veered away at the last minute, landing with a crash on the laden tea trolley, which had managed to survive the chaos until that moment. It crumpled in half under the blow, spinning fine china, treacle tart, and finger sandwiches in all directions.

So far as Alexia was concerned, that was *the last straw.* The infant-inconvenience inside her beat a tattoo of encouragement as she strode forward and whacked at the metal tentacle with her parasol and all her might. "Genevieve! Not the treacle tartlets!"

Whack, whack, whack. Twang!

It was, of course, a futile effort. But it made Alexia feel better.

The tentacle's tip flipped open, and a tube popped forward and out, becoming a bullhorn like those favored by circus ringmasters. The octomaton raised this to one of the slits in its eye. Madame Lefoux spoke into it.

Or at least it sounded like Madame Lefoux. It was odd to hear her cultured, slightly accented, mellow feminine voice coming out of such a big, bulbous creature. "Give me my son and I will leave you in peace, Countess."

"Maman!" yelled Quesnel to the octomaton. Realizing it was his mother and not some nightmarish monster, he began struggling in the vampire queen's arms. To absolutely no avail; she was much, much stronger than he would ever be. The countess merely clutched the boy tighter.

Quesnel began yelling in French. "Stop, Maman. They haven't hurt me. I'm fine. They've been very kind. They feed me sweets!" His pointy chin was set and his voice imperious.

Madame Lefoux said nothing more. It was clear they

were at an impasse. The countess was not going to let go of the boy, and Madame Lefoux was not going to let them go anywhere.

Alexia edged toward her sister, sensing that very soon the queen would have no recourse but flight. Leaving Felicity behind in this building was, unfortunately, not really feasible, appealing as the idea might be.

The house swayed on its foundation. Over half of it was now gone, with only the back section still intact, and there was very little holding that in place. The frame and supports were failing. Alexia had often thought London houses were built with far less structural integrity than even her cheapest bustle.

She waddled closer to the vampire queen, careful not to touch her. "Countess, I know you said practicality wouldn't come into it, but this would be an excellent time to swarm, if you could but try."

The countess turned eyes upon Alexia that were dilated black with fear. She drew her lips back in a shriek of wrath, exposing all four of her fangs: Feeders and Makers, the second set being ones that only a queen had. Very little of the sense was left in the woman's face. In this particular arena, clearly vampires could end up like werewolves, creatures of emotion, dependent only on the little that was left of their soul to save them.

Lady Maccon was not normally an indecisive individual, but in that second she wondered if she might have chosen the wrong side in this little battle. Even though Madame Lefoux was rampaging through London in a highly unlawful and destructive manner, the countess was behaving like nothing more than a child snatcher. Alexia knew she had the capacity to end this. She could reach out and touch the vampire, turn her human and utterly vulnerable and unable to hold on to the wiry and gyrating Quesnel.

She hesitated, for Alexia could not escape logic, even in crisis. The only diplomatic faux pas worse than a hive queen dying at the hand of a scientist would be if she did so at the hand of Lady Maccon, soulless, muhjah, and werewolf lover.

As if to settle the matter, a tentacle came crashing toward them. It knocked Alexia back. She tripped and stumbled on her weakened ankle and, for what felt like the millionth time that evening, fell back upon her bustle.

She landed next to Felicity and so wiggled over to her and slapped her about the face for a bit. Finally, her sister blinked blue eyes open.

"Alexia?"

The infant-inconvenience was rather sick of this kind of overactive, not to say violent, treatment on behalf of its mother. It thrashed in protest, and Alexia lay back suddenly with an "oof" of distress.

"Alexia!" Felicity may actually have been a little worried. She had never seen her older sister show any sign of weakness. Ever.

Alexia struggled to sit back up. "Felicity, we have got to get away from here."

Felicity helped Alexia to rise, just in time for them to see Lord Ambrose and two other vampires leap at the octoma-ton in one tremendous coordinated charge. They draped and strapped down a sheet of fabric, what looked to be a very large tablecloth, over the monster's head. Smart maneuver, for it momentarily blinded Madame Lefoux on the inside. She could neither steer nor attack. The tentacles flailed futilely.

With the octomaton temporarily disabled, the countess sprang into action. So did her drones. They all ran to the open side of the building, the countess moving at speed and clutching Quesnel tight to her breast. Without hesitation, she leaped over the edge and down to the rubble. Quesnel let out a holler of fear at the plunge, quickly followed by what could only be a whoop of exhilaration.

Alexia and Felicity tottered to the edge after them and looked down. Three stories. There was no way *they* could jump and survive, and there was no other apparent way to get down.

However, they did have an excellent perspective on the carnage and could watch the countess and her vampires race between the tentacles of the octomaton and dash away into the moonlit city, swarming at last. The drones followed a little more judiciously, climbing down out of what was left of the house by degrees and then running after, unable to keep up with the supernatural speed of their mistress.

The octomaton screamed, or Madame Lefoux did, and set its flaming tentacle to burn away the tablecloth that obscured its vision. As soon as it was gone, it took the inventor only a moment to realize that her quarry had escaped. Only Alexia and her sister still stood in the swaying building—a structure that was clearly about to come tumbling down.

The monster turned to track the fleeing vampires. Then it crashed off through the streets, heedless of who or what it crushed. Madame Lefoux either hadn't seen Alexia's plight or didn't care to help her. Alexia hoped fervently it was the former, or her friend was indeed more heartless than she had ever thought possible.

"Bugger," said Lady Maccon succinctly.

Felicity gasped at her language, even under such trying circumstances.

Alexia looked at her sister and said, fully knowing that Felicity wouldn't understand what she was talking about, "I'm going to have to arrest her, in the end."

The hive house yielded to gravity, tilting forward in a slow, reluctant creak.

The two women slid toward the edge. Felicity shrieked, and Alexia, in classic fashion given the tenor of her evening, lost her balance and tumbled forward, also yielding to gravity. She went right over, scraping and scrabbling at the splintered floorboards.

She managed to just hang on. Her parasol fell, landing among wall fragments, bits of art, and torn carpet far below. Alexia dangled, desperately holding on to the side of a wooden beam that stuck slightly out above the abyss.

Felicity had hysterics.

Lady Maccon wondered how long her grip was going to hold, grateful she'd removed her gloves. She was rather strong, but it had been a very long week and she wasn't up to her prepregnancy standards. Plus she was carrying a sizable amount of extra weight.

Well, she thought philosophically, *this is a very romantic way to die. Madame Lefoux would certainly feel cut up about it. So that's something. Guilt can be very useful.*

And then, just when she thought all was lost, she felt a puff of air behind her neck and a tingling stirring of the aether.

"What ho!" said Boots. "Can I be of any assistance, Lady Maccon?"

The basket-shaped gondola of Lord Akeldama's private dirigible came down out of the sky like some kind of fat and benevolent savior.

Alexia looked over her shoulder at him from where she dangled. "Not especially. I thought I might simply hang about here for a while, see what transpired."

"Oh, don't fuss about her," yelled Felicity. "Help me! I'm far more important."

Boots ignored Miss Loontwill and directed the pilot to float in until the gondola section of the basket was just under Lady Maccon.

The building lurched at exactly that moment, and Alexia, with a cry, lost her purchase on the beam.

She landed with a thud inside the basket. Her feet failed her and she went backward, once more onto the bustle, which had very little resilience left after the evening's extensive abuse. After a moment's consideration, Alexia just flopped right there on her back. Enough was enough.

"Now me, now meee!" shrieked Felicity, and she seemed to have good cause, for the structure was indeed falling.

Boots looked the young woman up and down, no doubt taking in the bite marks on her white neck. The remains of the house might well be tumbling down that very moment, but he hesitated.

"Lady Maccon?" Boots was a very well-trained drone.

Alexia sucked at her teeth and looked up at her sister. "If we must."

The pilot gave the balloon some lift and it rose. Tizzy put out his arm politely, as though escorting Miss Loontwill in to dinner, and Felicity stepped off the ledge and into the dirigible with all the dignity of a terrified kitten.

The building crumbled behind her. The pilot pulled one of his propeller levers hard, and the airship let out a great puff of steam and surged forward, just in time to escape a large chunk of roof as the last of the hive house crumbled to the ground.

"Where to, Lady Maccon?"

Alexia looked up at Boots, who was crouched over her in evident concern. The child inside her was continuing to express its distress with the night's events. Lady Maccon could think of but one place to go, with her husband out of commission and the moon still high and bright above them. All of her normal hidey-holes were inaccessible: Madame Lefoux's contrivance chamber was out of the picture, and the Tunstells were still in Scotland.

BUR, she was confident, would already be investigating the scene of the destruction below or chasing the octomaton as it crashed through the city. BUR had an arsenal of weaponry at its disposal—their own aethertronic Gatling guns, mini-magnatronic cannons, not to mention Mandal-son custard probes. Let *them* try to stop Madame Lefoux for a while. They probably wouldn't be any more successful than she, given the inventor's intellectual skills and mechanical abilities, but they might slow her down. Alexia, after all, had only a parasol. Then she swore, realizing that she didn't even have that anymore. It was lying below, probably buried under half a collapsed building. Ethel was secured in the reticule tied at her waist, but her precious parasol was gone.

"I'm certain you gentlemen would agree with me. It's at times like this that what a girl needs is some serious counsel on her attire."

Boots and Tizzy looked with deep concern at Alexia's sorry state of dress, her bustle flattened, her hem filthy, her lacy trim soot-covered and burned.

"Bond Street?" suggested Tizzy seriously.

Alexia arched a brow. "Oh, no, this is a profound clothing emergency. Please, take me to Lord Akeldama."

"At once, Lady Maccon, at once." Boots's face was suitably grave behind the muttonchops. The dirigible floated up a little higher and, with another violent puff of steam, set a brisk glide north toward Lord Akeldama's town house.

CHAPTER FIFTEEN

Where Dirigibles Fear to Tread

Lord Akeldama had arranged for a dirigible landing green to be built on the roof of his town house. It was shifted off to one side, allowing room for his aethographor's cuspidor-like receiver. Lady Maccon wondered that she had not noticed this before, but then she didn't spend much time investigating rooftops as part of her daily routine.

The dirigible touched down as light as a meringue. Given that bipedal motion hadn't been doing her many favors that evening, Alexia reluctantly clambered to her feet. Much to her delight, Lord Akeldama had made allowances for a dignified exit from the transport here at its home base. A drone bustled over with a specially designed peaked stepladder that flipped over the side of the gondola basket and then telescoped out to the required height on each side. This permitted one to climb up one side and down the other with great solemnity and aplomb.

"Why," wondered Alexia, "don't you float around already carrying that little ladder?"

"We thought nobody would be disembarking before we returned home."

Felicity climbed out after her sister and stood in haughty disapproval to one side. "What a way to travel! One can hardly countenance how acceptable floating has become. So unnaturally high up. And to land on a roof! Why, Alexia, I can see the tops of buildings. They are not landscaped properly!" All the while complaining, Felicity patted at her hair to ensure it hadn't been disturbed by air travel or her near-death experience.

"Oh, Felicity, do be quiet. I have had quite enough of your prattle for one evening."

Summoned by that secret instinct possessed only by the very best of servants, who always know when the mistress is in residence, Floote appeared at Alexia's elbow.

"Oh, Floote!"

"Madam."

"How did you know I would be here?"

Floote arched a brow as though to say, *Where else would you possibly end up on full-moon night but on Lord Akeldama's rooftop?*

"Yes, of course. Would you please take Felicity here back to our house and lock her in a room somewhere? The back parlor. Or possibly the newly configured wine cellar."

Felicity shrieked, "What?"

Floote looked at Felicity with an expression that was as close to a smile as Alexia had ever seen on his face—a tiny little crinkle at one corner of his mouth. "Consider it done, madam."

"Thank you, Floote."

The butler took a very firm grip on Felicity's arm and began leading her off.

"Oh, and, Floote, please send someone to check around the rubble of the Westminster Hive house right away, before the scavengers get there. I believe I accidentally dropped my parasol. And there might be some nice bits of art lying about."

Floote didn't even flinch at the knowledge that one of the most respected residences in London was now in ruins. "Of course, madam. I assume it is now permitted to give out the address?"

Lady Maccon gave it to him.

He moved smoothly off, dragging the protesting Felicity behind him.

"Sister, really, this is uncalled for. Is it the tooth marks? Is that what has you overset? There are only a few."

"Miss Felicity," Alexia heard Floote say, "do try to behave."

Boots, finished mooring down the dirigible, came up next to Alexia and offered her his arm. "Lady Maccon?"

She took it gratefully. The infant-inconvenience really was being quite troublesome at the moment. She felt as though she'd swallowed a fighting ferret.

"Perhaps you could take me to the, uh, closet, Mr.

Bootbottle-Fipps? I feel I ought to lie down. Just for a moment, mind you. There is still a loose hive to deal with. I suppose I should try to determine where Countess Nadasdy has gone. And Madame Lefoux, of course. She should not be allowed to rampage."

"Certainly not, my lady," agreed Boots. Who clearly felt, as Alexia did, that rampaging under any circumstances was uncalled for.

They had barely made it off the roof and down the staircases toward Lord Akeldama's second-best closet when a panting drone appeared before them. He was a tall and comely fellow with an affable face, a mop of curly hair, and a loose, floppy way of walking. He also had the most poorly tied cravat Alexia had ever seen within walking distance of Lord Akeldama. She looked with shock at Boots.

"New drone," Boots explained to Lady Maccon before turning amicably to face the young man.

"What ho, Boots!"

"Chip chip, Shabumpkin. Looking for me?"

"Rather!"

"Ah! Need a mo' to see her ladyship squared away properly."

"Oh, no, not just you, my dear chap. Looking for Lady Maccon as well. Care to follow?"

Alexia looked at the young man as though he had crawled from somewhere smelly. "Must I?"

"'Fraid so, your ladyship. Himself has called an emergency meeting of the Shadow Council," explained the drone.

"But it's full moon—the dewan can't attend."

"Several of us pointed this out to him. Niggling detail, said he."

"Oh, dear. Not at Buckingham, I hope?" Alexia clutched at her stomach, appalled at the very idea of any further travel.

The dandy grinned. "In his drawing room, madam. Where else?"

"Oh, thank goodness. Have Floote follow me there, would you, please? Once he's finished with his current line of business."

"'Course, Lady Maccon. My pleasure."

"Thank you, Mr., uh, Shabumpkin."

At which Boots straightened his spine, took a firmer grip on Alexia's arm, and guided her carefully down the next few sets of stairs and into Lord Akeldama's infamous drawing room. Once there, Shabumpkin nodded to them amiably and gangled off.

Lord Akeldama was waiting for her. Alexia was unsurprised to note that while she'd been dashing about London tracking an octomaton, the vampire had engaged in nothing more stressful than a change of clothing. He was wearing the most remarkable suit of tails and britches she had ever seen, candy-striped satin in cream and wine. This he had paired with a pink waistcoat of watered silk, pink hose, and pink top hat. His cravat, a waterfall of wine satin, was pinned with a gold and ruby pin, and matching rubies glittered about his fingers, monocle, and boutonniere.

"Can I get you anything, Lady Maccon?" offered Boots after seeing her safely ensconced in a chair, obviously concerned over her evident physical discomfort.

"Tea?" Alexia named the only thing she could think of that universally cured all ills.

"Of course." He vanished after a quick exchange of glances with his master.

However, when the tea was brought in some five minutes later, it was Floote who brought it, not Boots. The butler left quickly but Alexia was in no doubt he'd taken up residence very close to the outside of the door.

Lord Akeldama, in some distress, did not produce his harmonic auditory resonance disruptor, and Alexia did not remind him. She figured she might need Floote's advice on whatever occured next.

"So, my lord?" said she to the vampire, not at all up for dillydallying.

Lord Akeldama got straight to the point. Which was, in and of itself, a marker of his distress.

"My *precious* plum blossom, do you have *any* idea who is sitting in the back alleyway behind the kitchen *right this very moment?*"

Since Alexia was pretty darned convinced she would have spotted the octomaton from the roof, she took her second-best guess.

"Countess Nadasdy?"

"Behind the kitchen! By my longest fang! I—" He interrupted himself. "Gracious me, *buttercup,* but how *did* you know?"

Even coping with the violent kicking and squirming in her tummy, Alexia couldn't help but smile. "Now you know how I always feel."

"She swarmed."

"Yes, *finally.* You wouldn't believe what it took to chivy her out of that place. You'd think she was a ghost, so tightly tethered as to never be separated from her fixing point."

Lord Akeldama sat down, took a deep breath, and composed himself. "*Darling* marigold, please don't tell me you're responsible for...you know." He fluttered one perfectly white hand in the air, like a dying handkerchief.

"Oh, no, silly. Not me. Madame Lefoux."

"Oh. Of course. Madame Lefoux." The vampire's expression was arrested, deadpan at this latest bit of information.

Lady Maccon swore she could see the cogs and wheels of his massive intellect whirring away behind that effete painted face.

"Because of the little French maid?" He finally hazarded a guess.

Lady Maccon was enjoying having the upper hand for once. She had never dared to hope that someday she would have more information in a crisis than Lord Akeldama.

"Ah, no—Quesnel."

"Her son?"

"Not exactly hers."

Lord Akeldama stood up from his casual lounging posture. "The little towheaded lad the countess has with her? The one who ripped my jacket?"

"That sounds like Quesnel."

"What's the hive queen doing with a French inventor's son?"

"Ah, apparently, Angelique left a will."

Lord Akeldama tapped one fang with the edge of his gold and ruby monocle, pulling all the threads together right before Alexia's eyes. "Angelique is the boy's real mother, and she left him to the tender care of the *hive?* Silly bint."

"And the countess stole him from Genevieve. So Genevieve built an octomaton and destroyed the hive house trying to get him back."

"Upon my word, that's escalating things rather much."

"I daresay it is."

Lord Akeldama stopped tapping and began swinging his monocle back and forth while he took up a slow pace about the room. His white brow creased in one perfect line between the eyebrows.

Lady Maccon rubbed her protesting belly with one hand and sipped tea with the other. For once, the magic liquid was unable to disseminate any beneficial effects. The child was not happy, and tea was not going to pacify the beast.

The monocle stilled.

Alexia straightened up in her chair expectantly.

"The question remains, what is to be done with an entire hive skulking in my back alley?"

"Have them in for tea?" suggested Lady Maccon.

"No, no, not possible, little cream puff. They can't come in here."

Vampires were peculiar about etiquette. "Buckingham Palace? That should be relatively secure."

"No, no. Political nightmare. Vampire queen in the palace? Trust me, *darling,* it is never a good idea to have too many queens in one place, let alone one palace."

"To be really safe and buy us some extra time, we really ought to get her out of London."

"She won't like that at all, but there is *sense* to the suggestion, bluebell."

"How long do we have? I mean to say, how long does a swarming usually last?"

Lord Akeldama frowned. Concerned over whether he should give her this information, she suspected, rather than over any possibility of his not having it. "A newly made queen has months to settle, but an old queen has only a few hours."

Lady Maccon shrugged. Only one solution readily presented itself. It was the safest place she knew of—defensible and secure.

"I will have to take her to Woolsey."

Lord Akeldama sat down. "If you say so, Lady Alpha."

There was something in his tone that gave Alexia pause. He sounded like that when he had recently purchased a particularly nice waistcoat. She couldn't understand why he should be so self-satisfied with this predicament. As her benighted husband would say, *vampires*!

Someone had to do something. They couldn't let the Westminster queen simply cool her heels in an alleyway behind Lord Akeldama's and Lord Maccon's respective houses. What a scandal if the papers ever found *that* out! Alexia very much hoped Felicity was locked away. "It will only be until we can determine what's to be done with her. And how to resolve this situation with Quesnel. Hopefully without destroying any other perfectly innocent buildings." Lady Maccon tilted back her head and yelled, "Floote!"

The rapidity of Floote's appearance suggested he had, indeed, been waiting just outside the door.

"Floote, how many carriages do we have in town?"

"Just the one, madam. Just arrived back in."

"Well, that'll have to do. Hitch up the goers and have it brought round to the back, please. I shall meet you there."

"A journey? But, madam, you are unwell."

"Can't be helped, Floote. I cannot justifiably send a hive of vampires into a den of werewolves alone and without diplomatic assistance. The clavigers would never allow it. No, someone has to go with them, and that someone has to be me. The staff at the castle won't listen to anyone else, not on full moon."

Floote vanished, and Lady Maccon stood and began to make her way with stilted awkwardness out of the drawing room and through Lord Akeldama's house. The vampire followed. About halfway, however, she held up a finger at her host.

The baby inside of her had shifted. It felt a little lighter somehow. Well, who was she to question such a helpful adjustment? She patted her belly approvingly. However, she also rocked from one foot to the other. The infant-inconvenience had come to rest on a certain portion of her anatomy.

"Uh, oh, dear. How embarrassing. I really must visit your...uh...that is...um."

If he could have blushed, Lord Akeldama would have. Instead, he took out a red lace fan from the inside pocket of his jacket and fanned himself vigorously with it while

Alexia tottered off to see to the necessary business. She returned several long moments later, feeling better about all aspects of life.

Then she led the way onward through Lord Akeldama's house, behind the grand staircase and past the servants' stairs, through the kitchen, and out the back door. Lord Akeldama minced along solicitously after her.

Behind the house, past such shockingly vulgar objects as dustbins and a clothesline, the hive waited. Much to Lady Maccon's shock, there were gentlemen's undergarments on that clothesline! She closed her eyes and took a deep and fortifying breath. When she opened them again, she looked past the necessities into the delivery alley where a clot of vampires paced restlessly.

Countess Nadasdy was there with Dr. Caedes, Lord Ambrose, the Duke of Hematol, and two other vampires Alexia did not know by name. The hive queen was not in any condition to converse on any topic, mundane or otherwise. She was in obvious mental distress, her movements frenzied and her nerves overset. She paced to and fro, muttering and jerking at any noise. A startled vampire can leap to amazing heights and move at incredible speeds; this ability made the soft, round queen grasshopper-like. Sometimes she fought against one of her male counterparts as though trying to escape from the loose circle they formed around her. Occasionally, she would lash out at one of them, clawing at his face or biting hard into an exposed body part. The male vampire would only gentle her back into the center of the group, his wounds healed by the time she resumed her twitching.

Lady Maccon noted with relief that Quesnel had been transferred to Dr. Caedes's care. It was clearly not safe for a mortal to be near the queen. Alexia caught the young scamp's violet eye under his floppy thatch of yellow hair. He looked terrified. She gave him a wink and he brightened almost instantly. Theirs was not a long acquaintance, but she had once supported him in the matter of an exploding boiler, and he had trusted her implicitly ever since.

Alexia moved forward, only to pause, finding herself alone and Lord Akeldama left standing in a dramatic pose on the stoop behind her. Frankly, she had been surprised he even considered walking through the kitchen. He'd probably never even seen that part of his house before.

She turned back. "You aren't facilitating this conversation?" Never had she known Lord Akeldama to step aside when something significant was afoot.

The rove vampire chuckled. "My little *dumpling,* the countess would not tolerate my presence in her current condition. And I could hardly stand to endure such waistcoats as Dr. Caedes seems to favor these days. Not to mention the universal lack of headgear."

Alexia looked over the vampires with new eyes. It was true; the gentlemen seemed to have misplaced their top hats during the kerfuffle.

"No, no, my *cream puff,* this is *yours* to play now." He spared her a worried glance. She had not stopped clutching her protruding belly since she first reappeared in his drawing room. "If you are certain you can handle it with sufficient dexterity."

Lady Maccon took a fortifying breath, almost overbalancing. Responsibility was responsibility and no baby was going to prevent her from seeing everything right. Her world, currently, was in disarray. If Alexia Maccon was good at nothing else, she was good at putting things to rights and bringing order to the universe. Right now the Westminster Hive needed her managerial talents. She could hardly shirk her duty for so mere a trifle as pregnancy.

Without a backward glance at Lord Akeldama, she strode forward into the midst of the panicking hive. Or she would like to say she strode; it was more a gimpy kind of shuffle.

"Wait, Alexia! Where is your parasol?" Lord Akeldama sounded more concerned than she had ever heard him, devoid of both italics and pet names.

Lady Maccon gesticulated in an expressive way and yelled back to him, "Underneath what's left of the hive house, I suspect." Then she faced her muhjah duties full-on. "Right, you lot. I've had about enough of this waggish behavior."

Countess Nadasdy turned and hissed at her. Actually hissed.

"Oh, really." Lady Maccon was revolted. She looked at the Duke of Hematol. "Would you like me to sober her up?" She twiddled her naked fingers at him.

Lord Ambrose snarled and leaped, in one of those fantastic supernatural feats of athleticism, to place himself between Lady Maccon and his queen.

"Apparently not. Have you a better solution?"

The duke said, "We could not have her mortal and vulnerable, not in such an unprotected state."

Behind them, clattering through the alley behind the long row of town houses, the Woolsey carriage drew to a stop, the chestnut travelers hitched up rather than the parade bays. The countess leaped toward it as though it were some fearsome foe. Lord Ambrose held her back by snaking both arms around her from behind in an embarrassingly intimate gesture. It was only an old-fashioned gingerbread coach with a massive crest on its side and just that kind of superfluous decadence that would appeal to Lord Akeldama but that Lady Maccon had always felt was ever so slightly embarrassing for Woolsey. It was built to make an impression, not for speed or nimbleness. But Alexia hardly thought even such grandiose ugliness warranted a vampire attack.

"Well, then, as Lord Akeldama will not invite you in for tea and a sit-down, I was thinking I might suggest we retreat to Woolsey for the time being. Take refuge there."

All the assembled vampires, even the countess, who seemed to have only a limited ability to follow what was going on around her, paused to look at Lady Maccon as though she had just donned Grecian robes and begun hurling peeled grapes at them.

"Are you certain, Lady Maccon?" asked one of them, almost timidly for a vampire.

The doctor stepped forward, elongated and frail-looking, for all he held the struggling Quesnel as though the boy weighed no more than one of Madame Lefoux's automated feather dusters. "You are inviting us to stay, Lady Maccon? At Woolsey?"

Alexia did not see the source of their persistent confusion. "Well, yes. But I've only the one carriage, so you and the boy and the countess had best come with me. The others can run behind. Try to keep up."

Lord Ambrose looked at Dr. Caedes. "It is unprecedented."

Dr. Caedes looked at the Duke of Hematol. "There is no edict for this."

The duke looked at Lady Maccon, rolling his head from one side to the other. "The marriage was unprecedented, and so is the forthcoming child. She but maintains her brand of tradition." The duke moved toward his mistress. Cautiously, careful not to make any sudden movements.

"My Queen, we have an option." He spoke precisely, careful to enunciate each and every word.

Countess Nadasdy shook herself. "We have?" Her voice sounded hollow and very far away, as though emanating from the bottom of a mine. It reminded Alexia of something, but with the child inside her creating a fuss and the prospect of a long drive ahead, she couldn't remember what.

The countess looked to Lord Ambrose. "Who must we kill?"

"It is an offer freely given. An *invitation*."

For a moment, Countess Nadasdy seemed to return to herself, focusing completely on the faces of her three most treasured hive members. Her supports. Her tentacles. "Well, let us take it, then. No time to spare." She looked around, cornflower-blue eyes suddenly sharp. "Is that *laundry?* Where *have* you brought me?"

With a nod to Lady Maccon, Lord Ambrose hustled his queen into the Woolsey carriage. Quicker than the mortal eye could follow, he ducked back out again, his movements made smoother without the need to monitor a hat. He leaped to the driver's box, unceremoniously dismissing the perfectly respectable coachman who sat there and taking up the reins himself. Lady Maccon arched a brow at him.

"Pardon me?"

"I once raced chariots," he explained with a grin that showed off his fangs to perfection.

"I do not think it is quite the same thing, Lord Ambrose," remonstrated Alexia.

Dr. Caedes and Quesnel climbed inside next. And then, reluctantly, Lady Maccon. She struggled a bit with the steps, and no vampire was willing to offer her any kind of assistance, no touching, not even for politeness' sake. Once inside, she was unsurprised to find that the vampires were seated together on one bench so that she must sit alone on the other.

Lord Ambrose whipped the horses up and they took off at a canter, far too fast for the crowded streets of London. The clattering on the cobbles was awfully loud, and the carriage seemed to gyrate around the turns far more than Alexia had noticed before. Her belly protested the swaying.

It ordinarily took just under two hours to reach Woolsey from central London, less time for a werewolf in full fur, of course. The Count of Trizdale once claimed to have run it in his highflyer coach in only an hour and a quarter. Lord Ambrose, it seemed, was intent on trying to break that record.

Within London, the streets were worn enough into ruts for relatively smooth travel, and even though he had been tethered to Mayfair for hundreds of years, Lord Ambrose knew the way. Plenty of time to study maps, Alexia supposed. They took the lesser used road toward West Ham. However, upon exiting the city, everything went awry.

Not that the evening's events prior to that moment had been all sugared violet petals. But still.

First, and worst, so far as Lady Maccon was concerned, they hit the dirt road of the countryside. It had never bothered her overmuch before, and the carriage was well sprung and padded inside. But the fast pace combined with more-than-was-normal jiggling did not amuse the infant-inconvenience. Fifteen minutes of that and Alexia felt a new bodily sensation commence—a dull ache in the small of her back. She wondered if she had damaged herself during one of the evening's many bustle-crushing dismounts.

Then they heard Lord Ambrose yell and smelled acrid smoke. Here, away from looming shadows of the city buildings and under the full moon's light, everything was much easier to see. Alexia watched through the window as one of their vampire escorts put on a burst of speed, drew alongside the carriage, and leaped. The coach lurched but did not slow, and there came the sound of the roof above them being beaten viciously.

"Are we on fire?" Lady Maccon shifted herself into a better position, drew down the window sash, and stuck her head out into the rushing air, trying to see behind them.

It might have been difficult for her to make out their enemy, had there been a man on horseback or another carriage behind them, but the thing skittering after them over the fields and between the hedgerows was doing so on eight massive tentacles. Well, seven massive tentacles—it had the eighth in front of it spurting fire at the carriage. It was also several stories high.

Alexia pulled her head back inside. "Dr. Caedes, I suggest you have your charge there show himself. It might prevent Genevieve from actually killing us."

The carriage lurched again and picked up speed. The vampire on the roof, having succeeded in beating out the flames, had jumped off. But they were moving nowhere near as fast as they had initially—the horses were tiring, if not becoming winded and destroyed by such cruel speed.

The octomaton was gaining on them, and Woolsey still a good distance away.

Dr. Caedes changed his grip on the boy and tried to force Quesnel to stick his head out of the carriage window. Quesnel was not at all inclined to do anything any of the vampires wanted. Alexia gave her friend's son an almost imperceptible nod, at which point he did as directed. He stuck not only his head but also one skinny arm outside, waving madly at the creature behind them.

The ache in Lady Maccon's back intensified and she felt

her stomach lurch, wavelike. She'd never experienced such a sensation before. She let out a squeak of alarm and fell back against the padded wall of the coach. Then it was gone.

Alexia poked at her stomach with a finger. "Don't you dare. Now is most inopportune! Besides, arriving early to a party is disrespectful."

The octomaton fell back just far enough to allow the carriage to slow, but if Alexia knew Madame Lefoux, this was only giving the inventor time to come up with a new plan of attack. Genevieve must realize Alexia was also in the carriage and that they were headed to Woolsey. There was no other reason to be on that road at that time, for aside from everything else, no one traveled to Barking at night and no one *ever* traveled to Barking *at speed.*

"Oh, my goodness." Lady Maccon had the most uncomfortable feeling that she had lost some of her legendary control, over the physical, if not the mental. A wet sensation in her lower area indicated that her bustle, and quite possibly the rest of her dress, really was not going to survive this night. Then came that wavelike feeling again, starting at the top of her stomach and working its way down.

Dr. Caedes, who wasn't a real doctor, was nevertheless perceptive enough to see that the tenor of Lady Maccon's distress had changed.

"Lady Maccon, have you commenced? That would be most unfortunate timing."

Alexia frowned. "No, I absolutely forbid it. I will not— Oooh." She ended on a groan.

"I believe you have."

Quesnel perked up at this. "Bully! I've never seen a birth before." He turned big lavender eyes onto the now-sweating Lady Maccon.

"You're not going to tonight, either, young man," Alexia reprimanded between puffs of breath.

The countess, who was still twitchy as all get out and only partly paying attention to any conversation, looked with bright suspicious eyes at Alexia. "You can't. Not while I am here with you. What if *it* comes out and we have to touch it? Dr. Caedes, throw her out of the carriage at once."

Even with the strange wave sensation and a burgeoning pain, Alexia was quick enough to reach into her reticule and pull out Ethel before Dr. Caedes could stop her.

Not that he tried. Instead, he attempted to reason with the countess. "We can't, my queen. We need her to get us inside the house. She is our invitation."

Lady Maccon felt compelled to add, "And this is *my* carriage! If anyone is getting out, it's you!" She felt an additional downward pressure from the child inside her. "No, not *you*!" Then she looked wildly around. "This is not allowed," she said in a blanket kind of way, including both the imminent baby, the vampires, Quesnel, and the octomaton. She looked down at her belly. "I will not begin our relationship with disobedience. I get enough of *that* from your father."

The countess looked like she had eaten something foul, like a piece of fresh fruit. "I cannot be in proximity to an abomination! Do you know what might transpire?"

Now, this form of panic could be useful. "No, why don't you enlighten me?"

Too late. A crushing, grinding noise came from behind them. Alexia had no idea what the octomaton was up to, but when she stuck her head out of the window, she saw it was no longer following them. The carriage had turned off the main track, into the long weaving roadway that wended through Woolsey's grounds.

They were almost home.

Mere moments later, a tremendous crash came in front of them and the carriage slewed to one side and came to a rocking halt. Out of the window Alexia could see Woolsey just ahead atop its rise of ground, silvered under the moonlight, looking as though it had its own form of stone tentacles embodied in multiple flying buttresses.

It might as well have been a thousand leagues away, for the octomaton had felled a tree across the road before them. Lord Ambrose could not turn the carriage around, even if the high hedges permitted such a thing, for behind them the massive metal creature barred the way. The vampire escort, panting from their long run, instinctively formed a barrier before the coach, as though they could stop any attack by physically imposing themselves between the octomaton and their queen.

Alexia glanced around in desperation. She was among enemies, exhausted, and about to give birth. She was running out of options and would have to trust one of the vampires. Opening the carriage door, she yelled at the vanguard, "Your Grace, I have a proposition for you."

The Duke of Hematol turned to face her.

"We need some help, and we need a distraction if we are to make our destination."

"What do you suggest, Lady Maccon?"

"That we call out the hounds."

"And how do we do that? You definitely can't run to the castle from here, none of us can carry you to Woolsey, and no claviger will take the word of a vampire messenger."

"Listen to me. You tell them that Lady Maccon says it is *a matter of urgency*. The Alpha female requires her pack to attend her, regardless of their current state." *I will have to change the secret phrase now.*

"But—"

"It will work. You must trust me." She wasn't certain, of course. *A matter of urgency* was pack code for Lady Maccon acting as muhjah. She had rarely had to use the summons, and then only with a perfectly sane husband or Beta, never with only clavigers. Would the message even be understood?

The duke gave her one hard, long look. Then he whirled and ran, leaping the fallen tree with almost as much ease as a werewolf, heading directly for the castle, supernatural speed in full effect.

With one of their oldest and wisest gone and the great metal octopus looming above their unprotected queen, the vampires around Lady Maccon went ever so slightly insane themselves. Not as mad as the countess, but definitely wild. One of them charged the octomaton, only to be swept easily aside.

The metal creature raised up a tentacle to its eye slit,

once more opening the tip and flipping out the bullhorn that allowed Madame Lefoux to speak.

"Give me Quesnel. You are out of options." There came a short pause. "I can hardly believe it of you, Alexia, helping vampires. They tried to kill you!"

Alexia stuck her head out of the door-side window of the carriage and yelled back, "So? Recently, you also tried to kill me. In my experience, murder could almost be an expression of affection." It took an enormous effort to yell, and she fell back into the carriage, moaning and clutching at her stomach. She hated to admit it, even to herself, but Alexia Maccon was afraid.

Then came the noise, an eerie blessing of a sound, one that Alexia had grown to love very much over the past year or so.

Wolves. Howling.

CHAPTER SIXTEEN

A Clot of Vampires

The Woolsey Pack was a large collective, a good dozen strong. And a dozen werewolves is like two dozen regular wolves in size alone. Normally, they were also one of the better-behaved packs. When other packs were feeling snide, they called Woolsey *tame*. But no werewolf behaves himself on full moon.

Lady Maccon knew very well that she was taking a grave risk. She also knew her smell would attract her husband. Even in the throes of full-moon's curse, he would run to her. He might try to kill her, but he would come. He was Woolsey's Alpha for a reason, with enough charisma to hold his pack and drag them with him, no matter how strong the need to break away and trail blood and raw meat across the countryside. They would all follow him, which meant he would bring them all to her.

So it proved to be.

They poured out the lower doors and windows of the castle, howling to the skies. They evolved into a kind of cohesive moving liquid, flowing down the hillside as one silvered blob, like mercury on a scientist's palm. The howling became deafening as they neared, and they were swifter than Alexia remembered, full of eternal rage at a world that forced such a cost of immortality upon them. Any human would flee, and Alexia could see that even the vampires were tempted to run away from the massive supernatural force charging toward them.

At the front ran the biggest of the lot, a brindled wolf with yellow eyes, intent on but one thing—a smell on the evening breeze. It was the scent of mate, and lover, and partner, and fear, and something new coming. Near to that, twining with it, was the scent of young boy, fresh meat to be consumed. Underneath was the smell of rotten flesh and old bloodlines—other predators invading his territory. Dominating it all was the odor of industry, a monstrous machine, another enemy.

Lady Maccon stepped out of the carriage and slammed the door behind her, placing herself before the boy and the queen, knowing that she would be the last possible defense, that if nothing else, she had her bare hands.

Her legs, however, refused to obey her. She found herself leaning against the door, wishing she had her parasol for leverage.

The pack was there. The blur of fur and teeth and tail

turned into individual wolves. Lord Conall Maccon came to a sliding halt before his wife.

Alexia never quite knew how to handle her husband when he was in such a state. There was nothing of the man she loved in those yellow eyes, not during full moon. Her only hope was that he would perceive the octomaton as more of a threat than the vampires. That his driving instinct would be to defend territory first and eat later, thus ignoring her and Quesnel, who represented fresh meat.

Her hope proved to be the case, for Conall's yellow eyes flashed once, almost human, and he lolled his tongue out at her. Then the pack turned in a body and launched itself at the octomaton. One wolf per tentacle, the remaining four at the neck. Supernatural teeth were guided by instinct toward joints and arteries, even if those joints were made of ball bearings and pulleys and those arteries hydraulic steam-powered cables.

Alexia could only watch, admiring the grace in their amazingly high leaps. She held Ethel in one hand, but the gun dangled uselessly. She was nowhere near good enough to hit even something the size of the octomaton without also risking a wolf. The vampires made no move to help. This might have been because they were afraid a werewolf would take this ill and start attacking them, or it might be because they were vampires.

Lady Maccon could make out some of the pack by their markings. There was Channing, easiest to spot because of his pure white coat; and Lyall, smaller than the rest and more nimble, almost vampirelike in his speed and dexterity; and Biffy, darkest of all the pack with his oxblood stomach fur, abandoned and utterly vicious in his movements. But Alexia's eye was ever drawn, again and again, to the brindled coat of the largest wolf as he leaped up and savaged some portion of the octomaton, landed, and then leaped again.

To have had any real effect, the wolves should have all concentrated on one tentacle together, or all gone for the neck, but they were moonstruck. Even under the best of circumstances, only a few werewolves fully retain their capacity for human intelligence while in wolf form. Full moon was not the best of circumstances.

The octomaton was built for many things but not, apparently, for a full-pack assault. True, it was well armored and mostly metal, but Madame Lefoux had not used any silver, so it was vulnerable, especially in such numbers. But the Frenchwoman was not remaining idle. Oh, no. Madame Lefoux had those vicious tentacles in play, spraying fire and shooting wooden stakes. Alexia knew it was only a matter of time before the inventor became desperate enough to once more bring out the tentacle that shot lapis solaris.

Then Lady Maccon caught sight of a white floating blob behind the top of the octomaton, sailing the aether breezes swiftly in her direction—a small private dirigible.

Another contraction hit her hard. Alexia doubled over and slid down the side of the carriage, slumping to the ground, leaving the door vulnerable to attack. It was the first time the wave sensation had actually hurt. Curling against the involuntary movements of her own body, she looked up and over to the east.

She couldn't help but cry out—not from the pain but from what she saw. There was a distinct pinking to the cold silvery blue of the night sky.

She had to get them all to the safety of the castle.

She looked to Lord Ambrose, now standing over her barring the door, defending his queen. "We must bring the creature down somehow, buy us enough time to get to Woolsey. *The sun is rising.*"

The vampire's eyes went black with fear. The sun would stop werewolves in their tracks, turning them back to human shape. It would slow some of the younger members, making them vulnerable, and it would do permanent damage to Biffy, who lacked the necessary control. But it would kill the vampires, every last one of them, even the queen.

Alexia thought of something. "Find me a litter, my lord."

"What, Lady Maccon?"

"Tear off the roof of the carriage or remove part of the driving box. With one vampire at either end, you could use it to carry me to Woolsey. No one would have to touch me; there would be no loss of strength. We could make a break for it."

"Strategic retreat. Excellent notion." He leaped atop the driver's box.

Lady Maccon heard a loud ripping noise.

Above, she saw a bright flash of orange light emanate from the side of the dirigible and a loud clang as a massive bullet hit and tore through the mantle of the octomaton. The creature lurched at the impact but did not fall.

Lord Akeldama had sent air support. Alexia had no idea what kind of weapon the drones had, possibly a tiny cannon, or an elephant gun, or an aethero-modified blunderbuss, but she didn't care. It fired again.

By the time the second projectile hit its mark, Lord Ambrose was back, as was the duke. They rested a wide board on the ground next to Alexia. She managed to slide and squirm her way onto it.

They lifted her up. The queen and Dr. Caedes, carrying Quesnel, leaped out of the top of the torn and burned carriage, jack-in-the-box-like, and took off toward Woolsey, jumping the felled tree. The countess looked particularly odd performing this maneuver with her flowered receiving gown and dumpy figure. Lady Maccon's vampire litter bearers followed. Alexia could do nothing more than grip the sides of the board, desperate not to tumble off. The leap over the fallen tree was pure torture, and she was convinced she would fall when they bumped down, but she managed to hold on.

The wolves were providing enough of a distraction so that Madame Lefoux in the octomaton did not at first see them break for the castle. By the time she did, sending flames blasting after them, they were well out of range.

There was no need to bang on Woolsey's main door; it was wide open, with many of the clavigers and household staff assembled on the front stoop, mouths agape. They had binoculars or glassicals pressed to their faces and were riveted by the battle below. At Lady Maccon's imperious wave, they made a corridor for the vampires to run through, right up to the entrance, at which point everyone stopped abruptly. They waited with a ritual solemnity uncalled for in such dire circumstances.

"What is it *now?*" Alexia was annoyed beyond all reason. She was carried right to the door, like a dressed pig on a dinner platter. *Any moment now,* she thought in a flight of fantasy, *Cook will appear with an apple to stuff into my mouth.*

Lord Ambrose rested the bottom of the board down and the duke tilted it up so that Lady Maccon had merely to slide gently to her feet, finding herself standing.

A quick gesture had her supported on both sides by two of Woolsey's largest clavigers. Thus she managed to hobble inside the entrance of her home.

Still the vampires waited on the front stoop, like some bizarre parody of orphaned puppies—soulful eyed, pathetically scruffy, deadly fanged, immortal orphaned puppies.

Lady Maccon turned ponderously. "Well?"

"Invite us in to stay, Alexia Maccon, Lady of Woolsey, mistress of this domicile." The countess's words were singsong and hymnlike. She clutched a wide-eyed, blubbering Quesnel tightly to her breast—no trace of the scamp left, just terrified boy.

"Oh, for goodness' sake, come in, come in." Alexia frowned, trying to think. They had a goodly number of rooms, but where would it be best to put a whole hive of vampires? She pursed her lips. "Best to get you lot down to the dungeon. It's the only place I can guarantee that there are absolutely no windows, and the sun *is* about to rise."

Rumpet came forward. "Lady Maccon, what have you done?"

The vampires traipsed solemnly into the house. Alexia pointed out the appropriate staircase and they filed wordlessly down.

"You have invited in a queen?" The butler, normally quite a florid man, was ashen.

"I have."

The Duke of Hematol gave her a tired smile as he passed, showing fang, acknowledging the butler's fear as his due. "We can never go back now, you realize, Lady Maccon? Once a queen swarms and relocates, it is forever."

Lady Maccon finally understood Lord Akeldama's smile and why he refused to invite the hive in for tea. Alexia had managed to get his greatest rival out of London, for good. Not only was he potentate, and in charge of his own ring of very specially trained young men, but also he would now be the sole leader of fashion left in central London.

And Lady Maccon was stuck with vampires in her basement. "Curses, I have been rather neatly played."

Another contraction hit her, and she had no more thought for her present domestic predicament. She suspected this was somewhat akin to the pain her husband felt upon changing shape.

Rumpet put out a hand to steady her. "My lady?"

"Rumpet, there is an octomaton on our doorstep."

"So I noticed, my lady. And half of BUR has just arrived as well."

Alexia looked. It was true. Several of BUR's human members, on the octomaton's trail out of London, had finally caught up. She thought she could see Haverbink's tall, strapping form. "Oh, God. The pack will turn on them, they're food." And even as she watched, one of the werewolves left off fighting Madame Lefoux's creature and charged one of the BUR agents. "We must protect them. Get the pack members back inside!"

"Indeed, madam."

"Call up the clavigers. Tell them to bring the necessary equipment and open the silver cabinet."

"Immediately, madam." The butler moved toward a nested triangular alcove formed by the staircase. Next to the large cowbell that he rang at mealtimes there dangled a silver chain. At the end of that chain was a silver key. Next to it was a special glass box containing a large horn. Rumpet broke the glass with one swift punch of his gloved hand. He placed the horn to his lips and blew.

Not the most dignified of sounds emanated forth, a kind of farting noise. But it rattled through the castle in a way that suggested the sound had been manufactured specifically to permeate rock. The clavigers instantly assembled around Rumpet in the hallway. Pack policy dictated that every pack member have at least two clavigers. Lord Maccon had six these days, and there were a few extras loitering about as well.

Rumpet used the key to open the silver cabinet, an old mahogany monstrosity that gave no clue as to its true contents. Inside, instead of the usual household valuables—candlesticks, baby spoons, and the like—was the claviger kit. Displayed in neat rows and on special hooks were silver manacles, enough pairs for every member of the pack; silver knives; a few precious bottles of lapis lunearis; and, most importantly, the fishing nets. These were spun of silver cord, weighted at the corners, and used to capture and weaken a wolf without damage. Dangling from little hooks in each door were fifty fine silver chains with fifty fine silver whistles.

The clavigers, grim-faced, armed themselves and took up the nets. Each put a whistle over his head. They were so high-pitched that no human ear could possibly make out the sound, but wolves and dogs were violently affected by the noise.

Alexia thought of something. "Try to bring in Biffy first. Remember he's still susceptible to pup-stage sun damage. Take care—he'll be the most vicious. Oh, my goodness, what will I say if he accidentally eats somebody?"

Six of the biggest and best clavigers ran to the stables, and Alexia heard the roaring sound of the steam-powered penny-farthing wagons starting. Two clavigers per wagon— one to steer and one to cast the net—they roared out and down the hillside, steam trailing in a white cloud behind them. The other clavigers ran after.

Lady Maccon witnessed very little of the battle after that. She leaned against Rumpet and tried to watch, but contractions kept distracting her, and the fighting below was nothing more to her unfocused mind than a puddinglike mass of clavigers, wolves, and steam from penny-farthings and an octomaton. Occasionally, a spurt of fire jetted into the air or a glittering waterfall of silver net was cast upward.

Eventually she gave up. "Rumpet, help me to the bottom of the stair." The butler did so, and Alexia sank gratefully down onto the steps of the grand staircase. "Now, please go down and ensure that the vampires are locked in. The last thing we need is them on the loose."

"At once, my lady."

Rumpet disappeared and returned later, grim-faced.

"That bad?"

"They are complaining about the accommodations and demanding feather pillows, my lady."

"Of course they are." Alexia doubled over in pain as another contraction ripped through her. Dimly, she saw Lord Akeldama's dirigible float in to a graceful landing in the front courtyard of Woolsey. Boots and the airship company leaped agilely out of the basket and lashed the craft to a hitching post.

The first set of clavigers returned at that point, dragging a netted wolf with the aid of a penny-farthing wagon. It took four of them to get him up the steps and into the castle, even with the silver net burning him into submission. It wasn't Biffy, but it looked to be one of the other youngsters, Rafe.

Alexia's attention was refocused into moaning as her pains became, if possible, worse. She looked for Rumpet, but he was busy supervising the unloading, seeing to it that the young wolf was dragged down into the dungeon and locked away. Alexia spared a moment to hope that all the vampires had gone into one of the cells together, or things were about to get very complicated, indeed.

"Conall!" she yelled through the pain, even knowing he

was in wolf form and that he would be the hardest to catch and the last to return home. "Where is he?" She was irrationally convinced that he should be with her right that very moment.

At which juncture, a wide, cool cloth was placed across her brow and a soft reliable voice said exactly the right thing. "Here, madam, drink this."

A cup was pressed against her lips and Alexia sipped. Strong, milky, and restorative, exactly how she liked it best. Tea.

She opened her eyes, previously screwed closed in anguish, to see the fine lined face of an elderly gentleman, nondescript and familiar. "Floote."

"Good evening, madam."

"Where did you come from?"

Floote gestured behind him where the dirigible was still visible through the open front door. Tizzy and Boots hovered in the doorway, looking at Alexia in horror and with an air that suggested they would rather be anywhere else but there.

"I caught a lift, madam."

"Eep!" squeaked Tizzy as he was pushed aside by another group of clavigers dragging another netted wolf home. *Hemming,* thought Alexia. *Had to be.* Only Hemming whined like that. They muscled their captive through the hallway and toward the dungeon stairs without need of an order from the panting and writhing Lady Maccon.

The previous group came back up, passing them on the stairs.

"Back out," ordered their Alpha female, "and concentrate on finding Biffy. The others can take the sun."

"I thought werewolves could withstand sunlight?" asked Boots.

Alexia moaned long and low before answering. "Yes. But not when still learning control."

"What'll happen to him if he doesn't make it in?"

Rumpet reappeared at that juncture. "Ah, Mr. Floote." He acknowledged his butler peer with a slight bow.

"Mr. Rumpet," replied Floote. And then, turning his attention back to Lady Maccon, "Now, madam, do concentrate and try to inhale deeply. Breathe through the pain."

Alexia glared at her butler. "Easy for you to say. Have you ever done this?"

"Certainly not, madam."

"Rumpet, did all the vampires get sorted?"

"Mostly, my lady."

"What do you mean, *mostly*?"

The conversation paused at that while everyone waited courteously for Lady Maccon to let out another part scream part howl of anger as the agony rippled through her body. They all pretended not to notice her thrashing. It was very polite of them.

"Well, a few of the vampires spread themselves about. So we'll have to put some of ours in with them."

"What's the world coming to? Vampires and werewolves sleeping together," quipped Alexia sarcastically.

One of the clavigers, a cheerful, freckled blighter who had performed Scottish ballads for the queen herself on more than one occasion, said, "It's quite sweet, really. They've snuggled up with each other."

"Snuggled? The wolf should be tearing the vampire apart."

"Not anymore, my lady. Look."

Alexia looked. The sun was up, its first rays cresting the horizon. It was going to be a bright, clear summer day. It was all too much, even for the most sensible preternatural. Lady Maccon panicked. "Biffy! Biffy's not yet inside! Quickly!" She gestured the clavigers. "Get me up. Get me out there. Get me to him! He could die!" Alexia was starting to cry, both from the pain and from the thought of poor young Biffy lying out there, burning alive.

"But, my lady, you're about to, well, uh, give birth!" objected Rumpet.

"Oh, that's not important. That can wait." Alexia turned. "Floote! Do something."

Floote nodded. He pointed to one of the clavigers. "You, do as she asks. Boots, you take the other side." He looked down at his mistress. Of course, Alessandro Tarabotti's daughter would be difficult. "Madam, whatever you do, don't push!"

"Bring blankets," yelled Lady Maccon at the remaining clavigers and Rumpet. "Rip those curtains down if you must. Most of the pack is out there naked! Oh, this is all so embarrassing."

Boots and the freckled claviger formed a kind of litter by linking their crossed arms and hoisted Lady Maccon up. She threw an arm around each, and the two young men part

ran and part stumbled their way back out the door and down
the seemingly endless hillside toward the carnage below.

The octomaton was down, the result of too many of its
tentacles torn off during battle. As she neared, Alexia
could see the now-naked bodies of the pack lying fallen—
bloodied, bruised, and burned. Scattered among them were
the severed tentacles of the octomaton plus some of its guts:
bolts, pulleys, and engine parts. Here and there, a claviger or
BUR member who hadn't moved fast enough was limping
or clutching at a wounded limb, but thankfully none of them
seemed seriously injured. The werewolves, on the other
hand, lay floppy and nonsensical, like so much fried fish.
Most of them looked like they were simply sound asleep, the
standard reaction to full-moon bone-benders. But none were
healing under the direct rays of the sun. Even immortality
had its limits.

Clavigers were running around covering the ones they
could with blankets and pulling others back toward the
house.

"Where's Biffy?" Alexia couldn't see him anywhere.

Then she realized there was someone else she couldn't
see, and her voice rose in terror to a near shriek. "Where's
Conall? Oh no, oh no, oh no." Alexia's commanding tone
turned into a chant of keening distress only offset by the
need to scream as another contraction hit her. She loved
Biffy dearly, but all her worry was now transferred to an
even more important love—her husband. *Was he injured?
Dead?*

The two young men carried her, tripping and faltering, in

and around the wreckage until, near the great metal bowler
hat that was the fallen head of the octomaton, an oasis of
calm awaited them.

Professor Lyall, wearing an orange velvet curtain wrapped
about him like a toga and still looking remarkably dignified,
was marshaling the troops and issuing orders.

Upon seeing the amazing vision of his Alpha female,
carried by two young men, in clear distress—both the lady
and the young men—wending toward him, he said, "Lady
Maccon?"

"Professor. Where is my husband? Where is Biffy?"

"Oh, of course, preternatural touch. Very good idea."

"Professor!"

"Lady Maccon, are you all right?" Professor Lyall moved
closer, inspecting her closely. "Have you *started*?" He
looked at Boots, who raised both eyebrows expressively.

"Where is Conall?" Alexia practically shrieked.

"He's fine, my lady. Perfectly fine. He took Biffy inside,
out of the sun."

"Inside?"

"Inside the octomaton. With Madame Lefoux. Once she
realized, she opened the hatch and let them in."

Lady Maccon swallowed down her fear, almost sick with
relief. "Show me."

Professor Lyall led them to the octomaton's head, around
one side, and then *rat-tat-tatted* on it diffidently. A door,
previously invisible it was so seamlessly integrated into the
octomaton's armor plating, popped open and Genevieve
Lefoux looked out.

Lady Maccon wished fervently at that moment that she had her parasol with her. She would have greeted the Frenchwoman with one very hard whack to the head, friend or no, for getting them all into such a pickle. Justified or not, the inventor had caused everybody a good deal of unnecessary bother.

"Professor Lyall. Yes?"

"Lady Maccon, to see her husband." The Beta stepped aside to allow the Frenchwoman to catch sight of the sweating and clearly distressed Alexia and her improvised transport.

"Alexia? Are you unwell?"

Alexia was quite definitely *at her limit.* "No, no, I am *not.* I have been gallivanting all over London chasing you or being chased by you. I have watched the city burn and the hive house collapse and have fallen out of a dirigible— *twice*! I am in imminent danger of giving birth. And I have *lost my parasol*!" This last was said on a rather childish wail.

A different voice came from inside—deep, commanding, and tinged with a Scottish accent. "That my wife? Capital. She's just the thing to get the pup his legs back."

Genevieve's head disappeared with an "oof" as though she had been dragged forcibly backward, and Lord Maccon's head emerged instead.

The earl was looking perfectly fine, if a little sleepy. Werewolves usually slept the full day through after a full moon. It was testament to both Conall's and Lyall's strength that they were up and moving, although both were rather clumsy about it. Conall described being awake the night after as akin to playing tiddlywinks, drunk, with a penguin—confusing and slightly dreamlike. His hair was wild and unkempt, and his tawny eyes were soft and buttery, mellowed by battle and victory.

He caught sight of his wife. "Ah, my love, get inside, would you? No way to get Biffy back to safety without your touch. Good of you to come. Interesting choice of transport."

At which juncture, his wife threw back her head and screamed.

Lord Conall Maccon's expression changed instantly to one of absolute panic and total ferocity. He charged out of the octomaton and bounded to his mate. He tossed poor Boots out of his way with a mere flick of the wrist and took Lady Maccon into his own arms.

"What's wrong? Are you— You canna! Now isna a good time!"

"Oh, no?" panted his wife. "Well, tell that to the child. This is all *your* fault, you do realize?"

"My fault, how could it possibly . . . ?"

He trailed off as a different howl of agony came from inside the octomaton's head and Madame Lefoux looked back out. "Young Biffy could use your presence, my lord."

The earl growled in annoyance and made his way over to the door. He shoved Alexia inside first, following after.

It was very cramped quarters. Madame Lefoux had designed the guidance chamber for only two occupants, herself and Quesnel. Lord Maccon accounted for about that number on his own, plus the pregnant Alexia, and Biffy sprawled on the floor.

It took a moment for Lady Maccon's eyes to adjust to the inner gloom, but she saw soon enough that Biffy was burned badly down one leg. Much of the skin was gone—blistered and blackened most awfully.

"Should I touch him? He might never heal."

Lord Maccon slammed the door closed against the wicked sun. "Blast it, woman, what possessed you to come down here in such a state?"

"How is Quesnel?" demanded Madame Lefoux. "Is he unharmed?"

"He's safe." Alexia did not mention he was currently locked in a dungeon with a vampire queen.

"Alexia"—Madame Lefoux clasped her hands together and opened her green eyes wide and looked pleading—"you know it was my only choice? You know I had to get him back. He's all I have. She stole him from me."

"And you couldn't come to me for help? Really, Genevieve, what kind of feeble friend do you take me for?"

"She has the law on her side."

Alexia clutched at her stomach and moaned. She was being flooded by the most overwhelming sensation—the need to push downward. "So?"

"You are muhjah."

"I might have been able to come up with a solution."

"I hate her more than anything. First she steals Angelique, and now Quesnel! What right has she to—"

"And your solution is to build a ruddy great octopus? Really, Genevieve, don't you think you might have overreacted?"

"The OBO is on my side."

"Oh, are they really? Now that *is* interesting. That plus taking in former Hypocras members?" Alexia was momentarily distracted by the need to give birth. "Oh, yes, husband, I meant to tell you this. It seems the OBO is developing an antisupernatural agenda. You might want to look into—" She broke off to let out another scream. "My goodness, that *is* uncommonly painful."

Lord Maccon turned ferocious yellow eyes on the inventor. "Enough. She has other things to attend to."

Genevieve looked closely at Alexia. "True, that does seem to be the case. My lord, have you ever delivered a baby before?"

The earl paled as much as was possible, which was a good deal more than normal given he was holding on to his wife's hand. "I delivered a litter of kittens once."

The Frenchwoman nodded. "Not quite the same thing. What about Professor Lyall?"

Lord Maccon looked wild-eyed. "Mostly sheep, I think."

Alexia looked up between contractions. "Were you there when Quesnel was born?"

The Frenchwoman nodded. "Yes, but so was the midwife. I think I remember the principles, and, of course, I've read a good deal on the subject."

Alexia relaxed slightly. Books always made her feel better. Another wave washed through her and she cried out.

Lord Maccon looked sternly at Madame Lefoux. "Make it stop!"

Both women ignored him.

A polite tap came at the door. Madame Lefoux cracked it open.

Floote stood there, his back stiff, his expression one of studied indifference. "Clean cloth, bandages, hot water, and tea, madam." He passed the necessities in.

"Oh, thank you, Floote." The Frenchwoman took the items gratefully. After a moment's thought, she rested them on top of the comatose Biffy, since he was the only vacant surface. "Any words of advice?"

"Madam, sometimes even I am out of options."

"Very good, Floote. Keep the tea coming."

"Of course, madam."

Which was why, some six hours later, Alexia Maccon's daughter was born inside the head of an octomaton in the presence of her husband, a comatose werewolf dandy, and a French inventor.

CHAPTER SEVENTEEN

In Which We All Learn a
Little Something About Prudence

L ater on, Lady Maccon was to describe that particular
day as the worst of her life. She had neither the soul
nor the romanticism to consider childbirth magical or emotionally transporting. So far as she could gather, it mostly
involved pain, indignity, and mess. There was nothing
engaging or appealing about the process. And, as she told her
husband firmly, she intended never to go through it again.

Madame Lefoux acted as midwife. In her scientific way,
she was unexpectedly adept at the job. When the infant
finally appeared, she held it up for Alexia to see, rather
proudly as though she'd done all the hard work herself.

"Goodness," said an exhausted Lady Maccon, "are babies
customarily that repulsive looking?"

Madame Lefoux pursed her lips and turned the infant

about, as though she hadn't quite looked closely before. "I assure you, the appearance improves with time."

Alexia held out her arms—her dress was already ruined anyway—and received the pink wriggling thing into her embrace. She smiled up at her husband. "I told you it would be a girl."

"Why isna she crying?" complained Lord Maccon. "Shouldna she be crying? Aren't all bairns supposed to cry?"

"Perhaps she's mute," suggested Alexia. "Be a sensible thing with parents like us."

Lord Maccon looked properly horrified at the idea.

Alexia grinned even more broadly as she came to a wonderful realization. "Look! I'm not repelled by her. No feelings of revulsion at all. She must be human, not a preternatural. How marvelous!"

A tap came at the octomaton door.

"Yes?" Lord Maccon sung out. He'd decided to stop worrying about the child and was crouched down cooing over her and making silly faces.

Professor Lyall looked in. He'd apparently found the time to change out of the improvised toga and into perfectly respectable attire. He caught sight of his Alpha, who looked up and beamed proudly.

"Randolph, I have a daughter!"

"Felicitations, my lord, my lady."

Alexia nodded politely from her makeshift bed in the corner of the octomaton, only then noticing that she was resting against a pile of cords and springs, and there was some kind of valve digging into the small of her back. "Thank you, Professor. And it would appear that she is not a curse-breaker."

The Beta looked over at the child with a flash of academic interest but no real surprise. "She isn't? I thought preternaturals always breed true."

"Apparently not."

"Well, that is good news. However, and I do hate to interrupt the blessed event, but, my lord, we have several difficulties at the moment that could very much use your attention. Do you think we might repair to a more hospitable venue?"

Lord Maccon crouched over his wife and nuzzled her neck gently. "My dear?"

Alexia stroked his hair back from the temple with her free hand. "I'll give it a try. I would dearly love to be in my own bed."

Lady Maccon had to hold on to both her newborn child and Biffy as Lord Maccon carried her and Professor Lyall carried Biffy back up to the castle. At which juncture Conall declared that Woolsey *smelled rotten*.

Professor Lyall opened his mouth to explain but caught a sharp look from Alexia. So he refrained.

Predicting that his Alpha would find out soon enough on his own, the Beta carried Biffy down to a cell, tended to the pup's still-angry burns with a pat of butter, and chivied him in with the Duke of Hematol as the best of a bad lot of options.

Upstairs it was decided that Madame Lefoux should also be locked up.

"Put her into the one next to the countess and Quesnel," suggested Lady Maccon snidely to her confused husband. "Now, there will be an interesting conversation come nightfall."

"The countess? Countess who?"

Alexia contemplated letting Quesnel out—after all, the boy hadn't done anything wrong—but from previous experience, she saw no reason why having him underfoot might improve matters. Quesnel was an agent of chaos even at the best of times, and life was busy enough without his *help*. Plus, she suspected the best thing for him at the moment was some time with his maman.

"But I just delivered your child!" protested Madame Lefoux.

"And very grateful I am, too, Genevieve." Alexia was always one to give credit where it was due. "However, you rampaged through the streets of London in a massive octopus, and you are going to have to pay for your crimes."

"Preternaturals!" exclaimed the Frenchwoman, disgusted.

"At least this way you are near your boy. He was terribly upset by the attack," yelled Lady Maccon as her husband hauled the struggling inventor away.

Which was when Lord Maccon discovered the reason behind the funny smell. He had a hive of vampires living in his castle.

He came back upstairs fit to be pickled. "Wife!"

Lady Maccon had vanished.

"Floote!"

"She's gone upstairs, sir. To your chambers."

"Of course she has."

Lord Maccon stormed upstairs to find his wife abed, the

babe asleep in the crook of one arm. The child had already proved herself perfectly capable of sleeping through both her mother's and her father's vocal exertions. *A very good survival trait,* thought Alexia, wincing as Conall clomped into the room.

"There are *vampires* in my dungeon!"

"Yes, well, where else was I supposed to stash them?"

"The countess swarmed?" The earl leaped to the only possible conclusion. "And you invited them in? *Here*?"

Alexia nodded.

"Great. Wonderful! Brilliant."

Lady Maccon sighed, a kind of sad, quiet noise that calmed Lord Maccon where her yelling would only have aggravated matters. "I can explain."

Conall came to kneel next to the bed, his anger dissipated by her uncharacteristic meekness. His wife must be very tired.

"Very well, explain."

Alexia relayed the events of the night, and by the time she reached the concluding pack-versus-octomaton battle, she was yawning hugely.

"What are we going to do now?" wondered her husband. Even saying it, Alexia could tell from his defeated expression that he was already facing up to the truth—for better or worse, Woolsey Castle now belonged to the Westminster Hive. Or rather, the Woolsey Hive.

Alexia saw him blink back tears and felt her heart clench. She hadn't meant to make such a grave error in judgment, but the deed was done. Her own eyes stung in sympathy.

He nodded. "I rather loved this old place, buttresses and all. But it hasna been my home all that long. I can break from it. The rest of the pack, they are going to be difficult. Ach, my poor pack. I've nae served them verra well these last few months."

"Oh, Conall, it's not your fault! Please don't worry. I'll think of something. I always do." Alexia wanted to find a solution right then and there just to wipe that horrible expression of disappointment off her husband's sweet face, but she could hardly keep her eyes open.

The earl bent and pressed a kiss to his wife's lips and then to his daughter's little forehead. Alexia suspected he was contemplating going back downstairs to check in with Lyall, as there was still a lot to be done that afternoon.

"Come to bed," said his wife.

"You two ladies do look verra peaceful. Perhaps just a little kip."

"Lyall has both Floote and Rumpet helping him. They could run the empire, those three, if they felt like it."

Lord Maccon chuckled and crawled in on Alexia's other side, settling his big body down into the feather mattress.

Alexia sighed contentedly and nestled against him, curled about the baby.

He snuffled once at the nape of her neck. "We need to find a name for the wee one."

"Mmm?" was his wife's only answer.

"I'm nae certain that's a verra good name."

"Mmm."

*　　*　　*

"Sorry to disturb you, my lord, but the vampires are asking for you." Professor Lyall's voice was quiet and apologetic.

Alexia Maccon came awake with a start to the feel of her husband shifting behind her. He was evidently trying to extract himself from the bed without disturbing her. Poor man, stealth of movement was not one of his stronger character traits. Not in human form at any rate.

"What time is it, Randolph?"

"Just after sunset, my lord. I thought it best to let you sleep the remainder of the day away."

"Oh, yes? And have you been awake the whole time?"

Silence met that.

"Ah. Right. You tell me the lay of the fur, Randolph, and then you go catch some rest."

Alexia heard a faint howling. The younger werewolves, still unable to control change so close to full moon, were back in their fur and imprisoned below for another night. Locked away with vampires.

"Who is seeing to them?" asked the earl as he, too, registered the sound.

"Channing, my lord."

"Oh, blast." All pretense at subtlety abandoned, Lord Maccon jumped out of bed.

This jiggled the baby. A thin, querulous wail started up from just under Alexia's chin. She started violently, for she had, until that moment, entirely forgotten about the child. Her child.

She opened her eyes and looked down. Half a day's intermittent rest had not improved the infant's appearance. She was red and wrinkly, and her face got all scrunched up when she cried.

Conall, obviously still under the impression that Alexia was asleep, hurried around the bed and scooped the tiny creature up. The whining turned to a little snuffling howl, and there in his arms, instead of a child, lay a newborn wolf cub.

Lord Maccon nearly dropped his daughter. "God's teeth!"

Alexia sat up, not quite comprehending what she had just seen. "Conall, where's the baby?"

Her husband, mute in shock, proffered the cub at her.

"What have you done to her?"

"Me? Nothing. I simply picked her up. She was perfectly normal and then *poof.*"

"Well, she's unquestionably cuter in that form." Alexia was prosaic.

"Here, you take her." Lord Maccon put the squalling furry cub back into his wife's arms.

At which juncture she promptly turned back into a baby. Alexia could feel the bone and flesh shifting under the swaddling clothes. It seemed to be relatively painless, for the infant's cries did not modulate to those of real distress.

"Oh, my." Alexia thought she sounded rather sedate, under the circumstances. "What *have* we gotten ourselves into?"

Professor Lyall's voice was awed. "Never thought I'd live to see a real skin-stalker born in my lifetime. Amazing."

"Is that what it means?" Alexia looked down at the child. "How extraordinary."

Professor Lyall smiled. "I guess it must. So, what's her name, my lady?"

Alexia frowned. "Oh, yes, *that*."

Lord Maccon grinned, looking down at his wife. "With us for parents, we ought to call her Prudence."

Lady Maccon, however, did not seem to share the joke. "Actually, I rather like that. How about Prudence Alessandra, after my father? And then Maccon, because when Lord Akeldama adopts her, she's going to be an Akeldama."

Lord Maccon looked down at his daughter. "Poor little thing. That's a lot of names to live up to."

"My lord," interjected his Beta, "not that I don't see the importance of this particular matter, but can it wait? Biffy could use your proximity. And the vampires are kicking up quite the fuss. We've no justification for keeping them locked in the dungeon. What are we going to do about them?"

Lord Maccon sighed. "Sadly, it's not them we have to find what to do with—it's us. We can't stay living here, not with a hive in residence as well, and they can't leave. Not now. When you invited the countess in, Alexia, you gave them Woolsey Castle."

"Oh, no, surely not."

Professor Lyall sat down in a nearby chair. Alexia had never seen him look defeated before, but at that moment, Woolsey's Beta looked as close to crushed as any man she'd ever seen.

Lord Maccon looked grim. "Nothing else for it. We'll have to move the pack permanently into London. We will need to buy a second town house to accommodate us all and build dungeons."

Professor Lyall protested this decision. "Where will we run? How will we hunt? My lord, there is no such thing as an urban pack!"

"This is the age of industry, invention, and refined behavior. I suppose Woolsey really will have to learn to move with the times and become civilized." Lord Maccon was resolved.

Alexia looked at her child. "It would only be for sixteen years or so. Until Prudence is grown. Then we could look for a new territory. Sixteen years isn't all that long for a werewolf."

Professor Lyall did not look cheered by this shortening of his urban sentence. "The pack is not going to like this."

"I have made my decision," said his Alpha.

"The queen is not going to like this."

"We'll just have to persuade her it's in the best interest of the Crown."

"I think that's a very good idea," said Countess Nadasdy, entering the room at that moment, followed by Quesnel and Madame Lefoux.

Well, Alexia supposed, *it's her room now.*

"How did you three get out?" griped Professor Lyall.

The countess gave him a withering look. "Did you think I was queen of the vampires for nothing? We are the original inventors of the idea of a mistress of the domain. This is now my domain. No cell in all of Woolsey will hold me for long."

"Pish tosh. She can pick locks." Madame Lefoux crossed her arms and looked at the vampire queen witheringly.

"It was marvelous," added Quesnel, who seemed to be regarding Countess Nadasdy with real respect for the first time.

The countess ignored the Frenchwoman and her child and gave Alexia's baby a wary look. "Just keep that *thing* away from me."

Alexia rocked the newborn at her threateningly. "You mean this dangerous vampire-eating creature?"

The countess hissed and backed away, as though Alexia might throw baby Prudence at her.

Madame Lefoux wended her way to Lady Maccon's bedside to coo over the infant.

Countess Nadasdy said, "Woolsey is ours now, unfortunately. It is hardly to be countenanced. Me living near *Barking* in the *countryside*. Why, it is positively leagues away from everywhere."

Lord Maccon did not protest her claim. "We will need a few days to clear out. The youngsters of the pack can't be moved until the moon fades."

"Take all the time you need," said the vampire queen magnanimously. "But the soul-sucker and her abomination of a child must leave tonight." She twirled toward the door dramatically and then paused on the threshold. "And the boy is mine."

With that, she swept out, presumably to release the rest of her hive. "Oh," Alexia heard her say to no one in particular as she walked down the stairs, "simply *everything* will have to be redecorated! And those buttresses!"

Madame Lefoux stayed behind. She looked worn and tired from the events of the night before, not to mention her own trials. Quesnel was practically stuck to her side, his grubby little hand entwined with hers. Madame Lefoux had grease stains on her fingertips and a smudge on her chin.

"You can't let her take him away from me." The French-woman appealed to the assembled dignitaries with anguished green eyes. "Please."

Now, Alexia's subconscious had apparently given this conundrum some thought while she dozed. For a solution instantly proposed itself. "Speaking as muhjah, there is nothing we can legally do to remove him from the hive. If Angelique's testament is as they say, and you never formally adopted Quesnel under British law, then her claim is valid and legally recognized in this country."

Madame Lefoux nodded morosely.

Alexia pursed her lips. "You know vampires and solici-tors—practically indistinguishable. I'm sorry, Genevieve, but Quesnel belongs with Countess Nadasdy now."

Quesnel gave a little whimper at that statement. Madame Lefoux clutched him to her and looked wild-eyed at Lord Maccon. As though, somehow, he might save her.

Alexia continued. "Now, before you go off and build a gigantic squid, I should tell you that I also intend to give *you* to Countess Nadasdy, Genevieve."

"What!"

"It is the only viable solution." Alexia wished she had a judge's wig and a mallet, for she felt like she'd done rather well with this verdict. "Quesnel is what, ten? He comes into his majority at age sixteen. So, with Countess Nadasdy's approval—and I hardly think she'll object—you will serve as drone to the Westminster Hive for the next six years. Or, I should say, the *Woolsey Hive*. I can make a case with the queen and the countess not to press charges if such an indenture could be arranged instead. Given your distaste for the hive, this should be a rather fitting punishment. And you get to stay with Quesnel."

"Ah," said her husband proudly, "good plan. If we cannot bring Quesnel to Madame Lefoux, we bring Madame Lefoux to Quesnel."

"Thank you, my dear."

"This is a *terrible* idea!" wailed Madame Lefoux.

Alexia ignored this. "I suggest you take over Professor Lyall's sheep-breeding shed for your contrivance chamber. It is already rather well equipped and could easily be expanded."

"But—" protested Madame Lefoux.

"You can think of a better solution?"

"But I *hate* Countess Nadasdy."

"I suspect you have that in common with most of her drones and some of her vampires. I will have Floote draw up the necessary documentation and make the legal arrangements. Look on the bright side, Genevieve. At least you can temper the hive's influence over Quesnel. He will still have his maman to teach him how to make things explode and all the wisdom of the vampires at his fingertips."

Quesnel looked up at his mother, his big violet eyes pleading. "Please, Maman. I like to explode things!"

Madame Lefoux sighed. "I have gotten myself neatly
enmeshed, haven't I?"

"Yes, you have."

"Do you think the countess will approve such a bargain?"

"Why shouldn't she? She gets patronage, patent, and
control over your inventions for the next six years. Quesnel
stays with you both. Plus, think of the havoc Quesnel could
cause living in a hive house! Keep them all on their toes and
out of London politics for a while."

Madame Lefoux brightened slightly at that suggestion.

Quesnel's face lit up. "No more boarding school?"

Professor Lyall frowned. "This shifts England's vampire
power structures significantly."

Alexia grinned. "Lord Akeldama thought he'd have Lon-
don under his purview. I am merely balancing the scales.
Now my pack will be living in his territory full-time, and
Countess Nadasdy has Madame Lefoux working for her."

Professor Lyall stood, still looking a little sad. "You are a
very good muhjah, aren't you, Lady Maccon?"

"I like to be tidy about it. While we are on the subject,
Madame Lefoux, when you have cleared out your contrivance chamber, I thought that might be a good space for us to
build the pack a London dungeon."

Lord Maccon grinned. "It's big enough, and underground,
and easy to secure. An excellent idea, my love."

Madame Lefoux looked resigned. "And the hat shop?"
Even though the shop had been a front to cover over her

more nefarious dealings, she'd always had an affection for the establishment.

Alexia cocked her head. "I thought Biffy might do. You remember, my dear, we discussed that he was in great need of useful employment, and such a venture might suit him better than a position at BUR."

This time it was Professor Lyall who smiled in approval. "Wonderful notion, Lady Maccon."

"My darling wife," said Lord Maccon, "you think of everything."

Alexia blushed at the compliment. "I try."

So it was that the werewolf pack formerly of Woolsey Castle became the first ever to claim an urban hunting ground. In the late summer of 1874, they officially changed their name to the London Pack and took up residence next door to the rove vampire and potentate, Lord Akeldama. Where they kept their full-moon dungeon no one knew, but it was noted with interest that the new pack seemed to have developed a keen interest in lady's headgear.

It was a landmark summer so far as the tattle-mongers were concerned. Even the most conservative of the daylight folk took interest in the doings of the supernatural set, for the werewolf relocation was but the half of it. The Westminster Hive, having swarmed for the only time in recorded history, relocated to the countryside and changed its name to Woolsey. No one dared comment on the unfashionable choice. It was immediately suggested the government build a train track between the hive's new location and London. Even though Countess Nadasdy herself could not live at the heart of style, at least style could visit the countess. Protective measures were put into place and the vampires seemed to feel that isolation balanced out a known location.

The scandal rags were delighted by the entire ruckus, including the carnage caused throughout the city on that full-moon night by what was reputed to be a massive mechanical octopus. The hive house destroyed! The Pantechnicon burned to the ground! Indeed, there was so much of interest to report that a few key elements escaped the press. The fact that Chapeau de Poupe changed proprietors went unremarked upon except by such true hat aficionados as Mrs. Ivy Tunstell. The fact that the Woolsey Hive gained a very prestigious and highly valuable new drone escaped all but the scientific community's notice.

"Very, very nicely played, *my little plum pudding*," was Lord Akeldama's comment to Lady Maccon a few evenings later. He was carrying a paper in one hand and his monocle in the other.

Alexia looked up from where she sat in her bed. "You didn't think I would let you get away with everything, did you?"

He was visiting her in his third-best closet. Lady Maccon preferred to remain in bed for the time being. She was feeling a good deal recovered from her ordeal, but she felt she ought to lie low for a while. If people knew she was back in form, she might have to attend a meeting of the Shadow

Council, and the queen was reputed to be *not amused* by all the kerfuffle. Also there was Felicity to consider.

"And where is *my* lovely Biffy?" wondered the vampire.

Alexia clucked at her baby and jiggled the girl up and down a bit. Prudence gurgled good-naturedly and then spit up. "Ah, he has taken charge of Madame Lefoux's hat shop. He always did have a remarkably good eye. "

Lord Akeldama looked wistful. "Trade? Indeed?"

"Yes, it's proving to be a mellowing influence. And an excellent distraction." By the time Alexia had wiped the baby's chin with a handkerchief, the infant was fast asleep.

"Ah." The monocle twirled, wrapping itself around Lord Akeldama's finger until the chain was too short, at which point it began swinging in the opposite direction.

"You didn't actually want him to pine away and die, did you?"

"Well…"

"Oh, you are *impossible.* Come over here and hold your adopted daughter."

Lord Akeldama grinned and minced over to the side of the bed to scoop up the slumbering baby. So far Prudence was proving to be an unexpectedly docile child.

The vampire cooed over her in quite an excessive way, telling her how beautiful she was and what fun they were going to have shopping together, until he interrupted his own litany of italicized praise with an exclamation of discovery.

"Would you *look at that!*"

"What? What is it now?" Alexia leaned up in bed on one elbow.

Lord Akeldama tilted the child in her direction. Prudence Alessandra Maccon Akeldama had developed porcelain-white skin and a perfect set of tiny little fangs.

Acknowledgments

Sometimes the necessaries are not something that can be researched. With grateful thanks to those who, wittingly or unwittingly, found themselves tutoring my madness: Mom for the holly; Willow for the dates; Rachel my mistress of the emotional red herring; Erin coma goddess; the Iz of continuity; and Phrannish the best wing-chick evah!

extras

orbit

meet the author

New York Times bestselling author Gail Carriger writes to cope with being raised in obscurity by an expatriate Brit and an incurable curmudgeon. She escaped small-town life and inadvertently acquired several degrees in Higher Learning. Ms. Carriger then traveled the historic cities of Europe, subsisting entirely on biscuits secreted in her handbag. She resides in the Colonies, surrounded by fantastic shoes, where she insists on tea imported from London.

The Parasol Protectorate books are: *Soulless*, *Changeless*, *Blameless*, *Heartless*, and *Timeless*. *Soulless* won the ALA's Alex Award. A manga adaptation released in Spring 2012 and a young adult series set in the same universe—the Finishing School series—launched in Spring 2013. Gail is soon to begin writing a new adult series, The Custard Protocol (2015).

bonus material

A Very Alexia Christmas

Miss Tarabotti, as some of you may well know, is rather fond of comestibles. Thusly, the holiday season is one of great joy to her, from a food standpoint if nothing else. (The shopping, it must be admitted, she could very much do without. Her sisters are overly enthusiastic on the subject.) However, she has some tips for coping with the holidays Victorian-style.

1. Mincemeat pie. Sounds awful, looks revolting, tastes spectacular. The Americans have sadly neglected this part of their British heritage but there is much to be said for meat soaked in alcohol and then encased in pastry. If unwilling to venture in the mincemeat direction, how about exploring the fine art of Christmas pudding? (AKA plum pudding and no, there are no plums involved; don't ask.) A dense, fruity cake that is covered in alcohol and then set on fire. Fantastic.

2. Cloth-wrapped presents. Instead of paper, why not invest in some fabric remnants from a craft shop or colorful little scarves and then tie with a ribbon? All the fun of unwrapping, none of the waste, and perhaps it will encourage others to reuse as well. As an added bonus, cloth wrappers

can be used as emergency clean-up towels for the inevitable alcohol-related spill (see: inebriation caused by overconsumption of Christmas pudd, above.)

3. Roast goose. Benefits? Well, a goose is bigger than a turkey and more mean-spirited. Have you ever met a goose? The only bird nastier is a swan and, unfortunately, they are protected by Queen Victoria. Thus goose consumption gives one a sense of self-righteousness and satisfaction all rolled into one.

4. Frills and lace. Perhaps not a particular favorite amongst gentlemen for themselves (unless one is of a Lord Akeldama inclination) but for the ladies...Donning a pretty frock and perhaps a corset is bound to make one feel better ‒ a little constricted but definitely better. On the other hand nothing, I am convinced of this, is funnier than a werewolf with a doily on his head.

5. Which brings us back around to drinkies. Lord Akeldama suggests a Pink Slurp (champagne & blood), but he's a vampire and they have questionable palates. Alexia recommends substituting blackberry cordial for the blood, resulting in a truly excellent and festive drink. Alternatively, for those particularly cold nights, one might opt for mulled wine, which can be a most excellent way to disguise the quality of one's vino.

Bottoms up!

If you enjoyed this bonus material, check out orbitbooks.net and gailcarriger.com for more urban fantasy blog posts.

introducing

**If you enjoyed
HEARTLESS,
look out for**

TIMELESS

The Parasol Protectorate: Book the Fifth

by Gail Carriger

CHAPTER ONE

———

In Which There Is Almost a Bath and Definitely a Trip to the Theater

"I said no such thing," grumbled Lord Maccon, allowing himself, begrudgingly, to be trussed in a new evening jacket. He twisted his head around, annoyed by the height of the collar and the tightness of the cravat. Floote patiently waited for him to stop twitching before continuing with the jacket. Werewolf or not, Lord Maccon would look his best or Floote's given name wasn't Algernon—which it was.

"Yes, you did, my dear." Lady Alexia Maccon was one of the few people in London who dared contradict Lord Maccon. Being his wife, it might be said that she rather specialized in doing so. Alexia was already dressed, her statuesque form resplendent in a maroon silk and black lace evening gown with mandarin collar and Asian sleeves, newly arrived from Paris. "I remember it quite distinctly." She pretended distraction in transferring her necessaries into a black beaded reticule. "I said we should show our patronage and support on opening night, and you *grunted* at me."

"Well, there, that explains everything. That was a grunt of displeasure." Lord Maccon wrinkled his nose like a petulant child while Floote skirted about him, puffing away nonexistent crumbs with the latest in steam-controlled air-puffing dewrinklers.

"No, dear, no. It was definitely one of your affirmative grunts."

Conall Maccon paused at that and gave his wife a startled look. "God's teeth, woman, how could you possibly tell?"

"Three years of marriage, dear. Regardless, I've replied in the affirmative that we will be in attendance at the Adelphi at nine sharp in time to take our box. We are *both* expected. There is no way out of it."

Lord Maccon sighed, giving in. Which was a good thing, as his wife and Floote had managed to strap him into full evening dress and there was no way to escape that.

In a show of solidarity, he grabbed his wife, pulling her against him and snuffling her neck. Alexia suppressed a smile and, in deference to Floote's austere presence, pretended not to enjoy herself immensely.

"Lovely dress, my love, very flattering."

Alexia gave her husband a little ear nibble for this compliment. "Thank you, my heart. However, you ought to know that the most interesting thing about this dress is how remarkably easy it is to get into and out of."

Floote cleared his throat to remind them of his presence.

"Wife, I intend to test the veracity of that statement when we return from this outing of yours."

Alexia pulled away from Conall, patting at her hair self-consciously. "Thank you kindly, Floote. Very well done as always. I'm sorry to have drawn you away from your regular duties."

The elderly butler merely nodded, expressionless. "Of course, madam."

"Especially as there seem to be no drones about. Where are they all?"

The butler thought for a moment and then said, "I believe that it is bath night, madam."

Lady Maccon paled in horror. "Oh, goodness. We had best escape quickly, then, Conall, or I'll never be able to get away in time for—"

Clearly summoned by her fear of just such a delay, a knock sounded at Lord Akeldama's third closet door.

How Lord and Lady Maccon had come to be residing in Lord Akeldama's third closet in the first place was a matter of some debate among those privy to this information. A few speculated that there had been a negotiated exchange of spats and possibly promises of daily treacle tart. Nevertheless, the arrangement seemed to be working remarkably well for all parties, much to everyone's bemusement, and so long as the vampire hives did not find out, it was likely to remain so. Lord Akeldama now had a preternatural in his closet and a werewolf pack next door, but he and his drones had certainly weathered much worse in the way of neighbors, and he had certainly housed far more shocking things in his closet, if the rumors were to be believed.

extras

For nigh on two years, Lord and Lady Maccon had maintained the appearance of actually living next door, Lord Akeldama maintained the appearance of still utilizing all his closets, and his drones maintained the appearance of not having full creative control over everyone's wardrobe. Most importantly, as it turned out, Alexia was still close enough to her child to come to everyone's rescue. Unforeseen as it may have been when they originally concocted the arrangement, it had become increasingly clear that the home of a metanatural required the presence of a preternatural or no one was safe—particularly on bath night.

Lady Maccon opened the closet door wide and took in the sorry sight of the gentleman before her. Lord Akeldama's drones were men of fashion and social standing. They set the mode for all of London with regards to collar points and spats. The handsome young man who stood before her represented the best London society had to offer—an exquisite plum tailcoat, a high-tied waterfall of white about his neck, his hair curled just so about the ears—except that he was dripping with soap suds, his neck cloth was coming untied, and one collar point drooped sadly.

"Oh, dear, what has she done now?"

"Far too much to explain, my lady. I think you had better come at once."

Alexia looked down at her beautiful new dress. "But I do so like this gown."

"Lord Akeldama accidentally touched her."

"Oh, good gracious!" Lady Maccon seized her parasol and her beaded reticule—now containing a fan; her opera glassicals; and Ethel, her .28-caliber Colt Paterson revolver—and charged down the stairs after the drone. The poor boy actually squelched in his beautifully shined shoes.

Her husband, with a grumbled, "Didn't we warn him against that?" came crashing unhelpfully after.

Downstairs, Lord Akeldama had converted a side parlor into a bathing chamber for his adopted daughter. It had become clear rather early on that bathing was going to be an event of epic proportions, requiring a room large enough to accommodate several of his best and most capable drones. Still, this being Lord Akeldama, even a room dedicated to the cleanliness of an infant was not allowed to be sacrificed upon the unadorned altar of practicality.

A thick Georgian rug lay on the floor covered with cavorting shepherdesses, the walls were painted in pale blue and white, and he'd had the ceiling frescoed with sea life in deference to the troublesome child's evident unwillingness to associate with such. The cheerful otters, fish, and cephalopods above were meant as encouragement, but it was clear his daughter saw them as nothing more than squishy threats.

In the exact center of the room stood a gold, claw-footed bathtub. It was far too large for a toddler, but Lord Akeldama never did anything by halves, especially if he might double it at three times the expense. There was also a fireplace, before which stood multiple gold racks supporting fluffy and highly absorbent drying cloths and one very small Chinese silk robe.

There were no less than eight drones in attendance, as well as Lord Akeldama, a footman, and the nursemaid. Nevertheless, nothing could take on Prudence Alessandra Maccon Akeldama when bathing was at stake.

The tub was overturned, saturating the beautiful rug with soapy water. Several of the drones were drenched. One was nursing a bruised knee and another a split lip. Lord Akeldama had tiny soapy handprints all over him. One of the drying racks had fallen on its side, singeing a cloth in the fire. The footman was standing with his mouth open, holding a bar of soap in one hand and a wedge of cheese in the other. The nanny had collapsed on a settee in tears.

In fact, the only person who seemed neither injured nor wet in any way was Prudence herself. The toddler was perched precariously on top of the mantelpiece over the fire, completely naked, with a very militant expression on her tiny face, yelling, "Noth, Dama. Noth wet. Noth, Dama!" She was lisping around her fangs.

Alexia stood in the doorway, transfixed.

Lord Akeldama straightened where he stood. "My *darlings*," he said, "tactic number eight, I think—circle and enclose. Now brace yourselves, my pets. I'm going in."

All the drones straightened and took up wide boxer's stances, forming a loose circle about the contested mantelpiece. All attention was focused on the toddler, who held the high ground, unflinching.

The ancient vampire launched himself at his adopted daughter. He could move fast, possibly faster than any other creature Alexia had ever observed, and she had been the unfortunate victim of more than one vampire attack. However, in this particular instance, Lord Akeldama moved no quicker than any ordinary mortal man. Which was, of course, the current difficulty—he *was* an ordinary mortal. His face was no longer deathless perfection but slightly effete and perhaps a little sulky. His movements were still graceful, but they were mortally graceful and, unfortunately, mortally slow.

Prudence leaped away in the manner of some kind of high-speed frog, her tiny, stubbly legs supernaturally strong but still toddler unstable. She crashed to the floor, screamed in very brief pain, and then zipped about looking for a break in the circle of drones closing in upon her.

"Noth, Dama. Noth wet," she cried, charging one of the drones, her tiny fangs bared. Unaware of her own supernatural strength, the baby managed to bash her way between the poor man's legs, making for the open doorway.

Except that the doorway was not, in fact, open. Therein stood the only creature whom little Prudence had learned to fear and, of course, the one she loved best in all the world.

"Mama!" came her delighted cry, and then, "Dada!" as Conall's shaggy head loomed up from behind his wife.

Alexia held out her arms and Prudence barreled into them with all the supernatural speed that a toddler vampire could manage. Alexia let out a harrumph of impact and stumbled backward into Conall's broad, supportive embrace.

The moment the naked baby came into contact with Alexia's bare arms, Prudence became no more dangerous than any squirming child.

"Now, Prudence, what is this fuss?" remonstrated her mother.

"No, Dama. No wet!" explained the toddler very clearly, now that she did not have the fangs to speak around.

"It's bath night. You don't have a choice. Real ladies are clean ladies," explained her mother, rather sensibly, she thought.

Prudence was having none of it. "Nuh-uh."

Lord Akeldama came over. He was once more pale, his movements quick and sharp. "Apologies, my little dumpling. She got away from Boots there and hurled herself at me before I could dodge." He moved one fine white hand to stroke his adopted daughter's hair back from her face. It was safe to do so now that Alexia held her close.

Prudence narrowed her eyes suspiciously. "No wet, Dama," she insisted.

"Well, accidents will happen and we all know how she gets." Alexia gave her daughter a stern look. Prudence, undaunted, glared back. Lady Maccon shook her head in exasperation. "Conall and I are off to the theater. Do you think you can handle bath night without me? Or should we cancel?"

Lord Akeldama was aghast at the mere suggestion. "Oh, dear me no, *buttercup*, never that! *Not* go to the theater? Heaven forfend. No, we shall shift perfectly well here without you, now that we've weathered this one teeny-tiny upset, won't we, Prudence?"

"No," replied Prudence.

Lord Akeldama backed away from her. "I'll stay well out of range from here on, I assure you," continued the vampire. "One brush with mortality a night is more than enough for me. It's quite the *discombobulating* sensation, your daughter's touch. Not at all like your own."

Lord Maccon, who had been placed in a similar position on more than one occasion with regard to his daughter's odd abilities, was uncharacteristically sympathetic to the vampire. He replied with a fervent, "I'll say." He also took the opportunity of Prudence being in her mother's arms to ruffle his daughter's hair affectionately.

"Dada! No wet?"

"Perhaps we could move bath night to tomorrow," suggested Lord Maccon, succumbing to the plea in his daughter's eyes.

Lord Akeldama brightened.

"Absolutely not," replied Lady Maccon to both of them. "Backbone, gentlemen. We must stick to a routine. All the physicians say routine is vital to the well-being of the infant and her proper ethical indoctrination."

The two immortals exchanged the looks of men who knew when they were beaten.

In order to forestall any further shilly-shallying, Alexia carried her struggling daughter over to the tub, which had been righted and refilled with warm water. Under ordinary circumstances, she would have plopped the child in herself, but worried over the dress, she passed Prudence off to Boots and stepped well out of harm's way.

Under the watchful eye of her mother, the toddler acquiesced to full immersion, with only a nose wrinkle of disgust.

Alexia nodded. "Good girl. Now do behave for poor Dama. He puts up with an awful lot from you."

"Dama!" replied the child, pointing at Lord Akeldama.

"Yes, very good." Alexia turned back to her husband and the vampire in the doorway. "Do have a care, my lord."

Lord Akeldama nodded. "Indeed. I must say I had not *anticipated* such a challenge when Professor Lyall first suggested the adoption."

"Yes, it was foolish of all of us to think that Alexia here would produce a biddable child," agreed the sire of said child, implying that any flaw was Alexia's fault and that he would have produced nothing but the most mild-mannered and pliant of offspring.

"Or even one that a vampire could control."

"Or a vampire and a pack of werewolves, for that matter."

Alexia gave them both a *look*. "I hardly feel I can be entirely at fault. Are you claiming Sidheag is an aberration in the Maccon line?"

Lord Maccon tilted his head, thinking about his great-great-great-granddaughter, now Alpha werewolf of the Kingair Pack, a woman prone to wielding rifles and smoking small cigars. "Point taken."

Their conversation was interrupted by a tremendous splash as Prudence managed to pull, even without supernatural strength, one of the drones partly into the bath with her. Several of the others rushed to his aid, cooing in equal distress over his predicament and the state of his cuffs.

Prudence Alessandra Maccon Akeldama would have been difficult enough without her metanatural abilities. But having a precocious child who could take on immortality was overwhelming, even for two supernatural households. Prudence actually seemed to steal supernatural abilities, turning her victim mortal for the space of a night. If Alexia had not interfered, Lord Akeldama would have remained mortal, and Prudence a fanged toddler, until sunrise. Her mother, or presumably some other preternatural, was the only apparent antidote.

Lord Maccon had accustomed himself, with much grumbling, to touching his daughter only when she was already in contact with her mother or when it was daylight. He was a man who appreciated a good cuddle, so this was disappointing. But poor Lord Akeldama found the whole situation distasteful. He had officially adopted the chit, and as a result had taken on the lion's share of her care, but he was never actually able to show her physical affection. When she was a small child, he'd managed with leather gloves and thick swaddling blankets, but even then accidents occurred. Now that Prudence was more mobile, the risk was simply too great. Naked touch guaranteed activation of her powers, but sometimes she could steal through clothing, too. When Prudence got older and more reasonable, Alexia intended to subject her daughter to some controlled analytical tests, but right now everyone in the household was simply trying to survive. The toddler couldn't be less interested in the importance of scientific discoveries, for all her mother tried to explain them. It was, Alexia felt, a troubling character flaw.

With one last glare to ensure Prudence remained at least mostly submerged, Alexia made good her escape, dragging her husband behind her. Conall held his amusement in check until they were inside the carriage and on their way toward the West End. Then he let out the most tremendous guffaw.

Alexia couldn't help it—she also started to chuckle. "Poor Lord Akeldama."

Conall wiped his streaming eyes. "Oh, he loves it. Hasn't had this much excitement in a hundred years or more."

"Are you certain they will manage without me?"

"We will be back in only a few hours. How bad can it get?"

"Don't tempt fate, my love."

"Better worry about our own survival."

"Why, what could you possibly mean?" Alexia straightened and looked out the carriage window suspiciously. True, it had been several years since someone tried to kill her in a conveyance, but it had happened with startling regularity for a period of time, and she had never gotten over her suspicion of carriages as a result.

"No, no, my dear. I meant to imply the play to which I am being dragged."

"Oh, I like that. As if I could drag you anywhere. You're twice my size."

Conall gave her the look of a man who knows when to hold his tongue.

"Ivy has assured me that this is a brilliant rendition of a truly moving story and that the troupe is in top form after their continental tour. *The Death Rains of Swansea*, I believe it is called. It's one of Tunstell's own pieces, very artistic and performed in the new sentimental interpretive style."

"Wife, you are taking me unto certain doom." He put his hand to his head and fell back against the cushioned wall of the cab in a fair imitation of theatricality.

"Oh, hush your nonsense. It will be perfectly fine."

Her husband's expression hinted strongly at a preference for, perhaps, death or at least battle, rather than endure the next few hours.

*   *   *

The Maccons arrived, displaying the type of elegance expected from members of the ton. Lady Alexia Maccon was resplendent, some might even have said handsome, in her new French gown. Lord Maccon looked like an earl for once, his hair *almost* under control and his evening dress *almost* impeccable. It was generally thought that the move to London had resulted in quite an improvement in the appearance and manners of the former Woolsey Pack. Some blamed living so close to Lord Akeldama, others the taming effect of an urban environment, and several stalwart holdouts thought it might be Lady Maccon's fault. In truth, it was probably all three, but it was the iron fist of Lord Akeldama's drones that truly enacted the change—or should one say, iron curling tongs? One of Lord Maccon's pack merely had to enter their purview with hair askew and handfuls of clucking pinks descended upon him like so many mallard ducks upon a hapless piece of untidy bread.

Alexia led her husband firmly to their private box. The whites of his eyes were showing in fear.

The Death Rains of Swansea featured a lovelorn werewolf enamored of a vampire queen and a dastardly villain with evil intent trying to tear them apart. The stage vampires were depicted with particularly striking fake fangs and a messy sort of red paint smeared about their chins. The werewolves sported proper dress except for large shaggy ears tied about their heads with pink tulle bows—Ivy's influence, no doubt.

Ivy Tunstell, Alexia's dear friend, played the vampire queen. She did so with much sweeping about the stage and fainting, her own fangs larger than anyone else's, which made it so difficult for her to articulate that many of her speeches were reduced to mere spitting hisses. She wore a hat that was part bonnet, part crown, driving home the queen theme, in colors of yellow, red, and gold. Her husband, playing the enamored werewolf, pranced about in a comic interpretation of lupine leaps, barked a lot, and got into several splendid stage fights.

The oddest moment, Alexia felt, was a dreamlike sequence just prior to the break, wherein Tunstell wore bumblebee-striped drawers with attached vest and performed a small ballet before his vampire queen. The queen was dressed in a voluminous black chiffon gown with a high Shakespearian collar and an exterior corset of green with matching fan. Her hair was done up on either side of her head in round puffs, looking like bear ears, and her arms were bare. *Bare!*

Conall, at this juncture, began to shake uncontrollably.

"I believe this is meant to symbolize the absurdity of their improbable affection," explained Alexia to her husband in severe tones. "Deeply philosophical. The bee represents the circularity of life and the unending buzz of immortality. Ivy's dress, so like that of an opera girl, suggests at the frivolousness of dancing through existence without love."

Conall continued to vibrate silently, as though trembling in pain.

"I'm not certain about the fan or the ears." Alexia tapped her cheek thoughtfully with her own fan.

The curtain dropped on the first act with the bumblebee-clad hero left prostrate at the feet of his vampire love. The audience erupted into wild cheers. Lord Conall Maccon began to guffaw in loud rumbling tones that carried beautifully throughout the theater. Many people turned to look up at him in disapproval.

Well, thought his wife, *at least he managed to hold it in until the break.*

Eventually, her husband controlled his mirth. "Brilliant! I apologize, wife, for objecting to this jaunt. It is immeasurably entertaining."

"Well, do be certain to say nothing of the kind to poor Tunstell. You are meant to be profoundly moved, not amused."

A timid knock came at their box.

"Enter," yodeled his lordship, still chuckling.

The curtain was pushed aside, and in came one of the people Alexia would have said was least likely to visit the theater, Madame Genevieve Lefoux.

"Good evening, Lord Maccon, Alexia."

"Genevieve, how unexpected."

Madame Lefoux was dressed impeccably. Fraternization with the Woolsey Hive had neither a deleterious nor improving effect on her attire. If Countess Nadasdy had tried to get her newest drone to dress appropriately, she had failed. Madame Lefoux dressed to the height of style, for a man. Her taste was still subtle and elegant with no vampiric flamboyances in the manner of cravat ties or cuff links. True, she sported cravat pins and pocket watches, but Alexia would lay good money that not a one solely functioned as a cravat pin or a pocket watch.

"Are you enjoying the show?" inquired the Frenchwoman.

"I am finding it diverting. Conall is not taking it seriously."

Lord Maccon puffed out his cheeks.

"And you?" Alexia directed the question back at her erstwhile friend. Since Genevieve's wildly spectacular charge through London and resulting transition to vampire drone, no small measure of awkwardness had existed between them. Two years on and still they had not regained the closeness they had both so enjoyed at the beginning of their association. Madame Lefoux had polluted it through the application of a rampaging octomaton, and Alexia had finished it off by sentencing Genevieve to a decade of indentured servitude.

"It is interesting," replied the Frenchwoman cautiously. "And how is little Prudence?"

"Difficult, as ever. And Quesnel?"

"The same."

The two women exchanged careful smiles. Lady Maccon, despite herself, liked Madame Lefoux. There was just something about her that appealed. And she did owe the Frenchwoman a debt, for it was the inventor who had acted the part of midwife to Prudence's grossly mistimed entrance into the world. Nevertheless, Alexia did not trust her. Madame Lefoux always promoted her own agenda first, even as a drone, with the Order of the Brass Octopus second. What little loyalty and affection for Alexia she still had must, perforce, be a low priority now.

Lady Maccon moved them on from the platitudes with a direct reminder. "And how is the countess?"

Madame Lefoux gave one of her little French shrugs. "She is herself, unchanging, as ever. It is on her behest that I am here. I have been directed to bring you a message."

"Oh, yes, how did you know where to find me?"

"The Tunstells have a new play, and you are their patroness. I admit I had not anticipated *your* presence, my lord."

Lord Maccon grinned wolfishly. "I was persuaded."

"The message?" Alexia put out her hand.

"Ah, no, we have all learned never to do *that* again. The message is a verbal one. Countess Nadasdy has received instructions and would like to see you, Lady Maccon."

"Instructions? Instructions from who?"

"I am not privy to that information," replied the inventor.

Alexia turned to her husband. "Who on earth would dare order around the Woolsey Hive queen?"

"Oh, no, Alexia, you misunderstand me. The instructions came *to* her, but they are *for* you."

"Me? Me! Why...," Alexia sputtered in outrage.

"I'm afraid I know nothing more. Are you available to call upon her this evening, after the performance?"

Alexia, whose curiosity was quite piqued, nodded her acquiescence. "It is bath night, but Lord Akeldama and his boys must really learn to muddle through."

"Bath night?" The Frenchwoman was intrigued.

"Prudence is particularly difficult on bath nights."

"Ah, yes. Some of them don't want to get clean. Quesnel was like that. As you may have noticed, circumstances never did improve." Genevieve's son was known for being grubby.

"And how is he muddling along, living with vampires?"

"Thriving, the little monster."

"Much like Prudence, then."

"As you say." The Frenchwoman tilted her head. "And my hat shop?"

"Biffy has it marvelously well in hand. You should drop by and visit. He's there tonight. I'm certain he would love to see you."

"Perhaps I shall. It's not often I get into London these days." Madame Lefoux began edging toward the curtain, donning her gray top hat and making her good-byes.

She left Lord and Lady Maccon in puzzled silence, with a mystery that, it must be said, somewhat mitigated their enjoyment of the second act, as did the lack of any additional bumblebee courtship rituals.

introducing

If you enjoyed
HEARTLESS,
look out for

CHARMING

Pax Arcana: Book 1

By Elliott James

John Charming isn't your average prince...

He comes from a line of Charmings—an illustrious family of dragon slayers, witch finders, and killers dating back to before the fall of Rome. Trained by a modern-day version of the Knights Templar, monster hunters who have updated their methods from chain mail and crossbows to Kevlar and shotguns, John Charming was one of the best—until a curse made him one of the abominations the Knights were sworn to hunt.

That was a lifetime ago. Now John tends bar under an assumed name in rural Virginia and leads a peaceful, quiet life. That is, until a vampire and a blonde walk into his bar...

Prelude

Hocus Focus

There's a reason that we refer to being in love as being enchanted. Think back to the worst relationship you've ever been in: the one where your family and friends tried to warn you that the person you were with was cheating on you, or partying a little too much, or a control freak, or secretly gay, or whatever. Remember how you were convinced that no one but you could see the real person beneath that endearingly flawed surface? And then later, after the relationship reached that scorched-earth-policy stage where letters were being burned and photos were being cropped, did you find yourself looking back and being amazed at how obvious the truth had been all along? Did it feel as if you were waking up from some kind of a spell?

Well, there's something going on right in front of your face that you can't see right now, and you're not going to believe me when I point it out to you. Relax, I'm not going to provide a number where you can leave your credit card information, and you don't have to join anything. The only reason I'm telling you at all is that at some point in the future, you might have a falling-out with the worldview you're currently enamored of, and if that happens, what I'm about to tell you will help you make sense of things later.

The supernatural is real. Vampires? Real. Werewolves? Real. Zombies, Ankou, djinn, Boo Hags, banshees, ghouls, spriggans, windigos, vodyanoi, tulpas, and so on and so on, all real. Well, except for Orcs and Hobbits. Tolkien just made those up.

I know it sounds ridiculous. How could magic really exist in a world with an Internet and forensic science and smartphones and satellites and such and still go undiscovered?

The answer is simple: it's magic.

The truth is that the world is under a spell called the Pax Arcana, a compulsion that makes people unable to see, believe, or even seriously consider any evidence of the supernatural that is not an immediate threat to their survival.

I know this because I come from a long line of dragon slayers, witch finders, and self-righteous asshats. I used to be one of the modern-day knights who patrol the borders between the world of man and the supernatural abyss that is its shadow. I wore non-reflective Kevlar instead of shining armor and carried a sawed-off shotgun as well as a sword; I didn't light a candle against the dark, I wielded a flamethrower...right up until the day I discovered that I had been cursed by one of the monsters I used to hunt. My name is Charming by the way. John Charming.

And I am not living happily ever after.

CHAPTER ONE

———

A Blonde and a Vampire Walk
into a Bar...

Once upon a time, she smelled wrong. Well, no, that's not exactly true. She smelled clean, like fresh snow and air after a lightning storm and something hard to identify, something like sex and butter pecan ice cream. Honestly, I think she was the best thing I'd ever smelled. I was inferring "wrongness" from the fact that she wasn't entirely human.

I later found out that her name was Sig.

Sig stood there in the doorway of the bar with the wind behind her, and there was something both earthy and unearthly about her. Standing at least six feet tall in running shoes, she had shoulders as broad as a professional swimmer's, sinewy arms, and well-rounded hips that were curvy and compact. All in all, she was as buxom, blonde, blue-eyed, and clear-skinned as any woman who had ever posed for a Swedish tourism ad.

And I wanted her out of the bar, fast.

You have to understand, Rigby's is not the kind of place where goddesses were meant to walk among mortals. It is a small, modest establishment eking out a fragile existence at the tail end of Clayburg's main street. The owner, David Suggs, had wanted a quaint pub, but instead of decorating the place with dartboards or Scottish coats of arms or ceramic mugs, he

had decided to celebrate southwest Virginia culture and covered the walls with rusty old railroad equipment and farming
tools.

When I asked why a bar—excuse me, I mean *pub*—with a
Celtic name didn't have a Celtic atmosphere, Dave said that
he had named Rigby's after a Beatles song about lonely people
needing a place to belong.

"Names have power," Dave had gone on to inform me, and I
had listened gravely as if this were a revelation.

Speaking of names, "John Charming" is not what it reads
on my current driver's license. In fact, about the only thing
accurate on my current license is the part where it says that
I'm black-haired and blue-eyed. I'm six foot one instead of six
foot two and about seventy-five pounds lighter than the 250
pounds indicated on my identification. But I do kind of look
the way the man pictured on my license might look if Trevor
A. Barnes had lost that much weight and cut his hair short and
shaved off his beard. Oh, and if he were still alive.

And no, I didn't kill the man whose identity I had assumed,
in case you're wondering. Well, not the first time anyway.

Anyhow, I had recently been forced to leave Alaska and
start a new life of my own, and in David Suggs I had found an
employer who wasn't going to be too thorough with his background checks. My current goal was to work for Dave for at
least one fiscal year and not draw any attention to myself.

Which was why I was not happy to see the blonde.

For her part, the blonde didn't seem too happy to see me
either. Sig focused on me immediately. People always gave me a
quick flickering glance when they walked into the bar—excuse
me, the pub—but the first thing they really checked out was
the clientele. Their eyes were sometimes predatory, sometimes cautious, sometimes hopeful, often tired, but they only

returned to me after being disappointed. Sig's gaze, however, centered on me like the oncoming lights of a train—assuming train lights have slight bags underneath them and make you want to flex surreptitiously. Those same startlingly blue eyes widened, and her body went still for a moment.

Whatever had triggered her alarms, Sig hesitated, visibly debating whether to approach and talk to me. She didn't hesitate for long, though—I got the impression that she rarely hesitated for long—and chose to go find herself a table.

Now, it was a Thursday night in April, and Rigby's was not empty. Clayburg is host to a small private college named Stillwaters University, one of those places where parents pay more money than they should to get an education for children with mediocre high school records, and underachievers with upper-middle-class parents tend to do a lot of heavy drinking. This is why Rigby's manages to stay in business. Small bars with farming implements on the walls don't really draw huge college crowds, but the more popular bars tend to stay packed, and Rigby's does attract an odd combination of local rednecks and students with a sense of irony. So when a striking six-foot blonde who wasn't an obvious transvestite sat down in the middle of the bar, there were people around to notice.

Even Sandra, a nineteen-year-old waitress who considers customers an unwelcome distraction from covert texting, noticed the newcomer. She walked up to Sig promptly instead of making Renee, an older waitress and Rigby's de facto manager, chide her into action.

For the next hour I pretended to ignore the new arrival while focusing on her intently. I listened in—my hearing is as well developed as my sense of smell—while several patrons tried to introduce themselves. Sig seemed to have a knack for knowing how to discourage each would-be player as fast as possible.

She told suitors that she wanted to be up-front about her sex change operation because she was tired of having it cause problems when her lovers found out later, or she told them that she liked only black men, or young men, or older men who made more than seventy thousand dollars a year. She told them that what really turned her on was men who were willing to have sex with other men while she watched. She mentioned one man's wife by name, and when the weedy-looking grad student doing a John Lennon impersonation tried the sensitive-poet approach, she challenged him to an arm-wrestling contest. He stared at her, sitting there exuding athleticism, confidence, and health—three things he was noticeably lacking—and chose to be offended rather than take her up on it.

There was at least one woman who seemed interested in Sig as well, a cute sandy-haired college student who was tall and willowy, but when it comes to picking up strangers, women are generally less likely to go on a kamikaze mission than men. The young woman kept looking over at Sig's table, hoping to establish some kind of meaningful eye contact, but Sig wasn't making any.

Sig wasn't looking at me either, but she held herself at an angle that kept me in her peripheral vision at all times.

For my part, I spent the time between drink orders trying to figure out exactly what Sig was. She definitely wasn't undead. She wasn't a half-blood Fae either, though her scent wasn't entirely dissimilar. Elf smell isn't something you forget, sweet and decadent, with a hint of honey blossom and distant ocean. There aren't any full-blooded Fae left, of course—they packed their bags and went back to Fairyland a long time ago—but don't mention that to any of the mixed human descendants that the elves left behind. Elvish half-breeds tend to be somewhat sensitive on that particular subject. They can be real bastards about being bastards.

I would have been tempted to think that Sig was an angel, except that I've never heard of anyone I'd trust ever actually seeing a real angel. God is as much an article of faith in my world as he, she, we, they, or it is in yours.

Stumped, I tried to approach the problem by figuring out what Sig was doing there. She didn't seem to enjoy the ginger ale she had ordered—didn't seem to notice it at all, just sipped from it perfunctorily. There was something wary and expectant about her body language, and she had positioned herself so that she was in full view of the front door. She could have just been meeting someone, but I had a feeling that she was looking for someone or something specific by using herself as bait... but as to what and why and to what end, I had no idea. Sex, food, or revenge seemed the most likely choices.

I was still mulling that over when the vampire walked in.

PRUDENCE

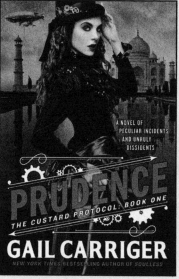

COMING MARCH 2015!

From *New York Times* bestselling author Gail Carriger comes a new novel in the world of the Parasol Protectorate starring Prudence, the daughter of Alexia Tarabotti.

When Prudence Alessandra Maccon Akeldama (Rue to her friends) is given an unexpected dirigible, she does what any sensible female would under similar circumstances—names it the Spotted Custard and floats to India in pursuit of the perfect cup of tea. But India has more than just tea on offer. Rue stumbles upon a plot involving local dissidents, a kidnapped brigadier's wife, and some awfully familiar Scottish werewolves. Faced with a dire crisis and an embarrassing lack of bloomers, what else is a young lady of good breeding to do but turn metanatural and find out everyone's secrets, even thousand-year-old fuzzy ones?

"RAVISHING." —Lev Grossman on *Soulless*

"CARRIGER DELIVERS SURPRISES WITH EVERY BOOK, AND THIS ONE IS NO EXCEPTION." —*Library Journal* on *Heartless*

"WITTY, SEXY, GRACEFUL AND UNPREDICTABLE." —*Fantasy Magazine* on *Changeless*

"I'M ALREADY HOOKED." —*Locus* on *Changeless*

"INTOXICATINGLY WITTY." —*Publishers Weekly* on *Soulless*

The fine art of
FINISHING OTHERS

FROM *NEW YORK TIMES* BESTSELLING AUTHOR
GAIL CARRIGER

Now in paperback

THE FINE ART OF
FINISHING OTHERS

ETIQUETTE
ESPIONAGE

GAIL CARRIGER

CURTSIES
CONSPIRACIES

GAIL CARRIGER

Hear the original song!
FinishingSchoolBooks.com
Available however books are sold

LB LITTLE, BROWN AND COMPANY

B0B618

You oughtn't keep a lady waiting...

GAIL CARRIGER

SOULLESS

REM

READ THE MANGA!
VOLUME 1 - 3
AVAILABLE NOW!

Soulless © Tofa Borregaard • Illustrations © Hachette Book Group

Yen Press

VISIT THE ORBIT BLOG AT

www.orbitbooks.net

FEATURING

BREAKING NEWS
FORTHCOMING RELEASES
LINKS TO AUTHOR SITES
EXCLUSIVE INTERVIEWS
EARLY EXTRACTS

AND COMMENTARY FROM OUR EDITORS

WITH REGULAR UPDATES FROM OUR TEAM,
ORBITBOOKS.NET IS YOUR SOURCE
FOR ALL THINGS ORBITAL.

WHILE YOU'RE THERE, JOIN OUR E-MAIL LIST
TO RECEIVE INFORMATION ON SPECIAL OFFERS,
GIVEAWAYS, AND MORE.

imagine. explore. engage.